For Ellen and Kate

Acknowledgments

As a character in this novel points out, you need help when you rip off a dangerous black-market dealer of stolen antiquities. Well, the same thing goes when you write a novel, and there are a lot of people I'd like to thank for their help along the way.

I'm incredibly grateful for the supremely good taste, good sense, and good will of my literary agent, Richard Parks, and my editor at William Morrow, Trish Daly. This book, and this writer, are better because of them.

The sales, marketing, and publicity departments at William Morrow and HarperCollins have been phenomenal. I keep waiting for the other shoe to drop and to discover that I've accidentally sold my soul to them (I do, now that you mention it, remember signing something in blood). In particular I'd like to thank the people I've had the fortune to get to know personally: Michael Brennan, Carla Parker, Jean Marie Kelly,

Danielle Bartlett, and Joanne Minutillo. And though she's gone to a better place now (upstate New York, I believe), I remain indebted to Peggy Hageman.

I make it a point to visit the places I write about (or, maybe, the other way around). I'd still be wandering lost in the highlands of Belize, or maybe in an Egyptian prison cell myself, were it not for the invaluable and gracious assistance of the friends I made at Chaa Creek and Lady Egypt.

A quick word about Belize and Egypt. You might gather, from this novel, that both countries seethe with murderous drug lords, exotic pet smugglers, and dangerous black-market dealers of stolen antiquities. They do! Well, not really. In my experience, the people of both countries are warm, friendly, and welcoming, and I can think of two no better places to visit on your next vacation.

The mystery-crime community—writers, readers, bloggers, magazine editors, and booksellers—has been a fantastic source of support and advice. I really can't overstate how much I've appreciated it, and I don't think I've ever encountered a group that has been so relentlessly generous and welcoming. There are too many people to thank individually, so I plan to buy each of them a beer in the hotel bar at the next Bouchercon.

This list is starting to drone on, I realize, and I don't want to be that costume designer at the Oscars who has to be dragged off stage as the orchestra swells. So here, without the elaboration they deserve, and in no particular order, are people I'm grateful to for one reason or another (usually multiple reasons): Dana Kaye, Jeremy Bell, Michael Sheresky, Ramses Ishak, Ben Jacobson, Frank Lunn, Jim and Katy Harrigan, Steve and Sue Ellen Harrigan, the Sanchez-Westenberg family, Thomas Cooney, Rick Klingenberg.

And finally I'd like to thank my wife, Christine, without whom I would be completely lost.

PART I

Chapter 1

The view from the veranda was a killer.

A sugar-sand beach, palm trees, the Caribbean glittering beneath a full moon. A wooden pier curved out over the water, with a thatch-covered *palapa* perched at the far end. Straight off a postcard.

Shake had bought the Sunset Breeze more than two years ago. You'd think he wouldn't even notice the view anymore, but he did. Every single time he stepped onto the veranda of the restaurant, *his* restaurant, that was still his first thought: *Straight off a postcard.*

Charles Samuel Bouchon was the name on his birth certificate, but he'd gone by "Shake" since he was nineteen, his first fall for grand theft auto, some twenty-five years ago now. One of the old black cons on the yard had started calling him "Vanilla Milk Shake." Just an offhand nickname, and not exactly affectionate, but that was a funny thing about life: you never knew what was going to stick.

Shake made his way over to the honeymooners to clear their empty plates. They were young, barely into their twenties, fresh and scrubbed and flushed pink from a day in the sun. Holding hands across the table.

"So how did that lobster treat you?" he asked.

"Oh my God!" the girl said. "It just . . ."

"It rocked!" the kid said.

Already finishing each other's sentences. Shake pointed it out.

"That's a good sign," he said.

"Is it?" the kid said. Earnest.

Shake shrugged. Sure, why not?

The kid dimpled with delight. The girl giggled and squeezed her husband's hand tight.

"So how long will you be in Belize?" Shake said.

"Not long enough," the kid said.

"I wish we could stay here forever," the girl said. "It's like paradise."

"It *is* paradise," the kid said.

"We're from Buffalo," she explained.

Shake smiled.

The girl gazed out at the moonlit sea, at the flames of the tiki torches snapping around in the breeze.

"Was it your dream?" the girl asked Shake. "To own your own restaurant? In a place like this?"

"It was," he said. Though he didn't mention where the dream had been dreamed. Long nights in the sweat-sour darkness of Block A, staring at the wall while his cellie in the tray above grunted and flopped in his sleep. It had been Shake's second stretch for grand theft auto, but twenty years down the line, Shake no longer a boy but a professional wheelman of some repute. And determined, once he walked out of the Mule Creek State Correctional Facility, to walk a straight path and never again wobble off it.

Well, that hadn't worked out exactly as planned. There had been a few wobbles. But now, finally, here Shake was. Palm trees and *palapas* and grilled lobster with a tequila lime sauce that did, if he did say so himself, rock.

"You really have the life," the kid said with a sigh.

Shake smiled again, tighter this time. "You don't know the half of it," he said.

IF SHAKE'S FIRST THOUGHT WHENEVER he stepped onto the veranda of his restaurant was *Straight off a postcard,* his first thought whenever he pushed through the double doors into the kitchen was usually *Shit.*

Tonight the waiter was cursing the prep cook in Spanish, the prep cook was cursing back in English and waving around a boning knife, and the grease trap was on fire.

Business as usual, in other words.

"Armando!" Shake yelled. "Roger!"

They shut up, but neither made a move for the fire extinguisher. Shake grabbed it himself and poured foam on the grease trap. When the flames were dead, he showed the fire extinguisher to Roger, the prep cook.

"Ever seen one of these before?" Shake asked. "Just curious."

Roger was a scrawny recovering alcoholic from Detroit who spent most of his shift recovering from the alcohol he drank on his breaks. He thought about the question.

"Fire extinguisher?" he said. "Shit. Sure I have. Hit a A-rab with one, one time. 7-Eleven store outside Gary, Indiana. Pissant tried to kick me in the nuts."

As hard as it was to believe, Roger was the best of the dozen or so prep cooks Shake had hired and fired over the past two years.

"Why he do that?" Armando, the waiter, asked. He was a mestizo from Guatemala, barely five feet tall. Not a drinker, just foul-tempered and forgetful. Exactly the qualities you wanted in a waiter.

"I was robbing him," Roger said. "And I dropped my screwdriver."

"Hijo jesu," Armando said. *"Pinche idiota."*

"Screw you, greasy little bean-eater!"

Shake felt a headache building, chugging toward him, a freight train ready to flatten him where he stood.

He'd worked in kitchens before. He'd known that running his own restaurant wouldn't be easy. But he'd never guessed just how unbelievably not easy it would turn out to be.

Fights in the kitchen. Fires in the kitchen. Crooked suppliers and corrupt inspectors. Third-world wiring and fourth-world plumbing. Tropical storms, swine-flu scares, cockroaches the size of lobsters. And, bane of Shake's existence, the Internet, where a single bad review on TripAdvisor could kill business like a stake through the heart.

Idaba, the hostess, pushed through the doors. A Garifuna woman in her sixties, with a tie-dyed head wrap and big gold nose ring, she was Shake's only competent employee. She made sure he never forgot it.

She looked around. "Problem?"

Shake studied her, but it was impossible to tell if she was being ironic. She had a hell of a straight face, grave and expressionless, her big block head like something the ancient Mayans had carved out of dark volcanic rock and killed sacrificial goats on.

"Problem?" He kicked fire-extinguisher foam off his shoe and raised his voice because Armando and Roger were still cursing each other. "Why would you think that?"

She might have frowned at him, might not have. Again, impossible to tell.

"The nine o'clock four-top canceled," she said.

Shake grimaced. That left them with only twelve covers for the night. Eight the night before. That put them deep in the red for the night, the month, the year. Ever since January, when the resort located just up the beach had switched over to an all-inclusive meal plan and sucked up half their business.

They'd been in the red even before then, to be honest.

Running his own restaurant in Belize was by far the most stressful job Shake had ever had. Driving getaway for the Armenian mob, a Humvee full of Salvadoran gangbangers trying to ram you into the Los Angeles River—that, by comparison, was like listening to soft jazz in the tub.

"You want me to comp their dessert?" Idaba said. "The honeymooners?"

"Are we sure they're really on their honeymoon?" Shake said. "Can we ask for proof?"

Idaba waited. Shake calculated how much the complimentary coconut pie would cost him, how much the chocolate cake, how much if the honeymooners wanted both.

"Fine," he said finally.

He needed some air, so he grabbed a bus tub full of dead lettuce and rotten mango and carried it out back. Out back was a weedy patch of crushed coral beneath a browning palm, with a Dumpster and a propane tank and a million or so of Roger's cigarette butts scattered everywhere.

Shake emptied the bus tub into the Dumpster, noticing that the floodlight above the kitchen door had burned out. He remembered he'd just changed the bulb, but before he could do anything useful with that information, a pair of hands grabbed his shoulders. The hands spun Shake around and slammed him so hard against the propane tank that Shake's teeth clacked together and rust puffed off the tank.

The guy who'd slammed Shake was big, and built, a dark-skinned bruiser in baggy plaid shorts and a Rasta tank top that said ONE LOVE. Shake recognized him, one of the thugs who hung around the bar that Baby Jesus owned down in San Pedro.

Shake had hoped this was just a random mugging. No such luck.

"Listen," he said, but instead One Love hit him in the stomach. Shake doubled over and the guy went for his kidneys, two hard chops that dropped Shake to his knees.

"You like that, *guna boi*?" One Love said.

"No," Shake said.

"Maybe you like another one, then."

Shake didn't follow the logic. He turned his body, thinking he might trap a kick to the ribs and bring One Love down.

But the kick didn't come. Shake looked up. One Love took a step back as a golf cart rolled up. The cart's shocks creaked as Baby Jesus heaved himself out. He was even bigger than One Love, enormous, like a Macy's Thanksgiving Day Parade balloon.

"Shake! My friend!" Baby Jesus held his arms wide. His face was round and smooth and alarmingly—for a guy that big, in his late thirties—cherubic.

Shake climbed unsteadily to his feet. "Friends," he pointed out, "don't punch friends in the kidneys."

Baby Jesus chuckled and wagged a finger at Shake. "Friends pay back the money that they borrow."

"Plus the point and a half a week, don't forget."

"Oh! Such onerous terms! Baby Jesus is such a bad man, yes?"

Baby Jesus arched his eyebrows and looked over at One Love, who nodded in agreement. Because yes, Baby Jesus—who ran the dope trade on Ambergris Caye and controlled a key leg of the lucrative cocaine distribution route between Lima and the Florida Keys—was in fact a bad man. Very.

Baby Jesus frowned at One Love and said something sharp in Kriol. One Love caught the drift and stopped nodding. He shook his head. "No!"

"No!" Baby Jesus said. "Of course not, Baby Jesus is not a bad man!" He wagged his finger again at Shake. "Tell me, Shake, who else would help you buy your restaurant? Who else would loan the necessary funds to—I am being honest here—a person of such dubious character and past transgression?"

Good question. Another one was why Shake, who should have known better, had borrowed money from a Central American drug lord known for shooting his rivals, breaking down their bodies like raw chicken for the fryer, and dumping the pieces at a place on the reef called Shark Ray Alley.

"Baby Jesus is who!" Baby Jesus said.

All Shake could say in his own defense was that he'd been at a difficult point in his life when he borrowed the money from Baby Jesus. When Shake found the restaurant for sale on Ambergris Caye, he'd recognized it as a miracle, a gift, a once-in-a-lifetime chance to slam the book shut on his past.

Unfortunately, the most recent chapter of that book had left Shake stone-cold broke, and Baby Jesus was right. Who else would have loaned Shake that kind of money?

"You know what?" Shake said. "I was just about to say 'Baby Jesus.' I was this close."

Baby Jesus rocked back on his heels, a parade balloon tugging on the guide wires, and surveyed the restaurant. "Business is good?" he said.

"Couldn't be better," Shake said.

Baby Jesus gave him a sweetly cherubic smile.

"I was barely a week late," Shake said. "First time in almost two years."

"Exactly," Baby Jesus said. "That is why we snip the problem in the bud. Yes? Snip, snip, snip!"

He brought two big fingers close to Shake's face and worked them like scissors. Shake made the mistake of watching the fingers and not One Love, who stepped up and hammered him with a blind-side roundhouse to the jaw. Shake hit the ground again.

When his vision cleared, Baby Jesus was crouched next to him.

"Next month's payment will be on time, yes?" Baby Jesus said.

Shake nodded.

"Excellent." Baby Jesus gave him a friendly pat on the cheek. "And you have learned your lesson?"

Shake remembered what the honeymoon girl had asked him earlier, if now he had the life he'd always dreamed of. He nodded again, but when he tried to speak, his jaw was still numb from the punch.

"What's that you say?" Baby Jesus said. "What is the lesson you have learned?"

"Be careful what you wish for," Shake said.

Chapter 2

Shake's flat above the restaurant faced east, toward the sea, so he never bothered with an alarm clock. The light came slanting in early, spreading like it had been dropped and spilled on the polished ironwood floor. When the dogs that guarded the bar next door woke up and started barking at the seabirds, Shake was already out of bed, sliding on his flip-flops.

He walked down to the end of the pier and put on a pair of swim goggles. You never knew what you might see out here in the crystal-blue water. Huge schools of tiny silver fish, swirling like snowflakes. A spotted ray banking and swooning. Shake stood for a second to let the sun warm him up, and then dove in.

Back in the States, Shake had taken long drives to relax. An empty stretch of country two-lane, the soothing sizzle of rubber on asphalt, a Flatlanders song blasting from the deck. But Ambergris Caye was an island only twenty miles long and half a mile wide. Almost everyone got around by bike or boat or golf cart. So now when Shake wanted to forget his troubles, he had to hit the water.

Usually his morning swim did relax him. This morning, though, no matter how hard he worked, he couldn't shake Baby Jesus. Who seemed to backstroke right along beside Shake, smiling sweetly, snip-snipping his big fingers like scissors.

Shake figured, best case, that he had two or three months for business to pick up. If it didn't, if he couldn't keep up his payments, Baby Jesus would take over the restaurant. He would take over Shake.

Shake picked up the pace and swam till he could barely lift his arms above his head. Finally, exhausted, he rolled onto his back and let the current carry him back down toward his pier.

When he climbed out of the water, Idaba was on the beach, supervising the little Kriol boy who raked up the sea grass. If the little boy missed a spot, Idaba would snap her fingers, loud, and make him go back and get it.

Shake dried off and walked over. Idaba handed him a cup of coffee.

"I'm gonna take the boat into town later," Shake said. "We need anything you know about?"

"Mangoes," she said.

"All right,"

"Good ones."

"You sure? I was gonna hunt around till I found some bad ones."

She looked at him. The boy almost grinned, Shake saw it building, but Idaba snapped her fingers at him and the little boy scooted off down the beach.

"You know what you need?" she asked Shake.

He sat down on the sand with his coffee and watched the waves smack and foam against the reef, half a mile offshore.

"What do I need?" he said.

"You need a woman."

He glanced over at her. "What?"

"How long it's been?" she said. "Since you have a woman in your bed?"

"Well," he said. He took a sip of coffee and pretended to muse. "I guess if you're offering . . ."

She snapped her fingers so close to his head that it made his ear ring.

"Be serious for one minute," she said.

"What I need," Shake said, "I need a prep cook knows how to prep or cook. Either way, it's an improvement. I need a roof that doesn't leak and wiring I don't have to say a Hail Mary every time I flip a light switch. I need TripAdvisor to delete that dipshit's review, the one said my conch ceviche was undercooked."

"A woman in your bed. That's the only way to fix when your heart been broken."

"I need to go back in time and kick my own dumb ass for borrowing money from Baby Jesus."

He turned to look at her.

"Who says I've got a broken heart?"

"You don't think I see?" She snorted. "I see it the first time I meet you."

"That wasn't a broken heart. That was a rough ferry ride from the mainland and a plate of bad huevos rancheros."

"Be serious. When a woman break your heart, you need to find a new woman. It's no good, a man all by himself."

That sounded like lyrics from a reggae song, but Shake knew better than to say so.

Idaba snapped her fingers again anyway, right next to his ear, like a gunshot going off.

"Hey!" he said. "What was that for?"

She was like one of those old nuns he'd known as a kid, growing up in New Orleans, who could read your mind like a book.

"You think I don't see?" she said.

She took his empty cup and headed back up to the restaurant. Shake stretched his legs out. It was true that he'd been suffering from more than bad huevos rancheros when he first arrived on Ambergris Caye. But that was two years ago. If his heart had been broken then, that didn't mean it was broken now. He no longer felt a stab of pain, for example, every time he thought about Gina. Every time he thought he smelled her shampoo on the pillow next to him. Every time he stepped onto the veranda of the restaurant and imagined how much she'd love the killer view.

Not every time.

He tried to remember how long it had been since he'd had a woman in his bed. Six months? He had opportunities. He was a decent-looking guy, he took care of himself, he owned a restaurant on the beach of a tropical island. A lot of the women he met were on vacation, far from home, ready to live and let loose.

But he could never work up much enthusiasm for it—a one-night stand with some divorced recovery-room nurse, too much makeup and a fresh dolphin tattoo on her ankle, she and her girlfriends three sheets to the wind and flying back to Louisville in the morning.

Shake called over the little Kriol boy with the rake and told him there were some homemade cinnamon rolls in the pantry, and to make sure he took a few home for his family.

"Thank you, Mr. Shake," the little boy said. Shake guessed he was about seven or eight years old, skin almost the color of the ironwood floor in Shake's apartment.

"I think she can read minds," Shake said. "Idaba."

The little boy shrugged, as if to say, *Of course she can, don't be foolish.* And then he went running up to the kitchen to get his rolls.

SHAKE TOOK THE BOAT INTO town, an eighteen-foot Wahoo that had come with the restaurant. The old Mercury outboard broke down on a fairly regular basis—usually when Shake had some expensive grouper sitting on ice—but today he made it to the municipal wharf without incident.

He tied up and walked to the market. A lot of visitors were underwhelmed by San Pedro, the only town on Ambergris Caye. Three streets, a few restaurants and bars, a layer of white sandy grit covering everything. Shake liked it. San Pedro felt like a real place to him, life going on, not like some of the other places he'd been to in the Caribbean. In San Pedro there were plenty of tourist traps selling T-shirts and scuba trips, but also places where you could buy plastic buckets or used bicycle parts or old romance novels written in Spanish. You could get your hair cut by a guy who worked out of his garage.

Shake located the fisherman he liked to use. The snapper looked good, so Shake took that and some lobster, some conch. The fisherman was about to make a run up to the northern resorts and agreed to drop off the fish on his way.

When the Garifuna ladies with the fruit carts saw Shake coming, they started clucking and cooing. In their brightly colored head wraps and skirts, they were like a flock of naughty tropical birds.

"Shake!"

"Come taste my fruit, boy!"

"Taste how sweet!"

"Shake, what's shaking?"

That last one always cracked them up. It never got old.

Shake bought mangoes and papayas. On second thought he also bought some plantains, thinking he might fry them up with the snapper tonight. He felt good about that until he remembered they had only seven reservations on the books for tonight, and not much hope of any walk-ins.

Shake paid for the plantains and walked over to his buddy Pijua's joint. It was early for lunch, but Shake hadn't eaten breakfast and Pijua turned out the best food on the island, probably the best in Central America.

Pijua's daughter sat him at a table inside, by the window, with a view of the marina. Shake tried not to guess what kind of phenomenal walk-in business Pijua did. He was shouting distance from the wharf, from all the bars, a quick golf-cart ride from the fancy resorts south of town. To get to Shake's restaurant from town, you had to take a taxi boat or the island ferry. Twenty minutes each way, minimum.

"Perfect spot," the guy who'd sold Shake his restaurant had assured him. "Quiet, romantic, secluded." Then the guy was on a flight home to Orange County before the ink on the deed was dry. Shake supposed that should have given him pause.

Pijua delivered Shake's pulled-pork empanadas and sat down across from him. Shake took a bite.

"What's a guy gotta do," Shake said, "to get the recipe for these?"

Pijua laughed. "Grow up in my mama's kitchen. Have her whack you on the head with a wooden spoon every time you fuck up."

Shake took another bite. "Small price to pay."

Pijua's real name was Manuel. He had been born in the Cayo highlands, on the border between Belize and Guatemala. Up there they had a little river shrimp that people called a *pijua*. A delicacy, hard to find and hard to catch. When Pijua was six or seven years old, it became his goal in life to catch one of those shrimp. When he finally caught one, he was so excited he ran through town yelling, *"Pijua! Pijua!"* That's what he'd been called ever since, Pijua, shrimp, the guy a head taller than Shake and built like a truck.

Shake glanced around the restaurant. There wasn't an empty table and it was barely eleven-thirty. Pijua read him.

"Give it time, amigo," he said. "Your food's good. Took me three, four years, my first place, before it really got going."

"Is that all?" Shake said.

Pijua put his palms up, conceding the point. "Everybody I know," he said, "I always send them up your way."

Shake knew it. "I appreciate it."

"Even though they come back and say, 'Why you can't do lobster like that, man?'"

"Now you're just bullshitting me," Shake said. "Which I appreciate as well."

Pijua let Shake eat for a minute.

"At least you didn't borrow no money from Baby Jesus," Pijua said. Watching Shake as he said it.

"Is that what you heard?" Shake said.

"Because you don't want to borrow no money from Baby Jesus."

"You don't have to tell me that." Which was true.

Pijua let it drop. His daughter hollered at him from across the room.

"Shit, man," Pijua told Shake. "Like I said, your food's good. Stick it out, you'll see. The wind turns around."

"The wind turns around."

Pijua slapped him on the shoulder and headed back to his kitchen.

• • •

ON HIS WAY OUT, SHAKE passed a woman seated on the outdoor deck. At a table by herself, going over the menu. She was in her late thirties or early forties, somewhere around there, and pretty. The paperback book next to her purse was one Shake had read when he first moved to Belize.

He walked past her, made it down the wooden steps to the street, and then stopped. He sighed. It was like he could feel Idaba watching him, with that carved-rock expression of hers that he could never interpret.

He turned around and climbed back up the wooden steps. What the hell.

"Hi," he said.

The woman glanced up from her menu. Shake decided that maybe her face was more interesting than pretty. Or maybe interestingly pretty. Her eyes were dark with a vaguely exotic tilt, like there was an Asian branch of her family tree. But she also had the rosy cheeks of a Minnesota farm girl and a square, all-American jaw.

"Not interested," she said. "Thanks."

Her bluntness took him by surprise. And then after a second he remembered the plastic bag of fruit he was holding.

Shake smiled. "I'm not selling anything."

"Awesome. 'Cause I'm not buying."

She smiled back at him, a helluva smile, like the sun sliding out from behind a cloud and lighting up the sky. Shake stood there like an idiot until Pijua's daughter rescued him by coming out to take the woman's order.

"Try the pulled-pork empanadas," Shake said, finding his footing again. "You won't be sorry."

"The fish tacos, please," the woman said. But when Pijua's daughter started to write the order down, the woman said, "Wait."

Pijua's daughter gave Shake a wink and headed back inside.

"My name's Shake," he told the woman. "I know you were just dying to know that, be honest."

The woman considered. She was wearing a UC Santa Cruz T-shirt and khaki cargo shorts that showed off a nice pair of legs.

"Evelyn," she said. "Shake?"

"A nickname."

"I hope so."

She hadn't asked him to sit down, but she hadn't asked him to leave either. Well, not in so many words. Shake decided to stay until she told him to leave, in so many words. He nodded at the paperback by her purse.

"So where do you stand on the scarlet macaw?" he said.

The book was a true story about the fight over a rare kind of bird. The government of Belize wanted to lower the cost of electricity by building a dam on a river where the scarlet macaws lived. Don't worry, the government said, the birds will be fine. A group of environmentalists called bullshit on that and said the scarlet macaws would not be fine. They suggested that eco-tourists would pay a lot of money to go watch the scarlet macaws, if the government would just be smart about it.

"Definitely pro-macaw," the woman said. "But don't ruin the ending for me."

The way she said it, the corner of her mouth turned up, Shake could tell she'd seen enough of the world to know how the story ended. The government built the dam, some government ministers made a whole lot of money, electricity prices went up, not down. And the scarlet macaws in Belize had disappeared.

"If you want to have dinner tonight," Shake said, and then stopped when he realized how that sounded.

"Most people do," she said. "I feel like I'm pretty conventional in that way."

"What I mean," Shake said, smiling again, "I mean I own a restaurant. I do the cooking there. If you're looking for a completely unbiased recommendation."

"I see."

"The Sunset Breeze. It's up north a little bit. You can take a taxi boat."

Pijua's daughter brought the pork empanadas. The woman pretended to reach for the bottle of ketchup on the table and Shake laughed. And then he realized she was serious. And then she laughed.

"You should have seen your face," she said. "I didn't think you'd fall for that."

"You'd be surprised what I fall for," Shake said.

She hit him again with that flash grenade of a smile.

"Good to know," she said, and Shake felt the back of his neck flush with heat.

WALKING BACK TO THE WHARF, Shake saw a thirty-six-foot Esprit cruiser slide by on its way to the Cut, between San Pedro and the north end of Ambergris. It had flames painted on the side and a couple of big Rasta bruisers lounging on deck. Baby Jesus's boat, the one he used to run product up to the Yucatán.

Shake didn't let the sight of the boat bring him down. He was still thinking about the woman back on the deck at Pijua's, that smile of hers. Evelyn. Whatever happened from here on out, Shake decided, his day had already turned out better than he'd hoped.

Chapter 3

Special Agent Evelyn Holly had been at the table for twenty minutes, nursing a diet Mountain Dew and keeping an eye on the shithead inside. She knew that she couldn't lurk around the restaurant much longer without ordering food, but she was on her own dime this trip, not Uncle Sam's, and everything on the menu seemed to cost twice what it should have.

She ducked behind the menu when the shithead walked past. But then he turned around and came right up to her table. Charles "Shake" Bouchon, smiling right at her. Evelyn almost burst out laughing. He'd already made her, less than half an hour after she'd begun tailing him? But she stayed cool and realized that the shithead was just hitting on her. That almost made her burst out laughing too.

Well, no time like the present. She'd been planning to approach him in a day or two anyway, strike up a conversation.

"I'm not selling," he said.

"Awesome," she said. "'Cause I'm not buying."

She hoped that might catch him on the wrong foot and it did. But Bouchon didn't get flustered like most guys would have. He didn't flee or try to force a clever comeback. Instead he just stood there, amused, and seemed to appreciate that she'd caught him on the wrong foot.

The waitress appeared. Evelyn bit the bullet and ordered one of the pricey entrées. And then realized, as she handed over the menu, what a knucklehead she was. Everything seemed to cost twice what it should have because the prices were listed in Belizean dollars. There were two Belizean dollars to every U.S. dollar.

"My name's Shake," Bouchon said. "I know you were just dying to know that, be honest."

Be honest, he was kind of a nice-looking guy for a shithead. Evelyn hadn't guessed it from the California Department of Corrections mug shot that she'd studied on the plane down from L.A. Grim stuff, that. Here in person, though, she saw that he had good sharp angles, chin and cheeks and brow. But the angles not *too* sharp, softened just so by the wry smile, the warm eyes, the wrinkles at the corners of his eyes. He had a touch of an accent that sounded like it had a little Brooklyn in it, but Evelyn knew it must be New Orleans, where his sheet said he'd been born and raised.

When he asked about the book she was reading and then told her about the restaurant he owned, Evelyn thought: *Wow, could this be any easier?* She'd arrived in Belize without much of a plan. Take a few days and just get to know the shithead a little, let him think he was getting to know her. Develop a bond. And then, when Bouchon let his guard down, *wham!* Evelyn would put the screws to him.

Evelyn loved that saying: *putting the screws to someone.* She loved doing it.

But at this point, Bouchon definitely had his guard up. Evelyn didn't let the wry smile and the warm eyes fool her. You didn't stay alive as long as he had, in the kind of company he'd kept, without staying on your toes. He'd only done two relatively light stretches in prison, which in his line of work was evidence that he was one careful shithead.

She reached for the ketchup. He laughed because he thought she was kidding. She wasn't kidding. The empanadas looked like something you might reasonably put ketchup on. He stopped laughing when he saw her face. So she laughed.

"You should have seen your face," she said. "I didn't think you'd fall for that."

"You'd be surprised what I fall for," the Shithead said.

Evelyn smiled. This would be so easy. It almost wasn't fair. "Good to know," she said.

SHE ATE THE EMPANADAS, ADMITTEDLY fantastic, talked herself out of dessert, and then drove her rented golf cart back to the resort.

From her bungalow, she called to check on Sarah. It was noon in L.A. Sarah told her that Andre had come by to take her to breakfast at the Farmers Market. Evelyn didn't say the approximately one thousand things she had to say about that. About how the sneaky asshole waited until Evelyn was out of the country to show even the slightest interest in his own daughter.

"Send me a text later," Evelyn said. "Tell me how much you miss me."

"Mom!" Sarah laughed. "You're such a dork."

Evelyn had been gone less than twenty-four hours and already she missed Sarah so much it ached.

"Don't text when you're driving. Don't borrow my yoga mat and lose it again. Don't join a cult."

"Check, check, oops," Sarah said. "Too late."

And don't believe anything that your asshole of a father tells you, Evelyn thought but didn't say.

"Does it seem like a nice cult at least?" Evelyn said. "Do they have a cute secluded compound in the desert?"

Her daughter was, literally, the last teenager in California who would ever join a cult. Or text while driving. Evelyn knew that Sarah would probably spend the rest of her weekend studying for the SATs, practicing her jump shot, and downloading recipes for healthy, delicious, one-pot meals. Maybe taking a break to learn Farsi and help inner-city kids create a sustainable dairy farm.

She wouldn't, in other words, be smoking pot or luring a skateboard punk rocker up to her bedroom or sneaking into a club to see Social Distortion. Nor any of the other myriad transgressions that Evelyn would have committed, sixteen years old and left more or less on her own for a week.

Sometimes Evelyn couldn't believe that she and Sarah came from the same gene pool. If they didn't have the same laugh, the same scowl first thing in the morning, the same gangly legs, Evelyn might have seriously wondered about some mix-up in the maternity ward, a nurse switching one baby for another.

"Text me," Evelyn said. "Every fifteen minutes if it's convenient, okay?"

"Mom!"

A few minutes after Evelyn hung up, there was a knock on the door. She took her firearm out of her purse, chambered a round, and checked the peephole. On the deck of her bungalow stood Cory Nadler, of all people.

Evelyn stuck the gun back in her purse and opened the door.

"Cory?" she said.

"Hi, Evi," he said. He looked cranky and sweaty. "Can I come in?"

"Sure. Of course." She took a seat on the edge of the bed. He sat in the wicker chair with the floral-print cushion. He was wearing a navy suit that looked way too hot for this climate. "What are you doing here, Cory?"

"I'm with DSS now," he said.

"Diplomatic security?"

"Out of the embassy in Mexico City. But I've been doing liaison work in Belize the last couple of months. I happened to be looking through passenger manifests this morning and I saw your name."

"Cory," she said, "take your coat off. That suit looks way too hot for Belize."

"It's fine," he said.

"Is it wool? You look like you're dying."

"It's tropical wool."

Evelyn cocked her head, dubious. "I don't think it is."

"Evi, shut up for a second, okay?" Cory was eight or nine years younger than she was, in his early thirties, but he'd probably been one of those kids who, in kindergarten, listened to classical music and wore sweater vests. The kind of man her daughter would probably marry someday. "You can't be here, Evi."

"I'm on vacation," she said.

"Vacation."

She shrugged.

"Did you pack a bathing suit?" he said.

"Maybe."

Cory sighed. "Evi," he said, "I've known you for how long?"

"So you know I need a vacation."

"I know you've still got a major, major hard-on for the Armenians, even after you were explicitly told to cool it with all that."

"Real girls don't get hard-ons, Cory. You've spent too much time in Bangkok."

"I know that Charles Samuel Bouchon, aka 'Shake,' alleged former wheelman for and close associate of the Armenian *pakhan* in L.A., allegedly owns a restaurant on this island. I know that you're still pissed off that your ex-husband—"

"Stop. Thank you. Right there." She didn't need anyone to walk her back through it. Seriously.

The short version was that Evelyn, a couple of years ago, had helped build a slam-dunk case against the Armenian mob. Evelyn had been *this close* to taking them down, top to bottom, *pakhan* to foot soldier, when the district attorney in Los Angeles blindsided her by negotiating a deal between the Armenians and the feds. It turned out that the Armenians knew the whereabouts of a fugitive Wall Street swindler that the Department of Justice was desperate to nail. So DOJ got their swindler, the Armenians got a time-out called on the racketeering investigation, and the asshole D.A. in Los Angeles—Andre Guardado, Evelyn's ex-husband—was the hero of the hour.

Well, that was then, this was now. Now, as far as Evelyn was concerned, whatever time-out the Armenians had earned two years ago had expired. Game on.

"Here's the thing, Evi." Cory leaned forward, the shoulders of his allegedly tropical wool suit coat bunching up. "DEA has been down here since October with a major, major ongoing. Okay? Serious stuff, a drug kingpin here in Belize with ties to the Zeta cartel. You have any idea how long it took me to get the Belizean government on board?"

"Good for you, Cory. I always thought you'd make an excellent liaison."

"DEA has put the kingpin together with Bouchon a couple of times. It's maybe nothing, it's maybe something. So help me God, Evi, if you step on this investigation, if you disrupt or compromise it in any way . . ."

"I'm not going to step on anything."

"Because you're on vacation."

"Exactly."

It had taken Evelyn almost a year to track down Bouchon. Alleged former wheelman for and close associate of the Armenian *pakhan*. Alleged, her ass. He'd worked with the Armenians for years, and his relationship with Alexandra Ilandryan, if the rumors were true, had been closer than close. With his cooperation, Evelyn could put her, and every Khederian, Ghazarian, and Bazarian, behind bars till the end of time.

Bouchon wouldn't *want* to cooperate. That was okay with Evelyn. She did her best work with shitheads who didn't want to cooperate. Back in elementary school she'd been a gleeful playground bully, taller and stronger and craftier than the other kids. Her brothers, whom she had bullied relentlessly, still called her Evil Lynn.

Cory was studying her. "And Mike," he said. "If I called your ASAC, he'd confirm that?"

She shrugged again. Mike was her supervisor, the assistant special agent in charge of the Los Angeles field office. "Mike knows I'm on vacation," she said.

"But not *where*, I bet."

Evelyn had learned early in life that the advantage of having a great smile was the impression you could make when you shut it off abruptly.

She did it now. Cory shifted uncomfortably.

"I'm not, you know, I'm not going to call Mike," he said. "I just want to make clear that if you stay down here—*on vacation*—you have to keep a low profile. It's critical. A low, low profile. And *stay away from Bouchon.*"

Evelyn turned the smile back on. "Of course," she said. "Absolutely."

Chapter 4

The young honeymooners from last night were back again. Shake told Idaba to seat them inside tonight, since the wind had picked up and the tables on the veranda were getting blasted. Plus, there was only one other customer so far, an older man eating by himself. Shake didn't want the dining room to look deserted if the woman he'd met at Pijua's actually showed up.

He didn't know if she would or not. She was a tough read. But it was still early, only a little after seven, so there was time. It occurred to Shake that a high percentage of the women he'd been attracted to over the years had been tough reads. He wondered what that said about him.

In the kitchen, Roger was explaining to Armando how soccer was a sport fit to be played only by homosexuals, and how that made anyone who watched soccer, like Armando, even more of a homosexual than the homosexuals who played it. Armando was asking Roger if everyone from Detroit liked giving the business to dogs and other stray animals, and getting the business from dogs and other stray animals, or was it just the *pendejos* like Roger? Neither Armando nor Roger was doing any work. They were lounging around and rolling a lemon back and forth across the floor.

Shake plated the conch fritters for the honeymooners and took the order out himself. The honeymooners were holding hands across the table again. They looked even younger and more sun-flushed than they had the night before.

"Good day?" Shake asked.

"Oh my God," the girl said. "It rocked!"

"We went ziplining," the kid said.

"This is the most amazing week of my life," the girl said. "I'm not even kidding."

"I know!" the kid said.

They started gazing into each other's eyes, so Shake left them to it. On his way back to the kitchen he stopped to check on the other table, the older man, who had ordered the lobster and a bottle of a good Argentine white.

"How's that lobster treating you?" Shake said.

"Let me ask you something," the older man said.

"Fire away."

"Harrigan Quinn, by the way." The man held out his hand and Shake shook it. "Call me Quinn."

"Shake."

The man kept his grip, strong, on Shake's hand. He was a youthful seventy or so, tall, tan, and fit, with craggy good looks and a full head of wavy white hair. He reminded Shake of someone, but Shake couldn't put a finger on who. He was wearing pressed khakis, a pale pink polo shirt, and on his tan wrist a Patek Philippe that could have paid off a lot of Shake's debt to Baby Jesus.

"This is your place, I take it?" the man said.

"For better or worse."

"All right. Here's my question." He finally gave Shake his hand back.

"You know what's the one thing, not music, that's the universal language? Not sex either."

"Food?" Shake guessed.

"Food. I'll tell you why."

He pinched the crease on his khakis and crossed his legs. Shake could sense him settling in for the long haul.

"Excuse me, Mr. Quinn. I should get back to the kitchen."

"Harry. Please. I'm not your high school principal, am I?"

The woman Shake had met at Pijua's entered the dining room. Shake watched Idaba lead her to a table.

"Harry," he said. "Enjoy your meal and let me know if there's anything you need."

He escaped and crossed the room. He waited till Idaba handed off the menu and then stepped up to the woman's table.

"Evelyn," Shake said. "I was positive there was a remote chance you might show up."

She'd changed into a dress and her dark hair was down around her bare shoulders. In this light—tabletop candles and the lanterns on the wall turned low—her smile was even more dazzling.

"I had to see it for myself," she said. "The kind of place that the kind of guy like you would own."

"The kind of guy like me?"

She looked around the room, taking her time and not missing anything. Shake had a feeling, he couldn't explain it, that maybe her father had been a cop, maybe her brothers and uncles too.

"I see you've got a 'ye olde sailing ship' thing going on."

"That was the previous owner," Shake said.

"A little on the nose for a place on the beach, don't you think?"

"Like I said."

"But I dig the—mermaids?"

She pointed toward the wall at one of the few additions that Shake was responsible for. Hung there were half a dozen folk-art figures made from painted coconut shells, leather, old tin cans.

"The kind of guy like me?" he asked again.

She opened the menu. "So. How good are the conch fritters?"

"On a scale of nine to ten?" Shake pondered. "Hard call."

She started to answer but stopped because Armando, the waiter, had come up next to Shake. Armando tugged at Shake's sleeve. Shake wasn't thrilled by the timing. He was warming fast to Idaba's advice about getting a woman in his bed, if that woman turned out to be this woman.

"What?" he said.

"He want you, boss," Armando said.

"Who?" Shake looked around. The old guy, Harrigan Quinn, was flagging Shake down. He had pulled his chair over and was sitting now with the young honeymooners. Shake wondered how they knew one another.

"Tell Idaba to take care of it," Shake said.

"He say it got to be you, boss."

"All right." Shake turned back to Evelyn. "Don't go anywhere."

"Don't worry," she said. "I'm not through with you yet."

Shake paused, then hurried back across the room. Idaba was watching him with what might have been interest.

"How's everybody doing over here?" Shake said.

"I want you to hear this too, Shake," Quinn said. Saying it like he'd known Shake all his life. Making Shake almost believe it. "You're going to love this."

Shake forced a smile. He decided that Quinn, with his craggy good looks and alert blue eyes, looked like he could have acted in B-movie westerns when he was young, the handsome deputy who took a bullet for the girl he loved.

"I'll tell you what," Shake said. "If you could just give me a—"

"A while back I was in Nicaragua on business," Quinn said. "My first time in Central America. Like the lovebirds here, that's why I thought of it. Anyway. I get invited to a big shindig at a mansion outside Managua, beautiful place, amazing view of the volcano. This would have been the late seventies, before the Sandinistas. The shindig was a surprise birthday party for the *commandante* himself, Somoza. The whole nine yards, fountain filled with champagne and a stripper popping out of a cake."

Shake looked over at the honeymoon couple. They were looking at him. Shake realized that they didn't know Quinn at all, that he must have invited himself over to their table.

"Next thing I know," Quinn went on, "wouldn't you know it, I'm in the back of a limo barreling up the volcano. Me and Somoza—'Tachito' everybody called him—and the stripper that popped out of the cake. She's the one driving the limo, still naked as a jaybird, nothing on her but a little chocolate frosting. She must've been doing a hundred, hundred and ten, laughing like crazy and coked out of her mind. Somoza's bodyguard, he's about to have a coronary. So he says, '*Commandante*, maybe we should slow down.' So Tachito, Somoza, nice and calm he snaps open his holster and pulls out his piece, Beretta 92F. And he points it at the stripper's head—she's got us up to a hundred and ten by now, remember—and he tells his bodyguard, 'You want to slow down? *No problemo.*'"

Quinn chuckled and took a sip of his wine. The honeymoon girl was looking at her husband, telling him with her eyebrows to do something. He was pretending he couldn't speak eyebrow.

"Quinn," Shake said, but that was all the edgewise the old guy gave him.

"Now, I'm about to have a coronary, you've got my word on that. Because if Somoza pulls that trigger and shoots the stripper, we all go flying off the side of the volcano and the monkeys down in the jungle below will be picking us out of their fur for the next few days."

Shake hoped Idaba would know what the hell to do with this guy. He turned to motion her over. Instead, though, he found himself staring at a man in a ski mask.

A man in a ski mask. With a gun.

Shake was so surprised that he just stood there when the man in the mask stepped past him, lifted the gun, and leveled it at Quinn.

"So long story short," Quinn was saying, "the stripper looks back at the gun Somoza has pointed at her, and she just keeps laughing. You know what she says?"

Quinn noticed the man in the ski mask. The honeymooners did too. Time stopped for one fat, floating second, like even the gunman was waiting to hear the end of the story.

And then everything sped up to a blur. Shake grabbed the gunman's arm, the gunman pulled the trigger. The explosion of the gun going off was like plate glass shattering inside Shake's head. The bullet blew a hole through the wall behind Quinn, about a foot above his head.

The honeymoon girl screamed and Quinn ducked down behind the table. Shake tried to hold on to the gunman's arm, but the gunman was stronger. He yanked his arm away before Shake could get his other hand on the gun.

Shake was dead. Just standing there, breathing, thinking how quick it was going to be, all the lights going out.

But the gunman ignored Shake. He swung the gun back around and fired at Quinn again, missing again, smashing a lantern. Quinn was on the move, crawling fast across the floor toward the next table over. The gunman blasted away at him, but either he was nervous or a terrible shot or both. Plates exploded, wood crunched, one of the glass portholes in the kitchen doors blew out. Quinn made it to the table and then went crawling for the next one.

Shake ducked down and scooted over to the honeymooners. The girl was still screaming, the pitch rising and falling like a car alarm. He pulled the table over on its side to provide some cover for the three of them. It wasn't much cover, but you had to play the cards the dealer flopped.

Across the room, Evelyn had pulled a table over too. Smart girl—Shake congratulated himself on his taste in women. Though he doubted that this incident would speed along their relationship. Idaba and Armando were crouched behind the checkout stand. Roger hadn't emerged from the kitchen. Either he'd already fled halfway to San Pedro or was so drunk he hadn't noticed anything wrong.

Three more gunshots. *Bambambam.* More glass breaking, more wood snapping, more sparks showering everywhere when the gunman hit another lantern.

"Screw you!" someone yelled. It took Shake a second to realize that the gunman wasn't yelling at Quinn, Quinn was yelling at the gunman. "Screw you, punk!"

Are you kidding me? Shake thought.

Bambam. Bam. Bam.

Idaba peeked around the checkout stand and gave Shake a look that said, *Do something!*

Shake gave her a look back that said, *Yeah? Like what?*

The smart play, Shake knew, was no play. The gunman was after Quinn. When he got him, there was an excellent chance he'd leave without hurting anyone else. He'd already had a chance to shoot Shake and passed it up.

But the smart play meant Shake would have to sit by and watch an innocent unarmed man get gunned down in cold blood. He didn't think he could do that. It was, Shake realized, a dangerous defect of character.

When the shooting stopped, Shake snuck a look. The gunman was fumbling with a new clip. Shake didn't give himself time to think about what he was about to do. He darted out from behind the table, put his shoulder down, and hit the gunman hard from behind.

They both went down. The gun tumbled loose. The gunman bounced up first and grabbed it. Shake was long past his bouncing days, but managed to lurch up and sideways and grabbed the gunman's wrist.

Now they were back where they'd started. Once again, the gunman tried to yank his arm away from Shake. Shake held on. The gunman yanked again, harder. Shake held on again. The third time the gunman yanked, with all his strength, Shake stepped into it, steered, and helped the gunman bash himself in the face with his own gun. The gunman dropped the gun and stumbled backward, clutching his nose. Shake kicked the gun away. He didn't want to risk the guy coming at him when he bent down to pick it up.

The gunman glared at Shake and seemed to be thinking about coming at him anyway. His eyes, all that Shake could see because of the ski mask, blinked fast and watered.

"Be smart," Shake said.

Quinn had climbed out from beneath a table and was tucking his pink polo shirt back into his pants. His face was flushed, but the head of wavy white hair had not been ruffled.

"What are you gonna do now, punk!" Quinn said.

"All of us!" Shake said. Jesus Christ. "All of us be smart!"

The gunman edged back toward the veranda door, still holding his nose. When he got to the door, he turned and ran.

Shake went to the window. He watched the gunman sprint across the beach, stumble once, stumble again, and then make it to the pier. He ran to the end of the pier and jumped into a Boston Whaler that was waiting for him. A second guy in a ski mask was at the wheel of the Boston Whaler. The boat pealed away into the night, kicking up a big sheet of foam that hung, shimmered, and finally collapsed.

Roger, wild-eyed, stuck his head out of the kitchen.

"Yow!" he said. "Ho!"

"Everybody all right?" Idaba said.

The honeymoon girl was still screaming. Shake realized that she'd never stopped. His own heart kept hammering, hammering, like it might never stop either. Shake put a hand on the wall and leaned against it.

"Don't worry," Roger said. "I called the cops."

Oh, no, Shake thought. *Shit.*

OH, NO, EVELYN THOUGHT WHEN the sketchy dude in the stained apron stepped out of the kitchen and announced that he'd called the cops. *Shit.*

Well, of course he'd called the cops, or somebody had, but that didn't make Evelyn's current situation any less sticky. As a United States law enforcement official, a special agent of the Federal Bureau of Investigation, she had sworn duties and responsibilities. She took them seriously. Like, don't leave the scene of an attempted murder. Like, wait for the cops and answer their questions with truth and candor.

But, *shit,* if she waited for the cops and answered their questions, it would take Cory Nadler at DSS about a minute to find out where she'd been tonight, what she'd been up to. After telling her, and throwing such a hiss about it, to keep a low profile and *stay away from Bouchon.*

She rehearsed the conversation in her head.

"Cory, I was just having dinner."

"*Where* were you having dinner, Evi?"

And then he'd pick up the phone and call Mike, her ASAC back in L.A. And Evelyn would be in so much shit that she'd never slog her way out again.

Evelyn hadn't known that a human being could keep screaming for as long as the girl across the room had. The screaming girl and her husband appeared unharmed. So did everyone else. The hostess, a formidable-looking black woman with a gold ring in her nose and a sort of turban on her head, was gently trying to calm the screaming girl down. *Shhh, shhh, shhh.*

Evelyn probably would have just given the girl a slap. A gentle one.

When the shooting started, Evelyn had reached for her purse. And then remembered she didn't have her firearm. Cory had made her promise to lock it in the hotel room safe. Evelyn didn't need a gun on vacation, he'd pointed out, now, did she?

So that had left her—as she hunched behind the table and counted the shots from the shooter's Glock— armed with nothing but a steak knife.

She'd assumed, at first, that the shooter's target was the shithead— *her* shithead, damn it, just her luck. She wondered how in the world the Armenians could have known that she was there to flip him. They *couldn't* have known.

After a couple of quick peek-and-ducks, a stray bullet zinging past, she realized that the target was actually the old guy.

He was yelling at the shooter, taunting him. Evelyn was 1,000 percent certain nothing good could come of that. She was surprised the shooter hadn't hit the old guy yet, but not shocked. It happened sometimes. A shooter's adrenaline went crazy, the target kept moving, the gun kicked and jumped. Evelyn had seen TV footage once, caught by a local news crew, of a client trying to shoot his lawyer outside a courthouse. Point-blank range, but the lawyer kept moving, juking, ducking behind a tree. He'd survived, not a scratch on him.

Evelyn doubted he'd been taunting the shooter, though.

When she'd counted fifteen shots, the magazine empty, she started to make her move. To her surprise, Bouchon was already making one of his own. He tackled the shooter and knocked him to the floor. The gun came free, but Evelyn had to stay where she was. She could probably get to the gun before the shooter did, but that really wasn't something you wanted to be *almost* sure about.

The shooter got to the gun before Bouchon did. They wrestled and then the shooter punched himself in the face. Evelyn wasn't exactly sure how Bouchon arranged that, but the shooter dropped the gun and took off.

Now the sound of sirens began to drift in through the broken window. *Shit,* Evelyn thought again.

Bouchon had checked on the screaming girl, and now came over to check on Evelyn. He looked like he might want to say something clever, but finally he just ran a hand through his hair and sighed.

"You're bleeding," he said.

Evelyn reached up and touched the lobe of her ear. A sharp fragment of painted coconut shell had stabbed into the wall right next to her head. Bouchon worked the piece of coconut shell loose from the wood. It still had a little blood from her ear on it.

"Your poor mermaid," Evelyn said. The mermaid had been smashed to pieces by a stray bullet.

"Other than all that," he said, "it's been a pretty good day."

She smiled. She was finding it harder and harder to think of him as a shithead. He was, no question. In Evelyn's book, anyone who made a living from unlawful activity, past, present, or future, was a shithead. But she'd always been able to read people well. She'd known, for example, that her ex-husband was an asshole the minute she met him. Shake Bouchon just didn't seem that bad of a guy, for a bad guy.

She was still going to put the screws to him. It just wouldn't be quite so much fun now. Maybe.

"I'll go get the first-aid kit," he said. He left as the sirens grew louder.

Evelyn had to make a decision. If she stayed, she reasoned, she wouldn't be able to give the cops much. She hadn't seen anything that the other witnesses hadn't. On the other hand, her continued presence here would definitely jeopardize the case against the Armenians, who were surely a much greater threat to society than some lone gunman with terrible aim. Right?

Her earlobe started to sting. She made sure that no one was paying attention to her and slipped out the front door.

EVELYN SAW LIGHTS FLASHING ACROSS the water—the cops were coming by boat. So she headed inland until she found an unpaved road that ran parallel to the beach, behind the resorts and restaurants. She walked along that for half an hour or so, tripping in the darkness and fighting off mosquitoes. When she figured that she'd gone far enough, she cut back toward the beach to a hotel pier, and from there she caught the ferry to town.

Evelyn sent Sarah a text from the ferry.

Howzit, sweetpea? Everything here is great but miss u. Love, mom.

It was eleven o'clock by the time she got back to her resort. Her dress was torn and her hair was a mess. Not to mention the mosquito bites on her legs and the wounded earlobe, caked with dried blood. The female desk clerk in the lobby gave her a sour look. Assuming, no doubt, that Evelyn was just another debauched gringa tourist, fresh off some wild, booze-soaked sexual encounter.

Evelyn wished. She ducked her head and hurried past.

Chapter 5

Maybe Shake was just feeling sorry for himself, but each bullet, it seemed, had managed to cause the maximum possible damage to his restaurant.

He frowned at yet another ugly gouge in the floor. One bullet had hit the paneled wall in such a way that the wood cracked, splintered, and split apart, floor to ceiling. Two lanterns had been blasted to pieces. Two windows broken. An antique ship's wheel had fallen off the wall and crushed an antique ship in a bottle.

Cops swarmed all over the dining room, digging bullets out of the walls and bagging shell casings and dusting every surface for fingerprints. This was the most excitement the San Pedro Police Department had seen in years. They were having the time of their lives.

"It was a robbery," one of the cops sitting with Shake said.

"It wasn't a robbery," Shake said. "I told you. He was shooting at the old guy."

"Why?" the other cop asked.

"Ask him," Shake said.

Quinn was sitting across the room with another cop and the chief of police. He had his legs crossed and was doing all the talking.

Shake didn't much care why the gunman had been shooting at the old guy. Shake had bigger worries. His restaurant was trashed and he couldn't afford to shut down, not even for a minute. Baby Jesus would expect his next payment, rain or shine, no excuses.

Shake watched Quinn pour himself a glass of wine. Miraculously, his bottle of Argentine white had survived the mayhem. When Shake had gone to see if Quinn was okay, right after the gunman fled, Quinn had waved the question off. "Hell," he'd said.

"Please describe the robber again," the cop told Shake now.

Shake sighed. "Six two, two hundred pounds or so, a white guy."

"He was a white guy."

"He was a white guy."

"But you said he was wearing a mask!" The cop leaned forward, eyes shining. He'd seen too many reruns of *Law & Order.*

"It was a ski mask," Shake said. "I could see part of his nose and some of his forehead."

"And that was white?"

"And around his eyes. Yes. It was white."

The other cop made a note in his notebook.

Shake looked around the room. The woman, Evelyn, had disappeared. He didn't know what to make of that. She'd been gone when Shake returned from the kitchen with the first-aid kit for her ear.

He spotted the reporter from the island newspaper taking photos of a smashed lamp. Shake jumped up, crossed the room, and grabbed the guy by the arm.

"Hey!" the reporter said.

"No," Shake said. "No, no, no."

He propelled the reporter out onto the veranda, and then off the veranda.

"Take it easy, man," the reporter said. "No harm."

"No harm?" Shake said. He saw a crowd of lookie-loos on the beach, drawn from the bar next door by the flashing police lights. "Get out of here!" he yelled. "Free beer next door!"

A couple of people chuckled, but nobody moved. Shake went back inside.

The police chief came over. He seemed glad to take a break from Quinn. "He don't shut up," the chief said. "I'm ready to shoot him myself."

Shake nodded. "He know why somebody'd want to take a shot at him?"

"He say he don't know," the chief said. "Who do you think? Was it a professional, you think?"

"I don't know," Shake said. If the gunman had been a professional, Shake didn't know what that said about the state of the profession. He shook the chief's hand and passed over the bills folded in his palms. "I appreciate all your help with this, Chief. I appreciate your discretion."

"My pleasure."

"You know what I mean?"

"Shake," the chief said. "You hear about that tourist last week? That fishing accident on the flats?"

"I didn't."

The chief waited. Shake caught up.

"Okay," he said. "Thanks. You want me to make you something to eat? Some rice and beans?"

"Later," the chief said. He saw Idaba approaching and hurried back to Quinn. There wasn't anyone on the island who wasn't scared of Idaba.

"They're ready," she told Shake.

"You think so?"

She shrugged. He followed her to the kitchen. The young honeymooners were leaning against the reach-in, sipping hot tea that Idaba had made for them.

"I'm glad you're both okay," Shake said, his opening argument.

"You think we're okay?" the kid said. Not so much in anger as in disbelief.

"Well," Shake said, Idaba scowling at him, "I just mean—"

"Oh my God!" the girl said. "We could have been killed! That was the most horrible, the most . . . the most . . ."

"It's our honeymoon!" the kid said. Angry now, but Shake thought it was mostly for the girl's benefit.

"Listen," Shake said. "I want to do what I can here. Okay? When are you supposed to go home? To Buffalo?"

"Tuesday," the kid said. "Why?"

"Why don't you spend a few extra days in Belize? I'll cover your hotel."

"Really?" the kid said.

"And your meals," Shake said. "You can eat here for free."

The kid was thrilled, but he needed to gauge his bride's attitude before he showed his hand. He turned to her.

"We don't have to have to *have to* be back home till Wednesday," he said.

"What if it costs money to change our flight?" she said. "It costs to change the flight even if it's a frequent flyer award."

"I'll cover that too," Shake said.

"That would rock," the kid said.

"And we'd want to do a snorkel trip," the girl said. "If we were going to be here a few extra days. There's that place up north?"

Holy shit. Shake was impressed. The girl was shaking him down like a pro.

"And I'll cover your snorkel trip too," he said. "As long as you don't mention any of this. All right? The shooting. You don't write about it on TripAdvisor."

They agreed. Shake went back into the dining room to see if the cops were done taking Quinn's statement, but Quinn was already on his way to the pier. The chief said he'd sent a couple of his men to escort Quinn back to his resort.

Shake caught up to them on the beach.

"There he is!" Quinn said.

"Mr. Quinn. If I could talk to you a second."

"You saved my bacon back there, Shake."

"Don't mention it."

"Don't mention it." Quinn turned to the cops. "You hear this guy?"

"Mr. Quinn," Shake said. "I'm just thinking. It probably doesn't do anyone any good, does it? Word of this gets around. You know?"

Quinn laughed and clapped a hand on Shake's shoulder, squeezed hard. "You hear this guy?" he asked the cops again.

The cops boxed Shake out and steered Quinn toward the pier.

Shake walked slowly back up to the restaurant. He felt exhausted all of a sudden, too dense for the earth's gravity. Idaba was waiting on the veranda for him.

"Well?" she said.

She and Shake watched the police boat with Quinn on board pull away from the pier.

"I think we're good," Shake said.

Chapter 6

Terry's nose hurt so bad he thought he was gonna pass out. It was like getting smashed in the face every time he took a breath or the boat hit a bump in the water. Blood and snot bubbling out. He wished he hadn't tossed the ski mask over the side, 'cause then at least he'd have something other than his sleeve to press against his nose. But Meg said they had to get rid of the evidence, don't be a goddamn moron.

She was driving the boat. Wind whipping her hair around, one hand on the wheel and the other fist on her hip, looking even more ferocious than usual. You wouldn't think that a little slip of a girl, just turned twenty-one years old, could look so ferocious. Barely five foot two, a hundred pounds dripping wet, with freckles and a cute button nose. But Meg never looked nothing but ferocious, even when she was sleeping. You didn't want to wake Meg up when she was sleeping, take it from Terry. He'd learned that the hard way.

She looked like a pirate right now, standing there at the wheel of the boat. In her cutoff jeans and wife-beater and bare little sun-brown feet with the nails painted pink. A sexy ferocious pirate.

"Goddamn it, Terry!" she said. He was sitting there right next to her, but she refused to look at him. Which meant either she had to keep her eyes on the water 'cause they had their running lights off and were going fast, or it meant Terry was in her doghouse big-time.

"Wasn't my fault, babe!" he said. "I ran out of bullets!"

"Swear to God, Terry. Who shoots off a whole clip and don't hit a goddamn thing?"

The boat bumped against the water, and Terry's nose blew out another big bubble of blood and snot. He whimpered. "I think my nose is busted," he said.

"Don't be a pussy," she said.

"But it hurts!"

"Pussy."

Terry climbed to his feet. Standing up hurt his nose even more than he'd expected it to, all the blood sloshing around in his face, but he didn't care. He walked to the back of the boat and stared out at the water foaming up behind them.

"Oh, for God's sake," he heard Meg say, and then louder, "C'mon, get back over here!" He walked back up to the front of the boat, but this time he was the one who refused to look at her. Two could play at that game. He admired the lights twinkling far off on the island.

"Stop that," Meg said.

"Stop what?"

"Feeling sorry for yourself."

"I'm not," he said. Though ask just about anyone, their nose got busted, if maybe they deserved a kind word or two. Just because one time Meg pulled a nail out of her own foot and then went right back to whatever she was doing, and another time didn't even know she had a cracked collarbone till the doctor told her. That didn't mean everybody else in the world was a pussy but her.

Though probably, Terry considered, everybody else in the world *was* a pussy, compared to Meg.

He'd made her go in and get a shot after she stepped on the nail. Everybody knew that your jaw could freeze shut otherwise, and then you'd starve to death.

"Get on over here," she said. He took a step closer, wary. She yanked him the rest of the way and then yanked again to bend him down. He was close to a foot taller than she was, unless she was standing on her tippy toes, or on the bottom rung of a bar stool. She reached up and kissed the bridge of his busted nose, her lips tender as a whisper.

"That feel better?"

He nodded. The first time he'd ever seen her, going on three years ago now at a bar in Anchorage, she'd been standing on the bottom rung of a bar stool, telling the bartender to pour her another goddamn shot of whiskey and hurry it up.

"Now sit back down and be still," Meg said. "Ain't nobody ever died of a busted goddamn nose."

She eased back the stick and turned the wheel. The boat drifted to a stop on the open water, facing sideways. She squinted her eyes and stared off into the darkness that they'd just come out of. Terry knew he better be quiet while she was doing that.

"I think we're all right," she said finally. "There ain't nobody following us."

"Maybe you just don't never hear about the ones that do," Terry said. " 'Cause they're the ones that died."

She looked at him. "What?"

"The ones died of a busted nose," he said. "So they're not around to tell you about it."

"Be still and don't monkey with that," she said.

She zipped open the backpack and rummaged around in it. Terry's nose was starting to feel a little bit better, so he gave it a tap, investigating. Oh, good Lord. The pain curlicued out all over and around his head, down his neck, like he was on fire and somebody was trying to stab out the fire with a butcher's knife.

"Goddamn it, Terry," Meg said. "What'd I just tell you?"

She found what she was looking for in the backpack. One of the crumpled-up foil packets of antibacterial wet wipes that Meg always carried. She didn't like to use the soap in public restrooms. She always said, "How do you know there wasn't some indigent homeless person right ahead of you just lathered up their pubes? And now you want to wash your hands with that same bar of soap?"

Terry thought that was a worst-case scenario. And more times than not, the soap was in a metal box bolted on the wall that you had to pump to get the soap out. But he wasn't about to start that argument again.

She tore open the foil packet and started cleaning his face with a wet wipe. Gentle strokes up and down and then side to side.

"I shoulda known better," she said, "a job this big. I shoulda gone in there, done it myself."

"Like hell I woulda let you done that," he said. "It was too dangerous."

"Not for nobody but you, it wasn't," she said.

She turned the wet wipe around and started using the other side of it. Terry kicked himself because she was right about how big the job was. It was their first real one. Up till now, the only work Meg's friend in Guatemala City ever used them for was to pick up a suitcase full of drugs over *here,* fly on a plane with it over *there,* then go on back to their dumpy hotel room and wait to do it all over again. The money wasn't bad, Terry supposed, but less than he'd been led to believe. And, shit, to be honest, it just wasn't the glamorous life of crime and sunny beaches that he'd imagined when they moved down from Alaska by way of Mexico eighteen months ago. Guatemala didn't even have beaches! Meg said that was all right, that's how it worked. You paid your dues, and when you got a chance to advance your career, you grabbed it.

When Meg's friend in Guatemala City called and asked were they up for something a little more challenging, Meg told Terry that this was it, this was their chance to advance their career and make a name for themselves. Her eyes gleaming, ferocious.

One time in Mexico, they'd been short on cash, so Meg found a drunk American businessman in a hotel bar. She'd told him she was on a mission trip with her high school Young Christian Leadership group, some Mexican had stole all her money, and now she had no way back to Memphis. The drunk businessman was already licking his chops. When Meg told him she was sixteen years old, he said he'd give her two hundred dollars if she came upstairs and let him take pictures of her naked with his cell phone.

When the drunk businessman unlocked the door to his room, Terry snuck up behind and pushed him inside. Terry was supposed to whack him on the head with the nearest thing at hand, but he couldn't find anything near at hand. So Meg took a glass ashtray off the coffee table and did it herself. The businessman was a giant compared to little Meg, but she wasn't scared at all. Meg, fearless and ferocious—the girl turned Terry on like nobody's business.

Terry realized Meg had been making fun of him. When she'd said going into the restaurant wasn't dangerous for nobody but him. Since the old man was supposed to get shot, and Terry was the one ended up with a busted nose.

"I winged him, I think," Terry said. "I bet I did."

"I swear to God, Terry. Tell me again why I love you? 'Cause hell if I know."

Terry smiled big, even though it hurt. "Me neither!"

She flicked the bloody wet wipe over the side of the boat. "It ain't supposed to make you happy, you goddamn moron, me not knowing why I love you."

"I don't care, babe," he said. "I'm just happy you do."

She sighed, exasperated, but then gave him another soft kiss on the nose. "It makes me so goddamn mad. What that son of a bitch did to your poor old nose."

She was talking about the chef at the restaurant. Terry knew he was the chef because of his white coat with the double row of buttons. Before Terry had gone to Alaska to work on the crab boats, he'd washed dishes for a time at a steak house in Plano.

"I don't take it personal," Terry said with a shrug. He didn't. He'd been mad as hell at the time, when the chef made him hit himself in the face with the gun. Now that he was calmed down, he saw it from the chef's point of view. Terry figured that if he had a restaurant and somebody tried to shoot one of his customers, he wouldn't like that much, either.

"Well, I do take it personal," Meg said. "Don't think I don't."

"Jorge ain't paying us but to take care of the old man." Jorge was Meg's friend in Guatemala City.

"Then he's gonna get a buy-one get-one-free, 'cause don't nobody bust up my baby's nose and live to brag about it." She kissed him again, this time on his mouth. He felt her hand tugging on his jeans, popping open the buttons one by one.

Terry didn't bear him any particular grudge, the restaurant chef who'd busted his nose. But he did like it when Meg got her blood all pumping away like this.

"Swear to God," she said, fishing around in Terry's boxer shorts until she pulled him loose. "I'm gonna stick my gun right between that son of a bitch's eyes and blow his brains every which way."

The wet wipe must have left some blood on Terry's face, 'cause now Meg had blood on hers from kissing him.

"You got blood on your lips," Terry said. "Like a vampire."

"Be still."

"A sexy vampire."

She sank down on top of him and closed her eyes. She made her humming sound. Terry was never sure it was a real song or not. He traced his thumb along her beautiful freckles.

"You just wait and see," she said, moving up up up and then down down down, her eyes still closed. "I'm gonna blow his brains to king-dom come."

Chapter 7

The last of the cops finally left around one. Shake spent the next few hours sweeping up broken glass and broken plates and fingerprint powder. He pried the splintered boards off the walls and tried to decide if the table that the gunman had shot up the worst was salvageable.

It wasn't. He dragged the table out back and heaved it into the Dumpster, along with a couple of chairs also beyond repair. Idaba worked most of the night too, even though he tried to send her home. She went at the floor with sandpaper until the gouges weren't quite so deep or so ugly.

"Get some stain in the morning," she said. "Put the stain on the floor."

"Sounds complicated," Shake said. "Can you write that down for me?"

She grunted at him and left. He went upstairs and slept till daybreak. He could have used a swim to forget his troubles, but instead he took the Wahoo straight into town. He spent the morning in San Pedro rounding up plywood, pine planks, paint, paintbrushes, wood filler, wood stain, and some batik fabric to cover the plywood he'd nail over the broken windows. He had to go to a different place for each item. The guy who sold paint was out of paintbrushes. The guy who sold plywood didn't sell two-by-twelve pine planks. That was the nature of a place like San Pedro. Charming until it was a pain in the ass.

Shake kept an eye out for Evelyn. He kept thinking about the slight exotic tilt to her eyes, her rosy midwestern cheeks. That smile. He liked how she hadn't fallen to pieces when the gunman started shooting up the restaurant. She hadn't fallen to pieces afterward either.

"Have I got a deal for you," Shake decided he might say if she came back to the restaurant tonight. He planned to offer her the same arrangement he'd offered the young honeymooners, hotel and meals if she agreed not to tell TripAdvisor about the gunman shooting up the restaurant. But Evelyn would get the VIP treatment—he'd insist on taking her to dinner personally.

Shake didn't think there was a chance in hell she'd come back tonight. But it was nice to imagine she might.

He was walking down Front Street, the main drag in town, when he spotted Baby Jesus up ahead. Baby Jesus was impossible to miss. Gigantic, parting the sea of tourists before him. He was wearing a white linen suit with no shirt underneath.

Shake slipped into a tiny shop that sold hair products. Marketed toward, judging by the faded posters on the wall, black people who lived in 1983. The shop was empty except for the Mayan woman behind the counter. She looked at Shake. He put a finger to his lips. She yawned.

Shake waited until Baby Jesus and his entourage of Rasta thugs rolled past, then waited another minute, just to be safe. If Baby Jesus didn't know about the shooting last night, he would soon. Shake guessed that Baby Jesus would take the opportunity to give Shake a hard squeeze. Probably he'd move up the payment schedule with some bullshit reasoning about being forced, unfortunately, to protect his investment. Shake wouldn't be able to do anything about it. He'd have to come up with the money or else.

Or else just abandon the restaurant and take off. Shake would be lying if he said that option hadn't occurred to him. All things considered, it was probably the safest option.

But—fuck that. Shake had put too much into the restaurant just to walk away from it. And not just the money. When Shake bought the place, it had been turning out bad Tex-Mex food, nacho cheese from a fifty-gallon can. Now it was a place that Pijua, best cook in the country, recommended to people, and not because he was Shake's buddy.

Shake just needed to get the restaurant back open tonight. And stay afloat until the real honeymoon rush in June, when he might be able to get out ahead of Baby Jesus and stay there.

He stopped by Pijua's place to borrow a dozen dinner and salad plates, a dozen wineglasses, a dozen water glasses. "We had a little breakage last night," Shake explained. Pijua just looked at him and didn't ask. He helped Shake carry the boxes down to the Wahoo.

Shake still needed fresh fish for the dinner service, so he walked to the market. He was looking over some nice grouper when he thought he heard someone yell his name. He glanced over and saw the old guy, Quinn, down at the other end of the market. Shake left the fish stall and walked the opposite way, but the crowd in the market slowed him down and Quinn caught up.

"Shake!"

"Hey," Shake said. "I didn't see you."

"Bullshit," Quinn said, but with a laugh and a twinkle in his eyes. Or maybe his eyes always seemed to twinkle, they were that kind of blue. He was wearing a pale yellow polo shirt today, and a different Patek Philippe on his wrist. "Let me buy you a cup of joe."

"Some other time," Shake lied again. "I'm in the weeds this morning."

"You've got time for a cup of joe."

Shake started to disagree, but Quinn put up a palm.

"C'mon, now," he said. "Is it gonna kill you?"

• • •

"I WAS OUT IN THE Philippines, working for the government. Well, not working for the government. You know what I mean. This was right after Ollie North, so everyone was in cover-their-ass mode. The law firm that hired me was friendly with Marcos, it was friendly with Aquino's people, at least any of Aquino's people hadn't been killed or thrown in jail yet. Hell, it was friendly with the separatists, the communists, the Chinese, everybody.

"Let me ask you a question, Shake. What's the most valuable commodity in the world? And it's not oil, or gold. It's relationships. 'We bring good folks together.' You remember that? That TV commercial? Before your time, maybe. It was an insurance company, phone company, I don't know. But the point is, the law firm that hired me, their slogan could have been 'We bring folks together that can't do business together in public, and we make sure nobody finds out about it.' Because there's big money in that, I don't have to tell you.

"The Iranians back in '79, for example. Who do you think got those American hostages out of Tehran? Not the firm I'm talking about necessarily, but one like it. It wasn't the striped-pants crowd at the State Department, in other words. No 'official channels.'

"Here's another one, while we're on the subject. Pablo Escobar, when the U.S. was looking for him. I had nothing to do with that, for the record. Anyway, guess who gives Escobar up? His own people do, of course. No surprise, but think about this. Who brokers that deal? You know, between a Colombian drug cartel and the government of the United States of America? Who brings those folks together? They can't all just sit down together, some banquet room at the Bogotá Ramada, with a nice buffet lunch afterward and handshakes all around."

Quinn paused to take a sip of his coffee.

Shake had no idea where to begin. "So," he said, "you were a lawyer?"

Quinn looked annoyed. "You're not listening."

"Doing my best," Shake said, and Quinn laughed.

"I'm a talker, I know," he said. "I like to talk. First words I remember, probably three years old back in Brooklyn, my mother saying, 'Shut up, already, Harry, for chrissakes.'"

He leaned back, pinched the crease of his khakis, crossed his legs. He was wearing deck shoes without socks. His ankles were as tan as the rest of him.

Shake thought Quinn seemed awfully calm, considering that someone had tried to kill him last night. Considering that person had come close, and was still out there. Shake turned his chair so he had a better view of the café entrance.

"Look here." Quinn had Shake lean over. Shake saw that Quinn was sitting so that he had an angle on the street outside the café. A mirror on the wall gave him an angle on the doors to the kitchen behind them.

If Quinn really wanted to play it safe, Shake wanted to say, he wouldn't be out having a cup of coffee in public. "So the police chief said you didn't know," Shake said. "Who might be after you."

"It's not my first time at the rodeo," Quinn said. "I'll be honest with you. I'm seventy-two years old and I've pissed off a few people along the way. But Belize? That's why I'm here, a fresh start. I've only been here—what? Three weeks? Four? I haven't been here long enough to piss anyone off."

Shake didn't say anything.

"Now you be honest with me," Quinn said. "I saw how you handled yourself last night, Shake. Cool as a cucumber. Tell me you've been a chef your whole life. Tell me that with a straight face."

"I'm all for fresh starts too," Shake said.

Quinn waited to see if Shake had more to add.

"Fair enough," Quinn said. "I've got a proposition for you."

Shake finished his coffee and stood up. "I need to be getting back, Mr. Quinn."

"What did I tell you about that?"

"Harry."

"You're coming to work for me."

"Not a chance."

Quinn chuckled and took a business card out of his wallet. He handed the card to Shake. It had a glossy color photo of a swanky resort on the beach, cabanas under the palms, a big pool with marble dolphins leaping, turning, spitting water.

"The place I just bought," Quinn said. "All the way up north, last property till you run out of island. The last resort—get it? That's what people want these days. Secluded, luxurious. Here's my slant, though. Fertility tourism."

Shake paused. "Fertility tourism."

"You bet. Gals these days, God bless 'em. But they've got careers, they want to sow their wild oats, they end up thirty-five, forty years old before they start trying to have kids. Forty-five, even. Now, let me ask you a question. Do you know what all that costs? Fertility drugs, in vitro, donor eggs, and doctors and nurses and blood tests? It's a trick question. Because what it costs in Seattle, that's not what it costs in a place like Belize. You see what I mean? For what it costs back home, just the office visits and the drugs, down here the gal gets the whole enchilada. A luxury resort, gourmet meals, procedures at a state-of-the-art medical facility."

"State-of-the-art medical facility?" Shake said. "In San Pedro?"

"Not yet," Quinn said. "And access to the finest fertility specialists in the world. Because a lot of these doctors, they studied in the U.S., they've got degrees from the best medical schools in the U.S. Some of them do, not those in Belize necessarily, but ones in Panama and Costa Rica."

"I wish you all the best," Shake said. He started to leave and then paused again. "What did she say? The stripper?"

"The stripper?"

"In Nicaragua. In the limo. When Somoza pointed the gun at her."

Quinn chuckled. "She said, 'But, *Commandante,* the party's just getting started!'"

Shake smiled and headed for the door.

"I owe you one, Shake," Quinn called after him. "Better not forget it."

Shake didn't look back. He planned, with all due respect, to try his best.

SHAKE GOT HOME AROUND ELEVEN. He worked his ass off throughout the afternoon. By four he was sweaty and sore and had accidentally hammered his thumb a couple of times. He was light-headed from paint fumes. But the dining room looked like a dining room again, more or less.

"What do you think?" he asked Idaba.

"Huh."

"I couldn't agree more."

"We gonna need those plates you borrowed from Pijua."

"You've got my attention," he said.

"Some German people staying up at the Pelican been complaining about the food up there." The Pelican's Roost was the resort up the beach that had gone all-inclusive right after Christmas and killed a lot of Shake's walk-in business. "Eight or ten German people. The Pelican want to know can they send them down to us for dinner, tonight and tomorrow and maybe a few days after that too."

"Tell them I'll have to think about it. Nothing worse than a crowded restaurant."

"Huh," Idaba said, and walked off.

Shake had thirty minutes or so before he had to start prepping, so he walked down to the *palapa* and climbed into the hammock. He didn't even know that he'd fallen asleep until he woke up, the wind rising and the hammock creaking.

He rolled out of the hammock. When he stepped off the pier, he saw Roger and Armando off in the distance. They were strolling together along the beach path, laughing and kicking at the garbage that had washed up with the tide. Both of them late, as usual. Shake was too tired to be pissed. He lifted a hand. Roger and Armando saw him and waved back. Shake turned, started up the beach, and his restaurant exploded.

Chapter 8

Shake saw the flash first, the restaurant windows blinking from dark to light, and then he felt the air around him sucked away, sucked out of him. The next thing he knew he was lying flat on his back in the sand. Watching with interest as a million tiny burning embers floated silently down on top of him.

Silently because the whole world had gone silent. Just Shake alone with his thoughts. A couple of seconds later his ears started screaming and he could make out a *thump-thump-whump*ing that sounded like the sail of a sailboat flapping in the wind.

He lifted his head. The *thump-thump-whump*ing was the sound of flames, pouring out of his restaurant.

He tried sitting up. A good idea in theory. The pain started at the top of Shake's head and radiated down to the soles of his feet. He tried again, more slowly, an inch at a time, and made it up onto one elbow.

Different kinds of pain started to distinguish themselves. Bare skin scraped raw. Head buzzing and throbbing. An iron hoop locked tight around his chest that made it hard to breathe. Getting tighter. That was the worst.

No, the worst wasn't even pain. The worst was that Shake couldn't think straight. He'd have a thought and then it would slip away, water through his fingers.

Like, *Get away from the flames. Get up and get away from the . . .* what?

The flames. Why was that, again?

Shake saw a figure emerge, hazy and rippling, from the smoke. Embers snowing down all around her. Her? A girl. A child. Striding out of the smoke toward him. She had a grim, fierce expression on her freckled face and reminded him . . . Shake tried to remember, in the cartoon strip, the name of Charlie Brown's friend with all the freckles.

Shake thought he might be dreaming. Maybe he was still asleep back in the hammock. He'd had dreams like that before, where he thought he'd woken up but really hadn't. He hoped he was still asleep, because he saw that Freckles had a gun. A big-ass .44 revolver. She'd stopped twenty feet away and was pointing the gun at his face.

She stared at him with that grim, fierce expression. Her lips moved, but Shake couldn't hear what she said. She looked like she couldn't be fifteen years old. The .44 was almost as big as she was. She used both thumbs to cock back the hammer.

This was the second time in less than twenty-four hours that Shake had teetered on the edge of his own life and gazed down into the darkness. It didn't get easier with practice.

"Drop your weapon!" a voice yelled. Freckles looked over. So did Shake. Another figure stood rippling in the heat, standing a hundred or so feet up the beach in the opposite direction.

It was Evelyn. She had a gun too, and was pointing it at Freckles. She looked just as grim and steady as Freckles did.

Shake knew for sure now that he had to be dreaming.

"Drop your weapon!" Evelyn told Freckles again. "Do it now!"

Freckles swung her gun toward Evelyn, and the restaurant exploded again. Shake was slammed back to the sand as gunshots rang out, three or four. A big black wheel of smoke rolled over him. His head felt light, too light, like it was being lifted delicately away from the rest of his body.

He closed his eyes and tried to take steady breaths. When he opened his eyes again, the smoke had rolled past and Evelyn was kneeling next to him. She pressed two fingers beneath his jaw, checking for a pulse. When she saw that his eyes were open, she smiled at him. Just the most dazzling smile he'd ever seen. "Never a dull moment at your place, huh?" she said.

He tried to say something.

She bent closer. "What?"

"Have I got a deal for you," Shake said as his head finally did float away, into a black empty sky.

THE WATER TAXI HAD DROPPED Evelyn off at the Pelican's Roost, a stop north of Bouchon's place. She didn't realize the mistake until she was already on the pier and the boat was gone. A little boy raking the beach said it would take thirty minutes to call another taxi boat, so Evelyn decided to hoof it. She wanted to surprise the shithead before he opened his restaurant, pop in and catch him off guard. If it was even open after what had happened last night.

Evelyn was about a hundred yards from the restaurant when it blew. She saw the blast knock Bouchon to the sand. A fireball rolled up into the sky and her first thought was *Un-fucking-believable.* She pulled her SIG Sauer out of her purse and sprinted down the beach. She hadn't left her firearm behind this time—no way. That was the story of her life in some ways: many mistakes, none repeated.

She reached the beach in front of Bouchon's restaurant just as a petite young woman stepped out of the smoke. She had so many freckles it looked like she was wearing a mask. Peppermint Patty walked toward Bouchon and pointed a giant Ruger .44 at him.

"Drop your weapon!" Evelyn yelled at her. Peppermint Patty glanced over. She didn't look scared or surprised by Evelyn's gun. She looked like a dog that wouldn't bother to bark, it would just bite you.

"Drop your weapon!" Evelyn told Freckles again. She took up her trigger slack. "Do it now!"

Peppermint Patty swung around. Evelyn fired at the same instant the restaurant blew again. She staggered and knew she'd missed. Peppermint Patty staggered and fired back. Evelyn fired again, two quick shots.

Evelyn had been a crack shot since her earliest days at Quantico, and even before that, eleven years old and out hunting quail with her dad. But she'd never had to hit a target staggering around, thirty meters away, while staggering around herself, heavy smoke and chunks of burning thatch whooshing down.

Peppermint Patty fired another wild shot at Evelyn and then took off running, so Evelyn kicked off her heels and gave pursuit. She gained ground. No little girl in Daisy Duke cutoffs was going to shoot at Evelyn and then beat her in a footrace. But Peppermint Patty veered suddenly. She ran straight toward the burning restaurant.

Evelyn had to pull up. The heat was so intense near the fire that it felt like her contacts were fusing to her eyes.

Peppermint Patty ran right along the wall of the restaurant, a crazy risk. A flaming beam rolled off the roof and just missed her. She reached the corner of the veranda and cut around it. Evelyn sprinted the long way around. When she got to the road that ran behind the restaurant, Peppermint Patty had disappeared.

Evelyn hurried back to Bouchon and checked his pulse. Steady, and his eyes were open. He hadn't been shot. He looked like he was going to be okay. "Never a dull moment at your place," she said, "huh?" And then she felt stupid, how cheesy that sounded.

He said something she couldn't hear.

"What?" He said it again and still she couldn't tell what it was.

Evelyn jogged back up the beach to find her purse, her cell phone. For a split second she thought about making another run for it, but even she—expert rationalizer that she considered herself—couldn't justify fleeing the scene of a gunfight she had actually participated in. She found Cory's number in her phone, hit the call button, and prayed for the sake of her career that he got there before the cops did.

Chapter 9

Terry heard the explosion off in the distance and just about jumped out of his shorts. Shitfire! He wondered how much of the dynamite Meg had used. They'd happened by a demolition site a week ago, first day they got to Belize, nobody around and the dynamite just sitting there. Terry didn't know what Meg wanted dynamite for, since they had the guns her friend Jorge in Guatemala City had given them. But Meg said the more the merrier when you aimed to kill a body, so they helped themselves to some dynamite.

It had come in handy after all, now they had two bodies to kill. Meg had said, I told you so, didn't I, and Terry admitted she had.

He was sitting alone in the golf cart, parked in the jungle. Meg rolled her eyes when he called it that, the jungle. Well, it was jungle to him. The middle of the island up here was one big mess of twisted-up trees and big vines hanging down and the leaves so heavy in places the sun could barely push through. And plenty of snakes, you could be sure of that.

All that made Terry think of Tarzan, and Tarzan made him think of Meg, standing there naked in front of him this morning, her hair slicked back from the shower and her body shining wet. An interesting fact about Meg's freckles was they were just mostly on her face, hardly anywhere else.

"I love you too damn much," she'd said, so quiet he could barely hear it. "It ain't good for me."

"I'll be good for you," he'd said. "C'mon over here."

She was back to her old self then. Pushing him flat on the bed and calling him a goddamn moron and saying it was a good thing he had such a big goddamn cock. Terry got embarrassed when she talked like that. The way he saw it, you couldn't get too proud about what you just came by lucky, never putting any work of your own into it.

There was another explosion, and some *pop-pop-popp*ing. Terry figured that must be gunshots. A second later he remembered that the first explosion was supposed to be his signal. *Oh, hell,* he thought. He had a good idea what Meg would say about it, he didn't get down there to pick her up on time. Terry cranked that golf cart, out of the jungle and down the sand road. You never saw a golf cart cranking along like that, he thought. Old Ironhead in his number three car up in heaven just looked down in awe.

Meg was waiting by the side of the road. "What'd I tell you to do, Terry?" she said when she climbed in. "The one thing?" They drove about a mile and ditched the golf cart. About another mile on was where they'd parked the boat, in a little cove you couldn't see from land or water. They drove the boat up the coast of the island to their hidey.

Their hidey was a little cement-block fishing shack with a metal roof, miles from anybody else. Jorge had rented it for them. It wasn't much to look at, but there was a bed and a shower and a little porch where Meg could sit in the breeze and paint her toenails.

"Did you get him?" Terry finally had the nerve to ask. Meg hadn't said more than two words on the trip to the hidey. Turn here, get in the boat, hurry up. Terry couldn't tell if she was furious or just her normal ferocious self, quietly working things out in her head.

"Go cover up the boat," she said. "I got to call Jorge." He went and covered up the boat. He could hear her on the cell phone talking to Jorge, but Terry couldn't tell what she was saying. When she hung up, he walked back up to the shack.

"Jorge says that ain't his real name," Meg said. "He did some checking on it."

"Ain't whose real name?"

"The son of a bitch broke your nose." The chef at the restaurant. They knew his name because Meg saw it last night on a sign at his pier. She'd called Jorge last night to say she was gonna kill the chef. Jorge said fine, kill who you want, just make sure you take care of the old dude, pronto. But now, Meg said after she talked to him on the phone, Jorge was saying hold on about killing the chef or the old dude.

"Jorge says that son-of-a-bitch chef ain't no chef at all. He says he used to work for some badass people back in California. For some Russians or Armenians, whatever kind of Mafia it is they have out there in Los Angeles."

This news made Terry feel a lot better about his broken nose, that it was a Russian or Armenian Mafia badass broke it and not just your run-of-the-mill chef.

"Jorge says he thinks the son of a bitch broke your nose might be the old fucker's protection. We got to lay low for a while. Lay low on the son of a bitch and the old fucker, both of them."

Terry might not know much, but he knew his darling redheaded girl inside and out.

"But we ain't gonna do that," he said. "Are we?"

Chapter 10

Shake woke up in a room he didn't recognize. Moonlight moved at a strange angle through the wooden slats on the windows. The air smelled like disinfectant.

He remembered the restaurant exploding. On fire. His first thought, with a jerk that hurt every inch of his body, was *Idaba*.

"Go back to sleep," she said. She was sitting in a chair by his bed, making a necklace by sliding wooden beads, one by one, onto a wire. He was so relieved to see her that he didn't mind how much it hurt to sit up.

"You weren't inside," he said.

"Do I look like I was inside?" She snorted, no evidence of an expression on her big stone face. He noticed, though, that she'd put the necklace down in her lap and had laid a hand on his arm. "Geraldine brought her new baby round to the Fish and Hook. I went over there to see if he was ugly as the daddy." Geraldine was one of the bartenders at the Fish and Hook, the bar next door to Shake's restaurant.

"Armando?" Shake said. "Roger?"

Idaba shook her head. "They're all fine. Nobody hurt but you. Now lay back down."

Shake lay back down. He figured out that he must be in the town clinic. He'd been here once before, a few months ago when he'd sliced off part of his index finger while chopping onions. It had been a different room from this one, but with the same yellow walls, the same smell of disinfectant.

"Doctor says you gonna be all right," Idaba said. "Just a concussion, and some ribs he thinks is cracked. Go back to sleep."

Shake could feel himself being tugged back under. "Okay," he said.

THE SHITSTORM THAT EVELYN GOT from Cory and the DEA guys wasn't as bad as she'd expected. As shitstorms went, and Evelyn was something of an expert, it wasn't bad at all. They parked her in a cramped little office in San Pedro, let her stew for a couple of hours, then yelled for a few more hours after that.

Evelyn remained respectful but defiant. As in, Yes, fellas, I appreciate why you're pissed off, and take it from me, I know what it's like to work your ass off on an investigation only to have it go sideways on you, but tell me, what was I supposed to do?

They told her. They had lots of suggestions, most of them vivid and profane.

When they finally calmed down, Evelyn pointed out that their investigation of Belizean drug kingpin Walter "Baby Jesus" Jenkins had not, in fact, gone sideways. Evelyn's actions on the beach when the restaurant exploded were the reason it hadn't.

When they finally calmed down again after that, Evelyn explained that if she hadn't chased off Peppermint Patty, she would have shot and killed the shithead.

"The fuck do we care some shithead got himself shot?" a DEA guy yelled, the one with the tight black T-shirt and ginormous biceps.

"The fuck does that have to do with our investigation?" the other DEA guy yelled, the one with the even tighter black T-shirt and even more ginormous biceps.

DEA guys, Evelyn thought. Maybe if they spent a little less time on the bench press and a little more time using the muscles in their muscle heads.

But Cory got Evelyn's point. "If Bouchon got killed on the beach," he said, "we can't sell the innocent little propane leak."

"So the fuck what?" both DEA guys yelled.

"Try banging your heads together," Evelyn said. "See if that helps you figure it out."

Cory scowled at Evelyn. As if to say, *And you wonder why people in other agencies think everyone in the Bureau is arrogant and condescending?*

Fair enough.

"The media would have been all over a murder on the beach," Cory explained to the DEA guys.

"The federal police would have come flying in like bats out of hell," Evelyn said. "And Baby Jesus would have closed up shop until everything cooled out again."

Was that not, by the way, the weirdest nickname in the world? *Baby Jesus?*

The DEA guys continued to fuss and fume, but in the end, they didn't call Mike in L.A. and rat Evelyn out. They might be typical musclehead DEA jerks, bitter enviers of the FBI, but they were no rats. And they knew Evelyn was right, even if they wouldn't admit it. They'd lucked out with the propane thing, thanks to her. They left her with a warning so long and involved and so filled with ominous threats that Evelyn stopped listening halfway through.

"Got it, fellas," she said. Whatever. On her way out, Cory stopped her. He started to say something, but then didn't bother.

Evelyn walked over to the town hospital, which was really just a clinic. She flashed her creds and told the night nurse that she was there to see the injured man who had been brought in earlier.

"Mr. Cleary?" the nurse said.

Quentin Cleary. The name on the shithead's fake passport.

"That's my boy," Evelyn said.

The nurse told her he was sleeping. Evelyn peeked into his room. He was sleeping. The formidable black hostess was sitting in a chair next to his bed, dozing too. Evelyn went back to the front desk. The nurse assured her that the patient was going nowhere until the doctor saw him again in the morning. Evelyn checked her watch and figured she'd better grab some sleep herself, while she could. She told the nurse she'd be back at seven.

She got to her hotel around four in the morning. She looked even worse than she had the first night. Bits of blackened thatch in her hair, face streaked with soot, another dress trashed: one of her favorites, the navy-blue forties-style slip dress with puffed sleeves that she and Sarah had found at a vintage place on La Brea last summer.

The female desk clerk gave her another sour look. Evelyn smiled back. "Two guys at once tonight!" she said. "Golly! More work than you'd think!" The desk clerk turned red. Evelyn went back to her bungalow, took a shower, fell into bed.

Chapter 11

Shake woke up again. Sunlight now, not moonlight. He was in the same room. Idaba sat in the same chair by his bed, still working on her beads. Now that it was light, Shake noticed the big full-color poster on the wall: an illustration of a human body with the skin peeled back so you could see the muscles and tendons. Another smaller poster showed the human eye in various states of disease.

He still had his watch on. Seven o'clock in the morning. Which meant he'd been out, for the most part, for the last twelve hours. Twelve hours ago his restaurant had exploded and . . .

"What happened?" he said.

Idaba kept working on her beads. She shrugged, annoyed. "I told you last night. I was next door at the Fish and Hook."

"That's what I'm talking about," Shake said. "Was Geraldine's baby as ugly as the daddy or not?"

That got a sliver of a smile out of her. Miracle of miracles.

"I didn't see a thing," she said. "Heard the first big boom and I came running. The second one about knocked me over."

"The police. Did they get the girl with the gun?"

"The which?"

"On the beach, right after the explosion. She was gonna shoot me."

Idaba glanced over at him. "Wasn't no girl on the beach when I got there. Just you."

"With freckles. And the other one. With the other gun. You remember the woman from the night before, the pretty one with dark hair? Evelyn. Her name was Evelyn. She was there too, with a gun . . ."

Idaba set the beads in her lap again and turned to give him a good look. "They gave you some drugs," she said. "For your ribs."

"I'm not imagining it." Or was he? He tried to bring into focus those blurry moments right before he blacked out. The girl with the freckles and the gun. Evelyn. *Never a dull moment.*

No, definitely. All that had happened. Shake was positive, drugs or no drugs.

"She thought I'd be in the restaurant when it blew. When I wasn't, she came over to shoot me."

"This Evelyn lady?"

"No. Freckles. Evelyn saved my life."

He wondered what Evelyn had been doing with a gun. She had to be a cop of some kind. American. What was she doing in Belize?

"Police say it was the propane tank that blown up," Idaba said. "A leak, maybe."

Shake couldn't believe it. "A leak."

"What they say."

"They're not seeing a connection. Between a gunman in a mask opens fire one night, and a restaurant that gets blown up the next day?"

Idaba frowned. "Freckles was the one in the mask?"

"No." If Freckles had been the one in the mask that first night, Shake was absolutely certain that she would have shot him when he grabbed for the gun. She would have shot Quinn. She wouldn't have missed. "The guy in the mask was her partner, maybe," he said. "I don't know."

"But he wasn't after you. He was just after that old man."

Not anymore, Shake thought. He could see Idaba thinking the same thing.

No good deed goes unpunished. Shake wondered if he'd ever get that through his head.

The door to the room opened. A nurse poked her head in. "Visitor," she said.

Baby Jesus and his Rasta thug in the ONE LOVE tank top walked in. Baby Jesus was so big that he had to turn sideways coming through the door, a nimble little dance step. "My friend!" he said. "When I hear this about your terrible misfortune of the propane leak, I came at once!"

"It wasn't a propane leak," Shake said.

"You must be very careful," Baby Jesus said, "with explosive substances in the household or business setting. I know this from my line of work too."

"It was a propane leak my ass."

"I do not care." Baby Jesus smiled sweetly. "What it was."

He cared that the restaurant was gone, Shake realized. He cared that the collateral against the money Shake had borrowed was gone.

"Leave us," Baby Jesus told Idaba. She didn't move. Baby Jesus tried out a glare, but it was halfhearted. Even he was afraid to tangle with her.

"It's all right, Idaba," Shake told her. "Give us a minute, will you?"

She slowly gathered up her beads, stood, and crossed the room with regal indifference. When she was gone, One Love removed a gun from the back waistband of his baggy shorts.

"Get up, *guna boi.* Let's go."

Shake thought about the girl with the freckles and the big .44 revolver. She didn't know it, but today was her lucky day. "Why don't we talk about this," Shake said.

Baby Jesus didn't answer. He'd noticed the poster of the human body with the skin peeled back. He studied it with a curiosity that didn't make Shake feel better about his situation.

"I am a businessman, my friend," Baby Jesus said finally, turning back to Shake. "I have a brand identity. You understand? Like Coca-

Cola, like the Apple computer. I've been reading about these things. Do you know, for example, that the Four Seasons hotel company will never lower their rates. Never! When they have rooms they must fill, when business is not so good, they might offer a special, three nights for the price of two. But they never lower their rates!"

Shake looked over at One Love. "You following any of this?"

"If I don't protect my brand identity," Baby Jesus said, "who protects Baby Jesus?"

"Get up," One Love told Shake.

"No one is who!"

"Up."

"Just listen to me," Shake said.

"Oh, Shake," Baby Jesus said. He gazed up at the ceiling, wistful, looking even more cherubic than usual. "I don't enjoy this."

Shake thought he probably did. "What if I told you I have the money I owe you," Shake said. "More."

Baby Jesus giggled again. "I would say fiddlesticks."

"Think about it." Shake didn't know what he meant by that. He just needed time to figure out his bluff. He knew it was going to be a weak bluff, no matter what he came up with.

"Think about what, my friend?"

"You're aware of my past associations."

"The Armenians. I know them. You think they come save you now?"

"That's not what I'm saying. I'm saying that when I left L.A., I didn't leave empty-handed."

Baby Jesus studied him. "Fiddlesticks. Because why, if you have so much money you steal from the Armenians, you have to borrow money from me?"

"Because I didn't want the Armenians to know I stole their money. If they find out about my restaurant, they're going to wonder where the money came from. Right? This way, if I borrow money from you . . ." Shake didn't finish the thought. Someone like Baby Jesus, anybody really, you let them feel good about figuring it out themselves.

"It look like you don't steal their money," Baby Jesus said.

Shake was hoping that Baby Jesus didn't know the Armenians as well as he claimed. If he did, he'd know that no one would ever be crazy enough to steal from them.

Well, *almost* no one would ever be crazy enough to steal from them—Shake thought of Gina and almost let a smile sneak away from him.

"That's right," Shake said. "I was covering my tracks."

"Fiddlesticks."

"Maybe. But you take me out in a boat and shoot me, you'll never know for sure."

"Shoot?" Baby Jesus asked mildly.

Shake tried to ignore that. "I've got two and a half million dollars, U.S."

Baby Jesus picked up the clipboard that hung from the foot of Shake's bed. He scanned it. "Here," he said. He tapped his ribs.

One Love stepped over and punched Shake in the ribs.

"And I suppose you tell me now," Baby Jesus said, "that these millions of dollars was not burned up with every other one of your possessions in the world?"

"Yes," Shake said. Grunted. Gasped. *Fuck*.

"Excellent." Baby Jesus clapped his big hands together. "We go now and get these millions of dollars."

"No."

"No?" Baby Jesus tapped his ribs again. The "One Love" thug stepped toward him.

"Wait." Shake gathered his breath. "I'll bring you the money. Give me twenty-four hours."

"So you can run away."

"So I can meet you in a public place and not end up dead after I hand over the money."

Baby Jesus settled down into the chair that Idaba had vacated, one massive haunch at a time. A guy that big, he did his best pondering while seated. "I don't think you have the money," Baby Jesus said. "But just maybe you do."

"And you're a businessman."

"If you think you will run away on your boat," Baby Jesus mentioned, conversationally, "you know we have your boat now."

Shake shrugged. Thinking, *Shit.* The Wahoo had been escape plan number one.

"And you know, my friend, I have eyes everywhere. The airport, the ferry. The police, of course."

"I want to pay my debt. I want to be square with you," Shake said. He glanced over and saw One Love yawning. "Are we boring you?" he said.

One Love looked like he was about to smack Shake in the ribs again, but then he saw Baby Jesus frowning at him too.

Baby Jesus pondered some more.

"Twenty-four hours," he said. "And if you don't have this money, Shake, you will pray you are already dead."

Chapter 12

Terry had the idea, once they got to town, that they buy some flowers. Or a teddy bear, to make it look better. "You don't think I didn't already think of that?" Meg said. But a while later, after he'd given her the silent treatment, she sighed and lifted up on her toes to kiss him. "I didn't think of the teddy bear," she said. "That's better than flowers."

Terry thought it was. People saw a teddy bear and they went, "Aw, ain't that sweet?" They put their guard down.

The clinic was in the middle of town. A place down the street sold flowers and get-well cards, but no teddy bears. Meg said that was all right, just focus on the job now. Her plan was Terry would walk into the clinic and tell the girl at the desk he wanted to visit his hurt friend. It would have to be Terry, because the chef would recognize Meg, he'd seen her on the beach. Meg would wait out in the alley while Terry went into the chef's room. The chef would ask who Terry was, and Terry would say he was with the Young Christian Leadership group there in Belize, and they went around visiting all the sick foreigners. Terry would ask had the chef abandoned himself to the Lord Jesus Christ yet? While the chef was thinking, *Oh, great, a Bible-thumper,* Terry would pin him down and put a pillow on his face so he couldn't yell out. Meg would come in through the window and shoot the chef in the face through the pillow. She said the gun wouldn't make so much noise that way. Then they'd both go back out through the window.

That's all Terry had to do, Meg said, did he think he could do it without being too much of a moron? Terry thought he could, no problem. He had a good twenty pounds on the chef, and the chef had bruised ribs to boot. That's what the girl at the clinic desk had said when they'd called to see if the chef was at the clinic. Meg had seen the explosion knock him down, and suspected he might have ended up there.

But Terry asked her again, did they really have to kill the chef? The broken nose was water under the bridge as far as he was concerned. Meg turned and looked at him. "I start what I finish," she said. "Don't nobody hurt the folks I love and get away with it."

Terry didn't think the chef had got away with anything much at all, seeing how his restaurant had blown to bits and with him in the clinic now, but Terry didn't make a fuss. He just wanted to get this done and get Meg back to the shack, get her shucked quick out of her cutoff shorts.

"Whatever you say, my darlin' redheaded girl," Terry said, and he picked out the biggest bunch of flowers he could find.

WHEN EVELYN WOKE UP, SHE ordered eggs from room service and sent her daughter a text. *I had the weirdest dreams last night.*

Sarah sent a text back. *Everybody has weird dreams, Mom.*

While Evelyn ate her eggs, she considered how her own position had improved. She'd come to Belize without much to squeeze the shithead with. The best she had in her bag was that good old standby: Talk to me or I'll let the Armenians know you're talking to me. You think they'll be happy to hear about that?

The problem was that Bouchon had already served out his full bid on a GTA at Mule Creek because he refused to play ball with the prosecutor. He wasn't a ballplayer and the Armenians knew it. They still might try to clip him, just to be safe, if they thought she was trying to turn him around, but that threat didn't have the weight she would have liked.

Now, though, Evelyn didn't need the Armenian threat. Somebody was already trying to clip Bouchon. His restaurant had been destroyed. If ever he needed a friend, he needed one now.

Evelyn planned to be that friend, a shoulder to lean on. All the shithead had to do in return was be a friend back and help her nail the Armenians. Easy.

And then what, Evelyn? Evelyn was disgusted with herself, with the little crush that she'd developed on Bouchon. Realistically? She and the shithead would hold hands as they shopped for bargain wine at the Trader Joe's on Pico? They'd pull weeds together in the garden and he'd thumb a smudge of potting soil off her upper lip before he kissed her? He'd show Sarah how to cook conch fritters while Evelyn sat on the sofa and luxuriated in the sound of their happy laughter? Maybe, while he was at it, cooking conch fritters with Sarah, he could instruct her on the finer points of car theft and evasive driving.

Shake. It was a better nickname than "Baby Jesus," but still kind of silly for a grown man. Charles was a perfectly good first name. Charlie. No, Charles.

Sorry, Charlie. I'm your only friend in the world now.

She finished her eggs and drank another cup of coffee. It was seven-thirty. She decided to head over to the hospital and deliver the good news.

Chapter 13

Shake sent Idaba to the post office. He kept his passport in his post office box, taped to the wall of the box so the box looked empty. He was lucky the passport hadn't been upstairs in his flat when the restaurant blew. Baby Jesus was right. Everything else that Shake owned had been.

He started to climb out of bed, but the pain froze him in place. "Oh, no, you don't," the nurse told him. She'd come into the room to bring him breakfast. She put the tray aside and helped him lie back down. "Not till the doctor comes in and says you can."

"What time?"

"Later." As exact as island time got. The nurse put a hand on Shake when he started to sit up again, so Shake waited till she left. He didn't plan to hang around till the doctor arrived, no matter how much it hurt to get out of bed. It hurt a lot. Every move he made was like another rib cracking. You'd think he had an unlimited supply of ribs to crack. He put on his pants, his T-shirt, got one sandal on, and then paused to take a breather.

The nurse poked her head in again. "What'd I just tell you?"

"I forget. Must be the drugs."

"You got another visitor." Shake thought, *Who the hell now?*

A second later Armando walked in. "How you feelin', boss?" he said.

"Help me with this," Shake said, pointing to his other sandal.

Armando frowned. "You need you rest, boss."

"Help me."

Armando helped him put the sandal on. Roger walked in. "You ask him yet?" he asked Armando.

"Idiota," Armando snapped at him.

"Oh," Roger said.

Shake sighed. "How much do I owe you?"

"Two weeks," Armando said.

"All right. See Idaba about it in the next few days."

"Thanks, chef," Roger said.

"Thanks, boss."

"Help me up."

"You think you wanna do that, chef?"

"C'mon. Both of you. Let's go."

Shake put a hand on Armando's shoulder. He was just the right size. It hurt to stand, but no more than sitting up. With Armando on one side and Roger on the other, Shake made it down the hallway. He thought the nurse might try to stop him, but she was having a conversation with a guy holding a bouquet of flowers. The guy, with his back to Shake, blocked the nurse's view of the lobby.

"I'm sorry," the nurse was saying. "You just gonna have to wait."

There was something vaguely familiar about the guy, the way he was standing. Shake didn't have time to worry about it.

OUTSIDE, SHAKE SAID GOOD-BYE TO Armando and Roger. Idaba was waiting for him on the corner of Pescador Street. It took Shake a while to get there. The grit was blowing around and the sun felt twenty or thirty degrees hotter than it should have. Shake noticed sweat popping out all over his body.

"You see him over there, don't you?" Idaba said as she handed Shake his passport.

"I do," Shake said. One Love, Baby Jesus's thug. Hanging out about halfway down the block, lurking in the shadows.

"I guess Baby Jesus don't trust you," Idaba said.

"I guess he shouldn't."

"Come to my house. My husband and I, we'll help you."

"Your husband thinks I'm a jackass."

She didn't deny it, or argue with her husband's conclusion. "Come to my house," she said.

"You think you can cover a couple of weeks' pay for Armando and Roger?" Shake said. "I'll pay you back when I can."

She nodded. They stood there for a minute.

"You sure you didn't see her on the beach?" Shake said.

"Who? The one with freckles?"

"The other one."

"The pretty one," Idaba said. Sly.

"I was gonna take your advice, believe it or not. About getting a woman in my bed. I was gonna give it the old college try."

"Be the first time you take my advice," she said. "No, I didn't see her."

Shake checked his watch. It was time to go. "And I'll send something for you too," he told Idaba, "soon as I can."

"I don't want no money."

"Your severance package." He braced himself. "Now let's have it. The part you've been waiting for."

She slapped him hard, no hesitation. He rubbed his cheek. He'd told her to make it convincing, but still.

"Hell, Idaba. You could have pretended you were pretending."

"Huh," she said.

From the corner of his eye he could see One Love watching them. "Now storm off. I don't want Baby Jesus bothering you."

"He won't bother me. You the one. Be careful, you hear me?"

"Go. Unless you're planning to slap me again."

"Be careful. You hear me?" And then she stormed off.

SHAKE RESTED FOR A MINUTE and then made his way over to Front Street. One Love followed, on his cell phone, reporting in to Baby Jesus.

Front Street was crowded. Tourists who were staying on the island, plus cruise-ship day-trippers tendered over from Belize City. Shake kept his eyes open. Golf carts were parked on both sides of the street and it didn't take him long to spot one with the key still in the ignition. Shake liked to call it Blissful Idiot Syndrome. He saw it all the time. You went on vacation to a place as beautiful as Ambergris Caye, and it never occurred to you that the rules of the real world might still apply.

He heard Gina's voice in his head before he could stop himself. "Blissful idiot?" she'd say, and wink. "Look who's talking."

Shake slid into the golf cart and eased it out onto the street. He went fast enough that it didn't seem suspicious, but not so fast he'd lose One Love, who hurried to keep up. It was the first golf cart Shake had ever stolen, after who knew how many Honda Accords and Cadillac Escalades and delivery vans big enough to accommodate, for example, a one-eyed safecracker flown in from Belfast, plus his entire safecracking rig.

Shake turned left on Black Coral Street. He turned left again, into the alley that ran behind the buildings on Front Street. One Love had to hang back on the corner. The alley was deserted and Shake would make him if he tried to follow.

Shake pulled over halfway down the alley. He parked the golf cart tight, scraping up against the stucco back of a building that fronted Front Street. He got out of the cart and walked back up the alley toward Black Coral Street.

One Love eased back into the shadows. Shake retraced, by foot, the route he'd just driven in the golf cart. Black Coral to Front Street, back down Front Street. One Love followed. He was trying to figure out what the hell Shake was up to, Shake knew it.

Halfway down Front Street, Shake stepped into the little shop that sold hair products to black people living in 1983. He calculated that One Love would wait outside the shop for a minute or two before he got suspicious and followed Shake inside. Before he wondered what Shake was doing in a shop that sold hair products to black people living in 1983.

A minute or two should give Shake enough time. He hoped so.

The same Mayan girl was behind the counter of the shop. "I'm going to borrow your back door," he called over his shoulder. He'd noticed the door the first time he'd been in the shop a couple days ago, a lifetime of professional habit at work. Old getaway drivers don't die, they just spot the nearest exit. "Okay?"

The Mayan girl yawned. Shake slipped out the back door. The stolen golf cart was parked a few feet away. He got in, pulled it forward, and parked again, this time flush against the back door of the shop.

Shake jogged, as fast as his cracked ribs would let him, back toward Black Coral. He'd been counting seconds in his head, another old habit. One Mississippi, two Mississippi. Sixty-two Mississippis after he entered the shop, he heard a sharp metal *wunk* as One Love tried to push open the back door of the shop and found it blocked by the stolen golf cart.

Wunk-wunk-wunk. Shake smiled. One Love wasn't getting through that door.

Pijua's little Toyota minitruck was idling at the corner of the alley. Shake rolled into the bed of the truck and pulled a tarp over himself, thinking how he wouldn't want to be One Love when Baby Jesus found out what happened. On the other hand, he supposed, One Love probably wouldn't want to trade places with Shake either.

PIJUA DROVE UP PAST THE high school and over the bridge that spanned the Cut. That part of the ride wasn't too hard on Shake's ribs. The next part, ten miles north on a rutted sand track, was.

For the first time it really hit Shake that the restaurant was gone. *His* restaurant. Shake remembered how for the first few weeks the local fishermen had tested him. Steering him toward the snapper with the milky eyes. Shake would toss the bad snapper back and say, "Would you feed this to your family?" He gradually earned their respect. Or else the fishermen just got tired of him making a scene every time, pain-in-the-ass *cabrón*.

And not just his restaurant gone, Shake realized. His life in Belize too. A life, for better or worse, that he'd expected to live for a long time. It felt like he'd lost his balance. Like he'd reached for the rung of a ladder, and the rung wasn't there. The ladder wasn't there. Maybe there'd never been a ladder at all.

Shit. Pijua hit a bump and Shake couldn't breathe for the next thirty seconds. Finally, though, the truck slowed and stopped. Pijua gave him an all-clear rap on the back window of the cab. Shake climbed out from beneath the tarp and out of the truck bed. Pijua came around to shake his hand.

"Thanks," Shake said. "I mean it."

Pijua looked around, dubious. They were in the middle of nowhere. "For what?"

"I know," Shake said.

"Seem like you gotta have a better option, amigo."

"Seems that way to me too. I agree."

"Might be tricky, you know, but we can get you over to the mainland." That had been Shake's original plan, when he thought he still had his Wahoo. Now, though, he realized he had bigger problems.

"That doesn't help me any," Shake said. "And it sure doesn't help you any."

Pijua slapped at a mosquito. "You thinking Baby Jesus got reach over there too. Somebody high up."

"Yeah." As much dope as Baby Jesus ran up into the Yucatán, the odds were good that he had a cabinet minister or two in his pocket. Maybe he didn't, but Shake would rather not test the theory by walking up cold to airport security at Goldson International in Belize City. Shake's passport was fake paper that he'd picked up a few years ago in Vegas. But it was in the name he'd been using while he was in Belize, so that didn't help him any.

"I need to find a way out of the country that Baby Jesus won't know about," Shake said.

"How much he want?"

"Two and a half."

"American?" Pijua slapped at another mosquito. "Shit."

"And then we'd have to start talking about the other people want to kill me. The girl with the freckles."

"Idaba said she didn't see no girl with the freckles."

"Idaba wasn't there about to get shot."

"How about," Pijua said, but then didn't finish the thought.

"This is my only option," Shake said. "I wish it wasn't."

Pijua sighed. "You in a pickle, amigo."

PIJUA GAVE SHAKE A MACHETE, promised he'd have his daughter say a rosary for Shake, and then drove back toward town. Shake began to hike north, hacking his way through the brush. There was a better path on the beach, just a hundred yards or so to his right, but it was too exposed. Shake couldn't afford to be spotted.

About an hour later, around three, Shake turned seaward. The resort was on the other side of some low dunes. There were a dozen or so small bungalows, white stucco and red clay tile roofs, grouped around the pool with the leaping dolphins. Farther on was the main, two-story building, with a long balcony that faced the beach and the ocean beyond.

The resort looked just like the glossy photo on the business card. Except—not exactly. Shake noticed, as he got closer, that the stucco was chipped and a lot of the roof tiles were missing or broken. The pool was empty. You could see the dry rusty tubes in the dolphin mouths, where the water used to flow. A flexible plastic drainage tube, a couple of feet in diameter, snaked from the roof of the main building down to the ground.

There wasn't anybody around. No guests, no staff. Shake asked himself if he was surprised by any of that. He wasn't.

He found Harrigan Quinn pacing the balcony of the main building, talking on his cell phone. He was wearing a peach-colored polo shirt and pressed khakis, deck shoes without socks. When he saw Shake down below, he didn't seem surprised at all. He killed the call and spread his arms wide.

"There he is!" Quinn said.

Here I am, Shake thought.

Chapter 14

Quinn explained to Shake that the resort was closed for renovations. Fertility tourism, you had to understand, was a top-shelf racket. You couldn't cut corners. You had to pamper the gals. They'd expect the very best, from Italian tile to Frette linens to a special kind of toilet made only in Japan. The special toilet squirted warm water up your ass and then blew your ass dry.

Shake let that pass. Quinn caught him thinking it, though. His eyes twinkled. "You think that's what I'm doing, Shake? Blowing hot air up your ass?"

"What happened?" Shake said, looking around, innocent. "The construction crew doing the renovations knock off early today?"

"Go ahead and ask," Quinn said. "I'll tell you the truth. It used to be simple, before nine/eleven. You wanted to move your money from here to there, you moved your money from here to there. Now, though,

Christ, the regulations and the government sniffing around. Whoever even heard of a forensic accountant, twenty years ago?"

They were sitting in the resort's outdoor café. Or what someday might be the resort's outdoor café. Right now it was just a concrete slab and a couple of plastic beach chairs, with a big faded umbrella advertising a brand of Italian liqueur Shake had never heard of.

"So, yes, I'm experiencing a liquidity issue," Quinn said. "I went deep on this place. I threw the bomb. Let me ask you a question, Shake. When you die, are you gonna look back and regret the things you did, or the things you didn't do?"

What Shake was starting to regret was this conversation. He was starting to think he should just take his chances at airport security in Belize City.

An old Kriol man, older than Quinn, shuffled out of the main building and handed them two cans of lukewarm Coke. Then he shuffled away.

"Who's trying to kill you?" Shake said.

Quinn leaned back and studied Shake. "I told you."

"They're trying to kill me now too."

"You?"

Shake told him about the restaurant blowing up, the girl with the freckles putting the gun on him.

"Because—what?" Quinn said. "What you did for me the other night?"

Shake waited.

"The why doesn't matter," Quinn said. "Okay. I see your point."

"The who matters. And no hot air up my ass."

Quinn drummed his fingers on the plastic arm of his beach chair.

"I might have an *idea*," he said finally. "That's all."

"Let's hear it."

"Back in the eighties, this was after Nicaragua, after Berlin, I did some consulting work in Southeast Asia. I told you before, the kind of people hired me. The business of relationships? Bringing folks together? Well, Vietnam back then, you remember maybe, it was the Wild West. The Reds had gone free market, Saigon was a boomtown. And Cambodia, with the Khmer Rouge gone. It was Filene's Basement on a Saturday afternoon. Anything you wanted, a five-hundred-year-old stone monkey demon chiseled right off the wall at Angkor. If you knew what you were doing. If you had the right connections."

"Long story short," Shake said.

"Hey. You want to tell it?"

"Go ahead."

"Anyway," Quinn said. "I got to know this kid at the U.S. embassy in Phnom Penh. Just starting out, assistant to the assistant something. Nice kid. I showed him the ropes. Showed him how to tie a few knots with the ropes. Okay? We made some money together. Sticky Jimmy. That's what everyone called him. Funny story, how he got that name. Let me tell you that story."

Shake almost stepped into it, before he realized Quinn was having fun with him.

"So jump ahead to the present day," Quinn said. "I'm reading the newspaper a few weeks ago. I turn the page and guess who's looking back at me from the financial page?"

"I'm gonna guess Sticky Jimmy."

"Sticky Jimmy. That's right. But now the kid's not a kid anymore, he's got his own company, natural gas, it's doing well. You ever heard of fracking? Getting the gas out of the shale? Anyway, our boy came up with a way to do that, a better way. Some engineer on his payroll did, I mean to say."

The sun had started to set during all this.

"Take it easy," Quinn told Shake. "What I'm telling you, Sticky Jimmy is legit now. Pure as the driven snow. You think he wants any of it coming back to him, what he was up to in Cambodia?"

"So he goes after you?" Shake was dubious.

Quinn shrugged. "I knew what he was up to. I'm the only one. We were up to it together."

"Why now?"

Quinn shrugged again. "You asked. It's just an idea I have. Jimmy's moving up the ladder, he's getting his picture in the papers. He's taking care of loose ends. I don't know."

Shake decided that the who probably didn't matter any more than the why. What mattered was the what.

"You know what William Faulkner wrote?" Quinn said. "William Faulkner the writer?"

"Not William Faulkner the astronaut? The light heavyweight?"

"He said, 'The past isn't dead, it's not even past.'"

"I need a favor."

Quinn lit up like Shake had just given him the best news of his life. "Name it," Quinn said.

"I have to get out of the country."

Quinn mused. "You think they'll take another shot at you? Maybe. But it's me they really want, right? So maybe if you lay low for a while . . ."

"It's not just that."

"There's someone else trying to kill you too?" Quinn looked impressed.

"I have to get out of the country quietly. I thought you might be able to help."

Quinn frowned.

He *frowned*.

Shake, already hot and tired and his ribs aching, felt the air go out of him. You knew you were in bad shape when even your worst option wasn't an option. He remembered what his dad used to say at times like that. He called it getting fired from the carnival. Because if you couldn't even meet the standards of the carnie riffraff who worked the state-fair midway, you were in some bad shape, pal.

But then Quinn laughed. "That's it?"

"What do you mean?"

"I owe you my life. You lost your restaurant because of me. Your livelihood and passion. Sticky Jimmy tried to have you iced because of me. And that's all you want? You want to get out of the country? I'm disappointed, Shake, I'll be honest with you. I don't even get to break a sweat with this favor."

Quinn's one employee, the old Kriol man, shuffled up to take the Coke cans away. Quinn waved him off. "Get out of here! You see we're having a conversation?" The old man shuffled away. Quinn turned back to Shake. "You have these kind of problems with your joint? The quality of the local workforce, I'm talking about. I don't want to sound like an asshole, but there it is."

"Can you help me?" Shake said.

"Where do you want to go? When do you want to go? How many beautiful blond girls you want waiting naked for you when you get there? Or brunettes, if that's what you like."

Shake put his elbows on the table and rested his head in his hands. Quinn laughed again. "Okay, okay. I get it, you're under a lot of stress and I'm not helping that, am I?"

"No."

"Here's what I can do. Okay? I've got a buddy lives on the mainland. The line of work he's in, let's just say he needs to come and go without attracting scrutiny. Into the country, out of the country. He knows where the back door is, in other words. He knows which windows are unlocked."

"Dope." Shake shook his head. If it was dope, then Quinn's buddy on the mainland probably worked for Baby Jesus, and Shake was out of luck again.

"No, not dope. Birds, snakes, that sort of thing."

"Birds and snakes?"

"Exotic pets. It's real money, believe it or not. And you get caught, it's just a slap on the wrist, not like dope."

Shake felt a stirring of what might actually be called hope. He'd have to find a way to the mainland, get to Quinn's buddy, but if the buddy really did know a back door out of Belize . . .

"Just a quick hop over the border," Quinn said, "and then we'll be drinking margaritas in Mexico, you and me."

Chapter 15

When Evelyn got to the clinic, Shake was already gone.

"You're joking," Evelyn told the nurse.

"No." The nurse looked as pissed about it as Evelyn was, so Evelyn didn't push. She left the clinic and went down by the water to sit and think. She supposed she wasn't that surprised by this new wrench thrown at her. She'd been shot at twice and reamed out by DEA. She'd ruined two of her favorite dresses. Why wouldn't the shithead choose this opportunity to disappear?

A scrawny Rastafarian with a *Cat in the Hat* hat asked her if she'd be interested in some smoke. She told him to get lost.

She was scheduled to fly back to L.A. in three days. Her hotel was already paid for. Evelyn decided to stop feeling sorry for herself and find the shithead. Do what she'd come here to do.

Evelyn went to the restaurant where she'd first met him. She waited till the lunch rush slowed, then asked to see the owner. He came out of the kitchen, wiping his hands on his apron, a barrel-chested Latino guy. He said his name was Pijua.

"I want to ask you a couple of questions about your friend. Shake Bouchon? You might know him as Quentin Cleary."

"Who?" he said, his expression flat.

"I want to help him."

"Me too. Who is he?"

"I really am trying to help him. I think he needs help."

He shrugged. Evelyn knew she wouldn't get anywhere with this guy. With who, then?

IT WAS ALMOST DARK BY the time Evelyn finally tracked down the formidable black hostess. The woman with the turban and nose ring was sitting in a bar called the Fish and Hook, just up the beach from where the shithead's restaurant used to stand. Now it was just a pile of charred timber that looked like it burned down a hundred years ago.

"What's good here?" Evelyn slid in next to the hostess. She guessed the woman was in her late fifties or so.

The hostess looked her over. "I know you."

"Evelyn Holly. I was at dinner the other night when all that excitement went down? I don't remember your name, I'm sorry."

"Idaba." She looked over Evelyn some more. "You up to something, ain't you?"

"Yep." Evelyn showed the hostess her FBI creds.

The female bartender asked Evelyn what she wanted to drink. The bartender held in her arms what had to be the ugliest, hairiest infant that Evelyn had ever seen.

"Belikin, please," Evelyn said.

Idaba seemed unimpressed by Evelyn's badge. "Huh. That's why."

"That's why what?"

"That's why you on the beach the other day with a gun. I thought he was on drugs."

"Shake?" Evelyn said.

Idaba got up and walked away. Evelyn took her Belikin and followed her outside.

"Just give me a minute," Evelyn said. "One minute."

Idaba turned to face Evelyn, arms crossed over her chest. "I don't know where he at, where he going, what he plan to do when he get there."

"I don't want to arrest him. I want to help him."

"Do you."

"I saved his life on the beach."

"So you can arrest him."

"I don't have jurisdiction here. I couldn't arrest him if I wanted to." Evelyn hesitated, and then decided she had nothing to lose. "I'm gonna put the screws to him in other ways, try to get him to help me."

Idaba looked at her with mild but renewed interest. Evelyn told her about the Armenians, and how she wanted to take them down.

"So?" Idaba said.

"That's important to me. I know Shake is important to you."

"Huh."

"I saw you in the clinic. Sitting there by his bed."

"Huh."

"And I really can help him, Idaba, if you let me. If he lets me. People are trying to kill him. I saw it. I was there. You ever heard of WITSEC? Witness protection? I just want to talk to him. If he doesn't want to cooperate, fine. I can't force him. I just want to give him the choice. He deserves a choice, don't you think?"

Idaba was still studying Evelyn. "I suppose he was right about you."

"About me?"

"That you pretty. You got parts of your face don't match up, though."

"My grandmother was Japanese. She married an Ozark hillbilly. And there's some Puerto Rican in there too, don't ask me how."

Idaba seemed to weigh the matter. Evelyn couldn't read Idaba for the life of her.

"If he gets mad at you for telling me where he is," Evelyn said, "I'll say it wasn't your fault."

"He ain't gonna be mad," Idaba said.

Chapter 16

Shake spent the night in the honeymoon bungalow at the last resort. There was no bed, only a mattress on the bare concrete floor. No electricity, just a kerosene lamp. The faded wallpaper was sloughing off the wall in big, rain-stained curls.

He would have had a hard time sleeping in any case. Every time a shutter banged in the wind, he jumped. Every time a dead palm frond scraped across the roof. Shake figured that Sticky Jimmy's hired guns knew where to find Quinn. Which meant that they knew where to find Shake too.

Last night, when Quinn started talking about the two of them drinking margaritas in Mexico, Shake had just stared at him. "What?"

"Margaritas or piña coladas, I don't know. Whatever you want."

"You're planning to come with me?"

"I owe you my life!" Quinn said, like that was supposed to explain it.

"You're planning to come with me? Out of the country?"

"I could just call my buddy on the mainland. Sure, I could. Just tell him to expect you. Tell him to take care of you."

"Yeah." Shake nodded. "That would be good. That's perfect."

"But what if there's a hink along the way? Right? There's always a hink."

There's always a hink.

Quinn leaned forward. "I've got to see this through, Shake," he said. "You know the Bushido code? The samurai? Doesn't matter if you do or you don't. The Bushido code is about honor. I spent a little time in Kyoto. You saved my life, so now your life is in my hands. Till I get you out of the country, till I've discharged my debt, you're my responsibility. A guy like you, you understand that."

Shake didn't understand. He didn't know why Quinn really wanted to come along, what his angle was. Whatever it was, Shake wanted to stay far away from it.

But it was Quinn's boat that would get him to the mainland. It was Quinn's buddy who knew the back door out of the country. Shake was in Quinn's hands, whether Shake liked it or not.

"It's a lot of trouble for you," Shake said. "You don't need to go to that trouble."

"Trouble? Ask the samurai, did they think the Bushido code was trouble."

And so on, until the wee hours.

When the sun rose, Shake gave up on the idea of sleep. He took a shower, cold, and then walked over to the outdoor café. Quinn was already up, looking fresh as a daisy, waiting for him. "I made some coffee," he said. "You ever been to Boquete? The coffee plantations there? Some people say the coffee out of Rwanda is better, but I've been both places and I'll tell you something about the coffee in Rwanda."

"Listen," Shake said. "I've been thinking."

"That's what I like to hear."

"You should get out of Belize. I agree. Whoever's trying to kill you, Sticky Jimmy, you're safer somewhere else."

Quinn looked around, annoyed. "Where the hell is he? I tell him to have breakfast ready for us at six-thirty. You think he has breakfast ready for us at six-thirty?"

"But why take the long way round with me?" Shake said. "You can go to town, go to the airport, get on a plane, you're in Miami in time for lunch."

"You think I don't know that?" Quinn waved it off. "I know that."

"I don't want to slow you down. I've got a couple of people want me dead, remember. A couple of different groups of people."

"My buddy on the mainland, he's the wary type. It's been a while since I talked to him. I worry if I don't show up myself, if I don't bring you folks together personally. That's a lot of it, you'd be surprised. The personal touch, these kind of things."

"How about you tell me how to find your buddy. In case we get separated along the way."

Quinn sipped his coffee and then set the cup down. "You don't want me to come with you, Shake, just say so."

"I don't want you to come with me."

"Good." Quinn's blue eyes twinkled. "I'm glad that's out of the way. You go on a journey with a guy, you don't want any bullshit between you. Let me tell you a story."

"Wait." Shake looked around. The shuffling old Kriol guy from last night. "You said he was supposed to bring us breakfast at six-thirty?"

"He's fired, don't worry about it. Minute he shows up. I'll let him make breakfast first, he's not a bad cook, but I've never met anyone lazier in my life. I don't care he's eighty-four years old. He was lazy when he was twenty, put your money on it. You think I'll be lazy when I'm eighty-four?"

Shake stood up fast. His plastic beach chair tipped over backward. "We've got to go," he said. "Right now."

BABY JESUS WATCHED HIS BOYS load the white lady, the *dama blanca* that had arrived on Monday. Very good product, the finest, from Peru. Or Bolivia. It didn't matter to Baby Jesus.

The white lady had been wrapped in plastic and then wrapped in old flour sacks and then those packets bundled together, four packets to a bundle, tied tight with string.

"Careful!" he called up to his boys. His boys, loading the boat, paid no attention to the scuffs and smudges they left on Baby Jesus's beautiful cruiser. "If this boat belong to you, would you treat her in such a way?"

Baby Jesus thought that if maybe he put a bullet in the head of the next boy who scuffed his cruiser, then the problem of future scuffs would be solved.

He was still hungry after breakfast, so he whistled Gabriel down off the boat and told him to go buy three or four barbecue chickens. Baby Jesus liked best the man on the beach who grilled his chickens in an oil drum he had sawed in half. This man was only on the beach most days, not all, and other times did not arrive until almost lunchtime.

"If he's not there," Baby Jesus told Gabriel, "go find him. Go to his house. Yes?"

Gabriel sulked. He believed, wrongly, that fetching the barbecue chickens was punishment for what had happened yesterday, Gabriel losing Shake in less time than it took Baby Jesus to remember it.

"If I want to punish you," Baby Jesus told him, "I don't send you for chickens. I put a bullet in your head."

Baby Jesus had not decided if he would put a bullet in Gabriel's head. According to *The 4-Hour Workweek,* a book Baby Jesus had reread several times, an über-successful individual must make the habit of accepting small failures so that he might achieve great victories. Baby Jesus was not sure yet if Gabriel's failure with Shake was small or large. Baby Jesus would wait until the situation was resolved before he decided whether to put a bullet in Gabriel's head.

"Fly away, birdie!" he told Gabriel. "Go!" But before Gabriel could go, one of Baby Jesus's other boys hurried up the dock.

"What."

"He want to talk to you."

"Who?"

"Him."

An old man shuffled toward Baby Jesus. The shifty old fart who used to mop the floors at one of Baby Jesus's bars, Baby Jesus couldn't remember which.

"Good morning, Grandfather," Baby Jesus said. He spread his arms wide and smiled. "How can I help you this fine morning?"

Grandfather slid his shifty eyes around everywhere but onto the face of Baby Jesus. "I hear you looking for a man," he said. "I know where he at."

Gabriel had paused on his way to get the barbecue chickens. All the boys on the boat and the dock had stopped to listen too. Baby Jesus took Grandfather's face in his hand. He turned it so that Grandfather looked at him. When Grandfather's eyes tried to slide away, Baby Jesus turned his face again, harder, and made the eyes stay still.

"Tell me now," Baby Jesus said.

QUINN'S BOAT WAS A TWENTY-TWO-FOOT Mako. It had come with the resort but was in better shape. Shake had checked it out the night before, fired up both Evinrude engines, made sure there was enough gas to get to the mainland.

Shake untied the lines while Quinn ran back inside to get his wallet and passport. He saw the opportunity to ditch Quinn right here, right now, and take his chances on the mainland. Shake scanned the horizon. The temptation was powerful. Before he could talk himself into a decision, or out of one, he saw Quinn come hustling up the pier.

Quinn jumped in, breathing heavy, wearing sunglasses now. Carrying a shaving kit and an overnight bag. Quinn saw Shake looking at the overnight bag. "What?" Quinn said.

Shake punched the throttle and they roared away from the pier. He didn't know how much of a head start they had. They'd need every minute of it, if Baby Jesus came after them in his big Esprit cruiser.

Shake should have been more cautious about the old Kriol man last night. He should have seen that coming. He wondered if he was losing his edge. On the other hand, it had been a long day yesterday, a long couple of days in fact, and he'd been on some pretty potent painkillers for his ribs.

Shake's plan was to head north along the reef, all the way to the far tip of Ambergris, and then cut around Bacalar Chico, across the bay toward the mainland. They made it about a hundred yards before one of the Evinrude engines kicked out. Shake stayed calm. This shit happened. It always happened. If you lost your cool every time . . .

The other Evinrude kicked out. *Shit*. The Mako began to drift with the current.

"You want me to drive?" Quinn asked. "I'm happy to do it. You know how to drive one of these babies?"

"I know how to drive," Shake said, jaw clenched. He looked at the console. Both fuel gauges read empty. Empty? He'd made sure, last night, they had gas. He'd made sure . . .

Shit. He climbed back, his ribs aching, to check the Evinrudes. Both fuel caps were missing. The tanks had been siphoned dry. The old Kriol man who'd dimed them to Baby Jesus.

"Turns out he's not so lazy after all," Shake said. He slapped his palm against one of the Evinrudes, hard, and then slapped the other engine even harder. "Damn it." He had to tie up quickly to a mooring buoy so the current wouldn't carry them into the reef.

"Uh-oh," Quinn said. Shake turned. A boat to the south, closing in on them.

Shake figured he had about three minutes to decide where he wanted to die, in the boat or in the water, trying to swim back to shore.

Quinn had lifted his sunglasses and was squinting at the boat. "Who was it you said is trying to kill you?" he said.

Shake squinted too. The boat closing in on them was another slow Mako, not the Esprit cruiser that belonged to Baby Jesus. And instead of Rasta thugs with heavy weapons, the boat was crowded with tourists in swimsuits, each of them holding a bright orange foam floatie.

"Hoo boy," Quinn said, "I see you've gotten mixed up with a pretty rough crowd."

"Funny." Shake waved the other Mako over. They needed to borrow some gas, and fast. "Hey!" he hollered. "Over here!"

In addition to the captain, there were eight or nine tourists on the other Mako. The tourists were busy squirting defogger into their masks, hopping foot to foot as they snapped their flippers on.

"You want me to handle this?" Quinn said.

"I don't," Shake said.

The captain of the other Mako was a little mestizo with his shirt off, smaller even than Armando but muscles everywhere. He throttled down, eased up, tossed Shake a line across the water. Shake pulled the line tight as the current bumped the two boats together.

"We ran dry," Shake said. "Think you can spare a few gallons?"

"No problem," the captain said.

"O Captain! My Captain!" Quinn said. He stood up and gave the little mestizo a salute. The mestizo didn't know what to do, so he saluted back.

"You gonna have to wait a little bit," he told Shake. "Till I get everybody in the water and everybody finish their snorkel."

Shake recognized the weary expression of a fellow professional service provider. Who knew if he didn't get everybody in the water, give them the full hour on the reef they'd paid for, they'd never let him hear the fucking end of it.

But Shake didn't have time for everybody to finish snorkeling, or time to siphon gas from one tank to the other. "Listen," he said. "I have a question about your boat."

"It's not belong to me," the little mestizo said. "It's belong to the hotel."

"We need to borrow it."

"Borrow it?"

"We don't want any trouble," Shake said. Meaning it.

The little mestizo tried to process. He rubbed a hand over his bare, muscular chest. "You wanna steal the boat?"

"I'm sorry. I know it's a pain in your ass, but—" Shake stopped. Quinn had stepped past him, a little hop onto the other boat. He was carrying his overnight bag.

Shake had time for two quick thoughts:

What the hell?

And then: *Fuck.*

"Ladies and gentlemen!" Quinn yelled. "Your attention, please! Do as you're told and nobody gets hurt!"

A few tourists looked over at him.

"Don't," Shake said. "Stop. Damn it." He made a grab for Quinn, but Quinn slipped it and climbed up onto a storage locker. He lifted the overnight bag over his head.

"We have a bomb!" Quinn yelled. "Everybody get your asses in the water, now, or we blow you to kingdom come!"

The tourists started screaming and jumping, their flippers smacking the water. The boat rocked back and forth. Shake wanted to throw Quinn's ass in the water, but instead he just stepped over into the other boat. He was committed at this point. He had been committed. The little mestizo just stared at Quinn, and then at Shake. Shake hoped he didn't have a knife, or try to use it.

"Let's just all be cool," Shake said.

"Out of the boat!" Quinn yelled at a couple of tourist stragglers. "Go! You want to see if I won't blow your asses to kingdom come?" The stragglers hit the water.

The little mestizo stayed where he was. He was thinking, Shake could be pretty sure of it, *You don't have no bomb*. But then he just shook his head. The boat belonged to the hotel, not him. *Fuck it*. He muttered something in Spanish, grabbed a couple bottles of Bud Light from the cooler by the wheel, and jumped into the water.

Most of the tourists were already swimming hard for shore, past the coral heads of the reef. All you could see of them in the water, mostly, were their bright orange foam floaties.

Two people were still treading water alongside the boat. Shake recognized them. They had recognized him. The young honeymoon couple from Buffalo. "Is this really for real?" the honeymoon kid said.

"Sorry," Shake said. *Think of the stories you'll tell your grandkids*.

"Go on," Quinn said. "Get out of here. Don't be a hero."

"It's only a few hundred yards to shore," Shake said. "There's a place with a phone when you get there."

The honeymoon couple drifted off. The kid looked dazed, like no way could this be happening again. The girl just looked mad. "I am so putting this on TripAdvisor," Shake heard her say quietly.

"The way to control a crowd of people," Quinn said, "buddy of mine worked state security in Budapest told me this once, is you just scare the living Jesus out of them. But you don't want to rile them up, it's a fine line."

Shake turned to Quinn.

Quinn lifted a hand. "Don't mention it," he said. "You're welcome."

"What the hell was that?" Shake said.

"It's called improvisation. It's called thinking on the wing. You think I've stayed alive this long without a little improvisation along the way?"

Shake, honestly, had no idea how Quinn had stayed alive this long.

"Cool your jets." Quinn sat down and settled in. "Sometimes you have to cut to the chase, Shake. My understanding is we're on the clock here. Let me know if we're not."

"Listen to me," Shake said, but he didn't finish. Quinn was standing back up and looking out over the water.

"Uh-oh," Quinn said.

SHAKE PUSHED THE SNORKEL BOAT they'd hijacked as hard as he could, but Baby Jesus's Esprit cruiser, no mistaking it this time, flew at them like they were sitting still. The snorkel boat—yesterday Shake's first stolen golf cart, today his first stolen boat—had maybe four hundred horses. Baby Jesus's cruiser had five or six times that.

"Step on it, Aunt Martha!" Quinn hollered over the wind blasting past. He seemed to be enjoying himself.

Shake knew they couldn't outrun Baby Jesus. Shake had been in this situation before, though never on water. The trick, in a car, was to minimize your disadvantage—take the chase to a parking garage, for example, where the souped-up Camaro trying to catch you wouldn't be able to open up and run.

Where was a parking garage, Shake wondered, when you needed one?

Baby Jesus was close. Shake glanced back and saw him at the wheel of his Esprit, a couple of his thugs up on the bow with what looked like semiautomatic rifles. They were close enough to open fire but didn't. That meant they wanted to make sure they had a clear shot, or that

Baby Jesus wanted Shake alive so he could kill him slowly. Probably the second one.

Shake got as close to the reef on his right as he dared. The coral heads, only a few feet below the surface, flashed past.

"Any time now!" Quinn hollered. "Whatever you got in mind!"

Shake waited, waited, waited, until Baby Jesus was right on them. "Hold on," Shake hollered. He cut the wheel to the left and eased off the throttle, hoping it would send them into something like a bootlegger's slide. It did, sort of, turning the snorkel boat broadside into the path of the cruiser.

Baby Jesus reacted instinctively. That was the biggest difference between a professional driver and an amateur. An amateur did the first thing his brain told him to do, without stopping to think about it. Baby Jesus didn't stop to think about it and cut his wheel hard to the right to avoid a collision. His Esprit sliced into the reef.

The cruiser grazed the first coral head but hit the next one flush. The sound was like nothing Shake had ever heard before—a crunching shriek, like someone was pounding a buzz saw against . . . well, the hull of a boat. One of the thugs on the bow of Baby Jesus's cruiser was flung into the water. The coral opened up the hull of the Esprit like it was a can of tuna, leaving a long jagged gash just below the waterline.

The cruiser started to list fast, taking on water. Baby Jesus tried to gun the cruiser off the coral head. He didn't stop to think about that either. The big engines roared, the teeth of the coral bit deeper, the long jagged gash got longer.

Shake hit the throttle of the snorkel boat and headed away from the reef. Apparently Baby Jesus had decided he'd rather have Shake dead quick than not at all. He yelled at his thugs and they opened up with their automatic rifles.

It was touch and go for half a mile. Shake heard—felt—a couple of rounds snap past. But he and Quinn stayed low. A few minutes later the Mako was safely out of range and they were in the wind, headed for the mainland.

Quinn dug around in the cooler and pulled out a beer. He settled back and put a hand up to shade his eyes. "Piece of cake," he said.

Chapter 17

Evelyn hired a taxi boat to take her way up north to the Crystal Shores resort. The driver asked if she knew that the resort had gone bankrupt several years before. Evelyn told him to take her there anyway. He shrugged. "Okay, you say so, *madame,* your money to spend."

When they reached the Crystal Shores, it was deserted. Evelyn walked around the whole place and poked her head into all the bunga-lows. On the sun-soaked patio of one bungalow she found an iguana the size of a golden retriever. Just lying curled up on the cracked tile, regarding her with drowsy indifference. She hoped it was indifference. Evelyn snapped a photo with her cell phone to send Sarah, and then got the hell out of there.

One of the suites, in the main building, looked like someone had been living there. Sheets on the bed, a closet full of clothes. Evelyn picked up a knockoff Patek Philippe watch from the dresser. It was an excellent knockoff, one of the best she'd ever seen. It reminded her of somebody, or something, but she couldn't place who or what. She returned the watch to the dresser and went back outside. She didn't think Idaba had lied to her, but if Shake had been here earlier, he wasn't here now.

Evelyn decided to leave a note in case he returned. Why not? She dug around in her purse until she found a pen and the wrinkled paper sleeve of her American Airlines boarding pass. She tried to think about how to start. *Dear Shithead?*

"Dear Charles," she wrote, and then stopped.

A lady in a one-piece, dripping wet and carrying a snorkel mask, came stomping across the cracked concrete slab toward her. "Is there a phone inside?" The woman looked pissed and exhausted.

"I don't know." Evelyn was too surprised to say anything else.

"Great," the woman said, and stomped past.

Evelyn saw more snorkelers straggling out of the ocean. She counted nine in all. A few collapsed to the sand and just lay there. A few began to straggle up the beach, heading toward the next resort over. Evelyn couldn't begin to imagine what was going on. She went down to the beach.

"Hey," she asked the snorkelers who had collapsed to the sand. "You guys okay?" They looked okay, just pissed and exhausted.

"They stole our boat," one woman said.

"What? Who did?"

Before the woman could answer, Evelyn saw more figures splashing toward shore, up to their waists in water. Four big black guys and one enormously big black guy. Each guy had an AR-15 semiautomatic rifle hanging from a strap around his shoulder, and each carried a brown burlap bundle above his head, to keep the bundle from getting wet.

Evelyn took her SIG Sauer out of her purse.

"Not them," the snorkeler on the beach said. "I don't know who they are."

"That's okay," Evelyn said.

The enormously big black guy was the first one to reach the beach. He saw Evelyn. He saw the gun she had pointed at him. "United States

Federal Bureau of Investigation," Evelyn said. "Keep your hands above your heads."

He had a weirdly small and round and smooth face, with delicate little Cupid's-bow lips. Evelyn understood it now, the nickname.

"Lady." Baby Jesus smiled at her. "Pretty lady. What is this?"

Evelyn smiled back, her best big warm smile. That seemed to surprise him. He'd probably never been outsmiled before. "One at a time," she said, "slowly, lower your hands and drop your weapons. You first."

After a second Baby Jesus lowered the burlap bundle to the sand. He straightened back up and moved a hand to the strap of his AR-15. If he went for his gun, if the other four guys dropped their bundles and did the same, it would be five guys with semiautomatic rifles against her one SIG Sauer. Not to mention the several gawking civilians behind her who would be mowed down when the shooting started.

"Do it now," Evelyn said.

"Lady," Baby Jesus said with a coy, sweet smile. "There is only you. You see this? And all of us."

Evelyn kept smiling back. "I'll shoot you before they can draw on me."

"But then what? What is the ending to that story?"

"I guess we'll never know," she said. "Either one of us."

He chuckled. His hand tightened on the strap of his rifle. "Lady," he said. "Pretty lady. I don't believe you will shoot me."

"Really?" Evelyn said. She turned her smile off—*boom*. Her gun stayed steady as a rock.

His smile faded. His brow knitted. He pursed his little cherub lips. Finally he shrugged the strap off his shoulder and dropped his AR-15 to the sand.

"No," he said. "Not really."

Chapter 18

Terry glanced over at Meg sitting on the other bench, her knees pulled up to her chest and her chin on her knees. She hadn't said a word to him in hours. She hadn't yelled at him once.

He cleared his throat. "Well. Could be worse."

And it could be. The jail they were in wasn't half bad, so far as jails went. One time Terry spent a week in a jail in East St. Louis, Illinois, which was like spending a week inside an asshole. This jail wasn't anything like that. It had a fresh sea breeze coming through the windows and the floor was swept clean. And they got to stay together, Terry and Meg did. A lot of jails, they put the men and the women in whole different parts.

The police station here on San Pedro didn't have any other parts. There was the front, with a couple of desks where the cops sat, and then, toward the back by a soda machine, a kind of cage made of iron bars, painted a cheerful shade of sky blue. Terry and Meg were locked inside that.

"Could be worse?" Meg said. She looked over at Terry. "That what you just said?"

Terry was happy to hear her voice again, to have her look at him. Even if he could tell she was so mad at him she could spit. "Hell, yes," he said. "You think about it. All they got us on is a little old possession charge. For pot! Why, just think what they coulda—"

"Terry," Meg said, sharp.

He shut up and looked over to the cop sitting at one of the desks. The cop was reading a magazine with a picture of President Obama on the front of it. Terry hoped that didn't get Meg started on President Obama. She could go on for hours, what a pussy she thought he was.

"Hey, over there!" he called to the cop. "What all they do to the people get busted down here on a little old pot charge? Ain't hardly nothing at all, is it?"

"Nobody does," the cop said, turning a page of his Obama magazine.

"Nobody does what?"

"Ain't nobody gets busted down here for pot except a goddamn moron," Meg said. "Ain't nobody goes up to a cop and asks him to light up his goddamn doobie."

The cop turned another page. "Nobody till now."

Terry didn't like it how they were teaming up against him. Not when the whole situation had been set in motion with a selfless endeavor on his part. He and Meg had just missed the chef they were going to kill, just by a whisker. He had already checked himself out of the clinic when they got there. Meg wasn't happy about that. She was steaming. So when Bob Marley down by the water asked Terry would he be interested in a little smoke, Terry thought a doobie might be just the thing to cool out Meg's nerves.

How was Terry supposed to know the cop he asked for a light was a cop? The cop just stood there watching Terry's whole transaction with Bob Marley without batting an eye. Terry figured he must be a tourist helper, the kind that wore uniforms and helped point tourists around to the various attractions. He was wearing short pants! What kind of cop wore short pants?

"I bet you a hundred dollars we don't get no more than a month or two," Terry told Meg. "For a little old pot charge. And I been in worse jails than this one, I can tell you that."

Meg's eyes just about set Terry's head on fire. Before she could say anything, though, the front door of the police station opened and a man walked in. He was American. Terry could tell it right away, and not just 'cause the man was white instead of black or Mexican. He had on a suit with his tie knot pulled away from his collar, and glasses that were just glass without any rims around them. He had the tallest, longest forehead Terry had ever seen in his life.

"Hi, sorry, sorry I'm late," the man told the cop at the desk.

"I knew it," Terry whispered to Meg. "I knew he was American."

"Be still," she whispered back.

The man opened his wallet and showed the cop something inside. The cop put down his magazine and walked over to the cage where Terry and Meg were sitting.

"Hi, guys," the man said to them as the cop unlocked the cage. "Sorry I'm late. It's a Saturday night, and usually, you know, well, since it's a Saturday night and all."

Terry looked at Meg. Meg was watching the man.

"Oh, right," the man said. "My name's Kevin Coover? I'm with the U.S. embassy in Belmopan? I'm the vice consul. The acting vice consul?"

"Stand up, please," the cop said.

Terry and Meg stood up. The cop put the handcuffs back on them.

"Sorry, guys," Kevin Coover said. "About the restraints? It's kind of a new deal we have. Just till we get you folks processed out? But we'll get you processed out ASAP. And then we'll get you on your way."

"What do you mean?" Meg asked.

"Well," Kevin Coover said, "you're American citizens and we have a, well, it's informal, an understanding with the Belizeans. A reciprocal agreement? Kind of a new deal. If it's not a huge, you know, if it's not murder or bank robbery or whatever." He made what Terry supposed was a machine gun with his two hands and pretended like the machine gun was kicking back on him as he fired all over the room.

"You mean to say you're gonna let us go?" Meg said.

"Well, I'll have to process you out. And that takes some time? Sorry about that. But then we'll get you on the next flight back home, courtesy of the United States government. And American Airlines? Because we have an agreement with them too."

Terry turned to Meg in happy wonder.

"Your lucky day," Kevin Coover said.

KEVIN COOVER TOOK THEM DOWN to the ferry and they all three of them rode the last ferry of the night over to Belize City. It wasn't a long ride, and smooth enough. The whole way Coover kept saying he was sorry about the restraints, sorry they couldn't go back to their place and get their personal belongings till later, sorry about how he'd been running late to get them out of jail.

Terry said, hell, they hadn't even known somebody was running to get them out of jail, so no apology necessary.

A couple of the other passengers glanced at the handcuffs. Terry didn't mind. He wasn't embarrassed. Everybody ended up in handcuffs, one time or another in their life. It wasn't anything to be ashamed of.

After the ferry, Coover put them in the back of a dark green SUV and drove them across town to a little office building. He had to stop and get out because the gate to the parking lot of the office building was locked. "Sorry," he said. "Everybody's gone for the weekend. Be right back."

While he was out unlocking the gate to the parking lot, Terry turned to Meg. "How do you like that?" he whispered. "They're gonna get us on the next flight home!"

"We ain't gonna get on no next flight home," Meg hissed back at him. "I'll tell you that right now."

"What?" Terry was pretty sure that was exactly what Kevin Coover had told them. "What do you mean?"

"I mean we got a job to do and we're gonna do it."

"But—"

"Don't you understand?" Meg's lips were chapped. "If we don't do this job, you think Jorge's ever gonna give us another one? You think anybody's ever gonna give us another one? We won't ever amount to shit, is what'll happen."

Terry didn't know what to say. On the one hand Meg was right. On the other hand, though, it did seem like a hell of a lucky day, getting pulled out of jail and put on a free plane ride home.

"We gotta look for the right moment," Meg whispered. "You hear me? If he tries to stop us, that's his own problem."

Coover got back in the SUV and pulled into the parking lot.

"Sorry about that," he said.

He took them up the stairs to an office on the second floor of the building. The office had hardly any furniture in it, just a couple of chairs and a big old steel filing cabinet and one computer monitor sitting on the floor. There was dust everywhere and Terry sneezed. Coover said his department was in the process of relocating to this office from another property where the rent had gone up. He didn't apologize about it, and Terry thought, *Hallelujah!*

Coover asked Meg if she'd mind taking a seat over in the chair by the big filing cabinet. She looked at him a minute, then did. He unlocked one half of her handcuffs and locked that half to the big steel filing cabinet. He explained he was sorry but the rules about processing said he had to interview them separately, in different parts of the office.

"He ain't goin' nowhere without me!" Meg said, so fierce that Coover took a step backward. "We don't go nowhere without each other!"

"It's the rules," Terry said. "Settle down, darlin'."

"It really is," Coover said. "And I'm sorry about the restraints, but that's the rule too. Because it's not business hours? If it was business hours, I wouldn't have to use the restraints. You could just sit here with the administrative assistant and chat. She's a hoot."

"Let me loose!" Meg said.

Kevin Coover looked like he was about ready to die, he felt so bad about leaving Meg restrained there in the front of the office. "I'm really, really sorry," he said. "We're just going down the hall for a minute. If you need anything at all, all you have to do is holler."

"Terry," Meg said, so soft all of a sudden that Terry could barely hear her.

"I'll be back in flash," Terry told her.

"I promise," Coover said. "You two won't be apart for long."

He led Terry down the hallway to another office. There was just one chair in there. Coover used another set of handcuffs to lock Terry to the chair.

"No apology necessary," Terry said, beating him to the punch, and they both laughed.

"So, Mr. Epperson," Coover said. "What was the purpose of your visit to Belize?"

"Vacation."

That's what Meg had told Terry to say, and not to add on anything else.

"Vacation?"

"Yes, sir."

"So you and your wife weren't hired by Jorge Nolasco in Guatemala City to perform a contract killing of Mr. Harrigan Quinn?"

Terry sat there. It felt like the whole room had tipped upside down on him.

"How'd you know 'bout that?" he said before he could stop himself.

Kevin Coover took his glasses off and put them in the pocket of his suit coat.

"I don't know nothing 'bout that," Terry said.

"Mr. Epperson," he said. "You mind if I call you Terry?"

"All right."

"Terry. My name's not Kevin Coover."

"It's not?"

"You can call me Paul. Paul Babb. That's what a lot of people call me."

"Okay."

"And I don't work for the American consulate. I work for the Federal Bureau of Investigation."

"That's the FBI."

"Yes. And I'm afraid you're in a lot of trouble."

"I told you. I don't know nothing 'bout no Jorge or no contract to kill nobody."

"We have your fingerprints on the weapon. We've got your DNA. The blood from your nose?"

"I don't know nothing 'bout that."

Damn it. Terry remembered now, his nose dripping blood all the while he ran out of the restaurant. They could get your DNA from blood. And then they could take your DNA and figure out all sorts of things about you.

"I'm afraid that you and your wife are going to prison for a very long time," the FBI man said.

Terry felt like he might burst into tears.

"Unless you cooperate with me, Terry. Okay?"

Terry nodded. He felt like he was so close to bursting into tears he better not open his mouth.

"Good. Now I want you to tell me what happened. That first night when you went to kill Mr. Quinn. I want you to tell me everything."

Terry told him everything, the words rushing out so fast that a couple of times the FBI man told him to slow down, back up. He kept asking about the restaurant chef, the one that broke Terry's nose and kept him from shooting the old man. Did it seem like the restaurant chef and the old man were friends? Did it seem like maybe the restaurant chef was really there to protect the old man?

"I think he was, come to think of it," Terry said. Watching the FBI man's eyes, wanting to make him happy. "Yes, sir. I know that for a fact! And I'll tell you another thing. That chef ain't no run-of-the-mill chef. He works for some people in California. Some Mafia people." Terry tried to remember what kind of Mafia people. Meg had told him—Germans?—but now he couldn't remember.

The FBI man was watching Terry real close.

"Armenians?" he said.

"That's it!" Terry said. "That's exactly it!"

"Okay," the FBI man said. He clapped his hands together once and then held them like that, clapped together. "I think we're done here."

Terry tried to think of what else he could say, his mind racing around.

"It was all me," Terry blurted out. "It wasn't Meg. She didn't have nothing to do with none of it. Jorge was her friend, but it was all my idea. Meg didn't want nothing to do with it, but I told her we had to. I'll say that to a judge too. So you go tell the FBI to let her loose."

"Oh, gosh, Terry." His mood seemed to lighten up and he laughed. "I don't really work for the FBI."

"You don't?" Terry saw that the FBI man who didn't work for the FBI had a switchblade in his hand. Terry didn't know where the switchblade had come from. It hadn't been there a second ago. The man clicked the switchblade open.

"What's that for?" Terry said. "I'm all confused."

BABB WIPED THE BLADE OF the knife on the carpet. He unlocked both sets of handcuffs and put them back in his pocket. He made sure there was no blood on his shoes. The boy wore a bracelet on his right wrist, different-colored strings braided together. Babb thought it looked festive. He cut the knot and put the bracelet in his pocket.

He screwed a suppressor onto the muzzle of his Heckler & Koch .45. He preferred to use the knife, but safety first. The girl was a firecracker. She was liable to bite his nose off if he got too close.

He walked down the hall and into the other room. The girl was gone. Babb bent down to examine the cuff. Still locked. Somehow the girl had managed to squeeze her hand out of the locked cuff. A person could squeeze out of a handcuff that wasn't locked tight—Babb had heard of it happening—but these cuffs had been locked tight. He always made a point to make sure. Babb considered how much it must have hurt for her to pull free. Probably the girl had torn off a good bit of epidermis and broken her carpometacarpal joints. Babb considered the force of will required to do something like that—to tear off your epidermis and break your carpometacarpals and still keep pulling. All without making a peep.

He chuckled. The girl was definitely a firecracker. She'd gone out the window, a fifteen-foot drop to the pavement below. Babb wasn't concerned. The boy had given him everything that he needed.

He called Gardenhire's private cell. Babb pictured Gardenhire—in a meeting, in a hotel conference room. Plastic coffee carafes on the table. Glasses of ice water sweating. Men and woman arguing, laughing, talking about "message alignment," "organizational positioning," "activation wheels."

Gardenhire was Babb's boss on this job. Gardenhire had a boss too. Babb wasn't supposed to know who that was—hush-hush—but of course he knew. Babb didn't take a job unless he had all the details.

Gardenhire answered his phone after three and a third rings. "What do you have?"

Babb guessed that Gardenhire had slipped out into the hallway to take the call. A carpeted hallway, a bank of elevators, a nice potted plant.

"Activation wheel," Babb said. "Message alignment."

"What?"

"Nothing. I spoke with the young man."

"And your conclusion?"

"I think it's possible."

"Likely?"

"Possible."

Silence.

"If the old bastard has real protection," Gardenhire said, "if he's tied up somehow with the Armenians . . ."

Babb heard Gardenhire sigh.

"You should have called me first," Babb said.

"I didn't think it was anything."

"You should have called me first."

"Is that what you want me to say?"

"Okay."

"I should have called you first."

"I'll take care of it," Babb said.

"I'll call you soon as I know something," Gardenhire said.

"Care will be taken."

PART II

Chapter 19

Halfway across the bay, Shake thought about turning north and trying to run the stolen Mako snorkel boat all the way up to Chetumal, just across the Mexican border. If he did that, he wouldn't need Quinn's buddy on the mainland. More important, he wouldn't need Quinn.

"How long you gonna stay mad at me, Shake?" Quinn asked. "I'd like to plan the rest of my day."

"Day?" Shake planned to stay mad about Quinn's improv performance a lot longer than that.

Quinn chuckled and followed Shake's gaze north across the water. "Fuerza Naval del Golfo y Mar Caribe," he said. "The Mexican navy. Buddy of mine, a few years back, he won the contract for their Polaris-class interceptor patrol boats. I consulted on the deal, I'll leave it at that. Nice boat, the CB90, I think it was called. Ungodly fast, you wouldn't believe it."

"Thanks for the insight," Shake said, testy. He didn't need Quinn to tell him that the Mexican navy patrolled the stretch of water between Mexico and Belize, or that the snorkel boat would never outrun them. A guy could dream, couldn't he?

"Paciencia y barajar."

Shake sighed. "What."

" 'Have patience and keep shuffling the cards.' Cervantes wrote that in *Don Quixote*. Cervantes the light heavyweight."

Shake didn't ask how Cervantes saying that applied to the current situation. He knew the explanation would be a long one.

" 'Better to lose by a card too many,' Cervantes wrote, 'than a card too few.' "

They reached the mainland a couple of hours after curling around Bacalar Chico and leaving Ambergris Caye behind. Shake found an abandoned pier, wood rotting, a few miles west of Sarteneja. He brought the stolen snorkel boat in and tied her up.

From there they walked a mile or so to the road. A pickup truck headed out of Sarteneja stopped for them around noon. Quinn asked the driver if he was going as far as Three Butterflies. He was going all the way to Orange Walk and agreed to drop them on the way.

Shake and Quinn climbed into the bed of the pickup. The road continued inland before turning south. Bouncing along beside a swampy lagoon, they passed a horse and carriage ambling by in the opposite lane. The guy driving the horse and carriage was white, with a big red beard and a flat, broad-brimmed straw hat. The woman next to him was white too, wearing a bonnet and a long dress.

"Mennonites?" Shake said. He remembered now reading about them when he first came to Belize, but he'd never actually seen any.

"Seventeenth-century Deutschland in the middle of Central America," Quinn said. "You can't make something like that up. They came down, it's my understanding, in the sixties, from Canada and Pennsylvania. The government of Belize cut them a deal on taxes and left them alone."

Another horse and buggy approached. *Guten Tag!* Quinn called out. *Wie geht es Ihnen?* The Mennonite driving the horse and buggy touched the brim of his hat.

Three Butterflies was a Mennonite settlement at the southern tip of the lagoon, a cluster of six or seven cement-block buildings with tin roofs. Little blue-eyed girls with braids and long plaid dresses chased each other, laughing, around the parked buggies.

The pickup stopped. Shake and Quinn climbed out.

"These are what you'd call the true believers," Quinn said. "No electricity, no phones, no modern defilements of the faith. The Old Colony, they call it. 'Altkolonier.' The more progressive bunch lives over in Blue Creek, you'll see them driving tractors."

"You know a lot about the Mennonites," Shake said.

"My buddy who's gonna get us out of Belize, I told you, he lives around here."

"He's a Mennonite?"

"What?" Quinn laughed.

An older woman with gunmetal-gray hair was watching the little girls play. Quinn walked over to her. Shake followed him. *"Guten Tag,"* Quinn said. *"Wie geht es Ihnen?"*

The woman answered. She and Quinn talked for a while in German. Or maybe it was Dutch, Shake didn't know. "Widow," Quinn told Shake after the woman left to go round up the little girls. He gave Shake a wink.

Shake waited.

"Don't worry," Quinn said. "She said my buddy's still around."

Shake hadn't known until now that it was a question, whether or not Quinn's buddy was still around.

"Just down the road a mile or so," Quinn said as he started walking. "Think you can keep up?"

QUINN'S BUDDY LIVED IN A cement-block house so buried by the jungle that it looked like a Mayan ruin.

"Benny!" Quinn hollered. After a few minutes, a man close to Quinn's age stepped out of the house, squinting in the sun. He had a big gray beard that fanned out and down and covered half his chest. He was wearing filthy denim coveralls, no shirt on underneath.

"There he is!" Quinn said.

Benny squinted at him. He frowned. "Quinn? The hell are you doing here?"

Perfect, Shake thought.

Quinn turned to Shake. "Benny and I have known each other since way back when. First time I came to Belize, back in the seventies, nobody had even heard of Belize. You remember that, Benny? We could've bought Ambergris Caye for fifty bucks and a bottle of Johnnie Walker."

"Get the hell off my property, Quinn."

Even better.

"I need a favor, Benny," Quinn said. "For old time's sake."

"Get the hell off my property."

Quinn laughed. "Stop screwing around, you old fart. Take us inside and pour us a stiff one." He walked up to Benny, gave the big gray beard a tug, and walked past him into the house. Benny scowled but didn't try to stop Quinn. He looked at Shake.

"You want me to get the hell out of here too?" Shake said.

"You'd better," Benny said.

Shake thought he knew what Benny meant. He shrugged. Benny shook his head, maybe with pity, and waved Shake inside.

EVERY WALL OF BENNY'S LIVING room was lined with wire cages and glass aquariums, stacked floor to ceiling, mostly empty. Shake saw two small toucans with enormous beaks and a Jesus lizard, the kind that could run so fast across water they didn't sink. Shake had seen them in action and it was fairly miraculous.

Curled up asleep on the sofa was what looked like a giant black pig, but with a weird long snout, like an anteater.

"Baird's tapir," Benny said when he saw Shake give the animal on the couch a wide berth. "Largest land mammal in Central America. The cow of the jungle, they call it."

"Is that right?" Shake said.

"Gentle, most of the time. Well, it's not an Irish setter. You want an Irish setter, go ahead and get one, not a tapir. I don't see the confusion. Tapirs don't need much exercise, that's another good thing about them."

Shake realized that Benny had misinterpreted his interest in the tapir. "I don't think I'm in the market right now," Shake said.

"I can make you a deal."

"Tell him, Benny," Quinn said, "about tapirs and natural predators."

"Tapirs don't have any. Not really. Crocs, if they're big ones. A grown jaguar, maybe, but that fight's still a pick-'em."

Shake was looking at Benny's beard. "I thought you weren't a Mennonite," he said.

"When the cops come around I am," Benny said. "Makes my life easier. The real broad-brims in town, the buggy humpers, they don't mind. I donate a few hundred bucks to the cause, whenever they need to build a new barn or what have you."

"Let's get down to brass tacks," Quinn told Benny. He nudged the tapir over with his knee and took a seat on the couch. "We need to get into Mexico without any noise and you're the guy, Benny. You know the back door, which windows are unlocked. You still have that four-by-four? The Land Cruiser can get through just about anything?"

"No," Benny said.

"No, you don't have the Land Cruiser?" Quinn said.

"No, I won't take you over the border. Hell no. You remember last time?"

"What?"

"What."

"I remember that if it wasn't for me, Benjamin, you wouldn't have this nice little racket selling exotic animals."

"That's how you remember it?" Benny said. The part of Benny's face that wasn't covered by beard, not much of it, flushed red.

"That's how I remember it because that's what happened."

"That's how you remember it?"

Shake, exhausted and hot and his ribs beginning to ache again, drifted for a moment. Left his body and felt the world go opaque. When he snapped back, Quinn and Benny were still arguing, the tapir was still grunting in its sleep. And Shake still had no idea how his life had come to this place, this moment. Shake wondered if twenty years from now he'd be the guy with the gray beard, sitting across from Quinn flushed with anger, asking, "Is that how you remember it? What happened in Belize?"

The odds weren't as long as Shake would have liked.

"All right, Benny," Quinn said. "How about this. Get us out of the country and I'll give you a grand."

"No."

But this "no" had less bite to it. Benny had started to comb his beard with this fingers.

Quinn saw it too. "Two grand."

"No."

"And you throw in the tapir."

"What?" Benny and Shake said at the same time.

"I'm kidding," Quinn said. "Does anybody here have a sense of humor but me?"

Benny narrowed his eyes. "Tell me why you want to get out of the country so bad," he said. "Out the back door and what have you."

"None of your beeswax," Quinn said.

"It is if I say it is."

"Like it's none of my beeswax that trouble you got into back in the States, Benny, why you came down here in the seventies. I'd never breathe a word of that to your friendly Mennonite neighbors."

Benny stiffened. He narrowed his eyes until they just about disappeared.

"Three grand and you keep the tapir," Quinn said. "Just a quick hop over the border. Don't tell me that's not fair."

"Four grand," Benny said.

"Two up front," Quinn said, "two when you get us to Mexico."

Benny combed his beard with his fingers. He combed and combed. Shake wanted to grab his hand and make him sit on it. "It'll have to be tomorrow," Benny said. "I can't make the run in the dark."

"That's fine."

"And you keep your damn mouth shut the whole ride, Quinn. You don't say a damn word."

"That's a deal," Shake said.

• • •

SHAKE AND QUINN ATE DINNER at the widow's house in town. Quinn had arranged for them to rent her couch and spare bedroom for the night.

"You don't want to sleep at Benny's," Quinn had told Shake. "You never know which one of God's creatures you're gonna step on, you have to get up in the middle of the night. You don't want to pull out your wang to take a leak, trust me, and then see a harpy eagle with his eye on you."

The widow's fried chicken was some of the best Shake had ever tasted. He could tell she used buttermilk, incredibly fresh and flavorful. If he'd still owned a restaurant, Shake would have begged for the recipe. Instead he asked Quinn how to tell her the chicken was delicious.

"Es schmeckt gut," Quinn said.

Shake tried it out. The widow and Quinn both laughed.

"It's the thought that counts," Quinn said, and put a hand on Shake's shoulder.

After dinner, while the widow cleaned up, Shake and Quinn sat out on the porch. They watched the sun, orange and trembling as an egg yolk, sink into the misty lagoon.

"Now, then," Quinn said. "Didn't I tell you we'd be off without a hitch?"

They weren't off yet, and by Shake's count they'd already hit multiple hitches. But he didn't say anything. It was Quinn's four grand that was going to get them over the border tomorrow, not Shake's. Shake didn't have four grand. He had about sixty-five bucks in his wallet, which meant he had about sixty-five bucks to his name. Sixty-five bucks, the clothes on his back. Shake wondered what he would do when he got to Mexico. And then he decided he'd better not wonder about that, not if he wanted to get any sleep tonight.

When Shake had walked out of prison three years ago, he'd known what he wanted. But what he'd wanted three years ago was vague, twisting away like smoke if he tried to close his hands around it. He'd just known, back then, that he wanted a different life than the one, up until that moment, he'd led. He wanted a different reason to wake up every morning and open his eyes. A reason.

Now the longing he felt was sharper, more specific. Shake could almost smell what he wanted. Peach-scented shampoo and tire rubber. The memory made him smile.

"It's a girl, isn't it?" Quinn said.

Shake glanced over, surprised. Quinn wasn't even looking at him.

"Let me ask you a question," Quinn said.

"I don't have any answers. Believe me."

Quinn chuckled. He had freshened up before dinner, taking a shower and putting on a clean polo shirt. This one was plum-colored. He had the collar of the polo shirt turned up, his white hair combed back in perfect waves.

"You ever see that one western?" Shake said. "The cattleman's son goes off and joins up with a different cattleman. The first cattleman hires a bunch of outlaws to help get his son back. Randolph Scott's in it, but there's this good-looking kid too, big head of hair. He gets shot early. A deputy, maybe."

"*Ten Wanted Men,*" Quinn said. "Richard Boone was the rival cattleman."

"Was that you?"

"What?"

"The kid who got shot. The deputy."

Quinn shifted to look at Shake like he was nuts, and then turned back to the sunset. He rattled the ice in his glass of iced tea. "So tell me about her," he said. "This girl you're mooning over."

"No," Shake said.

"Tell me why she dumped you. A guy can cook like you? A guy lives on the beach? You're emotionally guarded, maybe. My suspicion is you are. But women like that, I don't care what they say. They don't want some guy wears his heart on his sleeve. They don't want some guy starts weeping afterward and wants to cuddle."

"Good to know."

"Give me something, Shake. I didn't bring a book to read."

"No."

"All right, I understand. Let me tell you about this girl I knew in Istanbul. Long story, but we got time."

His eyes twinkled. Shake sighed.

"She was younger than me," Shake said. "Beautiful and smart and ambitious. Restless."

"Restless. Uh-oh."

"Restless. Me, on the other hand, I just wanted to own a little restaurant somewhere. Cook all day. I wanted to live somewhere nice and quiet and sunny. How long do you think it's gonna last, those two people in a relationship together?"

"You woke up one morning and she was gone."

"Something like that."

Shake had been an idiot. He'd known from the first minute he met Gina—well, maybe not the first minute, but pretty quickly afterward— that she was a woman who would never settle down, never stop moving. She was like the flow of electricity, like the universe expanding outward. Gina had told him, straight up, on more than one occasion, that she couldn't be trusted. She'd told him the truth, and for a long time Shake had refused to believe it.

Quinn nodded. Shake waited for the words of wisdom. "Well?" he finally asked.

The widow stepped out onto the porch. She said something in German or Dutch to Quinn and then went back inside. "She says she put fresh towels in the bathroom," Quinn told Shake. "If you want to take a shower."

"All right." Shake stood up. "You can have the bedroom, I'll take the couch."

"Take the bedroom. I might sleep out here in the hammock."

"Out here?"

"The breeze. Sure."

Shake realized that Quinn had a poker tell: he crossed his legs and then crossed them back the opposite way. Shake laughed. "Are you serious?"

"She's a nice lady. She's unattached. We're both adults. I don't see the problem."

"No problem at all," Shake said, and headed inside.

Chapter 20

The next morning Shake woke up with the barrel of a shotgun in his face.

"Get the hell up," Benny said. Shake got up. Quinn was standing across the room in a T-shirt and boxer shorts. Shake saw the widow peeking in at them from the hallway, a robe clutched tight at her throat.

"Benny," Quinn said. "You don't need to get your knickers in a twist."

Benny swung the shotgun around and pointed it at Quinn. "Shut the hell up. You've got exactly one minute to get out of here and never come back. Sixty seconds plus one more and then I start shooting."

The widow disappeared. Shake didn't want to guess what Quinn had done now. It was the widow, probably. She was most likely not a widow. She was most likely married to Benny. That was Shake's best guess.

"Come on, now, Benny," Quinn said. "Nobody needs to start shooting. Put the pump down and let's have an open dialogue about the situation."

"An open dialogue? Like the open dialogue where you forgot to tell me somebody wants the two of you shitbirds dead?"

So this wasn't about the widow after all. Shake didn't feel much relief.

"Like the open dialogue where you forgot to tell me what kind of number they put on you?"

Benny must have asked around last night in Belize City. He'd done his due diligence and found out that Baby Jesus was after them.

"That's right," Benny said. "The kite went up yesterday. My monkey guy in Belize City told me. He told me the kite went out far and wide."

Shit, Shake thought. Baby Jesus had wasted no time.

"How much is it?" Quinn asked, curious. "The number on us?"

"Thirty seconds left now. That's the number you better worry about. Before I start shooting."

"Put the pump down, Benny. Almighty Christ. What if it goes off by accident? You don't want to do something you'll regret."

"Who says I'll regret it?"

"Benny. Benjamin."

"Like the open dialogue where you forgot to tell me who it is in fact wants the two of you shitbirds dead? Hell. Hell. You're trying to get me killed too, aren't you?"

"It's me Baby Jesus wants," Shake said.

Benny kept the shotgun on Quinn but looked over at Shake. "You some kind of religious nut?"

"What?"

"Jesus can have you. And the apostles too. Sooner than later, if you don't start running and never look back."

Something wasn't connecting. "Who are we talking about here?" Shake said.

"Who are we talking about here?" Benny's laugh was like a bark. "Just about the last person you'd ever want to put a number on you, that's who."

Shake looked at Quinn. "I told you," Quinn said. "Sticky Jimmy. Kid I took under my wing, back in Cambodia. Got rich with natural gas, now he's moving up the ladder."

Benny laughed again. Bark, bark, bark. His long gray beard rose and fell.

Shake felt himself tightening up. "What ladder would that be?" he said.

Quinn frowned, like he expected better from Shake. "What else? A guy's got money, he looks good on TV, he knows how to bullshit."

"Politics."

"Fifteen seconds!" Benny said.

"He's gonna make a run," Quinn said. "He's *exploring* a run. Governor, I think. Maybe the Senate, I'm not sure. Anyway, he can't risk it, me coming out of the woodwork in the middle of an election, the old buddy who knew him when."

Natural gas, political aspirations. Shake had been on heavy-duty painkillers. He should have put it together before now. Mindful of Benny's shotgun, he tried to keep his voice calm, quiet. "Logan James," he said. "You're saying Sticky Jimmy is Logan James. Blackbird Energy?"

"Ten seconds!"

"That's right," Quinn said with a shrug. Like what does it matter, Sticky Jimmy's real name, or the name of the natural-gas company he owns?

"Logan James the billionaire," Shake said. "Logan James they say could be president someday."

"He'll always be Sticky Jimmy to me," Quinn said. "Benny, I ever tell you how he got that name?"

"Five seconds!"

Logan James.

Shake felt like he was back on the snorkel boat, speeding across the bay, except now the ride wasn't so smooth. The hull was smacking and shaking and splitting open. Shake was dropping down through the depths like a rock.

Over the years Shake had ended up crosswise with some very formidable people, some big swinging dicks. Baby Jesus was just the latest on the list, and not even at the top of it. But Logan James. The billionaire natural-gas magnate who might, someday, be president. This was a different order of crosswise, a completely different magnitude of swinging dick.

"Time's up!" Benny said. "Now get the hell out of here and don't come back!"

"You have to help us, Benny," Quinn said.

"And have Logan James put a number on me too? I don't want any part of this."

"Draw us a map, at least. Let us borrow the four-by-four."

Benny pumped a shell into the chamber. "You think I won't shoot you? Just try me."

Quinn took a step toward Benny. Shake moved in front to cut him off. He didn't know what Quinn was planning and didn't want to find out, not with a twelve-gauge pointed at him.

"Benny," Shake said. "Work it through. You're already a part of this."

"Like hell I am!"

"You think a guy like Logan James does anything halfway?"

"That's why I'm running you off!"

"You think if you run us off, and a guy like Logan James catches up to us in Belize, he won't find his way back to you?"

Logan James. Jesus Christ. Shake still couldn't believe that he'd ended up crosswise with a guy like Logan James.

"I ran you off! I didn't have any part of this!"

"Tell him that. Logan James. Or whoever Logan James sends to take care of business. I'm sure that person will be a good listener."

"Shut the hell up!" Benny said. But Shake could see his mind working. The hand on the stock of the shotgun twitched. Shake needed to get Benny's hand off the stock of the shotgun.

"Benny," Shake said, "your best chance, you have to help get us out of the country, fast and quiet."

"Maybe I'll just give Mr. Logan James's people a call," Benny said. "You thought of that? Collect the number on you myself."

Shake thought of the old Kriol man who'd dimed them to Baby Jesus. Was there anyone of Quinn's acquaintance who wasn't ready to sell him out at a moment's notice? Lucky for them, Benny seemed more motivated by fear than greed.

"How much is it?" Quinn asked again. "The number? You never said."

"It's plenty," Benny said. "Don't you worry about that."

"Go ahead and make the call," Shake told Benny. "You know you won't see a dollar of that money. You know you won't see the sun come up tomorrow. A guy like Logan James doesn't do anything halfway. He doesn't leave crumbs on the table."

Benny looked sick to his stomach. "You don't know that for sure."

Shake shrugged. "What was it you said about the tapir and the jaguar? Pick-'em?"

Benny couldn't stand it anymore. He took his hand off the stock of the shotgun and combed his fingers through his big gray beard. To keep the shotgun steady he had to move his index finger on the other hand from the trigger to the trigger guard.

One quick step, a hard twist, and Shake had the shotgun. "You made the right decision, Benny," he said.

"Asshole," Quinn said. "Friends like you, Benny, who needs enemies?"

Chapter 21

After Benny drew them a map and gave them the keys to his 4x4, Quinn handed over two grand in cash.

"You said four!" Benny said.

"That was before you pointed a shotgun at us," Quinn said.

Benny scowled but took the money. "I bet my ass you never even had the four grand in the first place," he said. Shake was thinking the same thing.

Shake told Benny they'd leave his 4x4 in Chetumal, over the border in Mexico, keys on top of the back tire. Benny could take the bus up and retrieve the truck at his convenience.

Quinn told Benny he owed him one now, a big one, the Bushido code, Benny could cash in the favor next time he saw Quinn. Benny said next time he saw Quinn he planned to shoot first and ask about favors later. Quinn chuckled. He took a comb out of his back pocket and pulled it through the waves of his white hair. He gave the widow on the porch a wink and a tip of the comb.

"Now get the hell out of here!" Benny said. He was frantically combing his beard with all ten fingers by now.

Shake headed for the driver's side. Quinn wanted to have a discussion about that, but Shake just slid in behind the wheel and started to pull away. Quinn had to walk fast to catch the passenger door and climb in.

The map Benny drew was detailed and precise—he wanted that Land Cruiser back. A few miles from Three Butterflies they turned onto a dirt road. A few miles later Shake spotted a muddy track veering off into the jungle that he would never have noticed if he hadn't been looking for it.

They drove deep into the jungle, bouncing and rattling down one muddy track after another. Some stretches were just mud, no track. The Land Cruiser handled it all with no problem, which was a good thing—one fishtailing skid and they could have ended up sunk deep in the swamp. Maybe years from now someone would have found them, a rusting Land Cruiser and a pair of bleached skulls.

One of the skulls would still be talking, probably, about the year he spent in Latvia, back in the eighties, on business. Well, call it business. Quinn didn't need to spell it out for Shake, did he? According to Quinn, his buddy in Latvia worked for the Latvian version of the KGB. On the weekends, he and Quinn would take whatever skirts they'd managed to chase down out to an old abandoned Soviet prison camp, where the four or five or six of them would drink vodka and throw old Soviet hand grenades into the snowy woods.

And so on, on and on for hours, all the way through the jungle. Shake didn't say anything until finally he couldn't take it anymore. "Logan James," he said. "Jesus Christ. Why didn't you tell me it was him?"

"I told you!"

"I know why you didn't tell me." Shake had no idea what he was going to do next, with just sixty-five bucks to his name and Logan James trying to kill him.

"Speaking of all that," Quinn said. "I've got an idea."

"No thanks," Shake said. At least he knew what he *wasn't* going to do. Or, more specifically, who he wasn't going to do it with. He was absolutely clear on that.

"You're thinking you're better off without me," Quinn said. "Your chances of survival. You're thinking it's me Sticky Jimmy wants, maybe he'll forget all about you."

"Tell me more about Latvia. I can't get enough of that."

"I see your point, I'm not an idiot. But hear me out. I got you off the island, didn't I? I'm getting you out of Belize. I won't even mention I paid for your accommodations last night, your dinner."

"You want me to feel guilty, you'll need to do better than that."

"I don't want you to feel guilty."

"No?"

"What I want," Quinn said, "I want you to open your mind to a once-in-a-lifetime opportunity."

There it was. Shake didn't blame Quinn for trying. With an enemy like Logan James, Quinn needed all the friends he could get. Shake just wasn't going to be one of them.

"You think people really keep them as pets?" Shake said. "Tapirs?"

"You're trying to change the subject."

"Yes."

"I've got this angle I've been working, the last few weeks."

"I thought your angle was fertility tourism."

"Do you only put one piece of fish on the grill at a time? I didn't think so. This is a different angle. One better suited to our current circumstances."

"Let me guess. You've got a buddy somewhere."

"I didn't want to say anything till now, it's a lot of money at stake. But you've had my back, Shake. I've developed a certain degree of affection for you."

Shake knew Quinn was full of shit. It was just hard to tell how full, when Quinn himself didn't seem to know.

"I do have a buddy," Quinn said. "Yes. A guy I used to do business with in Egypt, way back when."

"Anywhere you didn't use to do business? Way back when?"

"Is that a serious question?"

"No."

Quinn considered anyway. "Argentina. Chile. I never made it down there. I never spent any time in South Africa either. That's all I can think of, top of my head."

Shake checked Benny's map. It was almost dusk. They were across the border and deep into Mexico now. In another mile or so they should emerge from the jungle and hit an actual road that would take them the back way into Chetumal, another twenty miles east.

And then he would say good-bye to Quinn. Don't keep in touch.

"My guy in Egypt, I knew him at the consulate, he runs his own private security firm in Cairo now. It's a big-deal operation—celebrities, heads of state, Saudi oil sheikhs flying in to get drunk and gamble. Anyway. A few weeks ago, out of the blue, first time in years, I get an e-mail from him. My guy in Egypt. I e-mail him back, we get on the phone, we shoot the shit. And then he tells me why he got in touch."

"Pass," Shake said.

"You haven't heard yet why he got in touch."

"I've heard enough."

Quinn swiveled around in his seat and studied Shake. "Look me in the eye," he said. "Tell me you believe in your heart that Sticky Jimmy will forget about you. What was that convincing argument you made back in Belize, Shake? About the kind of people who never do anything halfway?"

Shake turned his head to look Quinn in the eye. "I believe in my heart, whether he forgets about me or not, I'm better off without you."

He turned back to the road ahead, which was, finally, road. Two lanes, paved. Right where Benny's map said it would be. Shake swung the Land Cruiser east.

Quinn sat there silently, sagging in his seat, looking like he was a hundred years old, like Shake had just punched him in the gut. When he saw that wasn't working, Quinn straightened back up and rapped his knuckles on the dash. "Two million bucks," he said. "Are you better off without that in your pocket? That's the question. You want to stay a step ahead of Sticky Jimmy, you're gonna need resources. Look me in the eye and tell me I'm wrong about *that*."

Quinn wasn't wrong about that. But it didn't change Shake's position on the matter.

The sun was down. The light died fast. Shake flipped on the headlights.

"Pass," he said.

"The two million is just your cut of the action. I want to make that clear. My buddy in Egypt, he's got a client at the moment, his private security firm does. Some rich expat asshole, British, American, I don't remember. Anyway, he makes his money the old-fashioned way, buying and selling what other people steal. You've heard of conflict diamonds? Well, this rich expat asshole buys and sells conflict antiquities."

Shake couldn't stop himself in time. "Conflict antiquities?"

"That's right. A country has a revolution, riots, whatever. Like Egypt did a while back. Syria, Greece, wherever. Well, all that confusion, guess what falls off the truck? Gets lost in the shuffle? A nice ancient marble bust over here, a nice ancient gold bracelet over there. Nobody notices. Why would they notice? There's a riot going on. A revolution! There's a little museum in Crete, for example, my buddy in Egypt told me this, had one of the finest collections of early Minoan artifacts in the world. For example. During all that trouble Greece had, the austerity shutdowns—well. You know who has one of the finest collections of early Minoan artifacts in the world now? Some guy in China. Bought it from the rich expat in Cairo we're discussing. Who bought it from whoever bumped it off the truck in the first place."

"So what then?" Shake said. "Your buddy in Egypt wants to take down the rich expat?"

"That's right. He just put a new item on the market. I don't know what exactly yet, but it's worth six, maybe seven million. A conservative estimate. We take it, we sell it, we split the profit three ways."

"Why doesn't your buddy just steal it himself?"

"It takes a village, this kind of job. My buddy can work the inside, but he needs someone who can get the wheels turning. I told you, I knew him when he was at the consulate. He knows I know my way around the wheels."

Shake shook his head. "What's the catch?" he said.

"What catch?"

"What's the catch?"

"Well. The rich expat is connected."

"Of course he is."

"Two million apiece? Sure, it's gonna be a little tricky."

"And dangerous."

"I won't lie to you."

"All that and Egypt too," Shake said. "What's not to like?"

Quinn frowned. "Simple and safe. Is that what you want? How much fun would that be?"

"Fun?" Shake started to laugh, but then stopped.

Quinn caught it, studied him. "What?"

"Nothing."

"You look like one of those characters in the funny pages," Quinn said. "The lightbulb goes off over his head."

Shake realized that he'd drifted over into the oncoming lane. An old truck barreled toward them, headlights jiggling, and Shake jerked the Land Cruiser back into his own lane. How had that happened? When was the last time he'd been so distracted that he'd drifted over into the oncoming lane? Never.

"I'm gonna pass," Shake said. "End of story."

"Just sleep on it," Quinn said. "Promise me that, that's all I'm saying. Snuggle up with her and see what she looks like in the light of day."

Chapter 22

They found a hotel in Chetumal. A nice enough one, more like a bed-and-breakfast, down by what passed for a beach. The owner of the place, a leathery blond woman from New York, checked them in and gave them keys to their rooms. She said she'd bought the place a year ago, betting that the tourist boom would eventually stretch south from the Riviera Maya.

"Tulum used to be just a little fishing village before the tourists discovered it," she said. "And look at it now! A lot of people say Chetumal will be the next Tulum."

Shake thought it was probably just the guy who sold her the place who said that, but he didn't want to rain on her parade.

"Don't you think?" she asked, her eyes pleading.

"You bet," Shake said.

He'd been planning to sleep on the beach, but Quinn insisted on paying for Shake's room, no strings attached.

No strings attached.

But Shake didn't argue. It was late, he'd been driving through the jungle all day, he was tired. Too tired to sleep on a beach, too tired to argue with Quinn. And besides—Shake planned to be long gone first thing in the morning, on a bus to Mexico City before Quinn even woke up. Before Quinn started pulling strings.

So why couldn't Shake get to sleep, if he was so tired? His room was quiet and cool, the sheets were soft. But he tossed. He turned. He kicked off the top soft sheet and then pulled it back on.

Even as hard up as he was at the moment—no cash and no prospects, stuck in Mexico and gazing back with fond nostalgia on a time when it was just Baby Jesus who wanted him dead, not Logan James—Shake wanted nothing to do with Quinn or his Egypt scheme.

The six or seven million had to be a wild exaggeration. Probably, Quinn's buddy in Egypt was as trustworthy as his buddy back in Belize had been. Probably, the rich expat selling the black-market antiquity had his own private army to protect it.

Shake had no desire to visit Egypt. He pictured deserts. Women in black, their faces covered. And he couldn't imagine that the food was very interesting. A lot of hummus, probably. Kebabs.

"Simple and safe," Quinn had said. "Is that what you want? How much fun would that be?"

Fun. Shake's previous career had involved a fair amount of risk. But a good professional wheelman tried to minimize that risk—a good day on the job was a boring day on the job. It had always escaped Shake, how anyone in his right mind could put together *tricky* and *dangerous* and come out with *fun*.

How anyone in *her* right mind.

He tossed and turned some more and then got out of bed. He took the coin out of his wallet, a Panamanian balboa he'd picked up a few years back and carried with him ever since. He flipped it, called it. The coin came up tails. Two out of three, he told himself, but then said, "Fuck it." He knew he was going to make the call, no matter how the coin landed.

Shake went down to the front desk. The leathery blond owner had gone to bed, but an old Mexican lady sweeping the floor nodded when Shake asked if he could use the phone on the desk. Shake checked the clock on the wall. It was midnight in Vegas.

Jasper answered on the first ring. Shake could hear the throb of music in the background. "Who that?" Jasper said. "What you want?"

"A nice quiet life," Shake said. "No surprises and lots of fresh fish."

The was a moment of silence, just the music throbbing. Shake could almost recognize the song in the background, but not quite.

"Shake?" Jasper said. "Shit."

"Where y'at, Jasper?" Shake said, letting his hometown accent breathe a little.

He and Jasper had both grown up in New Orleans, only a few neighborhoods apart. But they hadn't actually met until many years later, in Vegas, when Shake clubbed Jasper in the head with a phone book and Jasper tried to shoot him. They'd managed to work out their differences, eventually, and were now on better terms.

"I'm all right," Jasper said. "What you want, Shake?" Jasper, not a man to waste words.

"So how you like it?" Shake said. "Running your own place?" Jasper owned a strip club on the north end of the Vegas Strip, the same club where he'd been second in command for years.

"Shit." Jasper sighed.

"Running your own place can be a headache."

"Brand-new one every day."

"I know it. How's the Lucy thing going?"

Jasper made a sound that could have been a growl, a sigh, or a chuckle. Or maybe all three. "What you want, Shake?"

Shake didn't want to ask the question he'd called to ask. Jasper figured it out fast.

"Shit," Jasper said. "Gina."

"You know where she is these days?"

"Why you wanna know that?"

"Still in Vegas?"

"She out in San Fran," Jasper said. "Last I talk to her."

"San Francisco? What's she up to out there?"

"No good, be my guess."

"The girl knows trouble."

"Yeah, you right."

"You have an address for her?"

Jasper didn't answer.

"C'mon, Jasper. Do a homeboy a solid."

"You best move on, homeboy."

"I just want to see her again."

"Move on, Shake. I know you ain't asked my opinion."

"I just want to take another shot. You of all people, Jasper, you should know. Everybody deserves another shot."

"Ain't mean they get it." But then Shake heard Jasper sigh again and set down his phone. After a second he came back on and read Shake an address in San Francisco.

"I appreciate it, Jasper," Shake said.

"Better wait and see 'bout that."

THE NEXT MORNING SHAKE FOUND Quinn in the breakfast room. Quinn was showing the owner how to properly work a French press. He had his hand on her hand to gently guide it. "Nice and easy," he said. "Like most things in life, right?" She blushed when she saw Shake watching and quickly excused herself.

Shake sat down. "Nice and easy. That's your secret?"

"I don't need a secret. That's my secret."

"I'll try to remember that."

Quinn crossed his legs and sipped his coffee. If he was surprised that Shake hadn't already hopped the first bus to Mexico City, he didn't show it. Shake was annoyed either way, Quinn not surprised or not showing it.

"I've got one condition," Shake said. "Nonnegotiable."

"Let's hear it."

"Your plan is we chop the pot three ways. You, me, your buddy in Egypt."

"That's the plan."

"The new plan, we chop it four ways, not three."

That caught Quinn off guard. "You want to bring in another party, you mean?"

"Equal shares," Shake said. "Whatever we come away with."

Quinn drummed his fingers on the table. Part of Shake, most of him, hoped Quinn would balk at a four-way split. If he balked, even for a second, Shake would have the opening he needed to get up and walk away and hop the next bus to Mexico City. He'd have the opening he needed to take Jasper's advice and move on with his life.

But Quinn didn't balk. Instead he lifted his coffee cup to make a toast. "The more the merrier," he said.

Chapter 23

Meg watched Jorge use his hip to push open the door of his apartment. He had a big paper bag in one hand and a bottle of orange Fanta in the other one. He was taking a drink of the orange Fanta. When he saw Meg sitting there in the chair by the window, he stopped still. He kept the bottle pressed up against his lips while he tried to think what he was going to say.

Meg let him think. She wasn't in any rush. Finally Jorge slid the bottle out of the way so he could give her a big smile. "Hey, *chica*," he said, "I been hoping you come by."

Meg shot him in the shinbone. "Hey," she said.

Jorge squealed and spit and fell to the floor. The bottle of orange Fanta rolled over into the corner. The paper bag had split open and now the apartment started to smell goaty and sweet, from the tacos Jorge always ate.

"*Chica,*" Jorge said, his teeth locked together hard. "Wait. Just wait. Wait. I can explain."

"Explain what?" Meg shot his other shinbone, almost missing because she had to hold the gun in her left hand and she wasn't used to that yet.

Jorge was praying to the Virgin Mary in Spanish, but it sounded more like he was cussing her out instead. Meg limped over to shut the door behind him. She didn't see anybody with their head stuck out into the hallway, wondering should they call the police. That was a handy thing about Guatemala, Meg had found out. People here already had enough trouble all their own, they didn't need to borrow any more.

"How the fuck you still alive?" Jorge said. Crying now. "Fucking *puta.*"

She showed him her right hand, purple and swollen up like an eggplant. "That's how."

Jorge looked confused. "I don't understand."

"I don't expect you do." Her hand was purple and swollen from yanking it out of the handcuff. Her ankle was swollen up too, though not as bad. She'd twisted it when she jumped down out of the office window in Belize City.

"Wait," Jorge said. "Just wait."

"I ain't going nowhere." Meg limped back over to her chair and sat down.

She'd known something was wrong the very second the man handcuffed her to the file cabinet. What kind of government official drove you to a deserted building in the middle of the night and handcuffed you to a file cabinet?

She should have figured it out sooner, on the ride over. Goddamn it. But Meg had been too occupied with all the evil she planned to do, and not occupied enough with the evil might be done to her and Terry.

When the man said he was taking Terry to the back room, the dread had welled up in Meg so suddenly she could barely breathe. "Terry," she'd said.

The man took Terry to the back room. Meg put both feet against the file cabinet to brace herself. She didn't care if she ripped off her whole arm, just so long as she got herself loose in time to save Terry.

She got herself loose finally, but before she could run to the back and save Terry, a strange feeling came over her and she knew it was too late. The strange feeling was like a whisper, a nudge, like a dog panting in her face. Like Meg was right there next to Terry, dying along with him.

Meg had crept down the hallway. From the doorway she saw Terry. She saw the man, his back to her, crouched down and wiping his knife on the carpet.

Terry was the love of Meg's life. Her life would now be without love, for however long it went on.

Meg had wanted to scream and cry, to run at the man and dig his eyeballs out of his head with her bare hands. He had the knife, though, and likely a gun too, and Meg knew he'd kill her before she could even get started on him.

She couldn't bear the thought of leaving Terry behind on that bloody carpet. But if she didn't run now, if she let the man who killed Terry kill her too, then he'd walk out of this office building without a care in the world. Meg couldn't bear the thought of that either.

So she crept back up the hallway and dropped down out of the window. As she ran through the night on her twisted ankle, she promised Terry she'd make the man pay for what he'd done, no matter how long it took her, no matter what it cost.

"He died for me. 'Cause he wanted to protect me."

"What?" Jorge said.

Meg shot him this time in the elbow. He cried and cussed the Virgin Mary some more. "Who was it came to kill us?" she said.

"I don't know him. I swear."

"Tell me how I can find him."

"I don't know. You think I know?"

"Tell me."

"Please. Meg. *Chica*."

"Second ago it was *puta*."

"I never talk to him, Meg. My boss talk to him, not me."

Meg figured that was probably right, unfortunately. "Okay," she said. "Tell me how I can find your boss."

"Find my boss?"

"Did I shoot you in the ear?"

"Be serious, Meg. My boss, he is a heavy man, Meg. Is that how you say? *Es un hombre muy poderoso.*"

"If he's so powerful, why don't your boss do his killing himself?"

"He will, Meg. If you go look for him, he will kill *you.* I say this as your friend."

Maybe I want him to kill me, Meg caught herself thinking, just for second. But she didn't tell Jorge that. Instead she pointed her gun at his good elbow.

"Okay," he said. "Okay, Meg. No problem. I tell you."

She stood up, limped over to the kitchen table, and found a pen. She limped back and tore a piece of brown paper from the bag of tacos that Jorge had dropped on the floor. She handed him the pen and the piece of brown paper.

"Write it down. Where your boss is."

"No problem, Meg. Okay?" Jorge wrote fast, his hand shaking. When he finished, Meg made sure she could read his handwriting and then she shot him in the head.

Chapter 24

The seatbelt sign dinged a little after noon and they began their approach to SFO. The plane slid from the bright blue sky at thirty thousand feet down into a layer of dark heavy clouds. When they finally broke through those clouds, the next layer down was even darker, even heavier. They taxied to the gate through sheet after sheet of billowing rain.

"'The coldest winter I ever spent was summer in San Francisco,'" Quinn said, leaning over so he could peer out the window. "Mark Twain wrote that."

Shake didn't say anything. He tried not to read too much into the weather.

During the flight, somewhere over West Texas, Quinn had asked Shake about their new partner. Shake told him her name was Gina.

Quinn had turned in his seat to study him. Shake's own nervous tell, he realized too late, was holding eye contact a little too long.

"This Gina," Quinn said. "She wouldn't happen to be the same girl you were telling me about? The girl broke your heart a couple of years ago?"

"That doesn't matter," Shake said.

"It doesn't matter."

But Quinn left it alone for the rest of the flight. He read the airline magazine cover to cover and finished the crossword, driving Shake crazy.

In the cab from the airport, Shake finally had enough. "Let's hear it," he said.

"Hear what?" Quinn said. Innocent.

"Let's get it over with."

"It's just my experience," Quinn said carefully, "but you need a clear head. The kind of angle we're working here."

"My head is clear."

"I never said it wasn't."

"I know what I'm doing."

"I've made the mistake myself, I'll be the first to admit it. Letting emotions cloud my judgment at a critical juncture in time. Putting myself in a position where I might potentially run that risk."

"It's a deal breaker," Shake said. "Either she's in or I'm out."

Quinn held up his palms. "She's always been in. Did I ever suggest otherwise?"

The cab sluiced through the drowned streets of the Outer Mission. Shake hadn't been to San Francisco in ten, fifteen years, but he remembered these hills. He remembered trying to drive a stick on these hills, in the rain. It wasn't much fun, not when you were trying to clear out after a bank job without attracting attention.

He didn't know what he was going to say to Gina when he saw her. He wondered if he'd be able to say anything at all.

"I'm fine working with amateurs," Quinn said. "Some people aren't, but I'm fine with it."

"She's no amateur," Shake said.

"Like I said."

"First time we met, she'd just knocked off the meanest bastard in Vegas for three hundred grand. She made me think she was a Mormon housewife, drugged me, robbed me, and left me locked to a pipe in a hotel bathroom. And I still ended up falling for her."

Quinn brightened. "I like her already."

"So, no, she's no amateur."

The cabdriver turned onto a block lined with old commercial buildings—auto-parts wholesalers and offset print shops—that had been converted to office space. He pulled to the curb in front of the last building before the street hit a dead end. Shake could just make out the faded paint on the grimy brick: O'CONNOR INDUSTRIAL CLEANING.

Quinn started to unbuckle his seat belt. Shake stopped him.

"What? I don't get to meet her?"

"Not now."

"Shake. Chef."

"No." Shake tapped the cabdriver on the shoulder. "What's the closest hotel?"

"I'll let you take the lead," Quinn said. "I'll be the soul of discretion."

"There's a Hilton on Guerrero," the cabdriver said.

"Go there," Shake told Quinn. "I'll meet you in a couple of hours."

Quinn frowned, but clipped his seat belt back on. Shake got out of the cab and ducked under the overhang. He waited until the cab turned around and went sluicing off in the rain.

There was a small brass plaque bolted to the side of the building. It read: TWO BIRDS INVESTMENT GROUP.

The door was tinted glass. Shake checked out his reflection. He looked okay. He'd showered and shaved before they left Chetumal. At the airport in Cancún he'd bought a new shirt, a nice pair of jeans, shoes.

His plan, in its early stages back in Mexico, had been to use Quinn's scheme as an excuse to see Gina again. To entice her with it. Most women were happy if you brought them flowers or chocolate. Gina, of course, wasn't most women. Shake thought he'd show up with something more her style, something tricky and dangerous and fun.

Now that he was actually here, though, he was having second thoughts. Third and fourth thoughts. He'd assured Quinn he knew what he was doing, but really, when it came to Gina, Shake had no fucking idea. He never had.

Shake took a breath, pulled the door open, stepped inside. A receptionist was sitting at a desk. Behind her was a big open space, the entire interior of the building, with skylights, wrought-iron columns, nice wood floors. A dozen people, maybe more, at high-tech workstations.

"Hi," the receptionist said. "Can I help you?"

Shake didn't know what he'd been expecting. Not this.

"Gina Clement?" he said.

The receptionist was young and pretty and wore stylish glasses that she probably didn't need.

"Do you have an appointment?" she asked.

Shake was surprised again. He shook his head.

The receptionist pursed her lips in a sympathetic way. "May I ask what this is about?"

"Just say it's a friend here to see her."

She waited for Shake to say his name. He didn't. The receptionist pursed her lips in a less sympathetic way and murmured something into her headset. She waited, murmured again.

"It'll be a few minutes," she said, and motioned Shake over to a leather sofa.

Shake sat down. At the far end of the office a group of people in suits were gathered around a giant plasma screen, somber and nodding.

May I ask what this is about?

Shake had the same question. Was Gina working an angle? The place looked legit, and definitely overkill for your typical long con. The only thing he could think was that maybe she was putting together the pieces for an inside score.

A young guy with spiky hair came over. "Hey, bro," he said.

Shake looked at him. "Hey," he said. "Bro."

"I'm Brady, Gina's assistant. Sorry, bro, she's totally jammed up today, back to back to back. But let's get something on the books?"

The meeting around the plasma screen started to break up. Two of the guys moved away and Shake saw Gina standing at the front of the group. Listening to two other guys and making them nod with whatever she said back.

It had been more than two years since Shake had seen her. Her hair was a darker blond now, and cut shorter, with bangs. She wore a tailored navy business suit and a white blouse open at the throat. Her shoes had heels, but they were barely an inch high.

The way she held herself seemed different too. Straighter, tenser, less cock to her hip.

For all that, though, she was still Gina. The strong-minded nose, dusted with freckles. The smile that managed somehow to be both wholesome and sly.

And she was still a knockout. Maybe even more so than Shake remembered, though he didn't know how that could be possible.

She glanced over and saw him. Shake thought her expression might have flickered with surprise, but she had it back together before he could tell for sure.

As Gina walked over, Shake finally placed the song that had been playing in the background when he called Jasper in Vegas. The song had been "These Boots Are Made for Walking," but the girl singing it had been singing in French.

"Shake," Gina said when she got there. "What a surprise."

Her smile was easy, pleasant. She held out her hand and Shake took it. What was he supposed to do with her hand? He held it for a second and then let go.

"Brady," she said. "Can you push back my lunch?"

"But, Gina," he said.

"I know. But I think I can spare ten minutes for an old buddy."

Brady gave a huff and a puff for Shake's benefit, then left.

"So," Gina said. "Wow."

"Not that old a buddy," Shake said. Testing the waters. Seeing if she'd make her usual crack about their age difference. She'd never missed an opportunity.

"You know what I mean," she said with a light laugh. "How have you been?"

Shake frowned. The laugh seemed genuine, the eyes matching it, but this was Gina after all. She could do genuine in her sleep.

Her eyes. A deep, clear, underwater green. Shake felt himself sinking.

"I don't mean to step on your action," he said. "Just showing up like this."

"My action?"

"All this is legit?"

"Venture investment," she said. "I couldn't decide the one place I wanted to put my money, so I started a company where I could put it lots of places."

"It was a lot of money." Testing her again. Half the money she was talking about, their score from Panama, had been his.

Again, though, no reaction. She just kept smiling pleasantly.

"Can we go somewhere?" he said. "Talk in private?"

"Why don't we?"

She led him up a set of cast-iron stairs to an enclosed loft area at the back of the building. Her office had a spectacular view, looking out over the bay.

She closed the door behind them and crossed to her desk. He followed her over.

"I missed you," he said.

He didn't know where that had come from. He'd been planning to say something else completely, about how spectacular the view of the bay was.

She turned back to him and smiled. A spark of light on metal caught his eye and he saw she'd picked a letter opener up off the desk.

"Oh," she said. "You're so sweet."

"Wait," Shake said. "Shit."

Chapter 25

Her mistake, Gina realized, was trying to stab him in the face. He was six inches taller than she was, and the extra distance the letter opener had to travel gave him a split second to grab her wrist and twist it away.

"I should have gone for the stomach," she said.

"Gina," he said.

"And then the face next. Don't you think?"

She aimed the heel of her Louboutin pump at his foot. He danced out of the way, but she'd been expecting that, knew he'd have to drop her wrist to do it.

His mistake, this time. She stabbed at his stomach.

He danced away again, just barely. The blade of the letter opener ripped his shirt but didn't break the skin. He grabbed her wrist again, and her other wrist this time too. She tried to head-butt him but he pushed her back against the desk and twisted her this way and that, her arms held high. Finally she dropped the letter opener.

"You fucker!" she said. She was so furious it amazed her. Her ears rang and her skin prickled. She thought she'd been furious for the past two years, but that was nothing compared to this. When she'd glanced over and seen him, sitting there on the sofa in reception, it was like someone had stabbed *her* in the stomach. Like they'd cut her open and emptied her out.

"You fucker. You just show up out of the blue?"

"Jasper thought it wasn't the best idea either."

"Let me go. I'm calm now."

He tightened his grip on her wrists. That grip, still so familiar. Oh, God, she was furious. He was turned to make sure she couldn't knee him in the crotch. She tried anyway.

"I'm sorry," he said. "I was sorry the minute it happened."

"It?"

"Gina."

"Like you were in the audience? Just an observer?"

"Gina."

"You left me a fucking note!"

Until that note, two years ago, Gina had never in her life been dumped. The possibility, to be honest, had never occurred to her. She didn't mean to be snotty, but—why would it ever occur to her? The closest she ever came to getting dumped was when a man proposed marriage on the second date, not the first.

That Shake might dump her, Shake of all guys, with a note, and then just disappear—it still seemed so stupidly inconceivable she wanted to laugh.

"Let me explain," he said.

"You don't have the right to explain."

"It was the biggest mistake I've ever made."

"The note? Or dumping me? I just want to be clear."

"Both. All of it."

They had been living together in Santa Monica. A cute little Craftsman bungalow just north of Montana Avenue, seven blocks from the beach. Every evening at sunset they strolled down to the Palisades to watch the sun set.

And then one morning she woke up and went to make coffee. Wondering, in only the most fleeting of ways, where Shake was. Thinking that maybe he'd driven out to Pasadena for a farmers' market. He did that a lot, coming home with fresh strawberries or designer garlic, grabbing her from behind and kissing her neck.

Instead she found the note on the kitchen table. The note said he was sorry, he had to go, he loved her. Terse, like one of the bad Bruce Springsteen songs he liked. Like he was checking items off a fucking list. He'd given her the number and password for the account in the Bahamas where he kept his half of the Panama score, three million bucks. She was sure he considered that the most gentlemanly of gestures.

"Did it make you feel all warm and fuzzy and noble?" she said. "Giving me the money that was really mine to start with?"

"I was scared you might leave me," he said.

She stared at him. *"What?"*

"Sooner or later. I thought it was just a matter of time."

She kept staring. "You thought I might leave you. That's why you dumped me?"

"Take it easy."

"Okay," she said, and tried again to head-butt him.

"The other kind of easy."

She tried again to knee him in the crotch.

"Walking away from you was the biggest mistake of my life," he said.

"Let me have that letter opener back and we'll make sure it was."

That made him smile. Which, even furious as she was, almost made her smile too.

"You fucker."

"Consider the mistakes I've made in my life," he said. "You should be impressed."

"You can let me go now."

He let go of her wrists, no hesitation, he knew her that well. The bastard.

She went over and sat down on the sofa next to the big picture window. She smoothed out her skirt. "So," she said brightly. "What's new with you?" Because she refused to give him the satisfaction, if she could help it, of seeing her so furious.

"Stop doing that," he said. He touched his side, where the letter opener had torn his shirt, and winced. Gina was hopeful that maybe she'd punctured something after all.

"Did I get you?"

"No. My ribs have had a long week."

"Stop doing what?" She gave him an even brighter smile.

He walked over to the desk chair, wincing, and eased himself into it. She started to ask if he needed a walker, a fella his age, but stopped herself.

"You don't really want to kill me," he said.

"No. Of course not. I want an expert to do it. You think Jasper might come out of retirement for one last hurrah?"

"I tried calling you, Gina. You know how many times I tried calling you?"

"Why are you here, Shake?" She felt tired, suddenly. Hollow.

She watched him think. She remembered how much she used to love watching him think, always taking his time. She turned her head and looked out the window at the bay.

"I've got a job lined up."

"A job."

"I thought you might be interested."

"In a job. With you."

"Six million, split four ways. In Cairo."

"Cairo?"

"In Egypt."

"I know where Cairo is, dumb-ass."

She gazed out at a freighter moving toward the port in Oakland. The water was almost the same pale gray as the sky, hardly any seam at all between them.

"Why would I want to do a job with you in Cairo? For—a million and a half? Have you looked around this place? My place? Does it look like I need to do a job for a million and a half?"

"It'll be tricky and dangerous," he said. "It'll be fun."

Gina turned back to him. She couldn't believe it.

"Really?" she said. "That's what you thought would work on me?"

"I don't know what I thought."

"You're such an idiot."

"That's been established."

He smiled, crooked. His eyes were warm and wry and clear. She wanted to walk across the office and kiss him. Just to see how it felt, if it would feel the same. But she knew it wouldn't feel the same.

"You had no right coming here."

"I know."

They sat there in silence for a minute. The rain had eased up a little and the office was washed in a pearly gray light.

"I'm not going to Egypt with you," she said. "Or anywhere. You understand that, right, even though you're an idiot?"

He nodded. She hated that about him. She loved it.

Gina smoothed her skirt and stood up. "Okeydokey," she said. "It's been great catching up. See you at the next class reunion?"

He stood up too, slowly. Brady knocked on the door. Perfect timing.

"Coming, Brady," she called.

But then the door opened and she was surprised to see it wasn't Brady. It was an old guy in khakis and a cream-colored polo shirt, tan and tall and handsome, with waves of perfect white hair.

Gina had no idea who the old guy was, but he grinned at her like he'd known her his entire life.

"There she is!" he said.

Chapter 26

The spiky-haired guy, Gina's assistant, darted after Quinn and tried to get in front of him.

Good luck with that, Shake thought.

Shake had concluded that his reunion with Gina couldn't have gone any worse. Now, though, as Quinn wrapped her up in a big hug, he revised that assessment.

Shake realized that he'd really never, in all their time together, seen Gina at a loss for words.

"Bro!" the assistant said to Quinn.

"Quinn," Shake said. "Let's go."

Quinn ignored both of them. He held Gina out at arm's length and looked her over.

"What a peach! I was not properly briefed on the matter."

Gina laughed. "I don't think I've been briefed at all."

"Bro!"

"Quinn. We're done here."

"Harrigan Quinn. Call me Harry." He gave Gina a wink. "Or sweetheart. Or sugar pie, I'll answer to either of those too."

She laughed again. "Gina Clement," she said. "Pleased to make your acquaintance."

"Bro!" the assistant said, his face red. "I'm going to have to ask you to leave."

"It's okay, Brady," Gina said. "I think."

She looked at Shake. Shake shrugged. Quinn had already crossed to the couch and made himself at home.

"Who's a guy gotta sleep with around here to a get an Arnold Palmer, on the rocks?"

"First one's on the house today," Gina said. "I'll let you off the hook just this once."

Quinn chuckled. "I knew I was gonna like you."

Gina nodded to the assistant. He hesitated, then headed for the door. Shake stopped him.

"Don't bother. We're not staying."

"Sure we are," Quinn said. "Mind your manners, Shake."

"Yes, Shake," Gina said. "Mind your manners."

Jesus Christ, Shake thought. He sat back down on the edge of the desk.

"I apologize for interrupting," Quinn said. "I know you two have a lot to talk about. Shake filled me in, the broad strokes. I told him I'd been there myself and I have. If you're human, you've been there. I'm right, aren't I? You go there, you come back, you hope the journey makes you a better person. I think it's made Shake a better person. I feel I can say that, Gina, knowing him now like I do."

"Quinn," Shake said, but Gina cut him off.

"Please, Harry," she said. "I'd love to hear more about Shake's journey."

"When I was young man, younger even than you are now, Gina, I went abroad to pursue a certain career opportunity. Thailand, the land of smiles. And—you ever been there?—land of the most beautiful women on the planet. Present company excluded, of course."

"Why, thank you."

Quinn shot a twinkling glance at Shake, like, *See how it's done?* Shake rubbed his forehead with the heel of his palm.

"Anyway, as I was saying, when a man gets his heart broken, the only thing he—"

"When a man gets his heart broken?" Gina said.

"Yes. When a man gets his heart broken—"

"Quinn," Shake said.

Quinn held up his palms. "Down to business, you're absolutely right. We've got a lot of ground to cover and we'll have plenty of time to chat about life and love. Now, Shake told you about the thing in Cairo?"

Gina was looking coolly across the room at Shake. "He told me his version of it," she said.

"Let me give you the broad strokes. I've got an inside guy in Cairo. He heads up security for a rich expat asshole who sells valuable antiquities on the black market. You can guess the rest, I bet, can't you?"

"She doesn't want in," Shake said.

"Doesn't want in?" Quinn said. Dumbfounded by the mere notion.

"Afraid not," Gina said.

"I don't blame you. Exciting adventures in enchanting foreign locales, a lucrative opportunity. Who needs it?"

"Not me, Harry. Not anymore."

"Did Shake tell you about my buddy in Egypt? The inside guy. His security firm is a big deal, big-deal clients. Celebrities, sheikhs, that crowd. What I'm saying, I'm saying we'll have every possible resource at our disposal. And wait till you take a felucca ride on the Nile at dusk, listen to the call to prayer. You haven't lived yet."

"I'll have to do that someday."

Quinn pinched the crease of his khakis and crossed his legs. "Gina," he said. "Let me ask you a question."

Shake didn't know how much longer he could sit there and look at Gina. Look at her and know he couldn't have her.

He stood up. "She said she doesn't want in."

Quinn hesitated, but then got to his feet. He took Gina's hand and kissed her knuckles.

"You're gonna let it simmer," he said. "This Egypt thing."

"Nope," she said.

"Promise me. One night, just let it simmer. Give it a taste in the morning, see if the flavors have come together. Is that too much to ask? And I'm asking for your sake, not mine. I hate to see anyone rush into a decision, I've seen the consequences."

"Harry, sweetie . . ."

"Promise me."

She smiled. "And then you'll give me my hand back?"

He kissed her knuckles again and dropped her hand, all but a single finger he hung on to. "Good faith," he said. "Now promise."

"Okay," Gina said. "I promise."

Quinn dropped the last finger and headed for the door.

"Take your time," he murmured to Shake on the way past. "Don't blow it."

Don't blow it.

After Quinn left, Gina turned to Shake.

"Zowee! Where did you find him?"

"Long story. He's one long story."

"You told him I broke *your* heart?"

"No. I didn't. I tried not to tell him anything."

"You're lucky I believe you."

"Gina," Shake said. "Two years, two whole years, and there wasn't a minute I ever stopped thinking about you."

She blew her bangs out of her eyes, a long sigh.

"I have a life, Shake. A happy life. I'm sorry if it hurts—and it's not me being mean, cross my heart—but I did, I stopped thinking about you."

She held up her left hand. It took Shake a second to realize she was showing him a ring, a simple gold band on her ring finger, a wedding ring.

Chapter 27

Gina was half an hour late to her lunch. She was the dog with the bone now, so no big wiggie. Gina still wasn't used to that, being the one with the money and everyone else trying to get it. Who would have ever imagined such a topsy-turvy development in her life? Gina loved it.

The waiter brought her poached salmon and a glass of sparkling water, her usual, without having to ask. Gina nibbled and listened to some Stanford professor describe the front-end hedge-fund management software he'd developed.

"Now listen to what I've done with modeling integration," he said. "This will really blow you away."

Gina sipped her sparkling water—from a special stream in the Dolomites, more expensive ounce for ounce than a pretty decent wine—and thought about the Gina she used to be, the Gina who seemed so far away now. That poor girl was exhausted, wasn't she? Always scheming and dreaming and making the most questionable decisions possible. It exhausted Gina, now, just to think about Gina then.

That girl would have jumped at the prospect of an exotic adventure, a lucrative score, a questionable decision. But not this girl. This Gina, here and now, would never dream of jumping at something like that. Why in the world would she? She'd promised the old guy, Harry, that she would sleep on it, but only because she could tell he'd never leave otherwise. He was a piece of work. The old Gina would have loved him.

"You're smiling," the professor said. "Does that mean we're on the right track here?"

Gina was smiling because she could imagine the professor's reaction if he ever found out who she used to be. If she worked it casually into the conversation. As in, "Hey, yeah, you know, your front-end hedge-fund management software reminds me of the time I got a job dancing in a strip club so I could rip off Dick Moby, the most dangerous man in Vegas. Funny story, remind me to tell you about it sometime."

"We might be on the right track," she said instead, checking her BlackBerry. Twelve messages, just since she sat down to eat. "Shoot Jason the specs and I'll talk to him about it on Monday."

After lunch, she drove back to the office and spent the afternoon listening to pitches, listening to pitches of pitches, listening to Jason, one of her business partners, talk about modulated risk.

What's the point of risk, she wanted to ask, *if it's modulated?*

A little after six she called it a day. She stopped by the apartment to throw on a cocktail dress, then headed out to the Legion of Honor. A fund-raising gala for this or that, she couldn't remember what exactly. Jason had said she needed to make an appearance. Gina couldn't remember exactly why that was either?

She stepped into the foyer of the museum and her friend Kelsey motored straight over. Kelsey worked in PR and never walked when she could motor instead.

"Oh, my God, G," she said. "Wait till I tell you who's here."

Gina nabbed a glass of champagne from a waiter drifting past. Kelsey was a sweetheart, bright without being smart, from one of the wealthiest families in the Bay Area. It would blow her socks off too if she ever found out about the old Gina. Kelsey thought Gina had gone to Arizona State and pledged Kappa Kappa Whatever.

Gina downed the champagne in one shot.

"Did I ever tell you about the time I got a job dancing in a strip club so I could rip off the most dangerous man in Vegas?" she said. "His name was Dick Moby, but they called him the Whale. The Armenian mob caught me and put me in the trunk of a car."

Kelsey squealed with laughter. "You're hilarious! Now shut up and let me tell you who's here." And then she squealed again, this time with shock. "Oh, my God!"

"What's wrong with you?"

"That!"

Kelsey pointed to Gina's hand. Gina had forgotten about the ring. She set her glass down so she could switch the ring from her left hand back to her right one, where it belonged.

"It's not what you think," Gina said.

"You almost gave me a heart attack! I thought you'd run off and eloped or something!"

"I just wanted to see what it felt like."

Gina had switched the ring when the old guy had left her office. She'd hoped that Shake wouldn't spot the pass, and he had not. She'd always been quick with her hands, a quite proficient picker of pockets in her day.

"I have a life, Shake," she'd told him. "A happy life. I'm sorry if it hurts—and it's not me being mean, cross my heart—but I did, I stopped thinking about you."

The ring was her being mean. You betcha. She'd wanted to know what it felt like to see Shake's face go slack, to see the surprise and pain in his eyes.

It had felt good. Mostly good.

"Timmy Biancalana," Kelsey said.

"Who? What? Why?"

"That's who's here tonight. You promised you'd let me introduce you."

"I doubt it," Gina said.

"Okay, but you need to meet him. You need to meet some eligible guys. You haven't been out on a date in like forever, have you?"

Kelsey didn't wait for an answer. She took Gina by the wrist and pulled her across the room, through the hum of conversation about start-ups and teardowns, the *tink-tink* of champagne flutes brought together in toast.

"Timmy, meet Gina. Gina, Timmy. Discuss." Kelsey motored away.

Gina smiled at the guy, mop-headed but cute, in a navy pin-striped Zegna.

"Kelsey," he said.

"Kelsey," Gina agreed.

"So. You're the mover and shaker behind Two Birds."

"Ta-da!"

"You funded one of the companies my firm does legal for. PNL-SimLok in Milpitas?"

"Oh, sure," she said.

"They've had some amazing breakthroughs with wafer inspection hardware?"

"That's right."

"Amazing stuff. And you wouldn't believe where they're going with it now."

Gina looked at him. He seemed like a perfectly nice guy. Now was the moment to embark on a perfectly nice conversation with him. Instead, here she was thinking about the old Gina, about Shake. It infuriated her, all over again, that Shake had just bombed down on her. He'd already wrecked her life once, and now he was trying to do it again. What right did he have?

Maybe, Gina considered, what she needed was closure. The little trick with the ring had been a nice start, but if she ever wanted to feel whole again, she needed Shake to understand how much he'd hurt her.

She realized that she'd just come up with a pretty good answer to the question she'd asked herself earlier.

Why in the world would I ever want to go to Egypt with Shake?

To teach him a lesson, that's why.

"Don't you think?" Timmy Biancalana said.

He was still talking about wafer inspection software. Was it possible that was he still talking about wafer inspection software?

"Do I seem like a perfectly nice girl to you?" Gina said.

He was surprised. "I," he said, "well. Yes?"

Of course she wasn't going to Egypt. No matter how tempting the thought of teaching Shake a lesson might be. No matter how desperately the old Gina might have been enticed by an exotic locale, a lucrative score, a questionable decision.

Gina reached for another glass of champagne.

"Please," she said to Timmy Biancalana. "Tell me more."

THE ONE RULE FOR A wheelman, the only rule, was to *stay cool*. No matter how hot the situation. Shake had learned that early, his first real job, when a back tire blew half a block from the check-cashing joint his partner at the time, Vincent, had just knocked over.

Stay cool. Because panic never had an upside. Panic was a sucker bet. With Gina, two years ago, Shake had panicked.

He'd loved everything about their life together in Santa Monica. Everything. And then one morning he woke up with aching knees and a few gray hairs and remembered that he was almost fifteen years older than her. Remembered what Gina had admitted to him soon after they first met, that she was the kind of girl who couldn't be trusted. As if— this was after she had double-crossed Dick Moby and triple-crossed the Armenians and handcuffed Shake to a pipe under a hotel sink—Shake needed a reminder.

For the year they lived together in Santa Monica, Gina had never done or said or even seemed to do or say a single thing that made Shake worry. Just the opposite. But then he woke up with those aching knees and gray hairs, feeling old, and panicked. He became convinced that she would leave him, and that it might hurt less if he left first. Or something like that. You don't think clearly when you panic—the problem with panic, the reason it's so important to *stay cool*.

He wrote the note fast, and left the house fast, and took the flight to

Belize because it happened to be the first one leaving from the international terminal at LAX.

Shake had read somewhere about scuba divers in the water at night who became disoriented in the dark and panicked. They thought down was up and swam the wrong way. They didn't stay cool and follow their air bubbles. They drowned.

That's what happened to Shake. He'd felt, in his panic, that he had to escape the pain that was coming, when in fact he was just swimming deeper and deeper into it.

The phone on the nightstand *bleep-bleep-bleep*ed. Shake picked it up.

"Sir," a man said, "this is the front desk."

"What time is it?"

"A little before midnight. Sir, I'm sorry to bother you, but there's a problem with your room. Would you mind coming down to the front desk, please?"

Shake got dressed and took the elevator downstairs. The front desk clerk just pointed across the lobby to the hotel bar and shrugged apologetically.

Shake sighed and walked over to the hotel bar. He saw Quinn sitting at a table in the back. And then he saw Gina. She was sitting next to Quinn, smiling pleasantly at Shake.

"Surprise!" Quinn beamed. "Guess who's decided she wants a piece of Egypt after all?"

Shake stayed cool. He sat down across from Gina.

"Harry here was very convincing," Gina said. "He's quite a salesman."

"Well," Quinn said. He tilted his head, modest.

"We were just going over the deal points," Gina said. "I want half, since I'm the one making the capital investment."

"The lady has resources," Quinn said, "that I don't have at the moment. I'm not embarrassed to admit it."

"So the other half split three ways now," Shake said.

"Plenty for everyone," Quinn said. "No need to get greedy."

"What else do you want?" Shake asked her.

"Whatever I think of, sport," Gina said. "Whenever I think of it."

Shake almost smiled, but he hadn't forgotten the ring. He felt it all over again, the wave of black nausea that ran over him when Gina first flashed the gold wedding band. He tried to get another look at it now. He did and he didn't want to get another look at it. Gina's left hand was under the table.

"Is that all?" he said.

"That's all," she said. "And a pony. With ribbons in his tail."

"This calls for a celebration," Quinn said. "Why don't I chase down a bottle of champagne so we can toast the beginning of a long and fruitful association?"

He got up and headed to the bar. Shake stayed cool. *Follow the bubbles. Don't drown.*

"What about your husband?" he said.

"What about him?"

"He won't mind? You run off to Egypt for a few days?"

She laughed. And laughed.

"'He won't mind?'" she said. "'You run off to Egypt for a few days?'"

A pretty good impression of someone trying to be casual but failing miserably.

She laughed some more.

Shake grimaced. "You're not really married."

"Don't you feel stupid?"

Mostly he felt dizzy with relief, with joy. But also wary. Because he had no idea, not really, why she'd changed her mind about Egypt.

"Why are you doing this?" he said.

She stopped laughing.

"I don't know," she said. She gazed off across the bar, serious now. "I don't forgive you for what you did. But I guess, when I'm honest with myself, I guess I understand it. I just think—I don't know. I'm not going to promise anything. You know? But if there's something still there, between us, maybe we should see."

She was gazing at him now. Her hand was on the table, almost touching his but not quite.

"Maybe we should see if there's something still there," she said.

It was perfect. Shake wanted to believe it. He would have believed it, if he didn't know her so well.

"So I guess that's why I'm doing this," she said. "If you want the truth."

Oh, shit, he thought.

Quinn returned to the table with a bottle of champagne and three glasses.

"So what did I miss?" he said.

Chapter 28

Evelyn had been back in L.A. for less than twenty-four hours and already she was bored out of her skull. And still facing a full week of vacation that Mike, her ASAC, had suggested she take. Suggested as in, "Take it or I'll give you beach time right here and now, after all the shit you pulled in goddamn Belize."

Irony: *beach time* was what the Bureau called getting suspended.

Lucky for Evelyn, all the shit she pulled in goddamn Belize had ended happily. First she personally busted drug lord Walter "Baby Jesus" Jenkins in the act of multiple criminal transgressions, and then she put the screws to him.

DEA hadn't wanted to let her take a crack at him, but Cory talked them into it. He knew how good she was.

"Walter," she said.

"What." He sat across the table from her, handcuffed and pouting.

They'd been at it, back and forth, for a couple of hours. Evelyn wanted Baby Jesus to think he was grinding her down.

"I just want to be your friend, Walter."

"Why you think I need a friend?"

"Because maybe you do."

"Go to the devil!"

Evelyn caught a flash of triumph in his eyes and could tell he was feeling better about himself. He was no longer embarrassed that he'd been busted by a lone FBI agent, a lone *female* FBI agent. No, now he was grinding that bitch down and telling her where she could go!

Evelyn sighed and pretended defeat. She gathered her notes and stood up. "Okay, Walter, you win. Have fun in Colorado."

She reached for the door handle and Baby Jesus said, "Wait." She turned around. He was staring at her. "What do you mean? Colorado?"

Evelyn pretended innocence. "You didn't know? ADX Florence. The federal supermax near Colorado Springs."

"Supermax?" he said, alarmed.

Evelyn knew he'd been thinking, worst case, that he might do a few years of soft time at Hattieville Prison outside Belize City. Where he was probably related to half the guards by blood or marriage and would be cock of the walk.

Evelyn had been happy to let him think that, until just the perfect moment. "They call it the Alcatraz of the Rockies," she said. "Shank Central."

"No!"

"No?" She frowned. "I'm pretty sure they do."

"No, you can't do that! You can't take me to America!"

"Sure can," she said. "Ever since September of 2009. The Treaty on Mutual Legal Assistance in Criminal Matters?"

There was only about a 1 percent chance they'd be able to extradite Baby Jesus to the United States, but he didn't have to know that. Evelyn reached again for the door handle.

"Wait!" Baby Jesus said.

Evelyn smiled and sat back down. Thirty minutes later—she pinched hard, she stroked gently, she pinched and stroked simultaneously—

Baby Jesus had agreed to name names, detail details, and become a confidential informant for DEA.

"I am a businessman after all," he said. "What other choice do I have?"

Shitheads, bless their hearts—they always seemed to need her validation at this stage of the game, a final face-saving benediction. Who was Evelyn to deny them?

"Absolutely, you're a businessman," she said. "Exactly. And you know what, Walter? I genuinely like you. I do."

"Thank you, Evelyn," he said.

"What was the name of that book again? I'm going to order that book on Amazon."

"The 4-Hour Workweek."

"Great. Thanks." Evelyn couldn't fathom why anyone would want to work only four hours a week. All that time left over for just you and—yourself. No, thanks.

After she finished with Baby Jesus, the DEA guys flexed their giant biceps and acknowledged, grudgingly, that they'd never seen such a skillful flip. This was the Zeta cartel, after all, that Baby Jesus worked for, some very scary hombres.

Evelyn let DEA and Cory Nadler take all the official credit, of course, for both the bust and the flip. She was no dummy. Her last night in Belize, the DEA guys took her out drinking and said to give them a call if she ever needed a favor. She told them to start counting the minutes.

Now, though, a favor from DEA couldn't save her from a full week of boredom, a full week alone with herself. Sarah was no help, in school all day and training therapy dogs for the disabled at night. Brokering a peace accord in the Congo. When Evelyn had raised the possibility that the two of them might drive up the coast for a few days, a mother-daughter road trip, Sarah had rolled her eyes.

"Mom," she'd said. "Finals week?"

Evelyn was confused. "That's next week, I thought."

"It is. Hello?"

Of course. Her switched-at-birth daughter studied for finals the week before finals. Evelyn should have been happy about that. She *was* happy. Just bored.

"You'd be climbing the walls if we drove up the coast too," Sarah said.

Her daughter. Always right, never wrong.

Evelyn squeezed the steering wheel of her Subaru and watched her knuckles flex and roll. She was stuck in line at the Bank of America ATM on Fourth and Colorado, behind some nimrod in a Porsche who appeared to be transferring his life savings to offshore accounts, one dollar per transaction.

She honked. The nimrod whipped around, furious. A Hollywood-agent type, black suit and blue shirt. Evelyn smiled sweetly and honked again.

Her cell phone rang. She answered. "Cory?"

"Hi, Evi."

"I thought you were delighted to be finally rid of me."

"I was. I am. Believe me."

"I believe you. Are you still in Belize? Are you still wearing that quote-unquote tropical wool suit? I am so incredibly bored right now, Cory, that this conversation is the shining highlight of my day."

"I'm back in Mexico City now. Shut up, Evi. I've got some information for you."

"Information?"

"About Shake Bouchon."

The nimrod in the Porsche ahead was working the ATM in exaggerated slow motion now, glancing back every now and then to smirk at her. Evelyn ignored him.

"Really," she said.

"This is all off-the-record. That part is very important. Okay?"

"You have to ask, Cory?"

"The passport he's using, I asked customs to flag it. Since, you know, you helped us out in Belize."

"Oh, Cory. I'll never make fun of your suit again."

"Bouchon is traveling with that guy you asked me to check out, by the way. Harrigan Quinn? He's an intriguing guy. Very intriguing."

"Cory! Get to the point!"

"They flew into San Francisco three days ago."

San Francisco. Evelyn looked at her watch. If traffic wasn't too bad on the 405, she could be in San Francisco by dinnertime. She jammed the Subaru into reverse and started to back out of the bank parking lot.

"And then they flew out again yesterday," Cory said.

"What?" *Shit.* "Do you know where they went?"

"I do know. That's the good news."

"What's the bad news?"

"Where they went," Cory said.

EVELYN DROVE HOME, OPENED HER laptop, and clicked on Google Maps.

Cairo.

She didn't know anything about Egypt. She knew about the pyramids, and Tutankhamen, and Mubarak getting kicked out. She also knew, because Sarah had done a project on them when she was in elementary school, that fennec foxes lived in the Egyptian desert. She wondered how hot Cairo was this time of the year. Her brainiac daughter would probably know.

Evelyn clicked over to the Delta Web site. That she was checking her SkyMiles balance, that she was even considering the possibility of following Shake Bouchon halfway across the globe, was probably enough evidence to get her officially beached, if not committed.

She sent Sarah a text. *U remember the fennec foxes in Egypt?*

Sarah's answer came back. *Sure.*

Do u think Cairo is hot this time of year?

June, July, and August are worse.

And then, a second later: *Why?*

No reason.

Mom!?! Why are you asking about Cairo?

Sarah, who knew her so well.

Just looking at colleges for u, Evelyn texted back. *U would look so cute in a*

Evelyn thought for a second.

What r they called?

Burkas. Or hijabs. Mom?!?

Evelyn had over a hundred and sixty thousand Delta SkyMiles banked. Flying back and forth to D.C., over the years, back and forth to New York. She clicked around to see if any award flights were available. Just for the hell of it, just for a laugh, she wasn't actually going to take one.

Cory had filled her in about Harrigan Quinn. He was an intriguing guy. Cory couldn't be positive, but reading between the lines of Quinn's résumé, he thought Quinn had probably done contract work for the CIA back in the eighties and nineties. And/or contract work for the kind of people that the CIA spied on.

And now Shake was on his way to Egypt with him. Shake, whose restaurant had just burned down, who someone was trying to kill, who needed money and fast.

Evelyn had a nose for stinky cheese, and this was definitely stinky cheese, whatever Shake and Quinn were into in Egypt.

One could make the argument, just for the hell of it, that Evelyn had an opportunity here. If she managed to catch Shake in the act of something untoward in Cairo, then she'd have some leverage on him. He'd have no choice but to give up everything he knew about Alexandra Ilandryan and the Armenians in L.A.

Mom! You are NOT going to Egypt?!

Evelyn saw that there was award availability on Delta to Amsterdam via JFK. And then from Amsterdam to Cairo on KLM, proud member of the SkyTeam Alliance.

What!? Evelyn sent back. *U think i'm nuts?*

BABB THOUGHT IT WAS JUST great. Mennonites! In Belize, of all places! He smiled as he watched the little girls in bonnets frolic in the square. He wished he had some candy to give them. Marathon bars. Did they even make Marathon bars anymore? Marathon bars had been Babb's favorite as a child, chocolate and caramel twisted into an interesting shape.

The old lady required a translator. Her English, she apologized, was poor. The translator was a teenage boy with his hair parted on the side and slicked down.

Mennonites! So fun!

The old woman told Babb that the two men had spent the night in her home. They had enjoyed her fried chicken. She was astonished to learn that they were dangerous fugitives. They had seemed like such nice men.

"They always do," Babb said, nodding gravely. The old woman thought he was Special Agent Kevin Coover from the FBI. She thought that Babb's target, Quinn, and the target's Armenian mob bodyguard, Bouchon, were escaped murderers, fleeing justice. "You'd be surprised," Babb said, "how often someone who seems nice really isn't."

He'd had an easy time tracking Quinn and Bouchon to Three Butterflies. The man who'd given them a ride in his truck heard about the money on their heads and called Babb's liaison in Guatemala. Babb wished the liaison had called a little sooner, but that was just the way the cookie crumbled.

The old woman told Babb, through the translator, that the two dangerous fugitives had a long conversation with a certain Mr. Benjamin Finley, who lived half a mile outside town. The old woman had not understood any of the conversation. Her poor English, you see. Babb asked how he might find Mr. Finley's place. The old woman said Mr. Finley was not there. He'd taken the bus to Mexico yesterday and would not be back until tomorrow.

"No problem," Babb said. "Is there a place I can stay in town overnight? I'd love to have a word with Mr. Finley when he gets back from Mexico."

The old woman said she'd be happy to rent him her spare bedroom. The same bedroom, in fact, where one of the dangerous fugitives had stayed, the younger of the two. Perhaps Special Agent Coover might find a clue in the spare bedroom.

"Where did the other fellow sleep? I wonder," Babb asked. "The older one?"

The teenage boy translated. The old woman pretended not to understand the question. Babb laughed.

"I'd be delighted to spend the night in your spare bedroom," he told the translator to tell the old woman.

The arrangement was perfect. Babb needed a place to stay for the night. And he wanted to ask the old lady a few more questions in private. He thought she might speak better English than she let on. He thought she might recall some of the conversation that Mr. Finley had had with Quinn and Bouchon. Sometimes people needed to be properly motivated to remember things that they thought they'd forgotten. Proper motivation didn't always work, but it never hurt to try!

Babb's cell phone rang. He checked caller ID. Gardenhire. The boss. Gardenhire, who had hired Babb to work in the garden. To do some pruning.

"I'm really sorry," Babb told the translator to tell the old Mennonite woman. "Do you mind if I take this?"

He stepped off the porch and away from the little girls in bonnets, still frolicking away.

"We got a hit on the passports," Gardenhire said.

"Where?"

"Cairo."

"Great!"

"Great?"

"The pyramids!"

Silence. Then: "Just get it done."

Gardenhire hung up. Babb climbed back onto the porch. He gave the old Mennonite woman his card and asked her to call him if she remembered anything about the two dangerous fugitives.

She said something to the teenage boy. The teenage boy asked Babb if he would still be staying the night.

"I'm sorry, no," Babb said. And he was sorry. He'd been looking forward to staying the night. "I'm afraid I have to run."

PART III

PART III

Shake had never seen traffic like the traffic in Cairo. No lanes, no lights, a thousand grimy cars locked tight together on a street that would have been crowded with half that many. Creep and lunge, creep and lunge, horns beeping. Every beeping horn on earth, it seemed. Shake, in the backseat of the cab with Gina, was closer to the guy in the car next to them than he was to her. Shake could have reached through the guy's open window and picked the dandruff flakes off his shoulder, that's how tight the traffic was locked.

Pedestrians, when they wanted to cross the street, waded in and took their chances. They darted when the cars crept, they dodged when the cars lunged.

Shake saw a grimy old Peugeot that had bumped into a wooden cart full of watermelons. A few watermelons had spilled onto the street and broken open, dark green rinds and dark red fruit. A guy in a long gown down to his ankles was trying to calm the donkey who'd been pulling the wooden cart.

Because, sure, the traffic in Cairo included donkeys pulling wooden carts.

"It's called a galabiya," Quinn said, turning around in the front seat of the cab. "The dress he's wearing. But don't call it a dress, he'll kick your ass."

What was kicking Shake's ass was jet lag. He felt fogged and loopy. They'd landed in Cairo last night around midnight. Shake had tried to sleep when they got to the hotel, but he was still on Belize time. And his mind was still working, trying to figure out what Gina had in store for him. He didn't nod off until almost dawn. When Quinn pounded on his door a few hours later, it was like being wrenched from the dead.

The signs on the buildings didn't help his jet lag, everything written in Arabic. Shake was in a dream where words had melted and gone squiggly.

Gina looked crisp and alert—in sunglasses, her hair pulled back, fresh lipstick—not fogged in the slightest.

Yeah, Shake thought, like she needed the extra edge on him.

"It's a beautiful city, isn't it?" Quinn said, turning around in his seat again.

It was dirty and hazy and chaotic, stack after stack of buildings the color of dirty sand, dirty bone, dirty butter. Though Shake did like all the mosques, the skyline bristling with minarets. He liked the donkeys in the street. He was prepared to admit that Cairo did have a certain exotic appeal.

"You know you're not in Kansas anymore," Gina said. "For sure."

"So my buddy with the security firm," Quinn said. "When I called him this morning, he says the clock's ticking. He says his client, the rich expat asshole, put it on the market a couple of days ago. Opened the bidding, already has an offer. Not a great offer, my buddy doesn't think, but these things move fast. We've got to make hay while the sun shines or we'll lose it."

"What is it?" Gina said. "The it?"

Quinn winked at her. "Just wait. I'm going to tell you."

The cab turned a corner, squeezed down a narrow street crowded with giant tour buses parked up on the curb, and then turned another corner. Suddenly Shake found himself staring straight at the pyramids, right there, practically on top of him. "Holy shit," he said. If he'd felt like he was in a dream before, he really felt like it now. The pyramids looked exactly the way you'd expect the pyramids to look. But even bigger, even more impressive.

There were a lot of people moving around at the base of the biggest pyramid, but you didn't notice them at first, they were so puny in comparison. The blocks at the base of the pyramid were taller than the tallest person.

"Sheesh," Gina said. "Somebody had a teeny pecker, didn't he, whoever built these?"

"You know who stood right here and gazed in awe at those pyramids, same way we're doing right now?" Quinn said. "Herodotus. Julius Caesar. Napoleon. Mark Twain. Among others. If that doesn't blow your mind, I don't know what will. Come on."

He paid the cabdriver and the three of them walked down another street lined with tour buses. That street led them to an enormous sandstone lion with the head of a pharaoh. The Sphinx. The pyramids were lined up perfectly in the background.

"Holy shit," Shake said again.

Gina hooked her arm through his. "It's sort of romantic, isn't it?"

He looked at her. "I know what you're doing," he said.

She laughed.

"I have a general idea of what you might be doing and possibly why," he said.

"Come over here," Quinn said. "Take a look at this."

Shake and Gina walked over. A tourist was taking a photo of her husband with the Sphinx in the background, a forced perspective that made it look like the husband was holding the Sphinx in the palm of his hand.

Quinn found a spot with an unobstructed view. "What do you think of that?" he said. "See the nose?"

"The nose?" Shake said. He must have been missing something, because the Sphinx was missing its nose. There was just a flat slab of stone between the eyes and the lips.

"Speaking of teeny peckers," Quinn said. "Napoleon. The story is, 1773, his troops are screwing around, taking target practice with their cannons, they blast the Sphinx's nose off. What really happened, though, the nose was already off by the time Napoleon ever showed up in Egypt. The Muslims, some Muslims or other, they're the ones knocked it off in the fourteenth century. Religious issues, I don't know."

Shake and Gina were quiet for a minute. Shake finally got it.

"The nose," he said. "We're gonna boost the nose?"

"It was in a museum, wasn't it?" Gina said, nodding. "And then it got stolen during the revolution. The rich asshole ended up with it."

Quinn looked at them both. "Have you been listening? The Muslims knocked the nose off seven hundred years ago. It's dust. It's long gone."

Shake was glad Gina looked confused too. "Why are we here, then?" he asked Quinn.

"Because we're in Cairo! I thought you should see the pyramids, the Sphinx. When's the next time you're going to be in Cairo?"

"Harry, sweetie," Gina said.

"Okay," Quinn said. "You're right." He paused for effect, turning his vintage-movie-star profile to them and lifting his chin. "The speech that saved Teddy Roosevelt's life."

Wonderful, Shake thought. Quinn didn't have enough material of his own, now he was gonna start delivering other people's speeches too.

Shake and Gina waited. Quinn didn't say anything else.

"The speech that saved Teddy Roosevelt's life!" he said. "That's what we're going to boost!"

THEY FOUND A TABLE IN the shade. A café with a view of the Sphinx.

Shake had never heard about a speech that saved Teddy Roosevelt's life. Shake had been forced to talk his way out of several hairy situations, and Gina had too. Gina probably couldn't even count all the times. But Shake couldn't imagine how a president of the United States ended up in the hair like that.

"That's not what I mean," Quinn said. "It wasn't Teddy giving a speech that saved his life, it was the speech itself."

Calling him Teddy, like they'd been buddies. Maybe they had been.

The waiter who brought their coffee could have been Quinn's twin brother, Shake noticed when he poured Quinn's coffee. Tall, tan, the same waves of white hair. The main difference, the waiter had dark eyes and a big dark mustache, and he walked with a bit of a stoop.

Shake watched Quinn frown at the ghost of his Christmas future.

"I'm not following," Shake said.

"Shocker," Gina said. But she wasn't following either.

"Teddy could give a speech," Quinn said. "I mean it. Two hours long, three hours. A fascinating historical figure, but long-winded as hell. Don't say it, I know what you're thinking. Anyway.

"Teddy's in Milwaukee, October of 1912, running for president again. He's on his way to give a campaign speech. He steps out of his hotel in Milwaukee and some whack job pulls a gun. Takes a shot at Teddy. But guess what? The bullet hits the speech Teddy has in the pocket of his overcoat. Fifty pages long, folded in half. The speech stopped the bullet. Slowed it down, at least. And I think there was a metal eyeglass case involved.

"Anyway, Teddy survived. The bullet only went in him about three inches, it didn't get past the chest muscle. It didn't hit the heart. That speech saved his life. And get this. Teddy went ahead and gave the speech, on schedule, before he let them take him to the hospital. He told the people in the audience about the bullet. His exact words: 'It takes more than that to kill a Bull Moose!'"

It was a good story, if it was true. But Shake didn't know what any of it had to do with Egypt or some guy selling conflict antiquities on the black market.

"It's a good story," he said. "Is it true?"

"Of course it is," Quinn said. "Teddy didn't win the election, though. It's a better story if he had. He never won another election, sad to say."

"What does Teddy Roosevelt have to do with Egypt?" Gina said.

According to Quinn, the king of Egypt, back when there was still a king of Egypt, right after the Second World War, was a nut for American historical memorabilia. He bought everything he could get his hands on. An oar from the boat George Washington used to cross the Delaware. Grant's last cigar, the stub of it. The bloodstained cards that Wild Bill Hickok was holding—the original dead man's hand—when he got shot.

When the king was forced to abdicate in the fifties, the new government didn't know what to do with his collection.

"We're talking a lot of valuable items," Quinn said. "The Smithsonian would have killed Wild Bill Hickok all over again to get their hands on those aces and eights. Not to mention the Bull Moose speech with the bullet hole through the middle of it. But the Egyptians were pissed, they're still pissed, as a matter of fact, because half of ancient Egypt is in museums somewhere else. The archaeologists who dug it all up, you know this, they were foreigners. They took the best pickings home. London, Berlin, Rome. You know where the Rosetta stone is right now? The most important Egyptian antiquity in existence? It's in London. The British Museum."

"So the Egyptians started their own museum," Gina said. "A museum of American historical artifacts."

"The lady gets a prize. Hardly anyone even knew about it. It was famous for a minute in the sixties. But who comes to Egypt to see Harry Houdini's handcuffs? They come to see the Sphinx."

He swept a hand across the view.

"And then the revolution happened," Shake said.

"That's right. Nobody paid any attention to some forgotten little museum. Well, somebody did. Somebody knew Teddy's speech was worth money on the open market and they nabbed it. Our rich expat probably picked it up for pennies on the dollar, and now he'll auction it off to the highest bidder."

"Let me get this straight," Shake said. "The conflict antiquity we came to Egypt to boost is a speech Teddy Roosevelt gave in Milwaukee."

Shake glanced at Gina. She'd lifted her eyebrows up above her sun-glasses.

"I know," Quinn said. "Not your usual everyday score."

"Well," Gina said. "That's our specialty."

She gave Shake a little bump with her knee and Shake couldn't help it—he caught himself wondering, for a second, if maybe she'd told the truth after all. If maybe she'd come to Egypt because there might still be something left between them.

She caught him wondering, and smiled.

"There's not a huge market for this sort of thing," Quinn said, "from what I understand. But the players have serious money. The kind of people who can have anything they want, so they want what they can't have."

Gina gave Shake another smile, another little bump with her knee.

Quinn stood up. "There he is!" he said.

A scrawny Egyptian guy, about Shake's age, hustled toward them, grinning. He had a big black mustache, a world-class mustache, and was wearing a dark gray suit two sizes too big for him. One of his teeth was missing.

"Mr. Quinn!"

"Mahmoud!"

Quinn stood up and they hugged. "How long has it been, you old son of a bitch?"

"Very long, Mr. Quinn, you old son of a bitch."

"Now, hold on one second. I am in fact an old son of a bitch. So you may call me a crazy bastard, not an old son of a bitch."

"Okay, you crazy bastard."

They laughed and grinned and stared at each other. Quinn eyeballed Mahmoud's suit, two sizes too big and shiny at the elbows. Mahmoud eyeballed Quinn and then eyeballed Shake and Gina.

"And where are the remainder of your associates?" Mahmoud said finally. "That you mentioned?"

Of course, Shake thought.

"Mahmoud here runs his own private security firm," Quinn said, pointing, watching for Mahmoud's reaction as he said it. "That's what he's been telling me."

"Oh," Mahmoud said. "Well. I should clarify, I think, perhaps."

Of course.

THE WHITE-HAIRED OLD WAITER, QUINN'S twin brother, brought tea for Mahmoud. Mahmoud sipped the tea and explained that no, he didn't technically own the private security firm, and technically the private security firm wasn't one. It was a catering company. Mahmoud was a bartender. Well, to clarify, he was an apprentice bartender.

Shake was not surprised to learn that the bullshit had been flowing both ways. Mahmoud, apparently, had been led to believe that Quinn worked for the CIA and would show up in Cairo with Ocean's Eleven.

"So, yes, I see," Mahmoud said when he finally had to accept the reality that this was the sum of Quinn's associates, just Shake and Gina, and no martial-arts expert back at the hotel unpacking his high-tech fiber-optic heist gear. "Ah. I see."

He was grinning still, but starting to falter under the strain of it.

Quinn was faltering under the strain of his grin too.

Serves the old son of a bitch right, Shake thought.

"Let me get this straight," Quinn said. "Mahmoud, my friend. A bartender? So the man you told me about, the black-market dealer with the item in question. Do we need to clarify any details there too?"

"Oh, no, Mr. Quinn!" Mahmoud said. "Those details are precisely accurate! It is since September I have been working for Mr. Devane. Exclusively so! At his house and his nightclub, both. I hear things, you see, as bartender. As apprentice bartender, the distinction is meaningless. I see things. I have seen, with my own eyes, the item in question. I have verified the value of the item. And it can be ours, Mr. Quinn, *inshallah.*"

"*Inshallah,*" Quinn said.

Shake didn't know what that meant. Judging by their current situation, he thought it probably meant something like "What the fuck, you never know."

"What's that mean?" Shake said. *"Inshallah?"*

"God willing," Quinn said.

Shake hadn't been far off.

"He's got a nightclub?" Gina said. "This Devane fella? I thought he worked the black market."

"He does, yes," Mahmoud said, turning his grin, with the missing tooth, on her. "But the club, you see, is one of the most exclusive in Cairo. You can guess its purpose, I think? I do not know how to say it in English."

"To launder his money," Shake said. Mahmoud looked blank. "Wash it. Make it clean."

"Exactly!"

"Let's talk turkey," Quinn said. "Okay?"

Mahmoud nodded uncertainly.

"Where's he got it?" Quinn said. "The item. At his house?"

"Ah. Yes."

"He's got a safe?"

"Yes."

"Security? Cameras?"

"Yes. Cameras. And men who watch the house. Two, I think."

"Just like *Ocean's Eleven*," Shake said.

"Exactly!" Mahmoud said. And then frowned, because Shake, it was tragically apparent, was no George Clooney or Brad Pitt. He was not even one of the lesser Eleven.

"Inshallah!" Gina said cheerfully.

GINA WAS ABOUT TO DIE she was so jet-lagged. She was about to die she was working so hard to pretend she wasn't. Because she wanted Shake to know she had the edge in every possible way.

He was onto her. He'd figured out that she'd come to Egypt just to torment him. And it hadn't taken him long. Which annoyed her—she thought she'd played it just about perfectly back in San Francisco.

Though probably, she admitted to herself, she would have been more annoyed if Shake hadn't caught on so quickly. This was a guy, after all, she'd been in love with. Think how poorly it would have reflected on her if she'd fallen in love with a total idiot.

It wasn't the end of the world that Shake was onto her. So what if he was? He still, Gina could tell, clung to a sliver of hope that she really would fall back in love with him. A sliver of hope that she'd forgive, forget, leap into his arms, pop the buttons off his shirt, et cetera.

Gina could work with that sliver of hope. It was shiny and very sharp. It could be very dangerous in the right hands.

"Well," she said in the cab back to the hotel. "That went well, didn't it?"

"He told me his firm handled security for the guy with the speech," Quinn said. "He told me explicitly."

"What did you tell him?" Shake said. He had his head propped against the window, his eyes barely open. "Explicitly? You told him you were bringing Ocean's Eleven, didn't you?"

Gina tried to keep her own eyes open. It was taking forever to get back to the hotel. Traffic was even worse coming than going. How was that possible? She noticed that a lot of the women on the street wore burkas and had their faces covered. Gina was cool with that—if that was what the woman wanted, and not what the woman's husband or father or preacher told her she wanted. In that case she was not cool with it whatsoever.

"It's a wrinkle," Quinn decided. "That's all." And, *boom*, he brightened right up again, just like that. Gina was impressed. She didn't think it was an act. "We iron it out, we move on. Let's not get our knickers in a twist."

"Move on?" Shake said.

"Sure."

"A safe, security cameras, at least two security guys watching the house. Our guy on the inside's a bartender. Apprentice bartender, though of course the distinction is meaningless."

"His knickers are twisted, Harry," Gina said.

"I know it."

"And a break-and-take to begin with," Shake said. "I'm a wheelman.

I was a wheelman. The only thing I know about a break-and-take is how to drive away from one."

"Whoever said anything about a break-and-take? Show me the transcript."

"Then what?"

Quinn didn't answer. Gina wanted to lend a hand, she liked the old fella's upbeat attitude, but really her knickers were just as twisted as Shake's.

"I loved the first one," she said.

After a beat Shake said, "The one with Sinatra, you mean?"

"No. The first new one."

"I didn't see the other new ones."

"The other new ones weren't as good. They used a different writer, I think."

"Let's put our heads together," Quinn said. "There's more than one way to skin a cat."

"Who's the cat in this scenario?" Shake said.

"C'mon," Gina said. "You're giving up so easy?"

Shake looked at her. His face surprised, wary, defeated.

She knew he knew what she meant.

"Shake and I should check out his nightclub, at least," Gina told Quinn. "See what we can see. My friends tell me I haven't been on a date in forever."

Shake glanced at her. Again he looked surprised, wary, defeated, and—just a little bit, that sharp silver, dangerous sliver—hopeful.

"Fantastic idea," Quinn said. "Now we're cooking with gas."

Chapter 30

Shake pulled the blackout curtains in his room and slept most of the afternoon, into the evening. When he woke up he felt better, his head clearer, the world more like the world as he knew it and less like a dream. He took a long, hot shower and that made him feel better too.

He didn't feel any better about Quinn's scheme. He felt worse about that. The downside, unfortunately, of a clear head.

The apprentice bartender, Teddy Roosevelt's speech with the bullet hole in it, this shadowy Devane guy, his house with the safe and the guards. All that was a disaster waiting to sail. No, it was already sailing, far from land, and Shake was standing right on the top deck of it.

But he was going to stay there. He had nowhere else to go, not as long as Gina was on the top deck of the disaster too. Whether or not there really was a chance he could get her back. Whether or not she was here in Cairo for the sole purpose of torturing him. The distinction for him, at the end of the day, was meaningless.

He went downstairs. The hotel, a former palace on an island in the middle of the Nile, was hopping. The lobby was packed with guys in galabiyas and guys in sunglasses and Armani and other guys, darker-skinned, in flowing snow-white robes with matching head wraps, the whole nine yards. These guys looked exactly like you imagined Saudi oil sheikhs would look.

Quinn had said Muslims from all over the Middle East came to Cairo to party on the weekends, since the Egyptians had a more relaxed attitude toward booze and girls and gambling. Nobody wore a tie with their suit and every Arab guy, it seemed, had a mustache. Were Egyptians Arabs? Some of the lighter-skinned guys looked more like Italians than Arabs. Shake didn't know. He'd have to ask Quinn.

He caught himself. *Christ,* he thought.

Shake spotted a couple of girls in high cork heels lounging on a red velvet sofa. Hookers, he guessed, probably Russian. Ukrainian. Beautiful pale eyes and cheekbones, bad sharp teeth. Eyes moving moving moving around the lobby while the girls put on lipstick.

He walked past the casino and skirted the garden, where a wedding was going on. On the other side of the garden were some shops. Shake found a shop with suits on the rack, pretty good ones. He tried on a charcoal two-button that fit just about right, but the tailor who ran the shop wouldn't have anything to do with *about* right. He kept Shake there for half an hour, chalking and tucking and snipping, Shake waiting in his boxer shorts and sipping tea. The tailor asked him if he wanted a tie too, but Shake said no. When in Cairo.

He charged the suit to his room—he didn't think Gina would mind—and told the tailor he'd wear it now. The tailor put Shake's other clothes and shoes in a bag and offered to hold on to them. It was almost ten o'clock by now, so Shake headed back to the hotel lobby. He took a seat on a red velvet couch across from the elevators and waited for Gina.

Shake had expected Quinn to cut in on their night out. Instead, though, he'd told Shake and Gina that he was hitting the hay early, have fun, let's all catch up at breakfast in the morning.

When in his life, Shake wondered, had Quinn ever hit the hay early? When had he headed south when the action pointed north? It was a cagey move. Maybe Quinn figured that his best shot, if he wanted to keep his scheme on track, was to keep Shake and Gina on track. Or not on track. Shake wasn't sure which. Maybe Quinn understood what was happening between Shake and Gina better than Shake did.

When Gina stepped out into the lobby—in a dark sea-green dress that tugged and shimmered, knee-high leather boots—Shake understood for sure that she'd come to Cairo to torture him.

About a dozen guys with mustaches stopped what they were doing to gawk at her.

"Well, well," she said, eyeing his new suit.

"Off-the-rack, but I did my best."

"You didn't want to disappoint."

"That dress," he said. "The color."

"Oh, that's right." She smiled pleasantly. "I forgot all about that."

Devane's nightclub was only a few blocks away, so they decided to walk. The night was warm but not muggy. Strange, since the river was so close by. New Orleans, when it was warm, was always muggy. Shake could smell the river, and burning charcoal, and jasmine, and garbage, and the fruit-flavored smoke drifting away from the *sheesha* cafés that lined the street.

"So tell me really," Gina said. "How did you end up with a piece of work like Harry?"

"You want the extended version?"

"Sure. Why not?"

Shake told her how he'd moved to Belize and bought his own restaurant.

"You did?" she said. "You did it!"

"It wasn't exactly what I'd expected."

"Your own place! What did you name it? Did you put your gumbo on the menu?"

"It was the Sunset Breeze when I bought it. I never got around to changing the name. And yes."

"I missed your gumbo more than I missed you. You didn't name the restaurant after me?"

"No. Sorry." Though Shake had thought about it, long and hard.

"That's probably good. It would have made you seem like some poor lovesick loser who'd made the mistake of his life."

"Do you want to know about Quinn or not?"

"Go on."

He told her about the masked man who tried to shoot Quinn and how Shake intervened to save Quinn. He told her how the people who wanted to kill Quinn now wanted to kill Shake too.

"Mr. Nice Guy," she said. "When are you ever gonna learn?"

"Not soon enough, apparently."

"This time, I'm thinking, it's like that fable. Is it Greek? The boy and the lion. The boy thinks the lion is going to eat him, but the lion has a thorn in his paw. The boy feels bad for the lion so he takes the thorn out."

"And then the boy can't get rid of the lion? The boy wishes he'd never touched that fucking thorn?"

"You don't wish that. You can't help it, that you're Mr. Nice Guy."

"I can wish."

"Androcles and the lion. I don't remember how it turns out."

Then Shake told her that the guy who wanted to kill Quinn, and now him too, was Logan James.

"Logan James the billionaire?"

"That's the one."

"Oh," she said. Quietly. "Fuck."

"Ask Quinn to tell you about it, next time you have a couple of weeks free. Bottom line, Quinn knew Logan James when he was just a kid, over in Asia. I don't know exactly what all they were into. Scamming NGOs, fraudulent government contracts, moving the shells around. Now Logan James is legit and he needs to make sure those days are gone and forgotten. That's Quinn's theory, at least."

"Logan James," Gina said. "Wow. How do you get yourself into these situations?"

It was a sincere question. This from a girl Shake had first met when he found her gagged and handcuffed in the trunk of a Lincoln Town Car.

"My dad had this saying," Shake said. "When you sank so low it was embarrassing. When people you thought were the worst at something suddenly looked down at *you*. He called it getting fired from the carnival."

She smiled. "Given the lofty employment standards of the carnival." And then, "Wait."

"That's right. When it comes to getting into situations, you're the carnival."

"Shut up," she said. They turned the corner onto a busier street. "You never told me anything about your dad."

"Nothing to tell. He wasn't around much, and then he wasn't around at all."

"The Bouchon men have commitment issues? Imagine that."

Shake stopped walking. "There's somebody on us," he said.

Gina didn't miss a beat. She turned back and put her arms around Shake's neck. Like she was about to kiss him, but really so she could look past and behind him.

"Are you sure?" she said. "I don't see anything."

He wasn't sure. It had been just a feeling. Shake trusted feelings like that, he was still alive because of them, but this one had passed now.

Gina's lips were inches from his, her breath warm in his face. That was all he could feel now.

"When did you quit smoking?" he said.

"Long time ago. New Year's Day two years ago."

"Good for you."

"I'm touched by your concern for my health."

"Still nothing?"

"No."

"It was just a feeling," he said.

She didn't laugh. "Keep me posted. You better not get me killed because Harry got you killed."

"I'll do my best."

Devane's nightclub was just across the street. The name of the place was in English, in blue neon over the door: THE WILD ROSE. The doorman took one look at Gina and fell over himself to let her in. She pulled Shake along with her.

Inside, the place was dark and crowded, the music hammering away. A DJ in a glass cockpit had James Brown's "Please, Please, Please" buried under some kind of weird pulsing electronic beat.

Please don't do that to James Brown, Shake thought.

"Not that busy yet," Gina said into his ear.

"It's not?"

"When's the last time you've been out to a club? Was everybody kung fu fighting?"

She wasn't far off.

"Hey," she said. "Our lucky night."

Shake saw Devane in the next instant. It had to be Devane.

A youngish white guy, early thirties, wearing a straw porkpie hat and spread out in a booth at the back of the club. He had girls on each side of him, girls in the laps of other girls, girls giggling and spilling out of the booth. Several of the girls wore skimpy dresses that seemed to be made from bandages they'd wrapped around themselves. Devane, nodding along to the weird electronic pulse, had his straw porkpie tipped down over his eyes.

Off to the side, back in the shadows, stood a pair of hard-looking Egyptian guys with mustaches. In suits, no ties, hands at their sides. Devane's beef.

"Shall we?" Gina said.

"Do we have a plan?" Shake said.

But she was already on her way across the dance floor, zeroed in on Devane.

DEVANE'S BODYGUARDS STIRRED WHEN SHAKE and Gina approached the booth. They had their eyes on Shake, not Gina. Their mistake, Shake thought.

"It's cool," Devane told them. He had his eyes on Gina.

"Hi," Gina said.

"Have a seat."

"Give me a break."

Devane considered, and then gave the girl on his left a nudge. She got up and then all the other girls got up too, like birds lifting all at once off a telephone wire.

Clearing the girls out was a move like you saw in movies. Shake thought Devane had probably spent a fair amount of time working on it.

The girls drifted out onto the dance floor and started dancing. Shake and Gina sat down across the booth from Devane. The bodyguards eased back into the shadows. They were even more hard-looking up close than they'd been at a distance. Shake wanted no part of them.

The bodyguards fit, but Devane wasn't what Shake had expected. At first glance—the stupid porkpie hat and the jeans with fancy embroidery up and down the legs, the boyish sunburned cheeks and blond hair—he came off more like a trust-fund brat than a high-end fence for stolen antiquities. But once Shake looked closer, he saw that Devane's eyes were cold, suspicious, alert, and in his own way he was just as hard-looking as the bodyguards.

"Americans," Devane said. "You are, aren't you? You don't see many Americans in Egypt since the revolution. The revolution, yeah right, what a joke. But Americans. Americans walk into a room like they own it, here we come, ready or not. This land is my land and all that."

Once he got going, he talked fast, using his hands. He used his hands to mime shit blowing up in the revolution, Americans walking into a room, Woody Guthrie playing "This Land Is Your Land" on a fiddle.

Shake might have thought he was coked up, and maybe he was, but his eyes didn't move at all. They stayed steady.

"What are you?" Gina said. "You sound American too."

"No, thanks. Canadian."

"We don't have to discuss health care, do we?"

"What do you want to discuss? Is your friend here a mute?" Devane mimed zipping his mouth shut. "I can tell right away that you two aren't together, not romantically."

"Because he's so much older than me? Because I'm so clearly so far out of his league?"

"That must be it," Shake said.

"Huh," Devane said, picking up on something. "Maybe you are together. Or were. I don't really give a shit if you are or not." He looked at Gina. "I wouldn't mind seeing you naked."

"I don't really give a shit if you'd mind or not," Gina said, friendly.

All this time, Devane had stayed settled back on his side of the booth, slouched down. Now he sat up and leaned forward.

He was coked up for sure, Shake decided, but smart and suspicious. Probably more suspicious because of all the coke.

"I know why you're here," Devane said.

"Of course you do," Gina said.

What? Shake wondered. He tried not to look like he was wondering. Gina would kill him if he did.

"Too bad," Devane said. "You're too late. Already off the market."

"I don't think so," she said.

"Where'd you hear about it? From Billheimer?"

"I don't know any Billheimer. You just made that name up."

"Okay."

"We were just in Morocco," Gina said. "We came for the waters, but would you believe it? No waters! Well, really we came to check out a little bronze dog, first-century Roman. Supercute, and a real bargain. Have you ever been to Rabat? *Très charmant, non?*"

Gina's ability to lie on the fly was scary. Shake had almost forgotten. She told lies like Italians spoke Italian, the words rolling off her tongue fluid and effortless.

Shake could lie when necessary, but he never enjoyed it. Once a Catholic altar boy, always a Catholic altar boy. If he had to lie, Shake liked to be prepared for it.

"I don't know anybody in Rabat," Devane said.

"They know you."

Devane slouched back and picked at the fancy embroidery on his jeans. "Who's your buyer?" Devane said. "Not you."

"Him," Gina said.

Fuck, Shake thought.

"The mute?"

Gina turned to Shake and smiled. And waited.

Fuck.

She knew exactly what she was doing. She knew all about his past as a Catholic altar boy, his mixed feelings about lying.

Shake tried to remember how Ziegler would put it. Ziegler was a Wall Street swindler, on the run from the feds, who Shake and Gina had encountered in Panama at the beginning of their relationship. Ziegler was the kind of guy who would drop six million dollars for Teddy Roosevelt's bullet-hole speech, he wouldn't think twice.

"I collect stories," Shake said. "Not objects. The object has to tell a story. What's the point, otherwise?"

He thought that was right. Gina was still smiling at him, winking without winking. Shake realized that he hadn't felt this happy, not once, in the past two years.

Devane was paying attention to Shake now, from beneath the brim of his straw porkpie, the first time he really had. "I've already got a buyer lined up."

"Lined up means the buyer hasn't bought yet," Gina said. "Lined up means the bidding is still open."

"Let me see you naked. You can keep the boots on." Devane mimed unzipping Gina's dress, and then turned to Shake. "That's smart. Why you brought her along. You think she'll distract me."

"Is it working?" Shake said.

"No. I'm never distracted. It's a gift."

"We'd like to examine the merchandise before we make an offer," Gina said.

"Oh, sure. What hotel are you staying at? I'll just leave it down at the front desk."

"Yuk, yuk," Gina said.

She stood. Shake stood too. Devane nodded along to the music. The DJ was now murdering James Brown's "Get Up off Me."

"Wait," Devane said.

One of the bodyguards stepped forward and handed Shake a business card. There was nothing on it but a phone number. "Don't waste my time," Devane said.

"Wouldn't dream of it," Gina said.

Chapter 31

Gina held it back for as long as she could, then started laughing as soon as they were outside the club. She couldn't believe it.

"Jesus fricking Cricket!" she said. "He dropped that right in our lap."

"He had help," Shake said.

"I'm good, aren't I? It's a gift."

She knew she was good, but so was Shake. Gina hated that. She hated how he'd managed to keep up with her when she put him on the spot. She hated it and she loved it. Gina couldn't count how many guys she'd been with who couldn't keep up with her. Or could keep up but got all pissy because they had to work so hard at it. But Shake never got pissy. He liked how hard Gina made him work.

She hated and loved that the two of them had fallen so quickly back into the same easy rhythm, that same hot blue spark arcing back and forth between them. One of Gina's brothers, growing up, had been into welding. The energy she had with Shake was still like that. As if the past two years had never happened. As if he'd never left her a fucking note and DUMPED HER.

"Fucker," she said.

He didn't say anything. They were walking down the street, his arm around her. He'd put it there and she'd let him, because that was the plan.

"Let's go walk down by the river," he said.

"Let's go back to my room," she said.

He didn't say anything, but at the next corner he turned right, toward the hotel entrance and away from the river.

In the hallway, outside the door to her room, she turned and put her arms around his neck again. Her boots had three-inch heels, so she only had to lift up onto her toes a tiny bit.

She brought her lips close to his. She could feel his thumbs resting lightly on her ribs, through the silk of the dress. Through the silk of the dress, she could feel him rocking a serious boner.

Gina had spent half the day in Cairo looking for a dress the same shade of green as the one she'd worn in Panama, that first night they'd had dinner together.

"You can't have me," she breathed into his mouth.

He opened his eyes.

"Sorry, Charlie," she breathed. "You blew it."

He looked down at her. Gina didn't know how long she could stay like this, up on her toes, her lips so close to his.

"That's my real name," he said. "Charlie. Charles."

"I know that." She had known that, she'd just forgotten.

"You blew it and you can never, ever have me again." Their lips almost touching. "Sucks, doesn't it?"

"This little trick will only work on me one time, you know."

"Doubt it."

He smiled. She wanted him so much. The flaw in her genius plan to teach him a lesson was becoming more and more apparent to her. "Maybe just one kiss," she said.

He hesitated, then sighed. "You almost got me again."

"Don't worry," she said. "I probably won't bang Devane just to teach you a lesson. I know that's what you were worried about."

He blinked. She smiled. He was worried about it now.

"And you can trust me on the business end too. I won't be looking for an opportunity to screw you over when you're at your most helpless and vulnerable. Probably."

She went into her room and shut the door and left Shake standing alone in the hallway. She peeped through the peephole and liked what she saw. She might be making herself miserable by making Shake miserable, but it was worth it. She just hoped he didn't think it was worth it too, because then where did that leave them?

"Rest easy, partner!" she yelled through the door. "See you at breakfast!"

Chapter 32

Meg checked into a fancy hotel in the business district of Guatemala City. It was the kind of fancy hotel Terry had always wanted to stay at. He said he'd heard that some fancy hotels had girls in little uniforms by the pool, and all they did was walk around and clean your sunglasses for you.

"Can you believe that?" he'd said.

"I believe there's somebody fool enough to do anything," Meg said.

Terry chewed on that. "You mean fool enough to put on a little uniform and walk around the pool and clean folks' sunglasses?"

"I mean fool enough to want to stay in a place like that."

But now here she was. She took the elevator up to the roof of the fancy hotel to see if Terry was right about the girls in the little uniforms. The pool was closed, though, because it was dark outside.

Meg went back down to her room and ordered a shrimp cocktail from room service. That was another thing Terry had always wanted to do. Meg had never let him, because room service in a hotel, whether it was fancy or not, cost you an arm and a leg.

She had plenty of money now. After she shot Jorge, she'd helped herself to the cash he had in his desk. Close to ten thousand U.S. dollars. Meg didn't feel bad about stealing the money. Jorge couldn't use it anymore. They didn't sell orange Fanta and greasy goat-smelling tacos in hell, did they? That was Meg's position on the matter.

Meg ate half the shrimp cocktail even though she wasn't hungry, and then rode a taxi out to where the rich people in Guatemala City lived. Not the very richest people, but the people a step or two down from that. She went to the address Jorge had scrawled on the greasy goat-smelling paper bag. Jorge's boss lived in a nice big house with flowers spilling down off all the walls. There were lights in the yard pointed up at the house. That way you wouldn't miss how nice the house was, how pretty the flowers were, even though it was dark.

Meg stood on the porch. She was here to make Jorge's boss tell her where she could find the man he'd sent to kill Terry. She'd planned to kill that man, and Jorge's boss too, for sending the man in the first place. But now it was like all the stuffing had gone out of her, like she barely had the energy to take one breath after another. She couldn't stop thinking about that room-service shrimp cocktail, and how much Terry would have loved the little forks that came with it.

She remembered the thought she'd had back at Jorge's, when he told her that his *muy poderoso* boss, the heavy man, would kill her.

Maybe I want him to kill me, Meg had thought.

Now, on the porch of the boss's house, she had a thought that was even shorter and got right to the point. It was just: *Kill me.*

She felt so tired. She felt heavy, though not the kind of heavy Jorge was talking about. Meg's kind of heavy was in her arms and legs and most of all in her heart. Like she had a bag of something dead and wet inside her, and there was just no way she could keep dragging it along, not for one more second.

An aunt of Meg's had told her once that life was like a movie and everybody thought they were the star of it. That's why dying was hard.

People didn't want to accept it, that the movie would go on without them.

Meg lifted her heavy, heavy arm and rang the doorbell.

BABB SAT ON A BENCH on the bank of the river.

I am sitting on a bench on the bank of the River Nile, he told himself.

He tried it in third person:

Babb sat on a bench on the bank of the River Nile.

Crazy!

Less than twenty-four hours ago he had been sitting in the Belize City airport. He had traveled, in less than twenty-four hours, across time and space and history. It boggled the mind. What would the emperors and popes and philosopher-kings of yesteryear have given to possess such power? Anything!

It was dark, after midnight. He had followed the bodyguard, Shake, and the woman he was with, back from the nightclub to the hotel.

Now he was just waiting for Gardenhire to call and give him the go-ahead. He would tell Babb the time line and explain what arrangements would be made.

Gardenhire, rumpled and ruffled, balding, bustling from conference room to conference room, drinking pots of bad coffee. He was under an enormous amount of stress at the moment. Big developments afoot.

The man who worked for the Man Who Would Be Senator. That was Gardenhire. Which made Babb the man who worked for the Man Who Worked for the Man Who Would Be Senator.

Big boats festooned with lights plied their way up and down the River Nile. Dance cruises. Music and laughter floated through the warm night air. The lights of the boats shimmied across the water. Babb thought the dance cruises looked like fun.

He felt his phone vibrate. He took it out of his pocket and checked caller ID. He was surprised. It was not Gardenhire calling with the go-ahead, as Babb had expected. Calling instead was the liaison Babb used in Guatemala City, Edgar Ramales-Llende, a real up-and-comer in the

Guatemalan justice department. The Man Who Worked for the Man Who Worked for the Man Who Worked for . . .

The real surprise was that Gardenhire had not already called with the go-ahead. Babb sensed that Gardenhire was struggling with the decision. Babb didn't know why and didn't want to ask. It really wasn't any of his business.

"Hello," Babb said.

"I have news," Ramales-Llende said.

"Great."

"The other account has been closed."

Babb thought for a second. "The girl's dead, you mean?"

Ramales-Llende was silent.

"It's okay," Babb said. "You're using an encrypted phone, aren't you? I am."

"Yes," Ramales-Llende said. "She is dead. She killed Jorge."

"Really?" Babb had definitely called that one—the girl was a firecracker.

"And then she came to my house," Ramales-Llende said.

"Did you kill her yourself? Did she put up a fight?"

"My bodyguard did. No, not really. She had a gun, but she did not shoot."

"Huh," Babb said. "Interesting." The complex workings of the human mind never failed to fascinate him. But he also felt a little disappointed. "I guess this is good news. But I feel left out, I guess is my immediate reaction. Though why should I feel that? It's stupid."

Ramales-Llende was silent for another moment.

"You would like a souvenir?" he said. "It can be arranged."

"A keepsake," Babb said. "That would be fun. If it's not too much trouble? The girl, I remember, she was wearing a silver ring on her ring finger. Was she wearing a silver ring on her ring finger?"

"I believe so, yes."

"If you could maybe FedEx me the ring she was wearing, that would be great."

Silence. Ramales-Llende cleared his throat.

"No!" Babb said. He laughed. "Not with the finger in it! I'm not some maniac."

"Of course not," Ramales-Llende said.

"Can you hold for just one second?" Babb asked. He had another call beeping in, the go-ahead coming in from Gardenhire. "I'll be right back."

Chapter 33

Quinn ate like a horse the next morning, dipping back twice into the hotel buffet and knocking down a pot of purple Egyptian tea that smelled like flowers. Shake wondered if the old son of a bitch had managed to get lucky again last night when Shake and Gina were off chasing Devane.

When Shake, more precisely, was off chasing Gina.

"Try this," Quinn said. "It's called *karkade*. Hibiscus tea. It'll lower your blood pressure."

"Do I need to lower my blood pressure?" Shake said. "Or do you?"

Quinn gave him a wink. "I did meet a nice lady at the hotel bar last night, yes. A corporate something-something from London, retired. A very nice lady, I'm a sucker for the accent. Any accent, tell you the truth."

Gina made her way across the dining room. She gave them both big friendly hugs, then sat down next to Shake, looking as dewy and innocent as a fresh-plucked rose petal.

"I like it," Quinn said after Gina filled him in on what happened at Devane's club. "It's perfect. Sometimes the best angle is the simple angle. Point A to point B, don't get fancy. Ask me about my time in Lisbon sometime, when I'm in an expansive mood."

"No," Shake said. "It's not perfect. This guy Devane, he's the real deal. He's smart. The suspicious type. He's gonna be thinking a step or two ahead, every step he takes."

Quinn looked at Gina. Gina nodded. That annoyed Shake, both the look and the nod.

"What?" Shake said. "You need confirmation?"

"Is baby cranky?" Gina said. When Quinn turned to flag down the waitress for another pot of tea, she whispered in Shake's ear. "Didja wake up with a big achy boner this morning? That would make me cranky."

Shake ignored that. "And those bad boys working for Devane," he said. "If we're still on the subject of why this isn't perfect. We don't want to tangle with them."

Quinn nodded. "Former SSI. State security. That's what my buddy Mahmoud says. After the revolution, the military broke up the SSI. All the meanest bastards in the Middle East out on the free market to the highest bidder. We do not in fact want to tangle with them."

"Great," Shake said.

"It's pretty perfect," Gina said. "It's as close to perfect as we're gonna get. Porkpie thinks we're buyers because he was the one who thought of it. Don't you see? He pulled, so we didn't have to push. So he's not suspicious now."

"He's suspicious," Shake said.

"You know what I mean. We're over the wall, at least. That's what I mean."

"She's not wrong," Quinn said.

"Fine," Shake said. "We're over the wall. He thinks we're buyers. Now what?"

"We use that to get him on the move," Quinn said. "We get the item out of the safe, out of the house."

Gina nibbled at the base of her thumbnail. Shake had never seen her do that before. Maybe she'd picked up the habit when she quit smoking.

"I don't know," she said. "A different situation, I'd say maybe that was enough. But Porkpie is totally the suspicious type."

"And Egyptian state security working for him," Shake said. "Let's not forget."

She nibbled her thumbnail. "He has to carry it in something," she said finally. "When he takes it around to show buyers. A briefcase or whatever. He's not going to carry Teddy Roosevelt's seven-million-dollar speech folded up in his back pocket."

"Aha!" Quinn said.

Shake saw where Gina was headed too, but wasn't sure it deserved an *Aha!*

"Harry," she said, "can your buddy Mahmoud get us the specs on the case Porkpie carries the speech in?"

"Mahmoud can get us the specs. He can get us measurements, pictures on his telephone, the whole shebang."

"It has to be exact," Shake said. "The specs. We'll have to hunt down an identical case."

"I know we'll have to hunt down an identical case."

"Then all we have to do is throw the bump," Gina said.

Shake shook his head. "If it doesn't go like clockwork, he'll know it's a switch."

"Bet your ass he will," Gina said.

She waited. Shake had to smile.

"Really?"

"Sure."

"When have you ever heard of something like that working?" he said.

"We turn a negative into a positive."

Shake noticed that Quinn was frowning.

"What's wrong, Harry?" Gina said. "It might work."

"Look here," Quinn said. "It's a good idea, but I don't like it that Devane thinks Shake's the buyer. No offense, Shake. But you're not my idea of a wealthy collector of illicit antiquities."

Shake didn't take offense. He doubted he was anybody's idea of a wealthy collector of illicit antiquities.

"Porkpie was tuning out," Gina said. "I had to get his attention. I had to put the buyer right there in front of him so he'd take us seriously."

Shake didn't know if that was true. Maybe it was. He knew it was more true that Gina had just wanted to fuck with him when she'd ambushed Shake by telling Devane that he was the buyer.

"You did a helluva job, young lady," Quinn said. "Don't get me wrong. I wish I'd seen you in action. What I'm saying is, it should be me. It's not too late. We call Devane up, we move the furniture around a little."

"It's too late, Harry," Gina said. "You know that. You're the bump. You have to be the bump. You're the only one he hasn't seen yet."

"The bump." Quinn scowled. "The bit part, you mean."

So that was it. Shake let Gina take this one. *Have fun, young lady.*

"Harry. Sugar pie. Suck it up, okay?"

"Okay, okay," he said. "Okay."

Now Shake frowned. He'd expected Quinn to put up more of a fight. He'd expected Gina to emerge at least a little worse for the wear.

"We have to move fast," she said. "What do we have? A couple days max?"

"That's probably the window," Shake said. "The other bid isn't great or he would have taken it. But it's a bid."

"I'll go see Mahmoud right now," Quinn said.

"I'll go with you," Shake said. The specs on the case had to be exact. That point had to be communicated very clearly to Quinn's guy.

"Fine," Quinn said. "Maybe there's a lightbulb you can help me change afterward."

"And I'll go see Porkpie," Gina said. "Make arrangements for the show-and-tell. I can get to know him a little bit, soften him up."

She gave Shake a sweet, rose-petal smile. Shake remembered her threat last night about sleeping with Devane. Not like he'd forgotten it.

"Why don't I go see Porkpie?" Shake said. "And you go with Quinn."

"No, I can handle it," she said. She leaned over to whisper in Shake's ear. "His boner, I mean."

"He'll start digging, you know," Quinn said. Ignoring them or not ignoring them, Shake couldn't tell which. "Once he has the name of the potential buyer."

Gina nodded. "Suspicious type that he is."

"Not to mention, look at our potential buyer," Quinn said. Meaning, Shake was nobody's idea of a wealthy collector of illicit antiquities.

"Harry."

"Okay, okay."

"My IT guy back in San Fran, I can have him put up a fake Web site, hack around and create a footprint. You know, for whoever Shake is supposed to be. John Q. Dingus, whoever. My guy can hack it so our John Q. Dingus shows up top of the page on Google. No, fuck it, hold on."

"Devane will dig deeper than Google," Shake said.

"He'll call around. Shut up, I know."

"Use a real name, for chrissakes," Quinn said. "Don't make one up. Find a shoe that fits, don't build one from scratch. That's how we always did it."

Shake and Gina looked at each other.

"Roland Ziegler," she said.

The Wall Street swindler Shake had channeled last night. *I collect stories, not objects.* Roland Ziegler was a doughy, pretentious weasel who made sure you knew in the first thirty seconds of a conversation that he owned two private islands off the coast of Panama and a building on Park Avenue. He was exactly everybody's idea of a wealthy collector of illicit antiquities.

"Ziegler's a fit," Gina told Shake. "You totally nailed him last night. You're already playing the part."

"Ziegler's in the federal pen. Small problem, don't you think? When Devane starts digging and—oh."

"Good boy. Keep going and you'll get a big hug at the finish line."

"Shut up. I get it."

"The way we play it," Gina said, "Ziegler *was* in the federal pen. Past tense. Until, let's see, a few months ago?"

"We say he cut a deal with the feds so they let him walk. He's done it before."

"He promised to rat out a few of his old Wall Street buddies."

"All of it very hush-hush," Quinn said, catching on. "They kept it out of the papers."

"I'll still have my IT guy do some hacking. You know? Drop a hint here, a hint there."

"Maybe," Shake said. "I don't know. What if Devane knows Ziegler? What if he knows the feds would never cut another deal with him after he screwed them the first time?"

"Bad for us," Gina said.

"And the case Devane carries Teddy's speech in. What if it's custom? What if we can't find a look-alike for it?"

Teddy's speech. *Christ.* Shake was doing it himself now.

"Shake." Quinn set his cup of tea down. "You got a better hand on the table, I'd love to see it. I mean that sincerely. But from where I sit, my perspective, your other hand on the table looks like dead broke and Sticky Jimmy trying to pop you."

"Sticky Jimmy?" Gina said.

"Logan James."

Gina laughed. "Oh, Harry, I'd want to kill you too, you gave me a nickname like that."

"I didn't give him the nickname. Well. Let's just say he earned the nickname."

"I bet he did."

"We have to play our hand, Shake," Quinn said. "Another opportunity like this, it won't drop down from the sky."

Quinn meant the money. Or maybe he meant Gina. Both. Either way, Shake knew he didn't have a better hand to play.

"The case he carries the speech in," Shake said. "We have to find one that's identical."

"Go ahead," Quinn said. "Tell me one more time so I don't forget."

Chapter 34

Shake and Quinn waited outside the hotel while a bellhop called them a cab.

At the lobby entrance was a metal detector manned by two Egyptian soldiers holding machine guns. Down at the end of the drive were two more soldiers, poking mirrors beneath the chassis of every car that wanted to come closer.

"So the military runs the show now?" Shake said.

"They always ran the show," Quinn said. "They own half the country. They own construction companies, factories, resorts. The hotel we're staying in, I wouldn't be surprised the military has a piece of that. They build roads, they make bread. I mean the kind of bread you eat."

"The military does?"

"They were always independent, more or less. Mubarak had his security forces, separate from the military. The SSI, remember? The guys work for Devane? During the revolution, the military sided with the people, not Mubarak. It's more complicated than that, you know what I mean. The honeymoon's over now, between the people and the military. Hell, the honeymoon's over between the people and the people, the liberals and the Muslim Brotherhood and al-Noor. Don't even mention the Christians."

Shake had to give Quinn credit. The old guy knew a lot about Egyptian politics. Or seemed to.

"That's the problem with honeymoons," Quinn said. "Sooner or later, they're over."

"Yeah," Shake said. That was something he knew about.

The soldiers down at the end of the drive finished checking over the cab. It pulled up. Shake and Quinn got in.

"*Sabah el kheir,*" Quinn told the cabdriver.

"*Sabah el kheir,*" the cabdriver said. "Where you go?"

"Qarafa. You know?"

The cabdriver looked at Quinn. Then the cabdriver waved over the bellhop and said a lot of things to him, fast, in Arabic. Shake hadn't made up his mind about Arabic. It was harsh but also at times musical, a lot of hacking up phlegm but also some sweet surprising lilts. It was like listening to a hard-core metal band do a cover of "Hey Jude."

The call to prayer, this morning, warbling and scratchy through the amplified speakers of the mosques nearby, had sounded a little to Shake like mournful mountain bluegrass.

When the cabdriver finished talking to the bellhop, the bellhop looked at Quinn.

"Please, sir," the bellhop said. "Am I mistaken? You wish to visit the City of the Dead?"

Shake looked at Quinn too.

"It's not what you think," Quinn told Shake.

Shake hoped not.

"Yes," Quinn told the bellhop and the cabdriver. "That's exactly what I wish. How far is it? Half an hour?"

"*Inshallah,*" the cabdriver said, and pulled away from the curb.

Shake tried not to think about Gina and Devane. Gina with Devane.

Shake didn't think she'd really sleep with a douche bag like Devane just to get back at him. The odds were about a million to one against. But they were still odds—that was the problem. Not to mention that Gina was such an expert liar. Even if she didn't sleep with Devane, she could convince Shake that she had.

Or the other way around. Shit. Shake came up a loser on this one no matter how fine you chopped. Gina knew it.

"Keep your head in the game," Quinn said.

"My head's in the game."

"What did I tell you? About letting your emotions get in the way because of some girl."

"Some girl."

"She is some girl," Quinn admitted. "Why in God's name did you dump her?"

"What about you?" Shake said. Anything to change the fucking subject.

"Me?"

"Were you ever married?"

"Yes," Quinn said, and nothing else.

Shake looked around for the Four Horsemen of the Apocalypse. "That's it?" he said. "No story it takes you an hour just to get started?"

"Keep your head in the game," Quinn said, and then nothing else again.

GINA USED HER BURNER CELL to call the number Devane had given her. The call went straight through to him. He sounded like he was in the shower. He sounded like he was in the shower with a couple of the girls from the night before.

Ick, Gina thought. You'd need a shower after showering with that kind of girl.

Devane said he'd send a car for her but Gina told him she'd make her own way over. She didn't want him to know where they were staying yet, and she didn't want to be trapped at his place.

Gina had no intention of banging Devane. No way. She'd only told

Shake that to make him suffer. Devane could not have been more un-appealing to her. There was something cold about him, both stiff and limp at the same time, like frozen fish you left in the fridge overnight and had only partway thawed by morning.

Ick. But she might get some fresh ideas, during her private visit with Devane, for teaching Shake a lesson. The interesting thing about being her, Gina had discovered over the years, was that she never quite knew what she was going to do, not until she actually did it.

The old Gina, that is. The new Gina, who always ordered the same poached salmon for lunch and listened to pitches all day, who attended charity fund-raisers and went out with perfectly nice guys, that Gina hardly ever surprised this Gina.

This Gina? Did that mean that the real Gina was the old Gina?

As mad as she still was at Shake, Gina had to admit that she was having more fun now than she'd had in a while. She felt—happier. Was that because of Shake, or was it because she loved wheels and deals and that tingle she always got when she stood on the end of a diving board, no idea how deep or how cold the water was far below?

Fuck. She didn't know.

And, okay, she had to admit that teaching Shake a lesson wasn't the only only *only* reason she'd come to Cairo with him.

She realized she was biting at her thumbnail again.

"So give me your address," Gina told Devane. "I'll grab a cab."

"Meet me on the river," he said. "There's a private *dehabeah* docked across from the Cairo tower. That's a boat, like a yacht. You can't miss it."

"That's where you live?"

"Yeah right," he said. "Like I'm going to tell you where I live."

"Really?" Gina said. "You're that paranoid?"

"Ha. I'm a lot more paranoid than that."

Good, Gina thought. She was counting on it.

THE CAB DROPPED SHAKE AND Quinn off at the edge of a slum that sprawled for miles. Most of the houses were small, almost miniature, crowded close together. Baking in the sun, crumbling, chunks of plaster dropped away to reveal the ragged gray brick beneath.

"Why do they call it City of the Dead?" Shake asked Quinn.

"You'll figure it out," Quinn said. "I have complete faith in you."

Shake guessed it was because a lot of the buildings looked like tombs. The place reminded him of the cemeteries in New Orleans, where they couldn't put people in the ground because the city was below sea level.

And then Shake realized that a lot of the buildings didn't just look like tombs, they were in fact tombs.

"It's an actual cemetery?" Shake said.

"Gold star."

But there were people everywhere, moving up and down the narrow dusty lanes between the tombs, kids kicking around a soccer ball, a guy selling fruit from a cart.

"People live here? In the tombs?"

"Twenty million people in Cairo, that's what they say. More than that, probably. Everybody needs a place to lay their head."

"In a tomb?"

"Cool in the summer, warm in the winter. Free rent and you don't have to worry about your roommates making a lot of noise. Come on."

They passed through a crumbling stone arch and entered the cemetery. Nobody paid much attention to them. Quinn called over one of the kids playing soccer. He gave the kid an Egyptian pound coin, fifteen cents or so, and the kid led them toward Mahmoud's house. His tomb.

"It doesn't bother you," Shake said. "Our inside guy on the score, the guy everything hangs on, he lives in a tomb?"

"It bothers me. Did I say it didn't? He told me he had a fancy office, he told me he was Devane's right-hand man. But if he can get us the specs on the case, if he helps us take off Devane, does it matter where our inside guy lives or which hand he wipes his ass with?"

Mahmoud came out of the tomb, grinning, that big hole where an eyetooth should have been. He shook Quinn's hand. "You crazy bastard!"

"You old son of a bitch!"

"Come in, my friends! Come in, please. These are only temporary lodgings, of course."

They went inside. The tomb was clean and cool. There was a mattress in one corner, a TV in another. Mahmoud put three teacups on the table in the center of the room, an old green stone slab that had faint Arabic markings carved on it.

"Why don't we do this outside?" Shake said.

Mahmoud looked confused, but Quinn didn't seem too thrilled about drinking tea off a gravestone either.

"Let's just cut to the chase," Quinn said. He asked Mahmoud if he knew what Devane used to transport Roosevelt's speech when he took it out of the house to show potential buyers.

"Oh, yes," Mahmoud said. "Of course. The attaché."

"The attaché?"

"Yes. Such as a businessman might carry? Leather, black. Many of the items that Mr. Devane sells, if the item is of a certain size and no larger, he prefers the attaché."

"Can you get us the exact specs?" Shake said.

"Specs."

"Dimensions. Size."

"Ah. Of course."

"We need to know the exact color of the leather. We need a photo. Okay? We need to find a case exactly like it. Devane can't spot the difference."

"But I will bring you the exact match!" Mahmoud said. "Leave this to me. I will bring you the very twin of Mr. Devane's attaché! My cousin Sayed, you must understand that this is his business. Do you understand me? Leather and luggage and such. Leave this to me."

Shake glanced at Quinn. Quinn cleared his throat.

"Mahmoud," Quinn said. "This is important. A little bullshit now and then, two old friends, what does it matter? But bullshit in a situation like this one, we blow a serious payday. Maybe worse than that. Do you understand me?"

Mahmoud assumed a grave expression. Shake waited.

"My old friend," Mahmoud told Quinn. "I need this money. If I do not get out of this shithole soon, I am going to die. That is no bullshit."

DEVANE'S YACHT WAS BIG, NO surprise. But it also had a British colonial charm that Gina hadn't expected, with teak decks and wrought-iron railings, and fat old-fashioned life preservers along the hull. Gina could picture Agatha Christie on the deck of a boat like this, chatting with a man in a white tuxedo. Katharine Hepburn playing Agatha Christie in a movie.

There was a guy at the gate to the dock. Another guy at the walkway to the boat. Different guys from the ones who had been with Devane at the club, but they wore the same dark suits, they had the same dead eyes, they held their hands the same way. The guy at the gate opened the door of the cab for her. He had a pale knotted scar that ran the entire length of his face.

Gina told the cabdriver to wait for her. He didn't look too thrilled about that, what with Scarface dead-eyeing him, but he nodded. Scarface led her onto the yacht and through it. The interior was surprisingly tasteful too, British desert colonial, but not obnoxiously so. Gina saw a Picasso she thought might be real.

Devane was lounging on the top deck, by the pool. A very tan naked girl was lounging next to him, her hand down the front of Devane's silk pajama pants. The naked girl was working away at Devane in a sort of vacant, absentminded way, like she was petting a dog while watching TV.

"Hope you don't mind," Devane said. "I got antsy and I knew you weren't gonna fuck me. You weren't ever gonna fuck me, were you? But you were gonna try to make me think you might. That's your game."

"Nailed it."

"Part of your game, I should say. I'm not stupid."

To illustrate "stupid" he used his hands to make a dunce cap. At least that's what Gina thought he was doing.

He was wearing a different straw porkpie today. Really? Was this still 2008?

The naked girl kept petting away. She looked like she was trying not to yawn.

"She'll go down on you if I tell her to," Devane said.

"I prefer my sex with a consenting partner. Crazy me."

"She'll consent if I tell her to."

"I think you're foggy on the concept. Hey," Gina said to the girl. "Whatever he's paying you, it's not enough."

The girl said something back to Gina in a Slavic language, not friendly.

Devane smiled. "You know what she called you?"

"I can guess."

Devane said something Slavic to the girl. The girl glared at Gina, fished her hand out of Devane's pajama pants, and stood up. She took her time shrugging on a red silk kimono. Hervé Léger, Gina guessed. What was it with Russian girls and Hervé Léger? The girl walked into the cabin, taking her time.

"She called you what you think she called you," Devane said, "but an even nastier version of it. Leave it to the Russians, how many different versions of it they have."

"So who are you, anyway?" Gina said. She was genuinely curious, how a douche bag like Devane had ended up dealing stolen antiquities.

He smiled again. "You're thinking I look like a spoiled rich kid."

"Educate me."

"I was a spoiled rich kid. You should have seen me in high school. I got kicked out of three different high schools. Drugs and girls and— other things. The last time, senior year, Dear Old Dad thought a change of scenery would behoove me. So he sent me to live with a college chum of his in Paris. A professor at the Sorbonne who, interestingly, had a town house in the Marais that no professor should have been able to afford. Imagine that."

"Dad's college chum was a dealer in black-market antiquities. You learned the business from him."

"Learned it? I *took* it. *Tout le kit*. The old fart didn't know what he had, the potential. He didn't have the stomach to make real money. He did look the part, you would have liked that. The tweed jacket, the pipe. But not my style."

Gina didn't need to ask what had happened to the old fart. She suddenly wanted this conversation to be over.

"Mr. Ziegler would like to examine the merchandise you have for sale," she said.

Devane's smile shifted just a little. "Ziegler? That's the mute's name you work for?"

"He loves it when you call him that."

"Roland Ziegler?"

"Does tomorrow work?"

"Roland Ziegler."

"At a time and place of your choosing, of course."

"I heard Ziegler got locked up again."

"He did." She smiled. He studied her. "You've got the number I called you from," Gina said. "If you want to pursue this opportunity, let me know."

She turned to go.

"Wait," Devane said.

"What?"

"You better not play with me," Devane said. "I know all the plays."

"I'm sure you do," Gina said.

SHAKE TRIED CALLING GINA BUT she didn't answer. He and Quinn ate lunch at a little restaurant on a hill overlooking the city. Shake counted two dozen minarets before he stopped.

Hummus, two different kinds of kebabs, french fries. Some kind of glop made from beans, onions, tomatoes, and chickpeas. Not bad, but come on. Shake promised himself that the next time he got tangled up in a hopelessly tangled scheme, he would do it in Italy, or maybe Thailand.

Gina phoned back during dessert, some kind of custard with cinnamon. Shake told her about their conversation with Mahmoud. "Now it's just wait and see," he said.

"Same here," she said, and told him about her meeting with Devane.

Shake asked where she was. She told him she was at the hotel spa and planned to spend the rest of the day there.

Was she really at the hotel spa?

"I know what you're thinking," she said. "How can I put your mind at ease? Oh. Mmm."

"What?"

"Mmm. That feels good."

"What does?"

"Nothing," she said. "Let's have a romantic dinner together tonight."

"So you can torture me some more."

"Okay."

"Fine."

"Nine o'clock in the lobby."

"Can we find someplace with Italian food? Or Thai?"

"You can have whatever you want. Even me. No, wait. Except me. No, wait."

"I love you," Shake said.

She didn't answer. He waited. She still didn't answer.

"Did I mention that Mahmoud lives in a tomb?" he said.

"Of course he does. See you at nine."

She hung up. Shake and Quinn finished lunch and took a cab back to the hotel. Shake went to his room and fell asleep watching CNN. He didn't wake up until after seven.

At nine he took the elevator downstairs and found his spot on the red velvet couch. He leaned back and closed his eyes and listened to two oil sheikhs chattering excitedly in Arabic. One of them must have just won big at the casino. You didn't need to speak the language to guess that.

A second later he felt someone sit down next to him. Shake caught a whiff of perfume. Gina didn't wear perfume, and this—delicate, expensive—wasn't the kind of perfume a Ukrainian hooker would wear.

He opened his eyes. Sitting next to him was the woman from Belize, the mysterious dark-haired woman with the amazing smile who had saved his life on the beach.

She gave him the amazing smile. The lights in the lobby dimmed.

"So," she said, "what's a shithead like you doing in a place like this?"

Chapter 35

Shake was so surprised to see Evelyn that his jaw dropped. Just a little, but still. How often did you actually see that? Someone's jaw dropping with surprise? Evelyn didn't think she'd ever seen it. She was delighted.

She'd arrived in Cairo yesterday and picked up his trail this morning. Easy. He was registered at the hotel under the name on his fake passport. Probably he thought no one knew about the fake passport. Probably he thought that no one, even if they knew about the passport, would ever be crazy enough to follow him to Egypt.

Surprise!

Evelyn had tailed Shake and the old guy, Quinn, when the two of them took a cab from the hotel to a slum in the city center. Evelyn had a great private driver that her hotel had hooked her up with, an enthusiastic Egyptian named Mohammed. Mohammed thought it was a blast, playing cops and robbers. A couple of times he was a little too enthusiastic and they almost blew the tail. But Cairo—the traffic, the general chaos—had to be the easiest city in the world to not blow a tail.

Evelyn and Mohammed had tailed Shake and Quinn to lunch and then back to the hotel. Evelyn had waited, waited, waited. She wanted to pick the absolute perfect moment to catch Shake off guard.

And she had, judging by the dropped jaw and the sustained speechlessness on his part.

Well, he had a lot to process.

Who is this woman?

Why is she here?

Did she just call me a shithead?

Whoever she is, she's even cuter than I remember, isn't she?

Well, maybe that last one was a bit of wishful thinking. Evelyn knew she wasn't at her absolute cutest. Who would be, after flying coach across six or seven time zones?

He cleaned up pretty well. In a suit! No tie, white shirt untucked, as seemed to be the style here in Cairo.

She kept smiling. She wondered which of his many questions he'd hit her with first.

He surprised her by not asking a question at all.

"You know," he said, "I thought all along you might be a cop. My original thought, back in Belize that first day, I thought your dad or brothers might be cops, and you picked up the demeanor from them."

"That's totally sexist," she said.

He smiled, wry. Evelyn couldn't believe how cool, after that first little jaw drop, he was able to keep himself.

"Which is it?" he said.

"My dad," she said. "Seattle PD. One of my brothers too."

"It's kind of a watchful demeanor I noticed you had."

"Like a professional wheelman might have too?"

"I did my bid. Three years. I'm a free man."

She laughed. A free man. He was a riot.

He knew why she was laughing and sighed.

"Did you call me a shithead earlier?" he said.

"Yes."

"I'd appreciate it if you called me Shake."

"How about Charles? Charlie?"

"That's fine. Charlie is. I think the last person who called me Charlie was a cop too."

"Was he a special agent with the Federal Bureau of Investigation?" She showed him her creds.

"Impressive," he said. "Special Agent Evelyn K. Holly."

"You can keep calling me Evelyn. You're dying to know why I'm here, aren't you, Charlie?"

"I think I prefer Shake. If you don't mind, Evelyn. Charlie makes me feel like I'm ten years old and the parish priest is yelling at me because I nodded off during Mass."

"A choir boy."

"Altar boy. Big difference."

"No doubt. Shake, I'm here because I want to be your friend."

"I can use all the friends I can get."

Evelyn laughed again because ninety-nine out of a hundred shitheads, guaranteed, would have tried to lay something tough on her, like Baby Jesus had. *Why you think I need a friend?*

"Is that why you ended up with Harrigan Quinn, international man of mystery?"

"Was he really in the CIA? He makes it sound like he was, but I don't know if he's full of shit or not."

"Who knows? The CIA is surprisingly secretive about their employment records, go figure. Probably he was. If you read between the lines. Hey, by the way, Shake—what are you and Mr. Quinn up to here in Cairo? Just some sightseeing? I'd love to hear the details."

She saw a faint ripple spread across the pool of his cool. The first ripple. Nice.

"I like your perfume," he said. "And your smile too, but I think I told you that back in Belize."

"I don't get tired of hearing it. But it can be hard too. Like in high school, when you're known as the girl with the great smile. Because, excuse me, nice eyes too. Right? And a brain. And come on, please. Has anyone even noticed these legs?"

"What else do you like about yourself? Self-confidence is always attractive in a woman."

"You should have seen me play drums in an all-girl high school punk band. I was entirely adequate at that."

"No doubt."

The danger with a guy like this, Evelyn knew, he could waste your time and you didn't even mind. You enjoyed wasting time with him, and then before you knew it, time was up and you hadn't gotten anywhere.

"I don't mind if you try to charm me, Shake. It's working. I am charmed, totally. But I feel like we've got a star-crossed thing going on here. Like you love the Giants and I'm all about the Dodgers? I just don't see a fairy-tale wedding in our future. Do you? I think we work better as friends."

He didn't say anything for a second. "Is this about the Armenians in L.A.?"

"Yes. I want you to help me take them down."

"You followed me all the way to Cairo because you want me to help you take down the Armenians in L.A.?" He laughed, amazed.

"I was on vacation and I was bored," she said, a little defensively. "I had a ton of frequent-flyer miles. My daughter's the kind of girl who studies for finals the week before finals, so she didn't want to drive up the coast for a mother-daughter getaway."

"So you followed me to Cairo."

"You've got everything on the Armenians, Shake. I know you do. If you help me, I can slam them. And then I can help you."

"Evelyn," he said. Mildly. "You know I did my full bid at Mule Creek because I wouldn't dime out Lexy Ilandryan?"

"You won't be stupid twice. I can tell you've grown as a human being."

"Stupid."

"She tried to have you killed a couple of years ago. That's what I heard."

"We worked that out. She had her reasons, actually."

"And I heard that the two of you, before that, were something of an item."

"It was star-crossed. You know how that goes."

Evelyn caught him glancing at his watch. He wanted to wrap this up for some reason, probably nefarious. That gave Evelyn the advantage. She could keep this going until he sweated through his shorts.

He'd caught her catching him glancing at his watch.

"How old's your daughter?" he said. Like he had all the time in the world to sit and chat. "What's her name?"

"Seventeen going on thirty-nine. A mature thirty-nine. Sarah."

"In high school I never studied for finals at all."

"Neither did I. I have this theory that she might have been switched at birth. Do you want to hear it?"

"I'm not going to dime out the Armenians."

"Somebody's trying to kill you, Shake."

"Not the Armenians."

"Somebody is. I was there, remember? I can help you with that."

"There's the carrot."

"What makes you think there's a stick?"

"That's been my experience."

"The Armenians won't be happy if they find out we're friends."

"I think three years at Mule Creek buys me the benefit of the doubt."

"Let me try another one."

"Another stick."

"It's your fault. You don't want to hear about my carrots."

"Whack away."

"Well, whatever you and the international man of mystery are doing here in Cairo, the Mysterious Mr. Quinn, my hunch is it's sketchy and delicate. My hunch as the daughter of a cop. My hunch, Shake, is it might suck for you if somebody clumsy like me barged around and upset the applecart."

Another ripple across his cool pool. Nice.

"The watermelon cart."

"Okay."

"You don't have jurisdiction here. Even if we were doing something sketchy."

"Which you're not. Yada yada."

Evelyn left it at that. He knew, and she knew, that she only needed jurisdiction if she wanted to arrest somebody. She needed no jurisdiction to barge around and ask questions and upset something delicate.

"Is her father in the picture?" he said. "Sarah's?"

"Define 'father.' Define 'picture.' Didn't you ever want to settle down?"

"I tried. Somebody blew up my restaurant."

"I can help you try again."

"Thanks for saving my life, by the way."

"My motives were mostly selfish."

"I'm never gonna dime out Lexy Ilandryan."

"Give me one good reason why not. Two good reasons."

He smiled, but then one corner of his smile lost energy. He shifted on the sofa. Evelyn glanced over. The elevator door had opened while they were talking. A woman stood inside, watching them. She was very pretty. Maybe thirty years old, slender, great boots, great bangs. Her boots and her haircut probably cost more, separately, than Evelyn's Subaru.

The woman walked over and looked down at Shake. She looked down at Evelyn, at Evelyn's arm along the back of the sofa behind him. She looked at Shake again.

She was even prettier up close. Howzah. Evelyn felt suddenly self-conscious. She felt too tall, awkwardly jointed, jet-lagged. But she also could tell, Shake shifting around on the sofa, that she'd discovered another one of his pressure points. This woman was it, somehow. Nice.

"Hi," Evelyn said. She gave the woman a big friendly smile. "Who the fuck are you?"

THE MINUTE THE ELEVATOR DOOR opened, Gina made the tall brunette as a cop. So why, then, was she snuggled up next to Shake on the red velvet sofa? Why—*the fuck*—was he giggling like a schoolboy and mooning all over her?

"Hi," Gina said. "My name's Gina. You have the prettiest smile!"

"Evelyn. I love your bangs. I can never pull off bangs."

The brunette cop's face looked to Gina like one designer had started the work but then another designer with a different aesthetic had been brought in to finish up. Asian contemporary over here, American traditional over there. Somehow, improbably, it all worked. Her smile brought it all together.

"Your forehead is wrong for bangs," Gina said. "It takes a certain kind of forehead."

"I know!"

Gina couldn't decide if it made her feel better or worse that the cop was at least ten years older than she was. Faint lines around her eyes, the line of her jaw starting to soften. But she still looked great. She was the kind of woman who would still look great at fifty, sixty, forever.

So what—*the fuck*—did it mean that Shake had been mooning over an attractive woman his own age?

Shake was trying to catch Gina's eye. Gina was making a point not to let him.

"So what kind of cop are you?" she said.

The question didn't seem to surprise her, but she waited a while before she answered.

"I'm trying to think of something funny to say but I can't," the cop said.

"Don't you hate that?" Gina said.

"FBI. I give up."

"FBI. Neat!"

Gina finally let Shake catch her eye. Now that he had it, he had no idea what to do with it. He gazed off into the distance.

"We've been chatting about the sketchy shit Shake and the Mysterious Mr. Quinn are up to in Cairo. You're not mixed up with them in any sketchy shit, are you? I just know you're not."

Gina turned to Shake. "You're mixed up in some sketchy shit? How many times have I warned you?"

"Let's go to dinner," Shake said. He stood up.

"Why don't you join us?" Gina asked the cop. "We'd love it if you joined us."

Gina thought that Shake was going to have an embolism trying to stay cool. The cop saw it too and laughed.

"We'll all hang out together another time," she said. "You have my word."

Chapter 36

S hake waited for Gina to unload on him. She let him wait.

They watched Evelyn cross the lobby and exit the hotel.

"I guess dinner's off," Shake said.

"Really?" Gina said. "But why?"

They took the elevator upstairs. Quinn was just leaving his room.

"We need to talk, Harry," Gina said.

"Absolutely," he said. "Though if this is something that can wait? I only ask because that nice British lady I met earlier, we were planning to have dinner in the gardens. They're serving this delicacy the Egyptians are famous for. They take a pigeon and stuff it with nuts."

Shake shook his head. Quinn couldn't have had a buddy with a scheme in Bologna or Paris or Bangkok? Somewhere people knew how to eat?

"Your boy Shake has an FBI agent on his ass," Gina said. "Did you know about that?"

Quinn frowned and led them back into his room. He shut and bolted the door. "He never mentioned that," he said. "No, in fact."

"I didn't mention it because I didn't know," Shake said.

"Really?" Gina said. "You two seemed awfully chummy to me."

"I know her. I didn't know she was FBI."

"The FBI agent on your ass is here?" Quinn said. "In Cairo? Now? God Almighty, Shake."

Gina took a seat. She seemed perfectly happy, for the moment, to let Quinn do the unloading on Shake.

"I was surprised too," Shake said.

An understatement. When he'd opened his eyes and seen Evelyn sitting there on the sofa next to him, he'd just about fallen off the sofa. He put it together pretty fast, that she must be some kind of cop, but when she told him she was FBI and that she'd followed him all the way to Cairo so he'd dime out the Armenians, he'd just about fallen off the sofa again.

"That's it?" Quinn said. "That's all you got to say? You were surprised?"

Shake sighed and filled them in. He explained how he met Evelyn in San Pedro. How he thought she was just your typical tourist. How she'd pulled a gun and saved his life on the beach after his restaurant blew up.

"Was the gun maybe a clue?" Gina asked. "That she wasn't your typical tourist?"

"I didn't give it a lot of thought at the time," Shake said. "There were so many people trying to kill me I was losing track."

"You never told me about some woman saving your life on the beach," Quinn said.

"I'm telling you now."

"What aren't you telling us now?" Gina said. "That's the part I'm curious about."

"I'm telling you everything."

Everything, of course, except that he'd been attracted to Evelyn back in Belize and was still attracted to her. Shake left that part out. Gina knew it already. Shake didn't know how long she'd been watching them from the elevator, but it had been long enough.

"Let me get this straight," Quinn said. "We're on the eve of a big score. Score of a lifetime, tricky and dangerous, as previously discussed. And suddenly we discover there's an FBI agent on your ass, and she's here in Cairo. Is that about the size of it?"

"Another thing I'm curious about," Gina asked Shake. "Were you and Miss FBI planning to do it right there on that couch? In the hotel lobby? I worry about your back is all, Shake. At your age. Because it looked like you were about to flip her skirt up and go to town right there on the couch."

Shake didn't think Gina was really jealous. Evelyn was pushing forty, she was a cop. She might be attractive and smart, tough and funny, and she seemed interestingly complicated in a way that only a woman pushing forty could be, but . . .

Shit.

"It gets worse," Shake said. To Quinn, but that put the brakes on Gina.

Shake told them how Evelyn had threatened to hink their score if he didn't agree to dime out the Armenians.

"Well, it's been fun, fellas," Gina said. She stood up.

"Now just hold on," Quinn said. "Let's think this through."

The guy, Shake had to give it to him, he never stayed down for long.

"It's not the end of the world," Shake heard himself saying. He thought it might actually be, in terms of their score, but he didn't want to see Gina walk out that door. That would be the end of the world for Shake. The end of something.

Or maybe, Shake worried, Quinn's demented optimism had rubbed off on him, God help us all.

"You're both cu-fucking-ckoo," Gina said.

"I'm just saying let's think it through," Quinn said. "Let's sleep on it. Because what does this change? We were gonna have to be extremely careful one way or another, whether there's an FBI agent on Shake's ass or not."

"She doesn't have any idea about Devane," Shake said. "Or Teddy Roosevelt's speech. She's just punching in the dark and hoping she hits something."

"Yeah she is!" Gina said.

"She doesn't have jurisdiction. I doubt she's even supposed to be here, not officially."

"She must be smitten."

"This FBI gal," Quinn said. "She's bluffing."

"Does she seem to you like the kind of gal who bluffs?" Gina asked Shake.

Shake hesitated. "No."

"I don't think so either."

"When's that ever scared you?" he asked her.

"Don't do that," Gina said. "Asshole. You have no right."

"God Almighty," Quinn said. "Will you two just go ahead and jump in the sack already?"

"This isn't about jumping in the sack," Gina said.

"No," Shake agreed. "That was never the problem."

"Then buy the girl an engagement ring, or you, tell him it's over for good and put him out of his misery. Both of you, I don't care, get your heads in the goddamn game."

Shake didn't say anything. Gina didn't say anything.

"I apologize for being brusque," Quinn said. "All I'm saying, I'm saying let's just all of us get a good night's sleep and in the morning we revisit the issue of the FBI gal on Shake's ass, decide in the light of day if it's a deal breaker or not. Okay?"

Shake waited to see if Gina would answer first. But he knew she never would, not in a million years.

"Okay," he said.

"Whatever," Gina said.

Chapter 37

Babb waited until a little after midnight, then strolled up to the hotel. The metal detector in the lobby didn't worry him because he didn't have any metal on him that might be detected. Gardenhire had made arrangements.

At the metal detector in the lobby, Babb pretended to be rumpled and ruffled. He pretended he needed a pot of coffee. That darn message alignment, harrumph, harrumph. The soldiers barely glanced at him. Babb collected his wallet and change from the tray and continued on.

Gardenhire had made arrangements for the gun to be placed behind an ice machine on the third floor. A suppressor too. Babb was ambivalent about an arrangement like this. It took a lot of the sauce off a job, to be honest. Some of the sauce.

He used the house phone in the lobby to request, in a rumpled, ruffled way, immediate housecleaning for room 519. Babb picked that number because May 19 was his birthday.

He went to the fifth floor and waited. A few minutes later a housekeeper pushed her cart out of the service elevator. She knocked lightly on the door to room 519. No answer. It was almost one o'clock in the morning. The housekeeper used her key to let herself into the room. Babb walked quickly toward the housekeeping cart she'd left in the hallway.

A commotion had erupted in room 519. What's going on? Who are you? So sorry! Housekeeping! What? So sorry! What's going on, honey? You called for housekeeping! We did not! So sorry!

Or so Babb imagined, since the commotion was in Arabic.

He plucked the clipboard from the housekeeping cart without slowing down and continued on to the privacy of the fire stairs.

The clipboard listed the names and room numbers of every guest in the hotel. Babb ran his finger down the list. Only about half the rooms were occupied. *Cleary, Quentin* was in room 1011. That was Quinn's Armenian mob bodyguard, Bouchon, the alias he used. Across the hall, in room 1012, was *Clement, Gina*. The woman Babb had seen with the bodyguard, she'd joined the gang in San Francisco. Next door to her, in room 1013, was *Atwood, Fritz*. That was Quinn, the primary target, his nom de guerre. There were no other guests on that side of the floor.

Babb always had a hard time deciding whom to kill first. It was a big decision! There were so many variables to consider. In general, logistical concerns aside, Babb liked to save the best for last. But that in itself, a definition of *best,* was complicated. And people could surprise you. Who tried to scream, who tried to fight back, who mutely accepted the cool breeze of fate, a look of sullen aggrievement in his or (usually, when it came to sullen aggrievement) her eyes. *Oh, fate,* those eyes seemed to say, *what shit have you pulled on me now?*

This hotel didn't have cameras in the hallways, and Gardenhire had made arrangements for a master key card to be left with the gun. Babb took the fire stairs up to the tenth floor. He slipped the master key card into the slot of room 1012. He'd decided to kill the woman first. It just seemed appropriate. Ladies first?

The lock turned green. Babb opened the door. It was not bolted. He was disappointed, a little. He knew several different ways, each of them simple and elegant, to get past the bolt of a hotel room door. He could have taught a child to do it. Hotels didn't want their guests to know how easy it was to get past a bolted hotel door.

He slipped inside the room. Dark, the drapes pulled. He could tell instantly that the room was empty, but he checked anyway. It was empty.

Okay, Babb told himself. *Hmmm.* Maybe the woman was across the hall in the bodyguard's bed. A double Dutch. That would add some sauce to the job.

Don't get your hopes up, he told himself.

Babb told himself, in the hotel on the bank of the Nile, not to get his hopes up.

He let himself into the room across the hall. That room was empty too. The bed was empty.

Well, crap, Babb thought. Because he'd gone and let himself get his hopes up.

He checked the bodyguard's closet and drawers. Empty. There was no toothbrush next to the sink.

Babb went back to the woman's room. Nothing in the closet, nothing in the dresser, no toothbrush next to the sink. The same situation in Quinn's room.

The three of them were gone.

But why? To where? Not too far. Babb had a feeling.

It was a mystery, but Babb didn't mind. He liked mysteries. He liked a job with sauce.

"MOHAMMED," EVELYN SAID. "HEADS UP. There they are."

Evelyn and her driver had been lurking for a couple of hours. Down the drive from the hotel, parked across the street, with a good view of the main entrance. Mohammed sitting on the hood of his spotless

Mercedes and working his way steadily through a pack of unfiltered Camels. Evelyn sitting next to him, using her hand to beat away the smoke. Assuring Mohammed that everything he'd learned about the FBI from American TV shows and movies was exactly accurate. Mohammed practicing his English by waxing nostalgic about his salad days as a dive instructor, long ago, in Hurghada, a city on the Red Sea.

Mohammed was close to fifty years old, but the joys of Hurghada made him squeal like a teenage girl. "Oh, my Gaaaawwwd, Evelyn! The water so clear! You do not believe it!"

Evelyn had started asking certain questions just to hear him squeal.

Was the fish tasty and fresh in Hurghada, Mohammed?

The fish, Evelyn, oh, my Gaaawwwd!

"I see them," he said. He took a long last drag of his latest Camel and flicked it away.

Gina had a roller bag, as did the International Man of Mystery. Shake was carrying a plastic sack. Evelyn had thought they might switch hotels after she dropped in on them. She loved being right.

She and Mohammed got back in the Mercedes. Mohammed started the car. They watched a hotel bellhop load the roller bags into the trunk of a cab. Shake, Gina, and the International Man of Mystery squeezed into the backseat. The cab looped around, drove down the drive, and turned left just across the street from where Mohammed and Evelyn sat idling.

Evelyn waited until the cab was a block away, two blocks. Mohammed eyed her.

"Yalla bina!" she said. Mohammed had taught her that phrase. He said it meant "Let's go!" in Arabic.

"Giddyup!" he said, the phrase that Evelyn had taught him back, as he swung into traffic behind the cab.

Chapter 38

Gina had forgotten to pull the drapes in the new room last night. Dawn went off like a bomb. She groaned and lifted her head off the pillow and squinted. She peeled a strand of her hair off her lips. Jet lag. She'd just about had it up to here, sister, with jet lag.

Their new hotel was even swankier than the last one, with fantastic toiletries in the bathroom. It had been Gina's idea last night to switch hotels, but the guys had been thinking the same thing too. Their new hotel was across the bridge and closer to the center of town, just off the main square.

She reached for the glass of water on the nightstand and drank. "Want some?" she said.

Shake was awake too, squinting and groggy. "We forgot to pull the drapes."

"Wonder why?"

"Give it."

She handed him the glass. He drank what she'd left him.

Last night they'd taken a cab to their new hotel and booked three rooms using the name on Gina's fall-back passport. *Katherine Keel.* Quinn had made a beeline for the hotel bar while Gina and Shake had taken the elevator upstairs together. They hadn't said a word to each other the whole way up.

"So?" Shake said when they got to their rooms. His room was across the hall from hers.

"So what?" she said.

"So are you gonna take Quinn's advice? Finally tell me it's over between us and put me out of my misery?"

"I like your misery."

He kissed her. She let him. Well, she did more than let him.

"What was that other thing Quinn said we should go ahead and do?" he said. "Something about the sack? Jumping in it?"

"I'm not jealous of Little Miss FBI. I want to make that clear."

"It wasn't already?" He looked genuinely surprised. He better have.

"It's over between us," she said, then kissed him again.

"That's a relief," he said, and kissed her back.

It took them about half a heartbeat to get from the hallway into her room and across the room and into the sack. It was like they'd teleported there, and out of their clothes.

Now, this morning, Gina didn't know how she felt about what had happened. It was hard to know how you felt about anything with a hard bright desert dawn exploding in your face.

She knew how she felt about the sex itself. The sex had been good. She'd been aching to feel Shake's weight pressed against her again, inside her, through her. She'd been aching to kiss him and taste him and burn her lips on the stubble along his chin. Plus she'd been pretty horny in a general sense too. It wasn't all soft-focus curtains billowing in the breeze.

Shake hadn't learned any new tricks in their two years apart. Or he was smart enough not to show them to her. She showed him a few new tricks of her own, just to make him suffer. Okay, okay, she doubted the new tricks had made him suffer much.

"This doesn't mean what you think it means," she said.

"What do I think it means?"

"That all is forgiven and forgotten and we're back together now."

He didn't say anything.

"If you buy me an engagement ring like Harry told you to," she said, "I really will kill you."

"Is it such a bad idea?"

"It is."

She got out of bed and walked to the window. Stretched. The warmth of the sun felt good on her bare boobs.

"Put your boots on," he said.

She turned, surprised. This was a first in her experience, if she did say so herself. "You want me to get dressed?"

"I didn't say that."

He smiled. She got back into bed.

Later, quite a bit later, they ordered room service and ate in bed.

"Next time I'm not going anywhere that doesn't have really good food," Shake said. "Italy or Thailand. Mexico."

"Next time."

"The hummus is decent. But I just can't get excited about hummus."

"This brings back memories, doesn't it?" she said.

"Yes."

"That was your plan."

"Yes."

"But last time, remember, everything ended up sideways."

She wanted to see how he'd respond to that. He went for the safe play.

"I think we can pull this off," he said. "There are a lot of moving parts, but Devane is too smart for his own good."

"Harry's a liability. You know that, right? I love the guy, Shake, but."

"All he has to do is stay on script."

She looked at him. He didn't say anything.

"Is it worse than I think?" she said.

"That first time in my restaurant, he kept calling the guy a punk, the guy who was trying to shoot him."

"While the guy was trying to shoot him?"

"And he hijacked a snorkel boat." He moved the room-service tray to the floor. "I need a shower."

"Shake," she said.

"What?"

"Tell me you haven't even considered it."

"What?"

He knew very well what she was talking about.

"I'm not cutting a deal with Logan James," he said.

"He wants Harry, not you. Give Harry up and it could save your life."

"That's debatable."

"It's worth a try."

"No."

"Why? Is Harry the father you never had?"

Shake laughed. "God help me."

"He drives you crazy."

"You think?"

"But you haven't considered giving him up to Logan James, not for a minute."

"I haven't."

She believed him. It astounded Gina, but she believed him. It also astounded her, it really did, that she wouldn't want Shake any other way. She scooted closer and laid her head on his chest.

"Tell me why it's such a bad idea," he said. "Getting you an engagement ring."

"You were right," she said after a minute.

"About what?"

"I would have left you."

He took hold of her chin and tilted her head up so he could look into her eyes.

"What?" he said.

She sighed. "You said you left because you were scared I'd leave you first."

"Go on."

"I mean, I wasn't planning to leave you. It wasn't, like, impending. And I wouldn't have just dropped a fucking note on the kitchen table and hopped a plane, by the way, let's get that clear."

"But."

This was the problem with the truth, Gina thought. Fuck the truth! When did telling the truth, or admitting it to yourself, ever make you feel anything but shitty?

She'd been so happy back in Santa Monica with Shake. She couldn't have been happier. But.

She twisted her chin loose from his hand and laid her head back on his chest.

"I was scared too," she said.

"That I'd leave you?"

"No! Are you kidding? I never in a million years thought you'd be that big an idiot."

"Okay. So what were you scared of?"

She had been scared of getting bored. She had been scared that she might already be bored. There was one kind of happiness that was a state of equilibrium, there was another kind of happiness that was—the opposite of that. That was the kind of happiness that Gina had always known and loved.

"You remember how we'd walk down to the Palisades every night and watch the sunset?"

"You didn't like watching the sunset?"

"I did. But sometimes you'd watch the sunset and I'd watch the planes taking off from LAX. I'd watch a plane take off for parts unknown and I'd get, I don't know, a tingle."

"Why didn't you say something?"

She just laughed.

"And now?" he said.

"I think I've changed."

"You're ready to settle down?"

"Exactly. It's just exactly that simple."

His warm hand rested on her shoulder. Her cheek rested on his warm chest. Underneath the smell of hotel soap and sex and swanky cotton sheets, he had a very distinct smell. Shake's smell was like coming home.

"You know I'm aware," he said. "What you might be doing right now. You should be aware that I don't care. I'll take it."

"I'm not doing it right now," she said. She needed to pee, but it felt so nice lying here with him. "Yesterday at breakfast, you were up at the buffet, Harry was telling me his whole big plan for fertility tourism."

"Lucky you."

"It's not the world's worst idea, actually."

"Gina," Shake said. "We're right for each other."

"So what if we are?"

"Would you say yes if I bought you a ring?"

"Probably not."

"But you don't know what you'd say."

"Don't buy me a ring. That puts a girl on the spot."

"Maybe I want to put you on the spot."

"Did you know it at the time, that I was watching planes take off from LAX and not the sunset?"

"I thought you were watching the Ferris wheel down on the pier. It was hard to tell, you always had sunglasses on."

"Sometimes I was watching the Ferris wheel. Most of the time I was watching the sunset."

Her burner cell, on the nightstand, buzzed. Devane was the only one who had the number.

"Looks like we're on, sport," she told Shake. "Better get your head in the game."

Chapter 39

Shake checked his watch. It was going to be a busy day.

Devane had told Gina he'd be at the hotel at three to show them Roosevelt's speech. Gina had tried to bump him back a few hours to buy them time, she'd tried her best, but Devane had said take three o'clock or leave it. Shake knew Devane wanted to put them under the gun. It was the smart, suspicious play. He deserved a tip of the porkpie hat.

So that gave them—Shake checked his watch again—less than five hours to make sure they had all their corners squared away.

Five hours. Like this wasn't gonna be hard enough already.

On the other hand, this kind of pace gave you less time to worry about one of Devane's Egyptian ex–secret service goons shooting you in the face. That was the silver lining.

Quinn's job was to hunt down Mahmoud. Who had not yet produced the exact twin of Devane's black leather attaché case as he had promised. Who had not returned the voice-mail messages that Quinn left him.

"I'm not worried," Quinn said, looking worried.

Gina was going to contact her computer hacker guy back in San Francisco. Devane had demanded they have proof, the minute he walked in the door, that Roland Ziegler possessed the necessary funds for a minimum bid. Seven and a half million dollars. Most of Gina's ready cash was tied up in her business, so she needed her computer guy to work his magic. Shake didn't understand the details, not a single one of them, but the gist was the computer guy would create some kind of shell account. A shell within a shell on a mirror. With lots of smoke blown across the surface of the mirror. Devane would open his laptop between 3:00 and 3:09 Cairo time, punch in some numbers, a password, and then see—"see"—that Roland Ziegler—"Roland Ziegler"— had plenty of cash ready to transfer.

Maybe. Fingers crossed.

Gina looked a little worried too.

"What is it?" Shake said.

"He'll need a little coaxing," she said. "My hacker. Hackers are total sociopaths, but they're scared to death of doing time."

Shake had his own job to do. Two jobs, both critical. Three jobs. What wasn't critical, at this point?

He walked through the lobby of the hotel and out into the heat, the honking. He stood there for a second before he remembered to wave for a cab.

He was trying to keep his head in the game, but it was hard not to drift back to last night with Gina, this morning, everything. He had hope. He was practically bouncing off the walls with it.

But that, in his experience, was when you needed to be most careful. When everything seemed to breaking just right for you, when the morning sun lit up a beautiful woman's naked body right in front of you, the woman you loved.

Shake remembered the real Roland Ziegler. The real Roland Ziegler had been feeling pretty good about himself back in Panama City three years ago, about to walk away with both the money and the merchandise, back to his private island in the Caribbean. Next thing he knew, his hopes had gone up in smoke and he was staring at twenty years in the federal lock.

It was like poker. You might be zooming right along, a killer hand, picking up speed on the flop and the turn. But the game wasn't over yet. That last card, the river, it could jerk you around fast. Shake knew it.

EVELYN SLEPT TILL NINE, HAD some coffee, and called Mohammed. She asked him to meet her in half an hour at the hotel.

"Your hotel?" he asked.

"Their hotel," she said.

Mohammed was alarmed. "No, Evelyn. I will pick you up!"

She told him no, she was going to walk. She needed the fresh air and cardio, what with all the secondhand unfiltered Camel smoke she'd sucked down yesterday.

Her hotel, as luck would have it, was only a couple of blocks from the new hotel that Shake and Company had checked into. Their hotel was much swankier than hers. Was it true that crime paid? If Evelyn had to break it down, based on her experience in law enforcement, she'd say it probably paid a fair amount of the time.

It took her half an hour to walk the two blocks. Cairo traffic—so much for fresh air.

Mohammed was waiting for her, parked down the block and across the street from the new hotel. They took their seats on the hood of the Mercedes. Mohammed stripped the cellophane off a fresh pack of Camels and Evelyn sent Sarah a text. *What time is it there? Luv u bunches.*

The reply came back a second later. *Midnight. Mom, I cannot believe you actually went to Egypt.*

Midnight!?! U r not in bed yet?! i m so disappointed in u!

I AM in bed. You woke me UP.

You forgive me.

Sarah didn't text back for a long time. Evelyn wondered if she'd fallen asleep.

Dad is mad at you. For going to Egypt and not telling him.

Why the fuck does he give a fuck? Evelyn thought.

OK, she texted back.

He said I could have stayed with him and Lilly instead of Aunt Katie.

What a responsible, attentive, considerate parent Andre was! The asshole.

Every guy has a mustache here. It's like Magnum PI wherever you turn. Don't be mad at him, Mom.

Mohammed nudged Evelyn with his elbow. Evelyn had already seen: Shake standing outside the hotel entrance, looking kind of stupefied. Finally he raised his hand to hail a cab.

Gotta go. Yella beena! Love you bunches.

They tailed Shake's cab through town and across a bridge. His cab dropped him off at the pyramids.

The pyramids! "My daughter would flip out," Evelyn told Mohammed.

He double-parked behind a tour bus. Evelyn got out and tailed Shake on foot. She gave him a block, just to be safe, even though there were tons of tourists milling around. He walked down the street and stopped in front of the Sphinx.

The Sphinx!

He stood for a long time in front of the Sphinx, just staring up at it. Then he walked over to a little café and took a seat at a table. He ordered coffee, or tea. Evelyn couldn't be sure which, from a distance.

What the hell was he doing? Sipping his coffee, or tea, and gazing up at the Sphinx. He didn't look like a guy mixed up in sketchy shit at all. After he finished his drink, he paid the waiter and found another cab. Evelyn and Mohammed tailed this cab back over the bridge. It dropped Shake off on the edge of a small crowded square, across from a big mosque. Shake crossed the square and turned down an alley.

"Ah," Mohammed said, peering through the windshield of the Mercedes. "Khan el-Khalili."

"Khan el-Khalili?"

"Yes! Very famous."

"For what?"

Mohammed pondered. "Souvenir."

What? A little sightseeing, some souvenir shopping. What the hell? Evelyn started to get out of the Mercedes.

"Wait," Mohammed said. "Listen to me. *La shukran.*"

"What?"

"*La shukran.*" He said it slowly. "Say it to me."

"*La shukran.* Why? What is it?"

"It means 'No, thank you.' Say it again, please."

She thought he'd lost his mind. "*La shukran,* Mohammed, *la shukran.*"

Evelyn crossed the square and turned down the alley that Shake had turned down. The alley was insanely narrow, crammed with shops and shoppers and shopkeepers. All the shopkeepers were men, with mustaches, most of them wearing the long cotton caftans that a lot of Egyptian men wore. They spotted Evelyn and, oh, wow, it was like the running of the bulls, but at her.

"Where you from?"

"Please look! No cost to look!"

"Special price! One pound only!"

"You like this, I promise!"

"No cost to look, please enter!"

"Where you from?"

"*La shukran!*" Evelyn said. "*La shukran!*"

The nearest shopkeeper feigned surprise. "You are from *la shukran?* I do not know this place! Where is this place?"

"*La shukran!* Hey! Watch it! *La shukran!*"

They didn't touch her, but if she stepped left, so did they. If she faked left and stepped right, so did they. Evelyn saw that Shake, about a hundred feet up the alley, had been waylaid too. A shopkeeper had dragged him over to his shop.

"Here, special price, you may hold it," a shopkeeper told Evelyn. He forced a stone jar into her hands before she knew what he was doing. The lid of the jar was the head of a—dog? Coyote?

"*La shukran,*" Evelyn said, trying to hand the jar back. But her shopkeeper had his hands behind his back now, and she couldn't just drop it.

Shake's shopkeeper was showing him one of the long cotton caftans, a sort of dusty lavender color, holding it up so Shake could see how snazzy it would look on him.

"Please, miss," Evelyn's shopkeeper said. "I make a special deal for you. Ten pounds. Have pity, miss. I must feed the mouths of my family. You have a very good eye, miss, you select the very most excellent jar. I see you know this business. This price, I lose money, I barely feed the mouths of my children. The quality is excellent, you can see that, I see. The jar is yours now, you have picked it, I cannot take it back. Please do not waste my time, I am a very busy man."

And then he gave her a wink, like this was all in good fun, of course.

And then he frowned, like of course it wasn't, he had to feed the mouths of his family.

And then he frowned differently, like she better buy the jar or else, all the time of his she'd wasted.

Evelyn was impressed. "You're good," she said. "You should go to Hollywood and be an agent."

"You are from Hollywood! I know Hollywood! My cousin lives there. I give you a special discount."

"How much is it?" Evelyn sighed. She knew when she was beat. "Ten Egyptian pounds? It's like two dollars, isn't it? I only have American."

"Ten pound *British,*" the shopkeeper said. "Oh, no. You have mistaken me."

"Oh, for God's sake," Evelyn said. She handed over an American five. Her shopkeeper looked scandalized, then wounded, then resigned. He trudged back into his shop to wrap up her dog-headed stone jar in newspaper. He brought back three more jars that he said completed the set, an extra five bucks each, how could she refuse, she had already agreed in principle, had she not, and he had already gone to all the trouble of wrapping them too.

Evelyn saw Shake buying one of the lavender caftans. Apparently his shopkeeper was as relentless as Evelyn's. Then Shake pointed to something inside the shop. The shopkeeper nodded. Evelyn watched Shake step into the shop and disappear.

EVELYN WAS GOOD. SHAKE GAVE her that. She did almost everything right. But of course he spotted her, about thirty seconds after he left the hotel. Shake had spent most of his professional life making sure he didn't have a tail, and shaking them when he did.

She'd surprised him once, yesterday. She wouldn't do it again.

The cabdriver who picked Shake up at the Sphinx was a young kid, midtwenties, his English as good as Shake's. Probably better. Shake said something about it and the kid told Shake that he had an engineering degree. With the economy tanking since the revolution, though, he was lucky to have a job driving a cab. Still, he was glad the revolution had happened.

Shake asked him if he knew where he could buy a—he forgot the word for a second. A galabiya.

"Sure," the kid said. "I know a place. It's close by. And it's quality stuff, not like most tourists buy. Locals shop there. It's just up the street. You could probably just walk, if you want."

"You need to get the hang of this cab-driving racket," Shake said.

The kid grimaced. "Tell me about it."

"Listen," Shake said. "Is there a place, like a shopping area, lots of shops, crowded? Lots of tourists? Is there a place like that where I can get a galabiya? As far away as you want, keep the meter running."

The kid checked him out in the rearview mirror. "Sure," he said.

He dropped Shake at a square across from a mosque and pointed him down an alley. Shake made sure Evelyn had time to catch up. He couldn't see her, she was good, but Shake knew she was there.

Shake walked up the alley. It was nuts. Tourists wall to wall and the vendors were ferocious. He wondered how they'd do with Quinn. Probably, five minutes with Quinn, these guys would be down on their knees in surrender, begging Quinn to just take the goddamn plaster pharaoh head, on the house, mister, just shut up about the one time you met a pharaoh and gave him the idea for the pyramids, unofficially, of course.

There she was.

Evelyn was six or seven shops behind him. Almost hidden by the crowd. Almost. Shake bought two galabiyas, plus some small stone beetles he thought Idaba back in Belize might like. He paid way too much for everything, forty bucks American, but the guy who ran the shop was now Shake's best friend for life, or at least for the next five minutes.

"Is that a door?" Shake said. "In the back of your shop? You mind if I go that way?"

"By all means, my friend." The guy thumbing the two twenties that Shake had given him to make sure they were real. "By all means."

Shake squeezed through the galabiya shop and pushed the back door open. He found himself in another alley, this one even narrower, but less crowded. Next to the door was a big steel trash barrel, just the right height. Shake dragged it over, tipped it up, wedged it under the handle of the door.

He tested it and nodded. Evelyn wasn't getting through that door.

Good-bye, Evelyn.

Shake moved fast up the alley, back toward the square. He'd told his cabdriver to circle around and meet him back at the square. But when Shake got to the end of the alley, the edge of the square, he stopped.

Evelyn was standing there, waiting for him.

"In your defense," she said, "I came this close to taking the bait."

"In my defense," he said, "it's worked before."

"What did you buy?"

"Galabiyas."

"Is that what they're called? I got four fake stone jars that weigh a ton and were probably made in China."

"Those guys are sharks. I've never seen anything like it."

"They're fucking hammerheads. Can I buy you coffee? Or is it tea?"

Shake sighed. "I could use a beer."

NONE OF THE JOINTS NEARBY sold alcohol. Finally they found a T.G.I. Friday's that did.

Shake tried an Egyptian beer, Sakara. Not bad. He might have enjoyed it under different circumstances.

"Did you ever think that one day you'd be having a beer at a T.G.I. Friday's in Cairo, Egypt?" Evelyn said. "Bet you didn't."

"And with an FBI agent. No." He shook his head. "Safe to say."

She took a sip of her beer. "How can a Muslim country make its own beer? I don't get that."

"Their beer is better than their food," he said.

"What are you talking about? Have you tried the hummus? It's fantastic."

He just grunted.

"And something they call 'old cheese' is good," she said. "Which, I agree, could use a more tempting name."

"What do I have to do to get you to stop following me?" Shake said. If he didn't lose her soon, and lose her for good, if he didn't make sure she was nowhere near the hotel when the deal with Devane went down, they were screwed.

"Lose the FBI gal," Quinn had said that morning. "Top of your list, okay?"

"What can you do to get me to stop following you?" Evelyn said. "Let's see. I know!"

"I'm never gonna dime out the Armenians."

"That's what you say now. But we haven't finished our beers yet."

"You're the fucking hammerhead shark."

"Stop. You're making me blush."

"I'm serious. Are you out of your mind? Coming all the way to Cairo?"

She looked wistful as she sipped her beer. "Probably a little I am. I've never been the greatest investigator. You know, the slow and steady, the paperwork, all the federal bur-ese. I probably should have washed out at Quantico. My first SAC actually told me that straight up. But what I'm great at is, I don't ever give up."

"Give up," Shake said. "Please."

"And I'm really pissed off at my asshole ex-husband. I think that might be a factor too."

"Your ex-husband?"

"I was so close to nailing the Armenians a few years ago. So close. But my asshole ex totally screwed it up for me. He's the asshole D.A. in Los Angeles."

"Don't take it out on me."

"I'm not! That's what you don't understand."

"You want to be my friend. I forgot." Something clicked and Shake looped back around. "Andre Guardado is your ex-husband?"

"You know him?"

"Not personally. Well, I met him once. Briefly."

"And?"

Shake didn't say anything. He didn't have to.

"See!" Evelyn said. "You thought he was an asshole too!"

"I barely shook the guy's hand," Shake said. But, yes, he had seemed like an asshole.

"It's okay if you think less of me for marrying him and letting him impregnate me," Evelyn said. "I know *I* do. And hey, on a separate topic, what's the deal, asking me to dinner back in Belize when you already had a girlfriend?"

She was trying to spin Shake around. And doing a good job of it.

"She wasn't my girlfriend then. She's not my girlfriend."

"You sound confused."

"I am."

"What were you doing at the Sphinx? I can't figure that out."

"None of your business."

"You're right. Did you and your maybe-girlfriend have sex last night? What positions? Were you a gentleman, if you know what I mean?"

"Evelyn," Shake said, "how long do we have to keep this up?"

"I'm not bluffing, Shake. I enjoy making your life difficult. I could do it all day."

"I believe you. But what's the point of doing that? If I'm never gonna dime out the Armenians?"

"Never say never. Maybe your life just isn't difficult enough yet."

Shake realized who Evelyn reminded him of right now. She reminded him of Lexy Ilandryan, *pakhan* of the Armenian mob in L.A. Superficial details aside, the similarities were uncanny. And frightening.

"I really do like you, Shake. That's not a lie. So work with me. There's got to be a place halfway."

Shake slid his glass of beer aside and leaned closer, elbows on the table.

"I don't know how to make you understand, Evelyn. There's not a place halfway for me. I won't dime out the Armenians. I'm not sure I can even explain why, but I would never do something like that. I was that way as a kid, early as I can remember. I got my ass kicked plenty of times for it, believe me. So do what you want. Make my life even more difficult than it already is. It's your call, no hard feelings, you've got a job to do. But I'm not gonna dime anybody out, ever."

She sipped her beer. "Nice speech. The violins swell." But he thought her tone might have softened a little. Maybe.

Shake stood up. That was it, that was all he had. "Thanks for the beer." He was almost out the door when he stopped and turned back.

"By the way," he said. "Back in Belize, when I asked you to dinner—"

"Stop," she said. "Don't. I don't want to hear it."

He nodded and left.

Chapter 40

Shake made it back to the hotel just under the wire, barely an hour before Devane was due to arrive. Gina and Quinn were waiting up in one of the penthouse suites.

Quinn was annoyed because the best penthouse suite, the presidential, had been booked. They'd had to settle for this one, only fifteen hundred square feet and a grand piano.

"If you're going to play the part," Quinn said, "you have to play the part. You know who would be in the presidential suite? The real Roland Ziegler. A part I should be playing, I'll just mention again, for the record."

"Put this on," Shake said. He handed Quinn one of the purple galabiyas he'd bought.

"We're good with the account hack," Gina said. "As long as Porkpie doesn't start poking around and run the clock out."

"We're good with the gaff," Shake said. "It only cost me a hundred bucks."

"That was some luck," Gina said. "Lucking into that in the first place."

"We're gonna need it," Shake said.

Quinn stripped down to his boxers, socks, and shoes. He pulled the galabiya over his head. Shake and Gina tried not to laugh. Quinn in the long purple dress, with his straight posture and white hair, reminded Shake of the lady in *Sunset Boulevard,* the one who said it was the movies that got small, not her.

"Feel free," Quinn said. "I'm happy to be the object of your derision."

Shake handed him the other galabiya. "Downstairs," he said. "The side entrance, back behind the lobby bar."

"All right," Quinn said. "Did you lose the FBI gal?"

Shake looked around the suite. He didn't see a black leather attaché anywhere.

"Do we have a bigger problem than that?" he said.

"Mahmoud will be here," Quinn said. "I talked to him. He was just waiting for his cousin to bring it over."

"Why rush?" Shake said.

"Did you lose her or not?" Gina asked him.

"I hope so."

Before she could say anything else, the doorbell chimed.

"You see?" Quinn said. He gave Shake a patient, indulgent smile and opened the door. Mahmoud stepped into the suite, grinning and sweating and looking scared out of his mind. He handed Quinn a black leather attaché but was so scared he forgot to let go of the handle. Quinn had to tap his knuckles to remind him.

The attaché was hard-sided, about the size of a regular briefcase, a few inches thicker.

"I am very nervous," Mahmoud apologized, grinning.

You should be, Shake thought.

"Nothing to be nervous about," Quinn said. "This'll be a piece of cake!"

Mahmoud grinned, nodded, and bolted, almost knocking over a housekeeper who was vacuuming the hallway. When he was gone, Shake took the attaché from Quinn. He lifted it, lowered it. Lifted it, lowered it. Gina was thinking the same thing.

"It's empty," she said.

"How many angels can dance on the head of a pin?" Shake said. "How much does a fifty-page speech with a bullet hole in it weigh?"

"Does it matter?" Quinn said.

"It might," Shake said.

Quinn nodded. "You're right, you're right."

Shake didn't see fifty pages of paper lying around. He opened the door and stepped out into the hallway. The housekeeper with the vacuum looked over at him.

"Shampoo?" he said. "Wash hair?"

She nodded. Shake grabbed a few little bottles of shampoo from her cart. He went back inside the suite and dumped the shampoo bottles in the attaché.

Shake lifted and lowered the attaché.

"Inshallah," Quinn said. Shake handed the attaché back. They had about twenty minutes left. Quinn started to leave.

"Wait," Shake said. "Let's just go over it."

"Go over what?"

"Just keep it tight. In and out, nothing unnecessary. No improvisation."

"Stick to the script, Harry," Gina said. "Okay?"

Quinn rose up to his full height. The effect was either more or less impressive because of the galabiya he was wearing. Shake couldn't decide.

"I'm a professional," Quinn said. "I've been a professional since before either of you was a goddamn twinkle in your mother's eye."

Shake was afraid to look at Gina. She was probably afraid to look at him too.

"Go get 'em, Harry," she said.

SHAKE CHANGED INTO HIS SUIT. Ten minutes till showtime. He took a seat on the couch next to the grand piano. Gina took a seat on the couch across from him. A minute passed. Another minute passed.

"I wish we had something to talk about while we wait," she said. "Don't you?"

Chapter 41

Evelyn sat next to Mohammed on the hood of the Mercedes. He'd parked in the shade, across from Shake's hotel, but it was still hot. A dry heat, though, not murderous. Sarah had been right. It was probably a lot worse in the summer.

"In Hurghada," Mohammed said. "The sea breeze is so niiiiice, Evelyn. Oh, my Gaaawd!"

They'd tailed Shake back from the Khan el-Khalili market. He'd entered the hotel and not come out again.

"Do you think I'm a little bit out of my mind, Mohammed?" she said.

He didn't answer. Maybe he didn't understand the question, or maybe he didn't care one way or another, or maybe he thought all American women were a little bit out of their minds.

Evelyn knew, if she was serious about this, that she should send Mohammed to cover the hotel's side entrance and have him call her if he saw Shake come out.

If she was serious about this.

Evelyn thought about what Shake had told her back at T.G.I. Friday's. How he'd never flip on the Armenians in L.A., or anybody else for that matter. She'd heard a version of that speech approximately a thousand times before. Baby Jesus, most recently, had given Evelyn a version of that speech, not long before he broke down and flipped on the Zeta cartel.

But Shake's version of the speech—it was the first time in a thousand times that Evelyn believed the guy giving the speech really meant it. She was pissed at Shake because of all the times she'd told a shithead, "I like you, I do"—also, most recently, Baby Jesus—this was the first time that Evelyn had really meant it.

She was pissed at herself. For coming all the way to Cairo. For going home with nothing. She knew exactly what Cory Nadler would say, his mouth agape in disbelief. He would say:

"Evi, you lunatic, you just busted and then flipped the biggest drug dealer in Belize, and now you're pissed because you couldn't take down the Armenians in L.A. the same week? For God's sake, Evi, what does it take for you to consider it a good week?"

"Busting and flipping the biggest drug dealer in Belize," she would have said back. "And taking down the Armenians in L.A." She would have considered that a good week.

But it wasn't like she was done with the Armenians. Not by a long shot. Shake might be a dead end, Cairo might be a dead end, but Evelyn had plenty more angles to work. She was going to work angles and take down the Armenians if it killed her.

That made her feel better. And, hey. She wasn't going home from Cairo with nothing, was she? She had four stone jars that she'd paid way too much for and would have to lug through three different airports. Mohammed had explained that they were canopic jars, replicas of the jars that ancient Egyptians used when they made a mummy. The lid of one jar was the head of a jackal. The ancient Egyptians put the stomach from the mummy's body in that one. The mummy's intestines went in the jar with the falcon lid, the lungs in the jar with the baboon lid, the liver in the jar with the pharaoh's head.

According to Mohammed, the ancient Egyptians didn't have a jar for the brain. They used a long needle to drag it through the dead person's nose, then tossed it. The heart stayed in the body, so the gods could weigh it in the afterlife and judge the dead by it.

Good for the ancient Egyptians, Evelyn thought. They had their priorities straight.

The driveway of the hotel was buzzing. Check-in time. Evelyn watched expensive cars come and go.

"What did the ancient Egyptians say about gracious defeat?" she asked Mohammed. "What was their position on that? I'm having a hard time getting my head around the concept."

He shrugged and lit another unfiltered Camel. Evelyn sighed and slid off the hood of the Mercedes.

"Okay, partner," she said. "We're done here. I'm going home. Let's get the *yalla bina* out of here."

Chapter 42

Devane called from the lobby a few minutes after three. Gina told him to come on up. Shake sent Quinn a text.

Shake didn't feel like a billionaire swindler who bought high-dollar antiquities. He felt like an ex-con ex-wheelman who used to own a struggling little restaurant in Belize. He felt like that guy, just wearing a suit and sitting in a penthouse suite.

Quinn was right. Quinn should be playing the part of Roland Ziegler. Shake was no good at playing parts other than himself.

The doorbell chimed.

"You'll do just great," Gina said, because she knew that would annoy Shake. She gave him a reassuring pat on the shoulder as she went to answer the door. She knew that would annoy him too.

"I was also a professional," Shake said, "before you were a twinkle in your mother's eye. Or close to it."

"Don't I know it," she said. "You're an old man, I'm well aware."

"I'm forty-four."

She smiled. "And?"

Shake smiled back. He was in a better mood than any guy in his situation had a right to be.

Gina opened the door. Devane, in his straw porkpie hat, was flanked by the two hard-looking Egyptians from the nightclub. He was carrying a black leather attaché case. It looked to Shake just like the one Mahmoud had procured for them. When Devane lifted the case up and set it down on the coffee table, though, Shake could tell it had something inside that weighed less than hotel shampoo.

Oh, well. That train had left the station. There was nothing they could do about it now.

Devane's two bodyguards were armed. They didn't try to hide the bulges in their suit coats. Shake wondered how they'd gotten through the metal detector in the lobby. He supposed it wasn't that hard when your boss was rich and you used to be state security.

"You didn't bring your charming naked Russian prostitute wife," Gina told Devane. "I assume she's your wife? You two seem like a perfect match."

Shake didn't know what any of that meant. He knew, whatever it meant, that Gina was giving Devane a little jiggle, trying to rattle his focus.

Devane glanced her way, cold, and then ignored her.

"Roland Ziegler," he said to Shake. "In the flesh. Last I heard, you were in prison. In the clink, the pokey. A guest of the American federal government."

Devane moved his hands a mile a minute. To mime the pokey, he turned a key in a lock and then threw the key away.

You heard right, Shake started to say. But then he stopped and tried to think how Ziegler himself, the smug smirking prick, would put it.

Fuck. He was taking too long to think. Devane watched him.

Shake tried a smirk. He wasn't good with smirks.

"Is that what a little birdie told you?" he said. "The little birdie didn't tell you the whole story, apparently."

Shake thought he could hear Gina exhale. A little.

"You cut a deal with the *federales*?" Devane said. "Okay. Sure. I heard that too. It's plausible. But how do I know, Roland, that you didn't cut a deal to give me up? Me, *moi*? How do I know you don't have a wire? Though it wouldn't be a wire. It's a patch they use now, a wireless transmitter."

That was calculated stupidity. Shake knew the real Roland Ziegler wouldn't even bother to respond to something that stupid, so Shake just smirked.

It seemed to work. Devane snapped his fingers at Gina. "Laptop," he said.

Gina set the computer they'd borrowed from the hotel on the coffee table next to the black attaché case. Devane sat down on the couch and opened the computer.

"Bank and account number," he said.

Gina handed him a slip of paper. Devane started tapping.

"This is just like in the movies," Gina said. "It's how you like to do things, isn't it? The girls in the club, the bodyguards, the British colonial yacht. Your life is a series of movie clichés."

"How can you stand this bitch?" Devane asked Shake without looking up from the keyboard. "I don't care what she looks like naked."

"Neither do I," Shake said. The biggest lie he'd told so far.

Devane nodded. He finished tapping, looked at the screen for a second, and then shut the lid.

"I know all the tricks," he said. "So if you think I'm gonna shut my eyes now and drift off to dreamland"—he mimed drifting off to dreamland—"just because I see you have some money stashed in some bank. No. Sorry. If you think I trust a wire transfer? I know all the tricks. That was just to see you're viable. I deal in hard cash only, bearer bonds, seventy-two hours to turn it around or the deal is off."

"What deal?" Shake looked at Gina. "Did you make a deal? I didn't make a deal."

She sent him a look that Shake took to mean *You're doing okay, but stop smirking so much, you don't know how to do a smirk right.*

Devane snapped open the attaché case and lifted the lid. Inside, cushioned by custom-cut foam, was Teddy Roosevelt's speech.

The speech was about half an inch thick. Heavy, good-quality paper, the color of old ivory. The corners of the top page had gone a little brown, and there was a brown crease where the manuscript had been folded in half lengthwise. The type was double-spaced, from an old-fashioned typewriter, the letters crowded together. There were a few handwritten notes, almost faded away, in the margins.

The manuscript had been folded when Roosevelt got shot, so there were actually two bullet holes, one on each side of the fold. Small caliber, a .22 or a .38, probably. Shake could see that the bullet had gone all the way through. One hole was neat and clean, almost like it had been drilled, while the other one was a little ragged and torn at the edges. That bullet hole was right above a line of type that read "experiencing a partial corruption of foreign blood."

"Imagine it," Shake said. He ran a finger along the top sheet. He could feel the dents the typed letters had made in the paper. "Just imagine. Teddy Roosevelt held this. He folded this. He put this in the pocket of his overcoat and stepped out in the Milwaukee autumn."

He leaned down to smell the pages. He thought that was a nice touch.

"Gunpowder," he said. "Or maybe that's just my imagination."

"Roosevelt also had a metal eyeglass case in his pocket," Devane said. "That slowed the bullet down too. Nobody knows what happened to the eyeglass case or the bullet. The overcoat. If you could find all that, you could write your own ticket."

"How do I know it's real?" Shake said.

That was calculated stupidity. Shake thought Devane might expect it from someone like Roland Ziegler.

"Ha, ha," Devane said. He closed the attaché case. "My other bid is for seven million, so you'll have to beat that by another million."

Where the fuck was Quinn?

"Another million?" Shake said.

"If I'm gonna piss off my other buyer, it's got to be worth my while."

The doorbell chimed. Finally.

Devane remained cold and slack on the sofa, but his two bodyguards clicked into action, tucking back their suit coats to clear their guns.

One bodyguard stayed by the sofa with Devane and the attaché case. The other bodyguard fanned out to get an angle on the door.

The doorbell chimed again. A fist pounded the door.

Who could that be? Shake started to say. But that was too obvious, a terrible oversell, no matter how he said it. So instead he just looked over at Gina. She looked over at Devane.

"If you try to screw us," she said, "your reputation will be dead. You will never sell another fucking thing in your life."

That rattled Devane. Just for an instant, and just a little. Gina's hard work finally paying off.

"Don't answer it," Shake said.

"Answer it," Devane said. Because he wanted to prove he wasn't trying to screw them. And if they were trying to screw him—well, he had two armed bodyguards. He knew all the tricks.

Gina walked across the suite and opened the door. Quinn stood there in his purple galabiya, looking agitated. "Where's Lauren?" he said.

"What do you want?" Gina said.

"I want my daughter!" Quinn said, and barged past her into the suite. "Lauren!"

The first bodyguard made a grab for him but Quinn barged past him too. Quinn made it all the way to the coffee table before the second bodyguard grabbed him. Quinn tried to shake him off and the two of them almost fell into Devane's lap. Devane had to shove them away.

"Lauren! I will not stand for this any longer! Come out here!"

The second bodyguard wrestled Quinn around so that Quinn could see the first bodyguard pointing a gun at his face. Quinn stopped struggling. The second bodyguard let him go.

"How dare you!" Quinn said to the bodyguard with the gun in his face.

Please take it easy, Shake thought. *Please. Nothing unnecessary. Just stick to the script.*

"Sir," Gina told Quinn, "I'm afraid you have the wrong suite."

Devane seemed coldly amused by all this, coldly suspicious.

"Are you doing his daughter?" Devane asked Shake.

Quinn turned to Devane and glared at him. He was not supposed to turn and glare at Devane. That was not in the script.

"Do you know who I am?" Quinn said. Neither was that.

The second bodyguard had his gun out now too.

"No," Devane said. "Who are you? What's your story, old man?"

Gina slid over and grabbed Quinn's biceps. Shake saw her fingers tighten as she tried to pull Quinn toward the door. Quinn pulled back. He glared at Devane and rose up to his full height.

Oh, fuck. Shake saw it all falling apart, just like that, a slow-motion unfolding of the future.

And then: Quinn glanced around the suite. He seemed to realize something. He cleared his throat. "I appear to have," he said, and then stopped. "I apologize for the intrusion."

That was in the script. Quinn played it perfectly—stiffly embarrassed, not overselling.

The next part of the script was Quinn leaving.

He left. Shake relaxed.

"I want to meet this Lauren," Devane said. "I want to pop a cork with her." He mimed opening a bottle of champagne, squirting the champagne everywhere. "Don't you? Don't you bet his daughter's a fun chick?"

Shake could see Devane's mind working. Devane was trying to decide if what had just happened was staged. The suspicious type, he would be inclined to think so. It was just too much of a coincidence otherwise. But if it had been staged, *why* had it been staged?

At least Shake hoped that was the road Devane was driving down.

"Forget it," Shake said. "No way I go an extra million. Why do I care if you piss off your other buyer? I'll go an extra quarter, final offer. And word to the wise? I don't bluff."

"Nope," Devane said.

He stood and picked up the attaché case. He nodded to his bodyguards. The bodyguards stuck their guns back in their hip holsters and buttoned their suit coats. The three of them moved to the door.

"Wait," Gina said. "Roland?"

"No," Shake said. "I'm not going higher than a quarter."

"Let me walk you down," Gina told Devane.

"Whatever floats your boat." Devane made a boat with his free hand and floated it along on invisible waves.

GINA RODE THE ELEVATOR DOWN with Porkpie and his goons. It was all on her now and she knew it.

"He'll go up another half million," she told Porkpie. "He'll go to seven and three-quarters, but you have to let him think he's outsmarted you."

"So he does indeed bluff."

"Are you kidding me?"

"Why are you telling me this? What's in it for the bitch?"

One goon was right behind her on the left, the other goon slightly behind her on the right. They stank of sweat and nicotine and bad cologne.

"I'm sick of Cairo," Gina said. "I've been here what—three days? Three days is all, and I'm already sick of it. I don't know how you can live here."

"I'm not moving off eight," Porkpie said. "And nobody outsmarts me."

"I said just let him think that. I'll handle all that."

The elevator reached the lobby. Porkpie stepped out. Gina followed. The goons followed her, staying right up on her ass.

"What kind of deal did he cut with the feds?" Porkpie said, crossing the lobby. Gina had to walk fast to keep up. "I'm just curious."

"A good deal."

"I bet."

They passed the soldiers at the metal detector and pushed through the doors outside. Porkpie headed for his car, which he had waiting down at the end of the turnaround.

"So do you always do it this way?" he said. "The tag-team approach that's supposed to throw me off my game? Good cop, bad cop? Does it ever work?"

"Listen," Gina said. "If he doesn't get this stupid speech, he'll pout and whine for months. He'll pout and whine to me. *Moi*. Come down a quarter and I'll make it happen. You still come out seven hundred and fifty grand ahead."

Gina was good at this, if she did say so herself. She could play any part.

"I don't want to come out seven hundred and fifty grand ahead," Porkpie said. "I want to come out a million ahead. And I want the infamous Roland Ziegler to understand that I'm smarter than he is. And what's wrong with Cairo?"

They had reached Porkpie's car. Gina was almost there, it was almost done.

"What's wrong with Cairo?" she said. "I just spent a week in Beirut. That's what's wrong with Cairo."

Devane opened the car door and then stopped. Turned. Looked at her.

It was like all his nervous, coked-up, hand-waving energy had been suddenly condensed down to a single humming laser pinprick, aimed at the pupil of Gina's left eye.

"What did you just say?" he said.

Chapter 43

The girl blinked. That was all. That was enough. Devane knew he had her.

"What did you just say?" he said.

She smiled like she didn't know what in the world he was talking about.

Did she really think she could smile her way out of this one?

Mohammed Number One picked up Devane's vibe and moved closer to the girl. He grabbed her arm. He was the number one Mohammed because he had a gift. He could always read Devane's vibe. Devane never had to nod or point or murmur under his breath, "Hey, Mohammed, the bitch is trying to game me."

Mohammed Number One nodded at Mohammed Number Two, who came around on the other side of the girl.

"Rabat," Devane said.

"What?" the girl said.

"You said, the first night we met, that you'd just come from Rabat. Morocco. Not Beirut. Rabat. *Très charmant,* remember?"

"We did," the girl said. She rolled her eyes, exasperated. Pretending to be exasperated. "We went to Rabat for a night after Beirut. Do you want a detailed itinerary? Do you want to know what I had for breakfast each day?"

"You're lying," Devane said.

Mohammed Number One picked up Devane's vibe and squeezed the girl's arm harder. Devane had seen him break a girl's arm just by squeezing it. Another gift that Mohammed Number One had.

"I'm so not lying."

"What's your game?" Devane said. "You thought you were so smart, didn't you?"

The girl rolled her eyes again. A convincingly exasperated roll of the eyes, but—Devane caught the nervous flick at the end of the eye roll, a nervous flick of a glance over his shoulder.

Devane turned.

There. The crazy old man in the purple galabiya. The crazy old man, purple galabiya and white hair, who'd pushed his way into the suite and hollered for his daughter.

He was walking away fast. Just about to turn the corner on the other side of the hotel. He must have used the hotel's side exit. And he was carrying, at his side, a black leather attaché case.

Devane stared at the old man. He stared down at the identical black leather attaché case in his own hand.

It was impossible. It was fucking impossible. There was no way they could have pulled a switch. Devane had kept his eye on the real attaché case the entire time.

His first thought—of course it had been his first thought, when the old man bulled his way into the suite—Devane's immediate first thought had been: *It's a distraction.* The oldest trick in the oldest book. Distraction, misdirection. It was the first trick a grifter learned. Look over *there,* while I do this over *here.* It was a trick that fucking pickpockets used. The wrench. The bump.

So when the old man in the purple galabiya had bulled his way into the suite, Devane had kept his eye on the attaché case. He didn't think the old man was really a bump. Who would try something that clumsy? But better safe than sorry. Devane lived by that motto. Guilty until proven innocent, and even then probably guilty. Right?

So he hadn't taken his eyes off the attaché case. He hadn't taken his hand off it!

Had he?

Devane watched the old man in the purple galabiya walking fast, almost to the corner, the black leather attaché case in his hand.

He remembered, back in the suite, the old man and Mohammed Number Two almost falling on him. Devane having to shove them off. A split second when he'd taken his eyes off the attaché case, when he'd taken his hand off it . . .

"Get him!" Devane told the Mohammeds. The Mohammeds looked confused. They didn't understand. Mohammed Number One tightened his grip on the girl's arm and she spiked her elbow into his stomach, hard.

Mohammed Number One was a brick wall, he barely moved. But the girl had slipped her leg behind his leg before she spiked him, and he moved enough backward to lose his balance. The girl chopped him with her other hand, the side of her palm to his Adam's apple. He dropped her arm and stumbled backward, gagging.

The girl bolted. Mohammed Number Two started to go after her.

"Forget her!" Devane screamed. He'd been screaming for a while and hadn't even realized it. "The old man in the purple! He's got the real case!"

Mohammed Number One understood, but he was still gagging. Mohammed Number Two looked even more confused. Devane grabbed Mohammed Number Two's gun and took off after the old man. The old man was just turning the corner, just about to disappear.

Mohammed Number Two finally understood and sprinted after Devane. Mohammed Number One sprinted after them, slower, still gagging.

Devane whipped around the corner. The old man in the purple galabiya was up ahead, turning another corner, down a tight alley. He was walking fast but not fast enough. There was no way he would get away.

Did those fuckhead Americans think they were going to pull this off? Typical arrogant Americans. Though they would have pulled it off, Devane realized, a chill rippling through him, if the girl hadn't fucked up the one tiny detail about Rabat and Beirut.

That fuckup was going to get them killed. Because once Devane had his case back, once he shot the old man right there in the street like a dog—the Egyptian cops? What Egyptian cops?—once he had Roosevelt's speech back, he would sell the speech and use every dime of the money to hunt down the girl, hunt down the other guy. After he hunted them down, Devane would let Mohammed Number One have them. Devane would bust a few rails, find a comfy seat in the theater, and watch the show.

They had to be magicians! To switch the cases that fast, that clean, in the one single split second that Devane had looked away.

Devane whipped around the next corner. The old man was boxed up at the end of the alley, trying to get past a couple of fruit carts.

You're a dead man, Devane thought. *Your friends will wish they were.*

He reached the old man and slammed him against the stone wall. He yanked the attaché case away from him. Devane was so locked into that, getting the case back, that it took him a second to realize that the old man in the purple galabiya had a mustache.

A mustache. A mustache?

Mohammed Number Two put a gun to the old man's head and then looked at Devane, surprised. "He's got a mustache," Mohammed Number Two said.

The man had white wavy hair, but also a mustache and dark eyes. He was Egyptian, not American. He looked like he was about to faint.

"It's not him," Mohammed Number Two said. "This isn't the man that was upstairs."

"Who are you?" Devane screamed at him.

The old man started mumbling and jabbering in Arabic. Devane had to slap him.

"Ask him who the fuck he is!" Devane screamed at Mohammed

Number One. Devane's Arabic was good, but he wanted to make sure he got this exactly right.

"He says he's a waiter. He says he works at a restaurant in Giza, by the Sphinx. He says a man paid him a hundred dollars if he would wear this galabiya and carry this case."

That's what Devane thought he had said.

"He says he doesn't understand what's happening," Mohammed Number One said.

Devane didn't understand what was happening. He was starting to understand.

"Let him go," Devane said. He shoved the old man away. Devane was starting to understand. He bent down and popped the clasps on the attaché case that the old man had been carrying. His heart was beating so hard he could barely breathe. It was like he'd done way too much coke. He opened the lid of the attaché case. Inside were a few bottles, small plastic bottles, of shampoo.

Mohammed Number Two looked confused. "That was not the man from upstairs," he said. "This is not your case."

"No," Devane said. He understood now what had happened. "No. No. No."

Chapter 44

S hake picked up the attaché case.

The real case, the case with the speech that had saved Teddy Roosevelt's life.

It was on the pavement next to Devane's car, in front of the hotel, right where Devane had left it when he and his bodyguards went running after the dummy case.

There was nobody around Devane's car. The car looked like somebody had jumped out for a second to deliver a package to the hotel. The front door of the car was ajar. The door-ajar warning bell was going *ding . . . ding . . . ding.*

Shake dropped the attaché case in a big plastic shopping bag. He'd already changed out of his suit and put on a baseball cap, sunglasses. He crossed the street, not rushing, and got into the cab that was waiting for him.

Quinn was in the backseat. He'd changed out of the purple galabiya and was back in a polo shirt and khakis. "I'll be honest," Quinn said as the cab drove off. "Now that we've come up roses. I didn't know if he'd go for it or not."

Shake hadn't known if Devane would go for the dummy case either. Devane was no dummy. But that was why, in the end, he went for it.

"Hoisted by his own petard, wasn't he?" Quinn said. "Too suspicious for his own goddamn good. Let me have a look."

Shake slid the attaché case out of the plastic shopping bag and opened it. Quinn ran a finger along the edge of a bullet hole.

"I don't understand it myself," he said. "It's a mystery. Why some people get so worked up by something like this. But I'm happy for them, if it makes them happy. God bless 'em."

"How do we sell it?" Shake said. "If Devane's the main dealer for things like this?"

"The main one, not the only one. Hell, we'll sell it back to him if we have to. It's the way the world turns, Shake. You should know that. We'll sell it to the real Roland Ziegler when he really cuts a deal with the feds and gets out of prison. How would you like that?"

Stranger things, Shake knew, had happened.

The cab took them deep into the Christian Coptic area of Cairo. Fewer minarets, but just as much traffic, just as many donkeys pulling carts loaded with watermelons, honeydews, big green flopping bunches of sugarcane.

Shake and Quinn got out of the cab across from an old Coptic church with a bronze dome. They went past the church, turned down a deserted cobbled street, turned down an even more deserted cobbled street, turned into the courtyard of an abandoned building.

Gina was sitting on a plastic bucket in the middle of the courtyard, eating a slice of watermelon. "It's not bad," she said. "But I've been to this place that has the best watermelon in the world. Rush Springs, Oklahoma. The watermelon capital of the world."

"Let me ask you a question," Quinn asked her. "Now that we've come up roses. Did you think he'd go for it?"

"Porkpie?" Gina said. "Sure. Well, I wasn't totally sure. I thought he'd go for it, but I also thought he might check the real case first."

"He was so sure he'd figured it out," Shake said.

"He was hoisted by his own petard."

"His what?" Gina said. "I never touched his petard."

Quinn started to say something. Gina laughed. "I'm kidding," she said. "Sheesh, Harry. I know what petard is. It's gunpowder, isn't it? It's when you get blown up by your own gunpowder."

"You sold it, young lady," Quinn said. "You came up all aces. Brava."

"You too, Harry. Now that we've come up roses, I can say you had me a little worried."

"I guess I just stood around and watched," Shake said. "I guess you two did all the work."

Gina came over and gave Shake a big, sticky watermelon-flavored kiss.

"I was a little worried about you too," she said. "Now let me see it again."

Shake handed her the shopping bag with the attaché case inside. She took the case out and started to open it.

"Pardon me," a voice said.

Shake turned. A man stood behind them, at the entrance to the courtyard. He had popped up like a ghost, not a sound. It was quiet here in the courtyard. The cobbled street that ran past was quiet. They should have heard him coming. They should have heard something.

The man had the tallest, longest forehead that Shake had ever seen. He was wearing cargo shorts and sandals and a T-shirt that said YOU BETTER BELIZE IT!

He had a pleasant, mild expression on his face. And a gun with a silencer in his hand.

"I don't mean to interrupt," he said. He stepped into the courtyard and looked around. "This is the perfect place!"

Chapter 45

They were fun. They had been a lot of fun. Babb wished he could give them something in return. Like what? He didn't know.

"You guys were a lot of fun," he told them. That was the least he could do.

Maybe he could let them pick whom he shot first? Whom he shot and whom he used the knife on? In what manner he used the knife?

No. Babb wasn't prepared to go that far. If that made him an ungenerous person, then that made him an ungenerous person.

"Don't move, okay?" he said. "If any of you move, I'll shoot that person in the stomach. If all of you move at once—you might be thinking that—in different directions all at once? I'll shoot all of you in the stomach. I'm a really quick shot."

They seemed to believe him. They didn't move. They should believe him. Babb truly was a quick shot.

"Was the watermelon tasty?" he said.

"It was," the woman said. "Would you care for some?"

"No, thank you. But it was nice of you to ask."

"I was just telling these fellas here, though, that it's not the best watermelon I've ever had."

"It's not your lucky day," Babb told her. "It's the fellas here I'm supposed to kill, not you. You're just in the wrong place at the wrong time. And eating watermelon that could be better."

"I'm the one you're supposed to kill," the old man said. "Kill me and let them go."

"What fun would that be?" Babb said. "You guys really were a lot of fun. I'm serious! I can't tell you how much I appreciate that."

"Kill me and let them go," the old man said. "Tell Sticky Jimmy no hard feelings."

"No hard feelings?" the other man said. Quinn's bodyguard. Who had not turned out to be much of a bodyguard, if that was what he was.

"Sticky Jimmy?" Babb wondered aloud.

"Ask him to tell you the story how he got that nickname," Quinn's bodyguard said.

"Maybe later," Babb said.

He had decided to shoot them all in the stomach, get them down and settled, and then work his way down the line with the knife. He would line them up and proceed by—height?

He wasn't worried about screaming. It was hard to scream when you'd been shot in the stomach. Mainly there was just a lot of grunting and groaning and—

A donkey kicked Babb hard in the kidney. It clapped loudly at almost the same time.

A donkey did? Did what?

Babb felt like he had been kicked in the kidney by one of the donkeys that dragged fruit carts around Cairo. He stumbled but didn't fall. He pressed his hand against the small of his back. When he pulled his hand away and looked at it, it was covered in blood.

"Ow," he said.

He felt two more kicks, he heard two more claps. He fell down.

Ow, he thought.

Chapter 46

Meg limped over. Wasn't a big limp, just a little one. Her ankle felt mostly better and her limping days were just about behind her.

The man who'd murdered Terry, the man called Babb, was dead on the pavement stones. He was lying on his side half curled up, like a baby in its mama's belly. He looked like the picture they showed Meg's sister when she went in to ask about an abortion, and it turned out that sneaky church people ran the clinic. You see what's growing inside you, sweetheart? The miracle of life! Why would you want to murder that?

Meg had been mad how sneaky the church people were, but she had to give them credit. Meg's sister ended up keeping her baby, and he was Meg's nephew now.

Meg had never been pregnant herself. And she never would be now, not by Terry.

The man, Babb, was dead, but Meg shot him again anyway. She shot him through his long tall forehead. Banana head.

"That's for what you done to Terry," she said. She saw that the man was wearing Terry's string bracelet on his wrist. Meg left the bracelet where it was. That bracelet was ruined for her now.

She looked up at the others. They were surprised. Meg supposed she didn't blame them.

"What happened was," Meg told them, "he was all caught up thinking 'bout the evil he planned to do. He wasn't thinking 'bout the evil might be done to him. I know. I made that same mistake myself, one time." She hadn't made any mistakes since then. Meg had been careful not to.

She'd felt so heavy that night back in Guatemala, on the porch at Jorge's boss's house. All she'd wanted, standing there, was to get it over with—her life, her part in the movie.

But then she rang the doorbell and said the hell with that. This movie wasn't rid of her yet. She always finished what she started, and she wasn't going nowhere till she gave Terry what he deserved.

The man who answered the door was younger than she'd expected, handsome in a way, with slicked-back black hair. He looked like a lawyer or a businessman.

"Yes?" he said.

"Are you Jorge's boss?"

"Who?" he said, but his face told Meg he was in fact Jorge's boss.

He had a bodyguard, but the bodyguard was back in the kitchen making French-press coffee for the boss.

Not the best use of a bodyguard, if you asked Meg.

The bodyguard, when Meg and the boss went into the kitchen, didn't give her any trouble. Meg had a gun out and the bodyguard didn't. He was still fooling with the French press and decided he'd rather not get shot. Meg told him she'd pay him a thousand dollars cash money if he wouldn't give her any trouble. All he had to do was go back in the den and watch soccer till she was done. Did he think he could do that? He surely did. He poured himself a cup of coffee, handed over his gun and cell phone like she asked, and went off into the den.

The boss wasn't too happy about that. Meg only had to shoot one of his shinbones before he told her the name of the man sent to murder her and Terry. The man was called Babb. He had been sent to "clean up the mess" in Belize and to "finish the job." Meg supposed that was fair. She and Terry had in fact made a mess of it. They had not finished the job. But they could have cleaned it up themselves. They could have finished it. And there had been no need in the world, in any case, to murder Terry.

Meg asked Jorge's boss how she could find this man called Babb. He laughed, until Meg pointed out that the boss had another shinbone just begging to be shot. The boss said please no no no please, and told her that he'd heard Babb was in Cairo, Egypt, now. But . . .

"But he's *muy poderoso*?" she said. "And he's gonna kill me?"

"Yes. He is very dangerous."

"Maybe he will kill me. Or maybe I'll get him first. I aim to find out, one way or another."

She didn't know where in the world Egypt was. Far away, she imagined. But that's why they made airplanes. She had close to nine thousand dollars left from Jorge. That should get her just about anywhere. Meg and Jorge's boss discussed the best way for her to find out exactly where in Cairo this man called Babb was. Meg knew she couldn't just set down in a foreign city and start wandering around.

Jorge's boss had some good ideas. Meg had to shoot his other shinbone to hear them, but he did. He was the one told her Babb always liked having a souvenir.

After the boss found out which hotel Babb was at and clicked off his phone, Meg shot him in the head. Then she went into the den and gave the bodyguard his thousand dollars cash. Meg always kept her promises.

Because here she was, wasn't she? Standing halfway across the world in a courtyard in Cairo, Egypt, with the man who'd murdered Terry curled up dead at her feet.

"I always keep my promises," she told them now. The old man, and the restaurant chef who'd busted Terry's nose, and a lady Meg had never seen before. She looked sharp as a tack and Meg thought she was the one, not the two men, she better watch out for.

"Holy shit," the restaurant chef said.

"What?" Meg said.

The restaurant chef just stared at her.

"You didn't expect to see me here, did you?" Meg said.

"No," he said.

"You two know each other?" the lady asked.

"He broke Terry's nose and now I'm gonna shoot him for it," Meg said. "'Cause I promised Terry I would."

"You mind if I sit down?" the chef said.

"I don't care."

The chef sat down on a plastic bucket. He shook his head. "Holy shit."

"Who's Terry?" the old man said. "Who are you? I'm sorry if I sound confused."

"The guy in the ski mask," the chef said. "Back in Belize. Terry was the guy in the mask."

"Terry was." The old man's eyes lit up. He had baby-blue eyes that matched his shirt. "He was the punk who tried to shoot me!"

"Please shut up," the chef said to the old man.

"Terry was the love of my life," Meg said. "Is what he was. And now he's murdered. This man here murdered him."

She gave the man called Babb a nudge with her foot.

"I ain't gonna shoot you," Meg told the old man. "That's all behind us. I'm off that job. As long as you keep your mouth shut."

"I appreciate that," the old man said. "And I'm sorry for your loss. I really am."

"Thank you."

"I ain't gonna shoot you either," Meg told the lady. "I got no issue with you."

"What's your name?" the lady said.

"Meg."

"Meg. My name's Gina."

"I don't care."

"Will you tell me why you want to shoot Shake?"

"I told you already. Who?"

The lady pointed.

"What kind of name is that?" Meg said.

"It just doesn't seem totally fair to me, Meg," the lady said. "Shooting him because he broke Terry's nose?"

"I don't care about fair." Meg pointed her gun at the black briefcase the lady was holding. "What you got inside there?"

"It's a speech," the chef said. The Shake. What kind of a name was that?

"It's not just a speech," the old man said. "It's the speech that saved Teddy Roosevelt's life."

Meg sneered. "I doubt that happened."

"It's worth eight million dollars," the chef said.

The sneer dropped off Meg's face fast. "You're full of shit."

"Take it, Meg," the lady said. "You can have it."

"Why would I want something like that?" Meg said. "That's a world of trouble, something like that. Eight million dollars? I don't want nothing to do with that. You can have all that trouble."

None of them said anything.

"Let me ask you a question, Meg," the old man said after a while.

"Please don't," the chef said.

"Let *me* ask you a question, Meg," the lady said. "Okay?"

"I don't care."

"What would Terry want you to do?"

"About what?"

"About shooting Shake because he broke Terry's nose."

"I only broke his nose because he was trying to shoot one of my customers," the chef said. "I'd like to point that out."

"Shut up," Meg said. She looked back at the lady. "What would Terry want me to do? I'll tell you. Terry wouldn't have no goddamn idea what he'd want me to do. Or if he did, it'd be the exact wrong idea, the goddamn moron."

Meg felt the tears boiling up in her. She missed Terry so much she could barely stand it. But she didn't want to die anymore. She was done with that. If she died, then Terry really would be gone forever.

"Would he want you to shoot Shake?"

Meg thought about it. "No," she said. "Terry never blamed him for it. He said he would've done the same thing, somebody came into his restaurant with a gun and started shooting."

"Okay, then," the lady said.

"But he wouldn't have. Terry wouldn't have punched anybody in the nose that had a gun and was shooting. He would've run and hid and probably peed his pants. He was the biggest goddamn pussy you ever seen in your life."

"Well, for fuck's sake, Meg," the lady said. "Compared to you he was, maybe. But who isn't?"

Meg looked at her. "That's just what he used to say."

"He wasn't a pussy," the chef said.

Meg almost told the chef again to shut up, she almost shot him right then and there, but she wanted to hear what he had to say.

"Meg," the lady said, "you know what? My theory as an amateur psychologist is that you haven't shot Shake yet because you know Terry wouldn't want that."

"Shut up," Meg told the lady. "I want to hear what this one over here has to say. The Shake."

"It's just Shake," he said.

"I don't care."

"Terry might have been a dumb-ass," the Shake said, "and he wasn't the world's best shot. But he wasn't a pussy. I can tell you that first-hand."

Meg didn't know was he lying or not. People, when they were about to be shot, would say next to anything not to be. Teddy Roosevelt had, apparently, whoever he was.

Meg didn't know why, but she thought the Shake was probably telling the truth. He seemed like the kind of person, you put a gun on him, he'd rather not waste his last breath on a lie.

"He was the love of my life," Meg said. "You only get one of them, don't you?"

She looked at the lady. Meg swore that if the lady lied to her, she would shoot the Shake.

"I think so," the lady said. "Yes. I'm sorry."

The Shake was looking at the lady like she was the love of his life. Meg didn't know if the lady loved him back the same way, it was hard to tell.

"I'd just like to say one thing," the old man said. "About the situation we're all dealing with here. About the universality of the situation."

Meg walked over to the Shake and lifted her gun and hit him in the face with it. He fell sideways off his plastic bucket. Blood ran down out of his nose and all over his chin.

"Is that fair?" Meg asked the lady.

"Yep," the lady said.

Meg looked down at the Shake.

"Terry says you're welcome," she said, and then she left.

Chapter 47

Next time we come up roses," Shake said, "let's make sure we've really come up roses."

"Zip it," Gina said. "You're getting blood and spit all over yourself and I can't even understand you anyway. It just sounds like 'honka honk honkhonk.'"

She held a cold wet towel to his nose. Shake didn't know if his nose was broken or not. He wasn't about to complain either way.

They'd found a room in a cheap hotel not far from the Coptic quarter. It was a shitty room, the AC barely panting along and big fat flies bouncing drunkenly off the windowpanes. They weren't staying long, though, just long enough to clean up. They had to head down to the river five minutes ago.

"That little girl," Quinn said. "My goodness gravy. I don't think I've encountered anyone or anything so ferocious in my entire life."

Shake could hear Quinn telling the story, far off in the future, cornering some poor innocent victim in a bar or restaurant somewhere. *Let me tell you about this one time, buddy of mine from Belize and I were in Cairo . . .*

But Shake couldn't argue his point about Freckles. Freckles had pointed a gun at him twice now, and twice now Shake had come out of it alive. He figured that must have used up about three or four lifetimes' worth of good luck.

"I'll tell you what," Quinn said, "if it had been her and not Terry who'd come after me, back at the Shake's restaurant in Belize? I can tell you this story would have had a different ending. This story would have been over a long time ago."

"For better or worse," Shake said.

"Honk honka honk honk," Gina said.

"I know what the Shake said," Quinn said. "And he doesn't mean it."

Gina smiled and tossed the bloody towel across the room, into the sink. It was the kind of shitty hotel room that didn't have a separate bathroom. The sink and the toilet were right next to the TV.

"I kind of liked her," Gina said. "Meg. Zowee. That girl doesn't take any shit."

It was almost six o'clock. "We have to go," Shake said.

They took a cab back toward the center of town. Traffic was balled up, as usual. Quinn told the cabdriver to cut over on the first bridge to the island, run up the island where the traffic might not be so bad, and then cut back over on the second bridge. They could save time that way.

Shake didn't love the idea. He preferred a straight line when he could get one. But the cab had been barely creeping for ten minutes, and this definitely wasn't a time for creeping. He told the cabdriver to go ahead and cut over.

Traffic on the island wasn't bad. They made good time. When they got to the second bridge, Shake told the cabdriver to take them back over. He said they wanted to take a sunset cruise on a felucca, just drop them off at one of the piers along the river on the other side, it didn't matter which one.

"No," Quinn said, interrupting. "Pull off right here."

"Here?" Shake said.

"On this side of the river, that pier down there." Quinn pointed to a pier just down the slope from the hotel where they'd stayed their first couple of nights in Cairo. "That's the pier we want."

They got there and got out of the cab. Shake looked at Quinn. Quinn was pink and beaming.

"What's going on?" Shake said. He'd started to tense. His nose throbbed. He wished Quinn wasn't pink and beaming. "You said we could hire a fishing boat anywhere."

Because that was the plan. The plan was, they'd steer clear of the airport and train station, anywhere that Devane might be looking for them. Devane was more connected, through his former SSI guys, than Baby Jesus back in Belize could ever dream to be. But Devane couldn't watch the whole river. The plan was, Shake and Gina and Quinn would hire a felucca or fishing boat in Cairo to take them up the Nile to a place called Beni Mazar. From Beni Mazar, Quinn said, they could catch a bus or taxi to Luxor. Devane would have no idea where they were. From Luxor they could take a direct flight to London.

"I've got a surprise," Quinn said.

Those were just about, at this or any point, the last four words Shake wanted to hear.

"Harry," Gina said. She was starting to tense too. "Tell us what's going on."

"Sure we could," Quinn said, "hire a fishing boat to take us up the river. Which is south on the Nile, an interesting tidbit, *up* on the Nile is *south*. Sure, we could hire some fishing boat that smells like fish and we're sleeping on hard planks, roasting in the sun. Or we could take a nice luxurious *dahabeah*. The most luxurious boats on the water, private, Cleopatra would feel right at home. Don't you think, after all we've been through, we deserve a little luxury? I had Mahmoud set it up for us, he's coming along too."

Mahmoud, who was supposed to be in the wind already, because it wouldn't take Devane long to figure out who the inside man had been.

Mahmoud, who would crack in half the minute Devane squeezed him.

Mahmoud, who wasn't supposed to know where Shake, Gina, and Quinn were.

Shake's nose throbbed. He was so mad at Quinn he felt dizzy.

"What?" Quinn said, and then the first bullet hit a wooden piling a few feet away, tearing it to splinters. The second bullet hit Quinn and dropped him where he stood.

The fishermen on the pier started to shout and scatter. Devane and his bodyguards, three of them, four, were a hundred yards away, running toward the pier. Shooting.

Gina helped Shake drag Quinn behind a felucca bobbing at the pier. The felucca, the way it was angled in the water, the distance from the bank, made for poor cover. The three of them had about a square foot each where a bullet wouldn't find them.

"We can't stay here," Gina said, crouched down. "We have to run."

Quinn was breathing rough and fast. He was still holding the leather attaché case. Shake saw a hole near the center of the case and couldn't believe it. Teddy Roosevelt's long-winded speech had stopped another bullet.

"Takes more than that," Quinn said, grimacing, "to kill a Bull Moose."

Then Shake realized that Teddy Roosevelt's speech had not stopped the bullet after all. The bullet had punched through the case, the speech, and Quinn's thigh. Out Quinn's thigh. Bullets were more powerful these days.

"Leave me," Quinn said.

"You don't have to ask," Shake said. "Damn it." But he looped Quinn's arm around his neck and heaved him up.

"Go," Shake told Gina. "The hotel."

She hesitated, nodded, took off. The girl could fly. Shake took off after her, dragging Quinn along with him, Quinn a couple of hundred pounds of dead dragging weight.

"Just leave me!" Quinn said. "God Almighty, Shake!"

A couple of bullets snapped past, wide. And then the shooting stopped. Devane and his goons had realized how easy this was going to be, catching Shake and Quinn.

Shake and Quinn made it about halfway up to the hotel. A couple of the goons got around in front and aimed their guns at them. Shake was out of gas anyway. He and Quinn went down in a pile.

Devane walked over and yanked the attaché case away from Quinn. When he saw the bullet hole punched through the case, through and through, he flinched like someone had slapped him. Devane ripped open the case. He was hoping, Shake supposed, that maybe the new bullet had passed miraculously through one of the existing holes in the speech. It hadn't. There were three holes now—two historic and the third one not at all.

"You fucking idiots!" Devane screamed at his goons. "It's ruined! I told you to hold your fire!"

He pulled a gun. Shake thought that Devane might actually shoot his own goons, he seemed that mad. That would have been Shake's vote. Instead Devane stalked over and jammed his gun against Shake's cheek.

"There!" Shake heard Gina yell, off somewhere in the distance.

Devane and his goons turned. Shake turned. Running toward them were three soldiers in dark green uniforms. The soldiers from the hotel lobby. They had their guns up and were yelling in Arabic.

Devane's goons yelled back in Arabic. There were four goons with guns and only three soldiers, but the soldiers had better guns, automatic rifles, and they seemed very young, very excited. Devane's goons dropped their guns. Devane dropped his gun. He started screaming at the soldiers in Arabic. Shake didn't speak Arabic, but he was pretty sure that Devane was saying something like "Easy, easy, take it easy."

"That man is in possession of stolen property that belongs to the people of Egypt!" Quinn yelled. He pointed at Devane, who was still holding the attaché case. "Arrest that man!"

Devane really started screaming at the soldiers now.

One of the soldiers spoke English. He translated for the other soldiers what Quinn had just said. The soldier who spoke English pointed at the attaché case.

A world of trouble, Meg had said about that case. *I don't want nothing to do with it.*

Devane dropped the case. "It's not mine!" he screamed at the soldiers. Screaming in English now, he was so worked up.

"Arrest that man!" Quinn said. The soldiers didn't hesitate. They grabbed Devane, jerked him around, zip-tied his hands behind his back. They grabbed, jerked, and zip-tied each one of Devane's goons, one by one.

"Bravo!" Quinn said. "Let me shake your hands, boys!" He stuck his hand out. One of the soldiers punched him in the sternum with the butt of his rifle.

And then the other soldiers zip-tied Quinn. They zip-tied Shake. They zip-tied Gina too.

Chapter 48

Shake had expected an Egyptian jail to be bad. It was, but not worse. The jail where the soldiers took him and Quinn was grim and filthy and hot. But so were the American jails, in Louisiana and California, that Shake was familiar with. This jail was hotter and filthier but not quite as grim. At least here there was more light, with windows high up on the stone walls.

The stink was almost exactly the same. The stink of a jail must be universal.

Shake was in one cell and Quinn was in the cell across from him. Shake's had a bare mattress on the filthy floor, Arabic graffiti scratched into the walls, and a brand-new gleaming stainless-steel toilet that only flushed intermittently.

A nurse had dressed and bandaged Quinn's thigh when Shake and Quinn first arrived at the jail. She'd given him a shot of antibiotics.

Every morning she came back to change the dressing and give him a new shot, but after the first day she hadn't given him anything for the pain. Quinn had started to turn a little green around the gills.

The soldier who brought the meals spoke some English. He told Shake and Quinn they were lucky to be in a military jail. You didn't want to find yourself in a jail run by state security.

The food wasn't bad. It was the glop made of tomatoes, onions, rice, and chickpeas. The food, like the jail, could have been worse.

The mess they were in could have been worse. They could be dead. That's what Shake kept telling himself, anyway. Trying to stay cool.

Shake didn't know what had happened to Gina. That was the worst part. The soldiers, when they arrested her, had put her in a separate truck from Shake and Quinn. They'd put Devane and his goons in a third truck. Shake didn't know what had happened to Devane and his goons either. He didn't give a shit about them.

Mahmoud was in a prison hospital, laid up with the broken jaw and ruptured spleen that Devane's goons had given him. He'd held out as long as he could before they cracked him, Shake gave the guy a lot of credit for that. The nurse had told Quinn that Mahmoud was going to be fine. Shake wondered if that was what Mahmoud would call it.

Shake didn't know what he and Quinn and Gina were charged with, or if anyone, other than the nurse and the soldier who brought the food, even knew they were here. He didn't know how long they'd go ripe in this jail before someone in charge came to talk to them. It was going on four days now.

"You all right?" he asked Quinn.

"I'm all right," Quinn said. "I've been better."

"I plan to cooperate fully with the authorities."

"Good idea."

"They have to let the State Department know about us, don't they?"

"Of course," Quinn said.

"They can't just throw us in here and forget about us."

"What worries me," Quinn said, but then stopped. Shake didn't ask him to continue. He didn't want to hear it.

A couple of hours later, just after the midday call to prayer, the soldier who brought the food showed up with another, older soldier. The older soldier, Shake could tell, was someone in charge.

He looked in at Shake. Shake was sitting on his mattress, his back against the wall.

"Mr. Bouchon," the soldier in charge said.

"That's me," Shake said.

"Permit me, if I may, to ask you a question." His English was excellent. He had a crisp accent that sounded vaguely Scottish.

"Okay."

"Does Egypt not have already enough problems of its own?"

"Without us coming over here and creating more, you mean."

"Yes."

"I would do it differently," Shake said, "if I could do it again."

He flicked his wrist at Shake. A weary, contemptuous flick.

"You have a visitor," he said.

EVELYN HAD BEEN ABOUT TO board her flight from Cairo to Amsterdam when her phone rang. She stepped out of line to take the call.

"You'll be glad you didn't go to Cairo," Cory had said.

An announcement in Arabic started to play over the public-address system. Evelyn covered her phone with her hand until the announcement was over.

"Like I would have ever gone to Cairo, Cory," she said. "Yeah, right."

"You considered it. Don't lie to me, Evi."

"Okay. Maybe I considered it. Why am I glad I didn't go to Cairo?"

"It would have been a waste of time," Cory said.

She wondered what he was getting at. He seemed to realize something.

"If I tell you," he said, "promise me again you won't go to Cairo."

Evelyn had to put her hand over her phone again. Another announcement in Arabic.

"I promise again," she'd said. "Tell me."

That was two days ago, when Cory told her that Shake and the others had been arrested by the Egyptians. Now Evelyn sat in a small hot room with no windows, a card table, a few metal folding chairs. She could hear the midday call to prayer off in the distance, faint.

A few minutes later a guard and the military official who ran the jail led Shake into the room. Shake had his hands cuffed in front of him. The military official pointed to the metal folding chair across the table from Evelyn. Shake sat down.

"Can we have some privacy?" Evelyn asked the military official.

"No," he said. He sat down in another chair, by the door. The guard kept standing, right behind Shake.

Shake didn't look so great. Evelyn had expected even worse.

He managed, somehow, to give her a wry smile. "We seem to keep running into each other, don't we?"

"How are they treating you?"

"Fine."

He'd picked up on her mood, but she knew he had to take the shot anyway.

"You know," he said, "I may be reconsidering my policy."

"Shake."

"About never diming out Armenians. I'm thinking there might be an exception, in light of recent developments."

"It's a no-go," she said. Because there was no point in dragging it out. The only point would be pointless cruelty, and Evelyn wasn't in the mood for that. "There's nothing I can do."

He nodded. "I didn't really think so."

"I tried." And she had. Without caring, really, whether Shake had reconsidered his policy on diming out Armenians or not. She'd never tell him that, of course. Or anyone.

She'd spent the last two days on the phone. Calling anyone and everyone who might have some torque with the Egyptians. Pulling every string. Evelyn had even fought back the poisonous bile and asked her asshole ex-husband if he could help, asked him if he knew of any other strings to pull.

He couldn't, he didn't.

Cory Nadler, after Evelyn's third or fourth call to him, stopped answering them.

Nobody had torque with the Egyptians, not the kind Shake Bouchon was going to need.

Evelyn, after two full days on the phone, torquing like crazy, was only able to get five minutes in a windowless room with the prisoner. And the guy who'd made that happen, a high-level congressional staffer Evelyn knew from college, who she'd probably have to boink after this, said it was a miracle she even got the five minutes.

"I appreciate it," Shake said. "You know anything about Gina?"

"They told me she's just next door," Evelyn said. "The facility for women. It's supposed to be not too bad down there."

"So."

"Yeah. You're in deep. You stole a priceless Egyptian antiquity?"

"It was already stolen. And it wasn't priceless. The guy we stole it from, he was trying to unload it for eight million."

"This Devane guy?"

"Yeah. And it wasn't Egyptian, the antiquity. It wasn't really even an antiquity. The Egyptians just used to have it in one of their museums."

She knew he knew, as he said it, that the last part was the salient part.

"Devane's in deeper shit than you are," she said. "If that makes you feel better."

"It gets deeper?"

"He's in just as deep. How about that?"

"One minute remaining," the military official said. He was studying his fingernails, intrigued by them.

"It was damaged beyond recovery," Evelyn said. "The antiquity or whatever it was. So, not a great development for you."

"No."

"I'll see if I can check on Gina for you."

He nodded. "I owe you one. Two. Three. I lost count."

"Are you counting the scar?"

She turned so he could see the lobe of her ear, where the gunshot splinter of painted coconut shell had dinged her, back at his restaurant in Belize.

"I don't see a scar," he said. "It's all healed."

"It's an emotional scar."

"I'll make it up to you. If I ever get out of here."

There was nothing else to say.

"Time," the military official said.

Evelyn followed him back through all the winding corridors. He dumped her, without a word, outside in the parking lot. She stood in the dazzling sunlight for a second. Going from dark to light, in this country, it felt like you'd been clubbed.

She didn't feel bad for Shake. She guessed she felt as bad for him as she'd ever felt for a shithead. But shitheads made their choices. Evelyn had never met one who hadn't. There was nothing else to say.

She walked across the lot to the Mercedes. Her driver, Mohammed, sat waiting on the hood, smoking his unfiltered Camels. "I do not like this place, Evelyn," he said. "This is a dark place."

She didn't answer because a black SUV with tinted windows was pulling into the parking lot. And another black SUV with tinted windows right behind it.

Two guys, they looked American, got out of the first SUV and started scanning. They wore badass sunglasses and clear plastic earpieces.

Evelyn couldn't imagine who they could be. They aimed their badass sunglasses at her, so she walked over. "Hi," she said. "You guys American?"

"We'll have to ask you to clear the area, ma'am," one of the guys said. American for sure, and young.

Evelyn showed him her creds. "FBI. Who are you?" She thought she saw the corner of the guy's mouth twitch, a little smile. He was not terribly impressed by her creds.

"We're nobody, ma'am," he said. "Now, if you don't mind. Agent Holly."

Nobody.

Evelyn knew she could push it, or not. She saw nothing to gain by pushing it. And a lot to lose. That was the message the guy had sent her when he said her name, the way he said it.

Do you like your job, Agent Holly? Do you like your career?

Evelyn didn't see anything to gain by pushing it, or she would have.

"Fair enough," she said, and walked back to the Mercedes.

THE GUARD LED SHAKE BACK to his cell. Quinn asked him what had happened. Shake told him. Quinn, Mr. Optimism, didn't have anything to say.

A few minutes later the guard returned.

"Up, up, up," he said. "Both of you."

Chapter 49

They took Shake and Quinn to a different room this time, a bigger room. The table was bigger, with more chairs. There was a window, covered by wire mesh bolted to the wall.

Shake and Quinn sat down. A few minutes later a female guard brought Gina in and sat her down next to Shake.

"Hi," he said.

"Hi."

Shake wanted to reach out and touch her—just put his hand on hers, anything—but the guard had cuffed him behind the back this time.

Gina's hands were cuffed in front, but the female guard was right next to her, watching Gina like a mean fucking hawk. Gina turned her foot, under the table, so that her leg pressed against Shake's.

The officer in charge walked in. He looked at Shake and Gina and Quinn with weary disgust, and then flicked his wrist. The guards left the room. The officer in charge followed them out.

"I don't understand this," Quinn said.

"How's your leg, Harry?" Gina said.

"It's been better."

"Are you okay?" Shake asked Gina.

"Sure."

Two young guys in futuristic sunglasses entered the room. They wore clear plastic earpieces. They looked around and then sat down on the opposite side of the table from Shake and Gina, leaving the chair between them empty.

A guy around Shake's age entered the room and took the empty chair. He was wearing a dark blue suit, like the young guys, but Shake could tell his suit was a lot more expensive. The way he wore it, though, the suit riding up all over him, it looked cheaper.

He was average height, average weight, with pale thinning hair. He looked tired, frazzled, annoyed.

Shake didn't feel good about any of that.

"You're going to spend the rest of your life in an Egyptian prison," the guy said. "And not this one. This one is the Ritz-Carlton of Egyptian correctional facilities."

Even better.

"And why do you think that is?" he said. "Why are you going to spend the rest of your life in an Egyptian prison?"

Shake wasn't sure who he was asking. He was looking up at the ceiling and shaking his head.

"Why are you such a little prick?" Quinn said.

The guy looked at Quinn, and then turned to Shake and Gina.

"My name is Daniel Gardenhire," he said. "You probably know who I work for."

"Sticky Jimmy," Shake said.

He grimaced. "Jesus. Don't ever call him that."

"Will I ever get the opportunity to?"

"No." He turned back to Quinn. "Why do you think?"

"Why do I think you're such a little prick? Maybe because you tried to have me killed."

"Leave," Gardenhire told the two guys in sunglasses.

They left. Gardenhire seemed to be gathering himself. Trying to control his anger.

"And why the fuck is that, Dad?" he said.

"Dad?" Shake said.

Gina's eyes went wider than Shake had ever seen them go.

"He didn't tell you?" Gardenhire said. "Classic."

Gardenhire looked nothing like Quinn. Or maybe he did, his blue eyes behind the glasses. The way he drummed his fingers on the table. Holy shit.

Shake was glad to see that life still had, at least, one more surprise left in store for him.

"He's your son?" he asked Quinn.

"He's a little prick who put a number on his own father."

"Did he tell you the rest?" Quinn's son asked Shake. "I'm just curious. What did he tell you?"

"He told me Sticky Jimmy did a few things, back in the day, that he'd rather forget about now. Logan James, sorry. In Cambodia."

"That's true," Quinn's son said. "Mr. James robbed UNESCO blind. And every other NGO in Cambodia in the nineties. He bung-holed them senseless. So far, so good."

"And now Mr. James, moving up the ladder, needs to get rid of the one guy who knows about what happened in Cambodia. So he put a number on him. He tried to have him killed."

Quinn's son waited. Shake didn't know what else to say.

"Is there more?" Shake said.

"I'm thinking," Gina said, "there might be."

"There's more," Quinn's son said. He took a good look at Gina for the first time. "Have we met?"

"I wouldn't have any idea," she said. "No offense."

"None taken."

"My name's Gina. Gina Clement. I have a very profitable venture shop in San Francisco."

"I know all that," he said. "I do my homework, no offense. I'm just trying to remember if I ever met you. Last year, maybe. A fund-raiser for the governor at Fort Mason?"

"Sure," Gina lied. "I remember now."

Shake was still trying to wrap his head around the idea that Quinn's son was the fixer for Logan James. That it was Quinn's own son who had tried to have him killed.

"I know all about you too," Quinn's son told Shake.

"Is any of that maybe going to help us here?" Gina said. "That I can be a very generous fund-raiser for Mr. James?"

"No," Quinn's son said. He turned his attention back to Quinn.

"Why don't you tell them the rest, Dad," he said. "I bet they're curious why they're going to spend the rest of their life in an Egyptian prison."

"The hell with you," Quinn said. "Sticky Jimmy, he's just doing what he has to do. You think I have a beef with him? I don't. Why would I? He was always a guy, he'd look you in the eye he had something to tell you. He's a straight shooter. You, on the other hand. Go ahead and put a number on your own father."

"My father tried to shake us down," Quinn's son explained to Shake and Gina. "Blackmail. He called me up a couple of months ago. First time in years, I should add. When he needed something. When he wanted something. That's when you can expect a call from Harrigan Quinn."

"That's not true. I called you plenty of times before that. You're the one who said, let me see, how did you put it? 'Stay out of my life.' Vail, Christmas Eve, 2005."

"Tell them why I told you to stay out of my life! Tell them how many chances I gave you! Your capacity to bend reality to your own selfish purposes is super-fucking-human, Dad."

Quinn's son turned back to Shake and Gina.

"He wanted a job with the campaign. He told me that if he didn't get a job with the campaign, he'd take all the dirt he had on Mr. James and dump it in public. I told him please, Dad, don't even joke about that. He said he wasn't joking. He said he had enough dirt on Mr. James to—let me see, how did you put it?—'bury him six feet deep.'"

"I wasn't really going to do it! For God's sake, Danny! I'm no rat. I may be a lot of things, I'm the first to admit it, but I've never been a rat. You ever heard of loyalty?"

"Loyalty? Classic, Dad."

"It was a bluff, Danny! A bluff!" Quinn turned to Shake and Gina. "You'd think he'd know how to play poker, wouldn't you, the line of work he's in? He's worked for two governors, a law degree from Harvard, top of his class, he'll be chief of staff in the White House one of these days, you just watch and see, and the kid could never play poker to save his life."

Quinn turned back to his son.

"Even when you were a kid, remember? Remember that summer in Virginia? I'd try to teach you Hold 'Em, it was like playing cards with a dog. Like the painting with the dogs in it? You'd flop a set of aces and your tail would start wagging."

"I was six years old that summer."

"You either know how to play poker or you don't."

Quinn's son chuckled. The chuckle, Shake realized, was another thing he shared with his father. "Do either of you happen to have any idea," he asked Shake and Gina, "how he's managed to stay alive this long? Because I don't."

"Not really," Shake said.

"I'd like to meet your mother," Gina said.

Quinn and his son glanced away at exactly the same time, Quinn to his right and his son to the left, like mirror images of each other.

Nobody said anything for a long minute.

"I would never have dumped any dirt on Jimmy," Quinn said finally. "Not really. I would never have done that to you. If you don't know that, I don't know what to tell you."

"Sure, Dad. You say that now."

"Guard!" Quinn yelled. "Return me to my cell, please!"

No guard came. Quinn's son took off his glasses and rubbed his face. He sat slumped down in his chair, looking even more tired, frazzled, and annoyed than when he'd arrived.

The moment of truth. Shake had never been sure why it was called that. Maybe because whatever way things broke, that became the truth. Your truth.

Gina pressed her leg harder against his. She knew it was the moment of truth too.

Shake realized that if he hadn't dragged Quinn along with him after Quinn had been shot, if Shake had left Quinn behind like Quinn had asked him to do, Shake and Gina might be free right now. Or they might be dead. Or they might still be sitting in an Egyptian prison and Quinn dead, Shake and Gina's only hope dead, their moment of truth long past.

"Here's the thing, Dad," Quinn's son said finally. "If you ever, ever, ever pull something like this again . . ."

Shake didn't hear the rest of it. Gina closed her eyes and leaned her head against his shoulder. Shake closed his eyes too.

Thank you, God, he thought, and for the first time since Shake was eleven years old, an altar boy at St. Frances Cabrini on Paris Street in New Orleans, he really meant it.

Chapter 50

Quinn got to his feet and began the speech of a lifetime, about how he'd never walk out of that Egyptian jail unless Shake and Gina walked out with him, that was the deal, take it or leave it.

"You know what the Marines say?" Quinn said.

"Dad," Gardenhire said. "Just—"

"The Marines say, and I know this because I spent a little time working with the Thirty-first MEU back in the day, one of the expeditionary units they have. Off-the-books, of course. The Marines say, 'You might kill me with my own rifle, but it won't be with my own bullets.' You know what that means?"

"Yes, I do," Gardenhire said. Shake had the impression that this wasn't the first time he'd heard it. "Dad, if you'd just—"

"It means you'll have to beat me to death with my rifle because I'll fire every last bullet in it. I'll go down fighting. That's what I'm talking about here, if you don't think I'm serious. Everybody walks or nobody walks, no negotiation. And I'll tell you why."

Gardenhire gave up trying to interrupt. When Quinn finally finished the speech, Gardenhire sighed. "They're walking too, Dad," he said. "It was never an issue."

"You better believe it wasn't. And Mahmoud too. He walks too."

Gardenhire sighed again. "Fine. Mahmoud too."

Shake wanted to know, but didn't ask, why Gardenhire was willing to make them part of the package. It would cost him, it would cost Sticky Jimmy—Shake had seen the Egyptians bargain at the market, and he doubted the top military guys would be any gentler.

Maybe Gardenhire was going to buy Gina because of her money and connections back in California. Maybe Shake would get a phone call down the line, in a few months or years, Gardenhire asking for a favor that Shake wouldn't want to do but couldn't refuse.

Or maybe Gardenhire just knew his father really wouldn't shut up unless Shake and Gina walked too. He didn't want to know what it felt like to get beaten to death with a rifle.

Shake didn't care what the reason was. He was just happy to walk out of the jail and into the blinding light.

"The Egyptians will need to cover their asses, you know," Quinn told Gardenhire when they were all in an SUV, speeding toward the airport. "They'll need someone to burn. But they've got Devane for that."

"Thanks for the advice, Dad," Gardenhire said. "I would never have thought of that."

"You have to keep your eye on the other guys when they look at their cards. Watch their faces and forget about your cards. You can look at your cards later."

At the airport, Gardenhire handed Shake and Gina their passports. He told them their flight to JFK left in two hours.

"I don't need to spell anything out, do I?" he said. "About keeping your mouths shut?"

"No," Shake said.

"Definitely not," Gina said.

"I'll be in touch at some point," he said. "I don't need to spell that out either, do I?"

Unfortunately not.

"What about me?" Quinn said. "I'm not on the flight?"

"We're going to D.C.," Gardenhire said. "I read Mr. Logan in on what happened and he wants to see you."

"So he can shoot me himself?"

Gardenhire took off his glasses and rubbed his face. He sighed. "No."

Quinn thought for a second and then chuckled. "He wants to hire me, doesn't he?"

"No," Gardenhire said. "No. It's not a job, it's just—it's a consultation. He wants to know what you know about Downey Cross."

"Downey Cross the pharmaceutical guy? I know everything there is to know about him! I'm not joking. This one time in Peking, I remember, he got so falling-down drunk that—well, I won't ruin the surprise, you need to hear the whole story from the beginning. Downey Cross! I did a lot of business with that old son of a bitch, way back when. He's got a lot of dough now, doesn't he?"

"What a coincidence!" Gina said. "I wonder if he's ever convinced to contribute to political campaigns."

"It's not a job," Gardenhire said again.

Quinn gave Shake a wink. "It's a consultation."

Gardenhire turned to Shake and Gina. "Don't miss your flight."

That meant get the fuck out of here.

Quinn gave Shake a big hug. He gave Gina a big hug.

"Good luck," Shake told Gardenhire as he and Quinn walked away.

Chapter 51

Gina was not pleased to see that Quinn's son had booked them into coach. Shake laughed. He could think of worse fates.

"How long is this flight?" Gina said five minutes after takeoff. "Are we there yet?"

"Who do you think Gardenhire will call first for a favor, me or you?"

"Me. But my favor will be easier to do."

"Were you worried?"

"When? Yes. Of course. Are you nuts?"

"Marry me," Shake said.

"No."

"Then think about it."

"I don't need to think about it."

"You love me too."

"So?"

"So marry me. We'll have kids. Do you want kids?"

"I don't know what I want. Neither do you."

"We'll figure it out together."

"A recipe for bliss."

"It might be."

Gina squirmed and wriggled and thrashed around in the confines of her coach seat, trying to get comfortable.

"If you're going to propose," she said, "do it right. With a ring, and not both of us smelling like an Egyptian jail. Not on an airplane. Not in coach."

"On the Palisades. At sunset. And then you'll say yes?"

"No. I'll still say no. But you'll feel better about yourself. You'll know you gave it your best shot."

The flight attendant braked her drink cart in the aisle next to Shake.

"What can I get you?" she asked him.

"Everything," he said.

"I'm sorry?"

"I don't have any money. My restaurant blew up. I don't have a place to live. I don't have any job prospects. I still owe back pay to the people who used to work in my restaurant. My ability to love any woman but the one sitting next to me has been permanently compromised."

The flight attendant glanced at Gina, smiled nervously.

"Give him a ginger ale," Gina told her. "Me too."

The flight attendant gave them ginger ales and moved on.

"If you need to crash with me for a while," Gina said, "all you have to do is beg."

"I'm begging."

"Whatever," she said, and put her headphones on. "Are we there yet?"

BOOKS BY LOU BERNEY

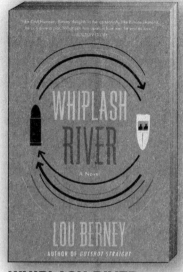

GUTSHOT STRAIGHT
A Novel

ISBN 978-0-06-176634-3 (paperback)

A Barry Award Nominee for Best First Novel

Professional wheel man Charles "Shake" Bouchon, fresh out of prison, is supposed to deliver a package to Vegas strip-club owner Dick "the Whale" Moby and pick up a briefcase for Shake's former boss. But when the "package" turns out to be Gina, a wholesome young housewife, Shake decides to set her free. Now Shake and Gina are on the run in Panama—looking to unload the briefcase's unusual contents. And Shake's learning that Gina is more complicated than he initially imagined.

"Like Carl Hiaasen, Berney delights in the cartoonish. Like Elmore Leonard, he can drive a plot. What sets him apart is how well he evokes love, making the romance at the heart of this cinematic book as compelling as the mystery."

—*Boston Globe*

WHIPLASH RIVER
A Novel

ISBN 978-0-06-211528-7 (paperback)

In this sequel to *Gutshot Straight*, Charles "Shake" Bouchon has finally realized the dream of owning a restaurant in a Caribbean paradise. He's left his life of crime behind for good—but business is slow, and to stay afloat he's borrowed money from local thugs. Things suddenly go from bad to worse when a masked gunman shows up, and before Shake knows what he's gotten himself into, his restaurant explodes in flames. Now he has no choice but to skip town with an eccentric old hustler, whose help comes at a price—Shake's assistance with a half-baked, risky score. And Shake only knows one person who could pull it off: his fearless ex-lover Gina. If she doesn't kill him first.